BLAIRE

Blaire - Part One

~

Anita Gray

Cover Design by Nero Seal

DISCLAIMER

COPYRIGHT 2016 (C)

This novel is a work of fiction by Anita Gray. Any character resemblance to people (fiction and non-fiction), places, incidences, or things is purely coincidental.

All rights reserved.

This story may not be reproduced in any form without the author's consent. Doing so will result in prosecution.

A FEW REVIEWS

Action packed, darkly erotic, and heart squeezingly good.

I dare any reader who likes dark romance and action not to love this.

I feel like I've been watching an intense movie for four days.

LANGUAGE INDEX

S'all right—it's all right
Tis—it is
Gotta— got to
Dunno—don't know
Wanner—want to
Gonna—going to
Kinda—kind of
Outa—out of
Сэр—sir, in Russian
Podgotovsja—prepare yourself, in Russian
Konchaj yego—end him, in Russian
Davaj, devochka—that's it girl, in Russian
Pizdets—this is the fucking end, in Russian
Jesucristo—Jesus Christ, in Spanish
Dios mío—oh my god, in Spanish
Falso—phony, in Spanish
Dios ayuda—god help, in Spanish
Snooker room—billiards room

PLEASE NOTE

Blaire is written in American style English with a few references still being British, as it is set in Britain.

I hope you're ready for this

*Blaire is not suitable for readers under 18.
Contains psychological impairment, dubious permission,
and violence.*

Bought. Conditioned.

My name is Blaire. I'm head of security to a man who controls the Russian underworld in Europe. His name is Maksim and he's my master. He bought me ten years ago and conditioned me with brutality to worship and protect him. And I have protected him. I've slain everyone who has tried to do him harm. Everyone but a man he loans me to; a man who threatens to break me and everything I believe in.

You're going to need a strong stomach and a strong heart to follow my story, because take my word for it, it's no fairy tale.

BLAIRE
(PART ONE)

1

I walk through Maksim's strip club like a ghost, under streaming red lights that flash in tune with the pounding music. The air smells potent with sweaty bodies and cheap perfume, a mixture of man and woman. Just how my master likes it.

Everything I see moves through my mind's eye in slow motion, my brain carefully and collectively scanning for danger. There isn't much out of the ordinary going on tonight; a few regulars lining the stage in the center of the club, all unaware of my presence. I know why. They're too focused on the strippers, beautiful European girls leisurely peeling off their clothes. I'm wearing the usual: black sports trousers, trainers, and a thin black leather jacket over a long sleeve sweater. Not exactly arousing attire but this is how I like it, being under the radar.

The strippers are the only people who do notice my presence. As I pass the stage, they each scowl at me with obvious loathing. I understand their loathing. I'm the only girl in Maksim's inner circle, and this lot—the strippers—hate it. They wonder why. They've always wondered why.

No danger here.

"Is сэр Maksim back there?" I ask a member of security in Russian, gesturing at the door he's standing in front of like The Great Wall of Man.

"Yes," he says in Russian, his pale eyes empty of emotion. "He's been waiting for you."

I nod, knowing I'm an hour late. I'm never late but my phone was on silent by accident and I didn't hear his text message. Fortunately, I couldn't sleep, otherwise I wouldn't have seen his message until early tomorrow morning and that would have resulted in a good, bloody hiding.

The security guy pushes open the heavy door with one hand and stands aside. I saunter down the red hall, turning left, and knock on Maksim's office door three times. The knocks echo, carrying over the music booming through the walls.

"Come in, my little pet," Maksim says through the intercom system in his thick Russian drawl.

I shiver as I normally do when I haven't spoken to him for a few days. His voice brings my entire body to attention.

Pushing with both palms, I force the door to creak open and go inside.

Maksim isn't alone.

I don't react—I never react to surprises. I briefly look to see who is accompanying Maksim, and though it's quite dark in here, I'm very aware of the powerful blue eyes watching me from the leather couch by the left wall, eyes that seem to be all over my body at once. Sharp little hairs race down my arms and legs. I haven't seen him before.

The notion that he's a stranger puts me on guard because Maksim rarely allows strange faces in his circle, let alone in his office.

I stop before Maksim's wide desk and fold my hands behind my back, feeling sheathed in darkness. He only has the desk lamp on and that isn't exactly bright. It just about illuminates his diamond shaped, iron face.

"You are late. My. Little. Pet." Maksim says each word with significant and singular meaning, speaking in Russian.

My blood runs cold when he's like this, mulling over something other than business. Today, it seems it's my timekeeping.

I keep focus, my gaze level and on him slouching back in his chair. He's a striking man with steady, hazelnut-golden, expressionless eyes, and shoulder length dark brown hair that smells like brut from the candles he burns. I remember the scent well. I remember the feeling of his hair on my face when he cuddles me after a beating.

"My phone was accidentally on silent," my voice is low, as per usual. "I'm sorry, сэр Maksim." I offer him a little head-bow of respect.

Leaning forward and resting his elbows on the desk, he entwines his fingers together, holding my gaze with soul consuming eyes. "No more keeping your phone on silent, Blaire."

I flinch subconsciously, stepping back. He only calls me by my given name when I've done something wrong and that usually means trouble for me is brewing.

Maksim cocks a brow at me. "You got that?"

I nod, taking his warning seriously. I might be in his inner circle but it takes just one bullet to remove me.

"What have you been doing for the past few days?" he asks in Russian, his tone husky and utterly terrifying.

"Nothing much," I whisper in our language, squeezing my hands together on the low of my back. "I've been training of course, went to the salon yesterday, and I went out to a club last night."

"Yes," he tips his head, "my men saw you driving through the countryside. Did you have fun?"

I shake my head, being honest. "I was just getting out of the apartment, сэр Maksim."

"Of course, my little pet. Of course. Though, next time you want to visit a club, you come here." He taps his desk with one finger. "You do not have to travel to strange places to have fun."

"Okay." I lift my lips in a forced, wary smile. "As you wish."

I like visiting strange places when alone. Everything in my life is a consistent bloodbath—the people and the work I execute. Sometimes, I just like a change of scenery.

I guess I don't like visiting strange places anymore.

Maksim gestures to the right, to the man sitting on the couch, and I know the conversation about my last two days is over.

"My little pet," he's speaking in English now, "meet my old friend, Mr. Decena."

Old friend?

It takes a lot of effort not to frown.

I've been with Maksim for ten years and I've never seen or heard of a Mr. Decena.

I look at Maksim's friend, my face blank of sentiment. Above him, a long tube light attached to the wall flickers on, buzzing with electricity, illuminating a tall, muscular frame.

"No matter what happens here tonight," Maksim says in sly Russian, "you are ordered not to challenge him."

The back of my neck pricks. Maksim never orders me to stand down.

Though nervous, I obey without question, nodding to show I understand his command. I then study Mr. Decena, surprised by how relaxed he is in his pose, sitting there in the middle of the couch with one arm draped over the back, long legs stretched out in front of him.

This is bizarre. No one is ever that relaxed in Maksim's company.

I reckon Mr. Decena is in his late twenties. He looks young wearing fitted jeans, tanned boots, and a black round-neck t-shirt that boasts solid muscles. He's nothing at all like Maksim who favors suits, but Maksim has a tall, athletic body for them. They are wearing similar watches on their left wrists with thick silver straps, but that's where their similarities end.

"Mr. Decena would like to ask you some questions," Maksim says.

I nod in response, still studying the relaxed pawn. Unruly ink black hair curls around his neck and face, abating hard features; a strong, square, clean shaven chin, and a blade of a nose. His black eyebrows are thick and long, framing prevailing blue eyes that stand against his naturally tanned skin. He's a good looking man, and judging by that lazy, narcissistic expression on his face, he's aware. He fancies himself.

He stares me up and down with slow meditation, taking in all my features from head to toe. I'm suddenly so uncomfortable that my stomach knots. I can't really explain it but he makes me feel naked to the bone.

I shift on my feet, trying to iron out my anxiety. A smirk lifts the side of Mr. Decena's lips then, a mischievous smirk that's full of promise.

"What do I call you?" he says, his voice deep yet calm. He's American but there's a sprinkle of Latin in his accent. "My little pet, or Blaire?"

Maksim nods to tell me I can answer.

"Blaire," I say.

There's a split second of silence before Mr. Decena tells me, "All right, you can call me Charlie."

Maksim's eyebrows shoot up but he doesn't say anything. I stand there like a statue, fighting not to react.

Another period of silence follows, then Charlie rasps out my name, drumming his fingers against the back of the couch. "Blaire, as in, field of battle?"

I screw up my face, unable to stop myself. What's he talking about?

Maksim chuckles under his breath like he's confirming something.

"You never mentioned how pretty she is," Charlie says softly, causing me to straighten out my features. "Nor did you mention that lovely, whispery voice."

"Ohhh, my friend," Maksim smiles cunningly at me, his golden eyes crinkling in the corners, "don't take it personally. I wouldn't boast of her to anyone."

"Why not? She's a nice looking girl." Charlie's voice lowers as he says, "I've always wondered about redheads..."

I swallow, hoping I'm not visibly sweating under the presence of these two.

"I wouldn't want you excited to see her," Maksim says, "for she is mine and mine alone."

"Hm..." Charlie hums, staring right at me with brazen audacity. I get the feeling he isn't a pawn in Maksim's game. He's too confident.

"She sounds kinda Russian," he says after a while, still tapping his fingers against the couch. "Where's she from?"

"She's not Russian," Maksim says, and I see that he shakes his head at Charlie.

Charlie nods once, understanding that head-shake. "How old are you, Blaire?"

I look at Maksim. He nods.

"Eighteen."

Raising his eyebrows, Charlie seems stunned. I'm not sure why.

"What'd you do, exactly?" he asks. "I've heard various stories."

Maksim gives me the go ahead, so I say, "I deal in technology."

"And she's also on my security detail," Maksim adds.

"This small girl is part of your security?" Charlie stops tapping the back of the couch, his eyes taut with confusion. A crease forms between his eyebrows. It makes him look evil.

"She is." Maksim smiles up at me again, knowingly proud. "She is a beauty in battle. Trained to defend me on instinct unless I say otherwise."

I am trained to defend him however I can, though I wouldn't just say I'm trained. I'd say I'm more... conditioned. My brain works to please and protect Maksim without me actually having to think. I used to find it disturbing. Now... I'm used to it.

Charlie doesn't believe Maksim—it's written all over his face—but that's good. This is Maksim's trick with me. I have always been the element of surprise for his enemies.

"And your parents?" Charlie says, still frowning at me.

I don't show my confusion to that question, just look at him.

"Erm, Charlie," Maksim starts to say but is cut off dead.

"I'm not talking to you, am I?"

My heart drops through me like a boulder.

"Don't you understand me, girl?" Charlie says with austerity. "Where are your parents? I won't repeat myself again."

I have no idea why he's being like this. It's not like I've done anything wrong.

Thumping the desk with a fisted hand, Maksim says, "Answer him, Blaire."

I cringe as he uses my name. "I only have cəp Maksim."

Silence.

Charlie's glancing between us, an air of frustration on his face.

8

"Where are her parents?" he demands to know, executing his attention on Maksim. "Dead? Did they sell her to you? Where are they?"

My eyes flitter between them, and I'm so confused. I don't get why he's being so ascetic all of a sudden or why he'd want to know if I have parents.

Maksim manages to give Charlie another curt head-shake, which Charlie also understands.

The next questions are sharp and snappy, like the tension that's now in the room.

Charlie states my address in London. "Is that where you live?"

I nod.

"Alone?"

I nod again, keeping it brief.

"Is the apartment yours?" He raises his eyebrows at me, making his blue eyes seem wider.

I nod a third time.

"And you drove here tonight on your own?" he gestures at the office door with a large, steady hand. "You have your own car?"

What kind of a question is that? What's it to him if I live alone or if I own my own car?

"Yes, the car is hers," Maksim answers for me, though he doesn't gain Charlie's attention. He is still looking at me.

"I have her on the payroll," Maksim explains. "She's not a prisoner like the rest."

"Is that right?" Charlie sounds like he's stuck in thought, his eyes flickering all over my deadpan face. "So, you trust her completely?" he breaks eye contact with me to focus on Maksim. "Because if you have any doubts... I can't risk having sloppy workers on the job."

Maksim doesn't hesitate. He says a powerful, "With my life," then it's quiet again.

Why do I feel like I'm being interviewed for something?

"Okay," says Charlie eventually, nodding to himself. He then summons my attention by rasping out my name. "Maksim tells me you can hack into any computer system."

Bingo. He is interviewing me.

"You can answer him," Maksim says. So I nod, my hands still firmly folded behind my back.

"How can you do that?" asks Charlie.

"My friend," Maksim butts-in, clearing his throat, "the details are better left unsaid. Just know that my little pet is masterful at-"

"I'll decide what details are better left unsaid," Charlie says. Sitting forward, he puts his elbows on his knees and narrows his blue eyes at Maksim. "I'll consider pardoning things that might make this girl feel uncomfortable but you'll tell me the finer details." His square jaw ticks, though when he stares up at me, that anger in his face... it... it vanishes. "How can you do that, Blaire?"

"I spent three years in a room with books, codes and computers," I say without thinking, and bizarrely without Maksim's permission. "I taught myself the things I know."

Charlie gives Maksim a baffled look, wrinkling his nose. "She actually thinks she became a hacker in three years?" No one answers him, and he runs a hand through his thick black hair, ruffling the strands at the back of his neck. "C'mon, don't try to take the piss outa me."

Maksim's face tightens with what almost looks like… fear? No. Can't be. He shakes his head at Charlie again.

"All right." Charlie lifts a hand, understanding Maksim's expression.

Is he hiding something from me? Why won't he just tell Charlie that he bought me from a man in Russia, or insist it's none of his business?

Digging into his jeans back pocket, Charlie pulls out a piece of paper and passes it to me between scissored fingers.

I glance at Maksim. He signals for me to take the paper, so I do. I briefly touch Charlie's fingers in the process and a warm, tingly sensation spreads through my body, causing me to snatch back my hand. Our eyes meet then in a moment of dead quietness. His are glowing like he knows what I just felt.

Everything around me becomes nonexistent. Even Maksim fades into the background. And I just look at this man who's invading our personal space with pure bafflement. He doesn't look away; doesn't blink. A pool of anxiety coils inside me, making my toes curl in my trainers.

I have a dark feeling he's going to turn the world as I know it upside down.

"It's the latest in technology for a certain CCTV system," he says softly, insisting I take the paper from him. "Here you go."

To break whatever the fuck *this* is, I pinch the piece of paper out of his fingers and scan the notes written down, mentally willing my heart rate to calm. It's the details for London's closed-circuit television system.

"Can you shut that down for fifteen minutes?" Charlie asks, his voice still unexplainably soft.

I've entered this system a few times before. Maksim likes to know that he can control a city for if trouble breaks out.

"Can you shut it down, my little pet?" Maksim says.

"I can shut this down for four, maybe five minutes before I get locked out." I lean over to give Charlie back the piece of paper, avoiding his touch—and his eyes. I have the contents of the note now stored in my memory.

Charlie shakes his head, screwing up the piece of paper in a large hand before tossing it across the office. "I need fifteen minutes." He exercises his eyes on Maksim, who seems a little uncomfortable, pulling open the top buttons of his shirt. "You said the redhead can get me fifteen minutes. I. Need. My. Fifteen. Minutes."

My protective instincts kicking in, I step closer to Maksim's desk. No one talks to my master like this with such contempt. No one.

I center my attention on Charlie. He's glaring at Maksim, his nostrils flaring.

I have to protect Maksim.

I have to ensure nothing happens to him.

Maksim is all that matters.

"Can you do it, my little pet?" Maksim says in a rush of words, visibly nervous—I hate that. "Can you get the fifteen minutes?"

"I'll need a few weeks," I whisper. I actually need more than a few weeks but I'll tell Maksim that over the phone. At least this way, if he gets mad at me, I have time to mentally prepare. Mad Maksim doesn't bode well for my ass.

Charlie nods, then Maksim tells me two weeks is fine, that there is no room for error. "Don't run over schedule, my little pet. You know what will happen if you do."

"I won't," I say. I do know what will happen, all too well.

Just as quickly as it bloomed, the tension in the room vanishes, though I stay by Maksim's desk.

Charlie pulls another piece of paper from his jeans back pocket. "For Maksim. Please, give it to him."

Maksim gives me the 'okay', so I take it from Charlie and put it on the desk.

"That's a Dark Web link. Don't lose it." Charlie gestures at the piece of paper. "To contact me the password is Guzmán Decena." He follows with saying out each letter of the password like we're fucking dyslexic or something. "Keep me updated regarding Blaire and the job. You can e-mail me any time and I'll get back to you within the hour."

Regarding Blaire *and* the job? Why would he need to be updated about me?

"Of course, my friend." Maksim touches his chest in a deceivingly composed approach. "Of course."

I feel Charlie is looking at me again, and my anxiety spikes when he asks, "Will Blaire be attending Rumo's poker game next weekend?"

I don't like how personally interested he is in me. It's... odd.

A few seconds of silence until Maksim says, "She will be." He smiles at me with an agenda, excitement gleaming in his eyes. "I might even put on a little show for you."

Charlie doesn't understand, so Maksim explains that he sometimes has me fight for entertainment. "Like I said a moment ago, she's a beauty in battle."

Chills run down my spine because I know what's going to happen. I know who he'll make me fight.

"You will come to the poker game, won't you, Charlie? You will come watch her fight?"

"Oh, I wouldn't miss it."

My stomach twists.

"Good. Very good, my friend."

While I stand here staring ahead impassively as not to draw attention to the fact that I'm sweating bullets, they chat about what's been going on in London over the past six years, which isn't much short of sex, crime, and murder. Charlie doesn't sound impressed as Maksim blathers on about his power in Western Europe. Seeming to have heard enough, he cuts Maksim off mid-sentence to say he needs to go. "Time's getting on."

Maksim focuses on me then. "Do you have any questions before you go, my little pet? Is there anything you need?"

"No," I whisper, devoid of emotion.

"I guess we're all done here then." He reaches over to shake hands with Charlie, his chair creaking under his weight. "It's good to see you again, my friend."

Nodding once, Charlie stands and fixes the hem of his t-shirt over his jeans. He's really tall—I'd say at least six foot two—and he's bigger than I thought: broad shoulders, a narrow waist, and hard muscles stretching under dark, olive skin. He looks like a Spanish soldier.

"If you're heading back to London, Blaire-" my name rolls off his tongue like satin, "-I'll get a lift with you."

What?

My heart does this weird doubling over thing.

I whip my eyes from Charlie to Maksim, who strangely nods. "You will have to forgive my little pet's attitude, as I am sure you will learn she has." Maksim chuckles under his breath. "She's as arrogant as a redhead comes."

Charlie laughs too, clearly amused. "I can handle one small girl, no matter how arrogant she might be. Don't worry about that."

My stomach is sinking with anxiety. This is a test. It has to be. Maksim would never leave me alone with another man.

Maksim tells me that I have to be polite to Charlie, that I'm not allowed to fight him. It isn't a request. It's an order. "You can speak to him, also, just not about me."

"Of course," I say, head-bowing to my master, hiding the fact that my anxiety is going through the roof.

I'm not allowed to fight him? What, *ever*?

BLAIRE
(PART ONE)

2

After bidding Maksim goodnight, I lead the way out of the club. Charlie isn't far behind—I can feel his distance on my shadow—but he's far enough for me to have a sense of mental space.

The club is still booming with music and heaving in perverted old men tossing money about. They're chanting over the music, "Take it off! Take it off!" because the girls are still performing on the stage, naked breasts and asses jiggling all over the place. I'm surprised Charlie doesn't want to stay and have a nice European girl for himself. Any normal man would stay.

At the exit doors, I nod to bid the doorman goodbye and steal out into the cold night, beneath a cloaking black sky sparkling in stars. My silver Porsche is parked under a flickering streetlight at the end of the car park. I open it using the key in my pocket. It flashes three times with a low, deep beep.

"This is a nice car for such a young girl," Charlie says, walking past me to open the driver's door. He rests his forearm on the top of the door and looks down on me, his head slightly cocked. "Did Maksim buy it for you or did you buy it for yourself?"

Maksim? That is so disrespectful. It's Maksim-Markov to those considered friends or work acquaintances.

"Do you want to drive or something?"

Charlie tips his head to the other side, his eyes glancing back and forth between mine. "Why'd you ask that?"

I gesture at my car. "You are holding my door open."

He laughs under his breath, flashing even white teeth. "Tis' called manners, Blaire."

I screw up my face. Holding my door open is considered manners?

"In you get." He nods at my car, amusement glittering in his eyes.

My neck arched back, I stare at him, baffled to say the least. He looks a bit different up close, more... I don't know. Beautiful? No. Handsome. He's too masculine to be beautiful. His lips are perfect, the lower fuller than the top, his cheekbones are sharp and high, and his eyes are deep set, a lagoon blue in this light.

"Do you want me to drive?" He nods at my car again without breaking eye contact. "I can if you want me to. I know where you live."

I scoff at the audacity of him, sink down into the plush leather and yank my door shut. He's laughing as he walks around to the passenger side, I'm guessing at me. I don't get what he finds so funny.

Pressing the power button, I fire-up the purring engine. My entire body vibrates as I rev to warm-up my pride and joy.

Charlie settles in the passenger seat, the leather creaking under his weight. He smells sweet and musky—a weird scent for a man but bizarrely appealing.

I peer at him from the corner of my eye. He's too big for my car; has to adjust the seat by sliding it back to give his long legs some room.

A quick glance, and he catches me staring; smirks at me. My heart almost jumps out of my chest but I save face by telling him, "Put on your seatbelt and then we can go."

He does, pulls it across his chest and plugs it in. I shift in gear to reverse out of the car park and head down the bumpy country lane. The car is easy to drive, even over all the potholes, the steering smooth and light. It's the best thing I've ever bought myself.

Though Charlie is blatantly watching me, he doesn't speak for about ten minutes. So I flick on the radio to drown out our silence and check the rear-view mirror. I notice twin SUV's on our shadow then with blinding headlights. They look suspicious; heavily tinted windows, both going at the same speed. I maintain my eyes on them, driving carefully as not to draw attention to us, but as I turn off to hit the clear motorway, they follow us.

Keeping one hand near my gun in my inside jacket pocket, my other hand on the wheel, I press down on the throttle to boot it out of Dartford, the force pressing me back into my seat.

"What's wrong, Blaire?"

"I think we're being followed," I say, reaching one-hundred miles per hour, dodging what cars are on the road. "Have you got a gun?"

"Have I got a gun?" Charlie laughs at me again, and when I look at him, he smiles. It's an utterly seductive, sly smile that makes me feel warm all over. "Relax," he says, "it's just my men. No need for guns."

"What?" I drop a gear to slow the pace. "If you have men with cars, why did you ask me for a lift?"

He doesn't answer my question, which I don't like. He diverts with, "How long have you known Maksim?"

Maksim-Markov! It really bothers me that he addresses my master like this.

"That's none of your business," I say. My voice comes out surprisingly calm.

"Well, I'm making it my business. How long?"

I try not to react to his cool, dominant approach, though it's hard. I want to punch his lights out because he's so fucking conceited.

"I cannot comment without his permission," I say in a flat tone.

He laughs at me again, though in a more mocking fashion. "You know, in all the years I've known your boss, you're the first of his girl's I've seen off a leash." Reaching over, he grabs my seat headrest, forcing intimacy.

I shift over in my seat, a little uncomfortable. I can feel the warmth of his large body at my side.

"Maksim must really trust you," he whispers, checking me out with obvious lust.

I don't say anything in response. Of course Maksim trusts me. I'm his most trusted devotee.

We fall silent again.

I glance at him a few times, sensing he's still staring at me with stark concentration. He is. I wish he'd stop. I'm already on guard and he's making the whole ordeal ten times worse with that penetrating gaze.

As a distraction, I turn up the radio.

"What are you allowed to say?" he breaks the silence, turning the radio down.

I shrug, steering off the motorway for London.

"Okay... How fast does your car go?"

Silence.

"You can answer me that, surely?" He sounds like he's being sarcastic. "Maksim said you can speak to me."

"Naught to sixty in five and a half seconds," I say, just to shut him up.

"And the color, did you pick it?"

Though his questions might seem ordinary, they're not. I know what he's doing. He's trying to get me talking by luring me into a false sense of security. I scowl to warn him off but he isn't bothered. He repeats his question.

"What is with you?" I snap my eyebrows together. "Why are you asking me these stupid, mundane questions?" My heart stutters with panic—Maksim said to be polite. "Sorry. I... I didn't mean to-"

"S'all right." He shrugs with one shoulder, still holding my headrest. "You can ask me a question if you want to." He pauses, then leans a little closer and whispers down my spine, "I won't tell Maksim."

I hold his stare for as long as I can, but then I have to center my attention on the road, on the cars.

"Why are you asking me these questions?" my voice is soft but demanding. "What's with the whole Spanish Inquisition?"

"The Spanish Inquisition, huh?" A wide grin spreads across his face. "I'm curious about you, Blaire," he says. "Even more so now."

I glance at him, puzzled, and he elaborates, "You don't wear a leash. You live outside of Maksim's house. You can apparently put up a good fight. You're educated..." the list of compliments is endless.

Why the fuck is he curious about me? And how the hell has he accumulated that much information about me in under an hour?

I don't ask why he's curious. I don't want to give him the satisfaction of my own curiosity.

"It seems Maksim wasn't lying when he told me you've got a bad attitude," Charlie says, chuckling to himself. His voice is so deep when he laughs like that. It's almost mesmerizing. Almost.

"I'm not gonna get anything outa you yet, am I?"

Yet? What makes him think he'll ever get anything out of me?

"No," I say. "You're not."

He doesn't say much more now, just wants to know if I like living on my own, that kind of thing. I shake, nod, and shrug a few times, but I don't actually answer his questions.

"Where would you like me to drop you off?" I ask, driving past my apartment building, curb crawling The River Thames.

"Here will do." He unbuckles his seatbelt.

I pull over with a sharp stop, desperate to get him out of my car. He doesn't seem to be in a rush to leave. He gives my body the once over, his eyes hooded and full of zest. "Maybe I'll stop by your apartment over the next two weeks to say hi."

"I wouldn't bother," I narrow my eyes at him, pushing my car in gear, "I won't answer the door to you."

He flicks up his eyebrows. "Sure you won't."

I snort with affront. Bar Maksim, I don't think I've ever met anyone so fucking smug.

He gets out of the car and leans down to look at me, causing that death black hair to fall around his handsome face, enhancing those diamond blue eyes. I feel trapped in a moment of visual connection with him, my chest constricting with unease.

Neither of us speak—I couldn't even if I wanted to. So I just hold his gaze.

I think he's contemplating something about me. I can't figure out why I come to that assumption. It's just that thoughtful expression on his face...

"I thought you said you had to leave? 'Times getting on', isn't it?" I try to rush him along when I find my voice, using his own words against him.

"I've always got time for a pretty girl," his tone lowers as he says that.

My stomach ties up in knots. I can't stand the way he talks to me, or the way he looks at me, as if he's mentally taking off my clothes. It's so personal.

"I'll see you very soon, Blaire," he says eventually, like it's a promise, breaking what can only be described as a spell.

In a fluster, I glance away, my chest so heavy that I can hardly breathe. He shuts the door and disappears into the city, one hand in his jeans pocket. I can't help watching him in quiet muse. He walks with purpose, his tall body sauntering at a relaxed pace like he has all the time in the world to get to his destination.

As soon as he's out of sight, I sag in my seat, the tension draining out of my body.

And I thought Maksim was intense.

When I can gather my wits after enduring Charlie, I steer into the underground car park of my apartment building. My phone buzzes in my jacket pocket. Pulling it out, I see it's James calling.

James is a *friend?* of mine. I'm very fond of him; known him since before I can remember. He plays a role much like mine with Maksim—security and devotee—but he doesn't reap luxury like a personal car and an apartment as I do. He drives a supplied security SUV, as all the other men do, and lives in Maksim's attic because Maksim doesn't trust him like he does me. That's never affected my opinion of James though. He is one of the good guys. I've lost count of how many times he's taken a beating trying to protect me from our master. How many times he's let Maksim fuck him in an effort to ensure he doesn't fuck me.

"Have you spoken to Maksim?" I step out of my car and lock it with the key. It beeps and flashes, echoing through the eerie car park.

"He just rang me about some bloke called Charlie," James says, his voice soft and husky. "Wants me to beef up security."

"Beef up security?" My eyebrows snap together. "Did he say why?"

"No. It was a brief call, and I wasn't about to start asking questions. Who is this Charlie?"

"I have no idea." I lean back against my car, poking my chin with the key in a musing fashion. "Maksim is nervous around him though." I'm quiet for a second, going over when Charlie told Maksim that he's not talking to him in such an aggressive approach. "I've never seen him so... I don't know." I pause again, still recalling things. "Charlie kept cutting him off from talking and Maksim just let him."

"What?"

"Yeah. And I will admit, I am nervous too. He makes me feel-"

"You're nervous?" James' voice goes up a notch. "But, you don't get nervous about anything."

"If you ever meet Charlie, you'll understand why. The way he looked at me in front of Maksim... spoke to me..." I get hot chills just thinking about it. "He said, and I quote, 'I've always wondered about redheads', like he was fantasizing or something."

"Seriously? And Maksim did nothing?"

"Yeah." I go right into detail about how much authority Charlie had over Maksim, how he insisted I drop him off even while he had drivers at hand. "Before that though, he interviewed me for a job; asked the oddest questions."

"What questions?"

"Wanted to know if I lived alone, drove my own car... It was ages before he asked about my skills."

"He's up to no good, that's why," James says, analyzing. I can hear he's pacing the attic. It's empty of things, other than his bed and a wardrobe. It heightens the slightest of sounds.

"I think so," I say. "I get that impression."

"Shit," he curses, then he's silent for a moment, I imagine thinking. "Keep your wits about you, Blaire. If Maksim is getting involved with people he's nervous about, it doesn't bode well for us."

"I know it doesn't." I nod at the empty car park. "I know."

Whenever Maksim gets in trouble with his dodgy dealings, one of us—his arsenals—takes the fall. It's always been this way.

"What job do they have you on exactly? Are you whacking someone?"

"No. Nothing like that." I tell him about the job in great detail—Maksim lets us discuss things with each other. While James isn't much of a hacker, he's a bloody good fighter—almost as good as me. I trust him implicitly.

"You could only get, like... what... four/five minutes last time, couldn't you?" he says, referring to my access to London's CCTV system.

"Ah-huh." I sound almost defeated because I am. It's going to be mentally taxing trying to grasp more time. "But I wasn't about to tell Maksim that face to face."

"No, I understand." James sighs in sympathy. "Just try and get his fifteen minutes. Try. And if you can't, before you confess to Maksim that you've failed, call me and I'll come over to your place, okay? Don't tell him anything while you're on your own."

My heart bleeds for this guy. There's nothing he wouldn't endure if it means he can spare me of pain.

BLAIRE
(PART ONE)

"Thanks, James," I say blank of emotion, knowing I'd never deliberately put him in the firing line. "I have to go." I shove my keys in my jacket pocket and head for the private elevator that leads up to my apartment. "I'll speak to you soon."

BLAIRE
(PART ONE)

3

For the next week, in my London apartment that overlooks a gray River Thames, I test myself to the limit.

I eat plain minimal foods to prevent feeling lethargic and scarcely sleep five hours a night because my mind is on overdrive. Eventually, I have to give up on the hypnopaedia—learning while asleep via a recorder—because I can't handle the overload of studying. I'll come back to it of course, once this job is complete. In my personal gym upstairs, I execute my usual combat routine for four hours a day—which steals time away from my work—but I have to train. Maksim would kill me if I let myself slip. It could cost him his life. The dark computer room at the back of my apartment, hidden behind fake white paneled walls, is my prized possession—except for my Porsche, that is. Spread across the back wall, ten computer screens in two rows glow over my freckly face. They offer the only source of light in here. From wall to wall, the floating desk boasts keyboards, black boxes, and other useful gadgets that help me safely link to The Dark Web.

27

BLAIRE
(PART ONE)

I work like a dog morning and night, occasionally nodding off in the wide office chair. By day four, I manage to gain access to London's CCTV for a maximum of eleven minutes, controlling the traffic lights, certain security gates, and the city cameras, but I cannot get a hold of no more than eleven minutes. The system locks me out.

Sweaty and hungry for real food, and frazzled to the max, I rub my forehead, then I bash the keyboard keys to put glitches in London's system, working through another night.

Now, I have one week and one day left to train, and to add to my worry, work commitments over the weekend set me back a little. I don't have any other choice but to accept what is though, as I'm on Maksim's security detail and his life comes before mine.

Friday night, James and I watch his back while he parties ruthlessly at a mansion in Kensington Palace Gardens. The mansion belongs to some Asian Prince who is largely in the public eye, but the public knows nothing of his taste for young girls and sex shows. They know only what the media allows them to know.

By ten o'clock, the party becomes hard to stomach—like most of the parties Maksim attends—because the Prince has a willing little Albanian brunette on all fours in the middle of his glorious ballroom. She's getting whipped before fucked by a man in a black leather mask, their flesh slapping together so hard I can feel it in the air. A collection of suits line the walls, waiting for their turn. Some of the onlookers masturbate, while the rest get their cocks sucked by their sex-slaves who are firmly on leashes—until it's their turn to fuck the Albanian girl, that is.

James and I remain behind Maksim with our eyes ahead, clasping guns over our laps.

Maksim is in seventh heaven, especially when the Prince offers him a cock-sucker, which James and I have front row seats to. The sound of the tiny blonde choking against Maksim's cock turns my stomach inside out, as he refuses to let her breathe by blocking her air passage. And to make matters worse, the godforsaken fuck show goes on until early hours of the morning, the ornate ballroom whispering with soft piano music. The music isn't loud enough to drown out her cries of pleasure/pain in Albanian, nor the men's moans of satisfaction as they each have a go on her. Deep moans that remind me of Maksim when he makes me please him.

I'm beyond uncomfortable internally. On the outside, I must look as cold as ice.

The show gets even harder to stomach when Maksim takes over—belts the Albanian girl to the point where her back bleeds before drilling her from behind—because in a moment of raw intoxication, he presses her face into the floor and looks me right in the eyes. It's like everything and everyone in the room evaporates, the earth closing in on me. I go stiff, my chest so tight that I can just about breathe. I don't know whether to look away or not. He's never done this before.

He doesn't look away. He smiles at me and takes the girl slowly, holding her hips like he's caressing her, humming with delight, his eyes hazy and full of lust.

I stare ahead, blinking above him, trying to avoid the devil's eye. Then, he fucks her with everything he has, making her squeal, skin smacking against skin.

James glances at me, then steps a little closer, putting us arm to arm. "Don't worry," he whispers, "I won't let him do that to you."

Though I appreciate his promise, it's empty. If Maksim wanted to do that to me, no one could stop him.

A fuss of voices draws my attention.

"Everyone, stay where you are," an American guy says, yelling over the party.

"If you move before we state otherwise, we'll shoot," another man calls out snappily. "Girls, get your fucking clothes on."

On alert, I glance about to assess the level of danger, as does James. A group of combat suited men are storming the ballroom with guns, and once they've got every man looking down their barrels, Charlie marches in, yelling for Maksim to stop. "Right now!"

My heart drops through me. I watch in dismay as the naked sex-slaves scatter like rats to get dressed, tripping over their dresses, and then one guy orders them to line up against the back wall; starts handing out bottles of water from the duffle bag he's holding. The men tuck themselves in, pulling up their pants and zipping up their trousers, and then they're lined up against the opposite wall to the girls, guns in their faces. Maksim staggers off the Albanian girl he's fucking to fasten his trousers, his cheeks tinted red with lust.

"What is going on?" the Asian Prince asks in terrible English, standing a few feet away from Maksim. He's looking through Charlie—who's got a blanket in one hand, a large gun in his other—and his men who are surrounding us all with a munitions store.

"That's Charlie Decena," I whisper to James, and he loads his gun.

I pull back the hammer on my gun too and step forward for Maksim but James catches my elbow, making me stumble to a stop.

"What are you doing?" I hiss, tugging to get free. "Let me go."

"Stay here. He's got over twenty men."

I gawk up at James in panic, then at Maksim who is face to face with Charlie in the middle of the room, and then back up at James. "We can't just leave Maksim."

"We don't want to start something if we can avoid it," James says, his eyes trained on the situation. "I've heard a rumor Charlie Decena doesn't enjoy things like this, so he's probably just putting a stop to the show."

"How'd you know that?" I ask, drawing in my eyebrows.

"What's the problem, my friend?" Maksim says, gaining my attention.

There's a moment of dangerous silence as Charlie towers over Maksim, tapering dominant blue eyes. "This is." He drops the blanket he's holding over the girl Maksim just fucked.

She's panting for dear life, understandably bested after being whipped and screwed by at least ten men, so of course I'm stunned when she says, "Why are you stopping the show?" She's gazing up at Charlie through scraps of chocolate brown hair. "Who are you?"

James and I look at each other, and then ahead at Charlie. He's dressed in jeans over black boots and a black long sleeve sweater, rather casual attire considering his men look ready for war. He passes the gun he's holding to his right hand man and crouches down to the girl, elbows on his knees. "You're Arjana, is that right?" he says, stroking her hair back out of her face.

She nods, an air of vulnerability coming over her.

"How do you know my name?" she says, descending into her shoulders. She's veiled in sweat and looks weak with trembling limbs.

He whispers something to her, his face soft and welcoming, and then wraps up her tiny naked frame in the blanket.

What the fuck's going on?

"Blaire," James says quietly, "does he have dealings with the Albanians?"

"I... I don't know," I stutter, trying to filter what's happening.

Standing with masculine poise, Charlie lifts the girl up into his arms, one under her knees and the other behind her shoulders, I think to avoid touching her wounded back. She huddles against him, seeming glad that he's here.

"Anymore of this bullshit," he warns, and leisurely pivots around, using the girl as a demonstration, "and we're all gonna have a problem—especially you, falso Prince."

He continues to scrutinize everyone, then his attention lands on me. His pale eyes widen and his jaw ticks. For the second time tonight, I don't know where to look.

"Charlie," Maksim says, ruffling his damp hair, "the girl is old enough and she's a willing participant. Tell him, Arjana..." he points out to her.

"Willing participant?" Charlie walks up to him, hunched at the neck. "She's stolen property. You of all people should know better than to fuck with the Albanians."

"She is payment for a debt owed to me," the Prince says, lifting his chin in an attempt to look proud.

"Debt or no debt," Charlie stalks over to the Prince, who cowers in his kameez, "we can all find ways to please ourselves without beating and gangbanging an eighteen year old girl." There's something eerie in the way Charlie is looking at the Prince. "Fuck her in a more private setting next time or find an older 'participant', as you so nicely put it, Maksim." He stalks back over to Maksim, holding that girl like she barely weighs a bag of sugar. "I mean, I'm all for a bit of sadism but this is bullshit." He practically spits in Maksim's face.

"It is just some fun," the Prince says, lifting his shoulders in a shrug.

"Fun?" Charlie raises his eyebrows at him, then he turns to his coward audience. "Maybe I should get all your wives here and have my men belt them and gangbang them for so long that their flesh shakes. How would you all like that?"

The ballroom is in quiet shock, and I'm just about to pass out with it when Charlie tells Maksim that he should send me home. "She doesn't need to see this-"

As he focuses on me, I grip James' arm.

"-You'll have her on all fours next," he continues, maintaining eye contact with me the entire time, "getting fucked by this brainless lot."

Maksim is stunned and humiliated, stuttering to defend himself but nothing worthy comes out.

I feel a surge of rage go through James. He steps forward for Charlie and the five men who are his armor lift their guns in our direction. I grab the back of James' sweater to stop him, my heart drumming in my ears.

Charlie isn't bothered by James' attempt at him—and why would he be? He's got an arsenal. He shakes his head at me, pity burning in his eyes. "Since when did men start having young girls protect them?" Before anyone can answer him, he turns away and leaves just as quickly as he came. His men follow out the double doors like a pack of wolves, and they shut us in.

No one is sure what to do—we're all just glancing at each other—but then Maksim rushes after Charlie, telling the Asian Prince, "I need to make sure there's no tension after this. That was Charlie Decena."

The Prince seems to know who Charlie is because he's gone white.

"What the hell was that all about?" James says under his breath, his eyes glued to the exit doors. "And why doesn't he address Maksim properly?"

"I have no idea," I say, dismayed by Charlie's bizarre act of kindness to save that girl.

Voices break through the silence, discussing Charlie and what he's just done. Some know who he is. Others don't. I try to listen in—I want to know who he is—but Maksim returns. He marches up to me, his expression tight with nerves. "Go home now," he orders in Russian. "I'll call you if I need you."

What?

"Do not stop to talk to anyone," he says in a charge of Russian words. He can't seem to relax, looking back and forth between the exit doors and me. "Just get in your car and leave."

James nudges me onward because I'm paralyzed with confusion.

Maksim grips my arm so tight I can feel his fingers digging into my flesh even through my combat sweater. "Get a move on."

I don't question him, even while I know this is out of character—he's never ordered me to leave before. Putting my head down, I walk through the murmuring ballroom, sort of thankful that I no longer have to endure the party.

What Charlie saw is nothing. It'll get darker as the night goes on.

BLAIRE
(PART ONE)

4

Saturday, and it's work as usual.

I pick up Maksim from his house and drive him to his friend Rumo's country manor. Maksim plays cards there once a month, but they always play at different times and days. Men like Maksim don't have routines. They say routines make them easy targets for their adversaries.

Maksim is on the phone throughout the drive—arranging a place for a few trafficked girls—so I don't have to endure a conversation with him. I'm glad. After coming eye to eye with him last night while he was having sex with that girl, I'll admit, I am a little nervous. There was something in the way he stared at me… in the way he touched that girl while staring at me…

Maksim hangs up the call as we pull up on Rumo's paved driveway. It's illuminated with floodlights. They're so bright that I have to squint. The redbrick house before us is a fortress; black iron bars covering the sash windows and a red laser security system surrounding the dwelling.

Two SUV's pull up around us, the rest of Maksim's security detail. No one can get to him without a war.

In the cold, I help Maksim out of my car by opening his door. I bow my head to him, clasping a heavy gun in one hand.

"You look lovely this evening, my little pet," he says in Russian, grinning at me with a cunning gleam in his eyes. "I haven't had a chance to tell you."

He looks good, too, in a sharp gray suit against a white shirt under a knee length black coat, his long brown hair curtaining his hard face. He smells nice—something spicy that makes my nose tickle as the night breezes against my face.

I don't thank him for his compliment, nor do I smile. I just bow a second time.

"Have you heard anything from Charlie Decena?" he asks, tipping his head. "After last night, I mean."

I nearly frown, peering up at him with innocent eyes. "No, сэр Maksim."

He studies me for a moment, scanning my expression. "So... he hasn't been to your apartment?" His golden eyes widen for an answer. "I know he fancies you."

"What? No, no! Of course he hasn't been to my apartment. I would have told you. You know I wouldn't-"

"Okay." Lifting a hand, he cuts me off. "That is good, I guess." He scratches his stubbly chin. I cringe at the sound of his bristly beard rubbing against his nails. "But he's up to something. I just know it. I don't get why he's come to me for help on a job..." he goes on and on about his confusion over Charlie's agenda. "And what he did at the Prince's party... that wasn't him. He wouldn't do something so thoughtful."

So... it isn't just me who thinks *he's* up to no good. That makes me anxious, and the fact that Maksim is questioning me over my loyalty makes me even more anxious. He should know I'd never keep anything from him.

I'm sweating in my uniform.

Maksim eventually asks, "What did you both talk about when you gave him a lift to London? Did he want to know anything about me?"

No hesitation, I spill my guts about the useless questions Charlie directed at me. "He waffled on about my car... how fast it goes... the color..." I tell him everything—leave nothing to chance.

James appears from one of the SUV's and I almost gasp out with relief. Maksim will focus on him for a moment. He's as fond of James as he is of me.

"Ahhh," Maksim breathes out with a broad smile, turning his attention to James. "He's here."

Wearing a black combat outfit just like I am, James walks up to us with steady composure and bows to Maksim, touching his chest.

"Hello, my pet." Maksim calls us both his pet; however, I'm his 'little' pet.

"Evening, сэр Maksim," James says. He's got a Russian peppered accent, his low notes deep and level.

"How are you this evening?" says Maksim, his eyes flaring with something that a man shouldn't express to another man.

James answers as courteous as ever with, "I'm great, thank you."

We never return Maksim's gestures. We're not allowed to. Maksim doesn't like having to explain his moods—not that he needs to. I can sense his moods a mile off. Tonight, he's thriving.

"Good. Good!" Maksim claps like a child in a sweetshop, grinning from ear to ear. "Well, let us get on with this evening. My best vodka is inside waiting for me."

Maksim turns his back on me and I internally shake my head. He drinks far too much.

James gently catches my hand and gives me a squeeze, causing me to peer up at him. He flashes his most affectionate smile, mouthing, "Are you okay?"

Nodding, I smile back. Then, we enter the house without an invitation—the front doors are open. James walks on Maksim's left while I walk on his right, both with a gun in hand. Maksim hides his away in his knee length coat. Though we're amongst friends, we're not at the same time. In this game, no one ever has a true friend.

The entrance hall boasts gleaming black and white marble floors, a huge white piano tucked away under the arch of the staircase on the right, and oak double doors on each wall.

"Maksim-Markov..." Rumo greets from the furthest doorway that leads into the snooker room. "You made it."

Smiling like the devil himself, Maksim heads for Rumo, extending a hand. "I am much looking forward to this evening's events, my friend."

"Ohhh, you should be. You should be." Rumo clasps Maksim's hand. "I bought a new poker table, as you requested. The chairs are a lot more comfortable and the table is softer."

Maksim nods a few times, saying that he's glad. "When *we* can afford luxury, why skimp on the finer details like a poker table?"

Entering the snooker room, they flannel on about some Albanian business.

James and I follow them in.

The brass lights hanging from the ceiling are dazzling, reflecting on the dark paneled walls in burnt orange tones. Behind the mammoth snooker table that commands the space, a poker table can seat six. They always play poker in this room. I've never seen any other part of the house.

Carl and Umberto await patiently, already sitting at the soft green table. Umberto greets Maksim from a distance with cool esteem. Carl simply nods.

Mucky cigar smoke clouds the air in streams of grays and browns, and it stinks. I hate the smell of cigars. I don't get the fascination.

James and I stay within touching distance of Maksim when he sits at the head of the poker table, draping his coat over the back of his chair.

"I hear you have Charlie on side, Maksim-Markov?" Carl says in awful English, flicking the head of his cigar in a crystal ashtray—he's Spanish.

"That's right, my friend."

"Even after what happened?" Umberto asks.

Maksim nods, scissoring a Cuban cigar between his fingers. "Yes, even after what happened. He forgives me."

Forgives him? For what?

James and I glance at each other.

"Just. Like. That?" Umberto pulls his thin gray eyebrows together. "You... you don't think that's... odd?"

Maksim laughs under his breath, biting the end of his cigar off. "Charlie isn't the kind of man to beat around the bush, is he, Carl?"

Carl doesn't respond to that sarcastic directed question. He doesn't even address Maksim.

"And besides," Maksim continues, "it is always good to have such a powerful man as a friend. Wouldn't you all agree?"

They go into a full blown tête-à-tête over Charlie and what he's about—loyalty, mostly. I come to understand that nothing else really matters to him. I also come to understand that Maksim double crossed him on some job a few years back.

I gulp at this point.

Rumo leans forward, staring at Maksim. "Just don't cross him again, Maksim-Markov. You know what he is capable of—you know he gears himself up with at least twenty armed men wherever he goes—and I can't get involved. I don't want to die."

"I know, my friend." Maksim squeezes Rumo's shoulder. "I know. I understand." He then grabs his crotch under the table. "Anyhow, why would I double-cross him again? I like my balls attached to my body."

They laugh out loud—well, everyone but Carl laughs.

This is strange. I've noticed before that Carl isn't Maksim's biggest fan—as has James—but tonight, his dislike for Maksim is coming off him in waves.

A tiny blonde girl wearing a red underwear set and shiny red stockings enters the room. She fills the men's glasses on the table. Umberto says he will fuck her after the game, emphasizing what he's going to do—whip her. She flinches when he grabs her ass with an open palm and I drop my eyes to the floor, feeling a pang of pity for her. It's not my job to save girls like her, as much as I wish I could. As much as I know I could. I'd slaughter this lot in minutes with my own two hands if I was allowed.

James gently touches my hand and I straighten, coming across deadpan.

"Five card draw?" Rumo says after the girl leaves, and everyone agrees.

So, they play cards, chatting lightly about girls they've abused and the wives they wish they could abuse. James and I keep quiet for the next two hours, antipathy radiating through us. We don't agree with what *they* do to girls. We have sneakily spoken about what we've seen and heard, but neither of us really knows what to make of it. We don't share their fancy for abuse, of course, but we know nothing else—we were so young when we came to Maksim. Once, James actually asked if he was wired wrong because he cannot bear to see girls getting mistreated—even if they do consent at times. He doesn't understand why Maksim enjoys being brutal. I couldn't give James an even answer. I just don't know if he's wired right or wrong. I know what I feel—what they do is immoral. But this sentiment only came over me when Maksim granted me freedom, and since then, I've lived in the world amongst the normal and with television and books. James has only ever lived under our master. He's never tasted what 'normal' might be; never felt that satisfaction of freedom that comes with living alone...

"Charlie spoiled our fun," Maksim says, and the mere mention of Charlie's name pulls me from my thoughts. "And he was mad as hell. I swear, if anyone questioned his actions, he would have shot us all."

He must be talking about the Prince's party last night.

"I heard about what happened." Umberto lifts a glass to have a sip of vodka. "The gossip has spread like wildfire. Glad I wasn't there. I know how excited Decena can get when angry."

Carl comes to life, telling stories about Charlie in his younger years. "If anyone so much as attempted to pull a gun on him, they'd be dead. He doesn't fuck about."

The tension in the room skyrockets, and I grip my gun a little tighter, remembering Charlie say he was coming to this poker game. Hopefully, he's changed his mind.

"Do not worry, my friends," Maksim lifts a hand, grinning from ear to ear, "I straightened things out. He wanted me to send Blaire home last night, so I did-"

My stomach rolls with shock. James gawps down at me.

"-And luckily," Maksim adds, "that girl we were fucking was old enough and willing to let us abuse her."

"Yeah, luckily..." Charlie says from the open doorway, gaining everyone's attention.

My eyes flicker to him and an overwhelming tightness forms in my chest. He's leaning against the doorframe on one shoulder with his arms crossed over a strapping chest, looking cool in his pose. Wearing a black shirt tucked into dark blue jeans, the collar unbuttoned to a hard, dusty chest. The sleeves are rolled up to his elbows, revealing masculine forearms tanned in black hair, thick with veins. He's got that silver watch on his left wrist, a minute statement of money.

Our eyes align for a split second, where he flashes me a cunning smile, showing even white teeth. I'm the one to look away, unable to endure his presence.

"Hola, Charlie." Carl pivots to him from the table. "Where have you been? We expected you hours ago."

Are they close friends or something?

Uncrossing his arms, Charlie saunters in and rounds the snooker table, his motions oddly graceful. As he passes James and I from behind, I hold my breath, and my toes fist in my trainers. I'm expecting him to do something—touch me in secrecy.

He doesn't but the fact remains. He puts me on edge—even more so with knowing Maksim has betrayed him somehow.

"Tis' good to see you, Carl." Charlie approaches the poker table; smiles coolly at Carl and only Carl. "Work kept me late. I'm sure I've not missed much."

I check him out from the corner of my eye. His hair is tied back, enhancing his gorgeousness—if that's even possible. It's so black and shiny; looks finger touching soft. I've never thought about touching a man before. Maybe I haven't because all the men I've been around are either on Maksim's payroll or at the end of my barrel.

Charlie shows no interest in anyone but Carl, though the other men fuss over him like he's some kind of god, offering up their chairs and their drinks.

"The end chairs are the most comfortable," Rumo says, giving Maksim a funny look, curtly nodding to the right, as if to say, 'get up and move'.

Charlie doesn't react to them with smugness—he doesn't really indulge their fussing at all. He simply shakes everyone's hand while asking Carl, "How's the wife?" acting as polite as ever.

I'm itching to know who the fuck he is, especially after he saved that girl last night. He's like the light and the dark; good and bad. It's so confusing because no one in this game is both.

"She's doing great," Carl says, cradling his whisky glass on the table. "We're on our third child. Her name is Gabrielle. She's the most perfect little thing."

"I'm sure she is perfect. Your wife is beautiful," Charlie says, though not in a smutty manner. He sounds like he genuinely thinks highly of Carl and his wife. "Tell her I said congratulations," he adds, then takes Maksim's seat by grabbing the back in a way of authority, forcing Maksim to move over one. James and I follow him to the right, staying behind him.

"A drink?" Rumo says to Charlie, appearing a little nervous, tugging open his silver tie.

Charlie nods, slowly taking to his chair. Then, his eyes flitter between James and me, causing my stomach to roll with anxiety. I don't meet his gaze. I stare past him, endeavoring to come across collected in my pose.

"Someone's got a thing for redheads," he teases, referring to James and I, flicking up his eyebrows at Maksim. "They've gotta be related..." Turning his head, he says to James, "What's your name, boy?"

Maksim waves out a hand and James states his name, his voice coming out cold and detached.

"And you're obviously part of Maksim's security alongside Blaire?"

James nods. "Yes, sir."

"Sir?" Charlie looks amused and pleased with James' word choice. "Well, it's been a while since I was called sir. You should have seen this boy last night," he winks at Carl from across the table in a sly manner, "actually tried to stand up to me and all my men-"

My heart sinks with unease but James looks confident in his domain.

"-Though I can't blame him," Charlie says. "He clearly thought I was mocking this one." He gestures at me and smiles. It makes him look so handsome and young, which is odd given how sovereign he is.

"Yes," Maksim drawls, "I used to have a hard time training Blaire because he didn't like my process. He is too fond of her."

"Aren't we all?" Charlie eyes Carl, who seems entertained with his daring.

Maksim doesn't respond to that. He ushers me forward by clicking his fingers, telling me to get Charlie a drink. "You still like brandy, don't you, Charlie?"

"Yeah," Charlie says, and I hate that I can feel his steady blue eyes on me; on my body. "Especially if she's making it."

On autopilot, I walk over to the bar in the corner of the room, put down my gun, and fix him a drink.

"You opened your new club yet?" Charlie asks. I assume he's addressing Rumo, given his club opened last week.

"Of course," Rumo says; blathers on about his new adventure—the whores, as he calls them. "They're filthy as fuck, and for you all, my close friends, they're free."

Men... I roll my eyes. They're so easily distracted with tits and ass.

"I think I'll pass," Charlie says. "Don't like whores. I prefer my women clean and exclusive with a bad attitude."

Carl chuckles.

I grab the brandy from the side and take it to Charlie. He's surveying me come to him. My stomach won't stop rolling with anxiety, but I try to save face by being as impassive as I can.

"Hello, Blaire," he says when I stop in front of him, his Latin infused voice bringing hot chills to my skin. "It's nice to see you again. Did you enjoy an early night last night?" He smiles at me with bold seduction, his blue eyes glancing back and forth between mine.

He's so fucking handsome it makes me sick.

I nod at him by a way of forced respect.

"I've gotta say, you're even prettier in the light—isn't she pretty, Carl?"

Carl agrees, sparking a lighter for his cigar. "Even when she was younger, she was a pretty girl."

Charlie smirks at Maksim with mocking enthusiasm. "You really have to fix the lighting in your office." He then smirks back at me, hypnotized in his gaze. "What's the point of owning something so lovely when you can't fully appreciate it?"

I gesture impatiently with the glass, urging Charlie to take it. He does, and he runs his thumb over mine, causing me to jerk away from him as that familiar tingly feeling spreads through my body. A black switch goes off in my head—the switch that says, *KILL!* The switch that flickers on when someone touches me.

I don't attack him. I don't know why.

I manage to keep my cool and step back behind Maksim, training my eyes on the wall behind Charlie.

James gives me a weird side-glance, I see from the corner of my eye.

"How's work coming along?" Charlie asks me. Pressing his feet into the ground, he slides his chair around to face me.

A few uncomfortable looks are thrown around but Charlie doesn't care. He simply sits back and drapes his hands over the arms of the chair, holding the glass in one hand.

"You can answer him, my little pet," Maksim says, centered on the cards in his hand.

"Things are coming along fine," I say, squeezing the gun over my lap in both hands, fighting for composure.

"Just fine?" he asks.

I step around so I can see Maksim's face—and also to get out of Charlie's line of vision.

Maksim nods at me.

"Things are running like clockwork," I lie. Now is not the time to confess that I'm not only failing to attain fifteen minutes, but behind schedule.

"Good." A devious grin reaches Charlie's eyes. He looks me up and down, leisurely and with intent. "Hmmm, I like what you're wearing."

Oh, of course he does. My combat outfit is tight and black, covering every inch of my small frame but my face.

I think my cheeks heat up but I don't show a reaction—well, not deliberately.

James is wearing the same, but I doubt Charlie will compliment him.

"Can you breathe in those trousers?" he teases.

I shoot him a wolfish glare and he winks at me.

I press my teeth together. Why does this bastard have to provoke me?

Rumo and Umberto lewdly compliment my clothes too, saying what dirty things they'd like to do to me, if they were allowed.

"That was a private joke," Charlie says, and the room submerges in silence.

I peer over at James. He's staring at me, baffled beyond belief.

"So, Maksim..." Charlie says after having a sip of his brandy, "about your offer to see Blaire in action..."

James and I look at each other—this is about the only communication we achieve in Maksim's company.

"In action?" Umberto's eyes light up. "Are we to enjoy a... a fuck show?" He hesitates to say the words, I assume because he's remembering what happened last night.

"No..." Maksim says in a deep note, lifting a hand. "No one is fucking my little pet."

"No, they're not," Charlie says.

Maksim blinks at him. James and I blink at each other. Charlie's presence is so intense—it's like walking on fire.

"So, what show?" Umberto asks, seeming at a loss with a stupid expression on his wrinkly face.

"Maksim was telling me Blaire is a good fighter," Charlie elaborates, speaking with his hands. "He offered to show me just how skilled a fighter she is."

I detest how he addresses Maksim, especially in front of his friends.

"Oh, I see." Umberto emphasizes that he's never seen a girl battle with such raw fighting skills. "She's like a fucking cheetah she's so quick. You never said she was fighting tonight, Maksim-Markov?"

"I was waiting on Charlie," he says. "It is a surprise."

My heart drums in my ears. I'm not often nervous but I don't often have time to get my head around having a fight. I usually do, rather than think.

"Why don't we retire to the ballroom?" Rumo says, rubbing his hands together. "There is plenty of space for her to fight. We should bet?" Everyone concurs, then Rumo adds, "I've never seen Blaire fight before but Carl has told me she's good."

"That's because she is," Carl says, though he doesn't sound as animated as the others.

Nonetheless, Rumo grins. "Well, then let us get a move on."

BLAIRE
(PART ONE)

5

Chairs scrape against the wooden floors as everyone stands up from the table, including Charlie. He's getting on my last nerve with all this curious bullshit. I'm desperate to ask Maksim if I can fight him just so I can kick his ass.

James and I follow Maksim and the rest of the men through the entrance hall, down a wide lobby, and into a huge open space—a ballroom. All these rich motherfuckers have them. The room oozes luxury with ivory paneled walls, a large sparkly chandelier hanging overhead, and decadent, highly buffed wooden floors. Their oxford shoes echo through the space as we go forth, stopping by the French doors that lead out onto the back garden.

"My little pet," Maksim calls in Russian for me to stand in front of him, waving me forward. He takes my gun and tells James to put his down on the window ledge. "You and James will battle until one is unconscious, is that clear?"

Charlie steps in front of us and crosses his arms. "Unconscious?"

My face drops. *He can speak Russian?*

Maksim nods. "It will be a good fight, my friend. You'll see."

"No way. I'm not up for seeing this little girl unconscious." Charlie points at me, then tucks his hand back into his crossed arms. "I just wanner see what she's made of."

I almost huff. I'm insulted, truly, but quite eager to see the shock in this bastard's eyes when I knock James out cold.

Shit, no. What am I thinking? I don't want to do that to James. I don't want to hurt him.

"Charlie, relax, my friend." Maksim pulls me under his arm. I lean into him, into his warmth like a cat getting petted. He always pets me before a fight. "James will not beat Blaire. She's too good."

"She is," Carl concurs.

Charlie frowns down at me. "Is that right?"

Tipping my head back, I peek up at Maksim, almost purring. Since before I can remember, I've been robbed of affection, so when Maksim is like this I bask in his touch. I bask in the way he holds me. I guess everyone needs affection at some point in their lives, even me.

"Don't look at him-" Charlie snaps, making me flinch.

Everyone is instantly on guard, glancing at each other.

"-Look at me and answer me, Blaire."

Maksim squeezes my arm to give me the go ahead.

"Yes, that's right," I whisper.

I can feel James' anxiety behind us coming off him in waves. It would usually make my stomach turn over with guilt. Now, however, I'm too preoccupied with Maksim. He's so warm and he smells like freshly burnt brut. At times like this, I can almost imagine myself as a different person, someone who can and will thrive in another's tenderness. No more brutality. Just, this.

"Okay, Charlie?" Maksim says, holding me tighter under his arm. He knows I enjoy his touch. I've told him many of times when he's asked.

Charlie grinds his square jaw. "Yeah, but if I call it to a stop, they have to stop. I don't wanner see her half dead."

Somehow, he's snapped me out of this needy trance. I'm not sure if I'm angry, affronted, or flattered by his demand.

I frown.

No one has ever broken me out of a trance when Maksim holds me.

"Blaire, you understand?" Maksim looks down at me. "If Charlie says stop, you will both stop."

I nod, innocently blinking up at him.

"You too, James," Maksim says, glancing back.

"Yes, сэр Maksim."

"Good." My master gives me another squeeze before saying in Russian, "Now, the both of you go on and take position in the middle of the room."

When I glance up at Charlie he nods at me. I'm not sure why.

Turning out of Maksim's embrace, I come face to face with James. He appears very deadpan but I know he's nervous—I can sense it on another level. I don't enjoy fighting my friend like this either, so I guess I am a little nervous too but I have no other choice. Maksim will beat the shit out of me if I refuse, and like always, I'll do nothing to stop him.

While the men light up cigars and place bets, James and I walk into the middle of the room and stand opposite each other. His face is pale against short red hair, his eyes a dark shade of blue under this light. My hair is tied back in a bun but that won't stop James from trying to get a good hold on me.

I won't let that happen.

"Form position!" Maksim calls out in Russian, modestly annoyed because we haven't done so already.

Raising our fists to protect our faces and opening our legs to create balance through our bodies, James and I nod at each other.

"Just go down," I whisper, holding his uneasy gaze.

"He won't like that," James mouths back. "He wants to show you off."

My heart sinks because he's right. Maksim won't like that. He's boasting.

"I'm sorry," I say truthfully. At least I tried to spare him, for this moment.

"Fight!" says Maksim in Russian.

James and I smile pitifully at each other to apologize for what is about to happen. Then, he goes in for the kill. He swings for my face with a few steady punches. I evade his onslaught with effortless grace, ducking and weaving to the left and the right, my muscles easing into my motions.

James always dishes out the first hit, I've noticed over the years. It gives me an advantage because one is off balance while trying to strike.

I've never told him of his bad-habit, since we often have to fight each other to train or entertain and it gives me a chance to put him down before things get bloody.

I dodge another punch, then James pounces at me. I catch his wrist and fling him across the room with all the strength I have, letting out a harsh breath. I then run at him and dish out meditated jabs, landing a few to his hard stomach when I can get through his fist attack. He gasps, twisting his face in pain, but manages to keep focus.

I don't stop there.

I dance him around in circles, lashing out athletic kicks to bat away his punches until I'm behind him.

I'm trained with Wing Chun, a Chinese Martial Arts way of fighting. Since I was... well, I don't really know how old I was when I first started fighting, but I was young, I've always fought this way.

My muscles now warm and loose, I beat James' kidneys with perfect clenched fists, exhaling for each strike. My assault puts him on his knees, groaning in agony. Clutching the scruff of his neck, I ceaselessly beat him into a bloody haze, my knuckles cracking and throbbing with pain. His eyes come up real good, red and bruised and puffy. He will look like hell tomorrow.

I boot him in the chest, knocking him over with brutal force. He doesn't get up, just lies there half curled up in a ball. So I wait, trying to filter the rush of adrenaline. I don't want to get lost in myself while fighting my friend.

The seconds tick by at snail pace. I can hear the men over there by the doors muttering amongst themselves, though I can't make out what they're saying.

James is still crippled on the floor. I steal over to assess him to make sure he's okay. He jumps to his feet and clouts me right in the face, whipping my head back and splitting my bottom lip. The pain is dull. I spit out a pool of metallic flavored blood and meet his blows with rapid movements, punch for punch, my knuckles smashing against his; my chest on fire with controlled breaths. "Aargh!" I scream through clenched teeth with every strike.

He's battling in his stride, and because I know I can't get through his ambush, I lash out a high axe kick, knocking his head back. Dizzy again, he stumbles about.

I pant through my nose, watching him strive to gather himself.

"She's fucking unbelievable!" someone yells, keyed up—I think it's Rumo.

When James is back on par, he darts at me, growling, "Gragh!" He kicks my feet and jabs through the air like he's going for gold, forcing me around the room.

With my forearms, I block his storm, left then right, amid punting away his lazy kicks. He's trying to knock me over by kicking my feet but he's not doing a good job of it. I'm a little angry with him. He knows I'm good with my feet.

I side-kick behind his knee to put him off balance, then I twirl around and flip him over, scissoring him between my legs. I land on my palms as we hit the floor with a heavy thud, my hands throbbing with pain. Unfolding my legs from around his body, I kick him away and leap to my feet, stretching out my thigh muscles.

James struggles to get up and when he does, staggers back, I assume to put some distance between us for a breathing moment.

The adrenaline rushing through me is intoxicating, tingly sensations swimming in my bloodstream—I'm slowly losing focus. My heart is pounding.

"What... what are you-you waiting for?" James pants, squeezing his eyes shut a few times.

Fast and smooth, I sprint at him. I land a nice clean blow to the center of his face, causing his nose to explode. My knuckles pulsate but the pain goes away after a few seconds of flexing my hand.

"That is it, my little pet!" Maksim chants in Russian. "Kill him!"

"Kill him?" I stop then to look at Maksim and James thumps me square in the face, knocking me clean into the air.

I'm in a haze for a moment, plummeting backward, wondering if Maksim actually wants me to kill James.

My back cracks when it hits the hard floor. I wince, arching over on my side.

Maksim's control over my mind doesn't always serve me well. One word—one click of his fingers—and I lose focus.

I don't want to kill my friend. I have to clarify this before I do.

Booting me in the stomach, James winds me. I cough up thick, warm blood, struggling to breathe for a moment. I manage to wrap my arms around James' ankles, ensuring he cannot kick me again.

"Not literally, Blaire!" Maksim shouts in Russian. "Fucking get up!"

James grabs a fist-full of my hair and pounds me in the face, sending shooting pains right through my skull. My head lashes back and forth but I'm still here. I'm not out cold yet.

"Stop the fight!" someone yells. "Now, Maksim!"

"Just wait," Maksim says. "Blaire, Podgotovsja! Konchaj yego!"

My senses come to attention.

Bent over me, James is weak in his stance. I dig my nails into the backs of his knees and yank him forward with a loud groan, putting him on his ass. His grip still in my hair, he drags me forward with him, making my scalp tear.

He's trying to get up now, at the same time shoving me into the floor.

I fight to my feet, spin out of his grasp in my hair and boot him where it hurts.

"Oh, fuck!" cupping his crotch, he goes down like a sack of shit, all the color draining from his face.

I step back, panting like a wild cat, wiping damp strands of hair back out of my face.

"Finish him!" Maksim yells.

James wobbles to his feet and I know this is my moment—any longer, and it'll be a bloodbath. I jump up into the air with facility, wrap my legs around his neck and flip over to put him down completely. I land on the floor with open palms, James' neck between my thighs. I use all my lower body weight to keep him facedown, tensing and gritting my teeth, pressing my hands into the cold wooden floors. The veins in my eyes feel like they might pop but I don't stop. I squeeze and squeeze and squeeze.

"Jesucristo!" someone shouts out. "I thought he had her!"

Gasping and wriggling, James tries to pries my legs open, digging his fingers into my flesh. He's fruitless. I might be small but I'm strong.

"Davaj, devochka!" Maksim yells, 'that's it girl'. "Put him to sleep!"

I do, my heart twisting with remorse. This doesn't happen often, me feeling a sense of guilt, but it's happening now.

I'm sorry...

After a few minutes, James falls limp in my thigh tight grasp.

BLAIRE
(PART ONE)

6

Gasping, I loosen my grip on James and roll onto my back, relieved the fight is over.

A round of applause breaks out, echoing through the large room. I don't soak up the ovation. Lost somewhere in my mind, I turn over onto my knees and push to my feet, lengths of hair sticking to my sweaty, bloody face. Standing there, I look down at James. He's battered, bruised and bested. My chest aches at the sight of him. I hate that Maksim makes us do this to each other. Training together in my apartment is fine because we stop when one calls for a ceasefire, but in moments like this, we have to fight until one is cataleptic, or worse...

...I've had to kill to entertain many times before.

"You weren't lying," Charlie says, sauntering toward me with a white towel in hand, his inky black hair curling around his neck and face. He's undone his ponytail. "She's extraordinary." Reaching me, he says softly, "Wipe yourself off." He shakes out the towel, I assume because I don't take it. I'm just glaring at him, a storm brewing inside me.

BLAIRE
(PART ONE)

"What's with the silence? Hm?" His blue eyes glow with uncertainty as they search mine. "Maksim said you can speak to me."

I huff under my breath, amazed by his impudence. He goads Maksim into making me beat my friend half to death and wonders why I don't want to chat?

"I don't need that," I refuse the towel. Crouching down, I pick up my friend from the floor, hooking my arms under his so I can drag him out to the car.

"Leave him-" Maksim says.

I glance up, my muscles straining under James' weight.

"-Go on. Leave him where he is." Maksim smiles at me with zealous wickedness, standing amid the other men who are patting him on the back.

"Okay," I say softly and without thinking. "Sure." I carefully put James back down on the ground and fold his hands in his chest.

"Don't worry," Charlie whispers, draping the towel over his shoulder, "I'll put your friend in his car."

"Don't you dare touch him," I warn under my breath and stand up to him in defiance, barely coming up to his chest. I have no idea why I feel I can talk to him like this, but I do. "You asked for this."

He hunches down so we're almost at eye level, hands on his knees. "I just wanted to see what you're made of."

"Well, now you've seen." I'm trying to be sarcastic but I can't keep the misery out of my voice. "Happy?"

A lick of blood slithers down the side of my face, over my cheekbone. I catch it with a single finger and wipe it off on my trousers.

"You in a lot of pain?" Charlie lifts a hand to touch me, ignoring my question. "I can get you some painkillers if you need them?"

I bat away his hand with such force it makes a slapping sound. "I'm not allowed painkillers."

His eyes widen. "Like hell you're not."

I ball my trembling hands, the storm inside me whirling like hurricane Katrina getting ready to explode. "Who are you to tell me what I can or cannot have?" I'm just about to tell Charlie to piss off and leave me alone, then-

"What are you two talking about?" Maksim asks, reminding me that Charlie and I are not alone, and James is still lying there at my feet.

On instinct, so I don't get in trouble, I say, "Charlie was just praising me, cǝp Maksim." I give Charlie a desperate, knowing look. "Weren't you?"

"Yeah, I was," he concurs loud enough for all to hear, and then whispers, "For that, I wanner talk to you before the night is over."

I frown at him, maintaining eye contact. What could he possibly want to talk to me about?

There's a faint vibrating sound not very far away. I realize it's Charlie's mobile when he pulls it from his jeans pocket.

He doesn't even check the screen to see who it is—he doesn't once look away from me. "What?" he answers, and because we're just staring at each other, I blink about in a fluster.

He leaves the room through another door, I see out the corner of my eye.

BLAIRE
(PART ONE)

This is so fucking weird. I've never lied to Maksim before, and I'd never be so blatant as to hold someone's gaze in front of my master.

"Come over here and have a drink, my little pet," Maksim says, and I'm assured by his relaxed tone of voice that he hasn't clocked onto anything.

I walk stolid across the room with a slight twinge in my back, smoothing scraps of hair back out of my face.

"There you go..." He gives me his glass and smiles with obvious elation. "Drink up. It will make you feel better."

I nod with a forced smile, taking the glass. It's cold against my palm and quite heavy. I scoop out a cube of ice and press it to my broken lip, blinking droplets of sweat over my lashes. Not just sweat. Blood. It makes my left eye sting.

"Told you she was good," Umberto says, his chin doubled because he's staring down at me from at least six foot.

"Yes..." Rumo's eyes thin as he looks at me. "You should put her in the monthly fights at my farm, Maksim-Markov. We could make some serious money off of her."

"No! No!" Maksim laughs, tipping up the glass to motion I have a sip. "It would be unfair on her opponents."

The vodka burns my throat; makes me gasp a little.

"You can say that again," Umberto says between chuckles. "Imagine, we would be accused of fixing the fights."

Everyone but Carl laughs at his silly joke, and then Rumo says they should get back to playing poker.

"Umberto now has an extra fifty thousand to burn as he bet on Blaire winning."

Of course he did. I'm not sure he's ever missed one of my fights.

"Go put James in the car, my little pet." Maksim leans in to kiss the wound on my eyebrow, causing me to wince internally. He then puts warm lips on my ear and whispers, "Be cautious of Charlie if you run into him, and when you are done with James, meet me in the snooker room where we will be playing poker."

Nodding, I pass him back the glass and walk over to James, a morsel of pain still in my back like needles in my spine. Must be due to landing on this hard floor.

James remains out cold, I see when I'm within touching distance, his hands still folded in his chest. He's not moved an inch.

Poor guy.

I have to block out the sentiment of guilt—it's the last thing I need to be feeling right now. I must keep my wits about me as I'm the only person inside Rumo's house who can protect Maksim, should he need me.

With both hands, I grab under James' arms. He's heavy like deadweight so I use my lower body strength to move him.

Charlie appears in front of me and takes James' forearms; tries to throw him over his shoulder.

"What are you doing?" I snap, standing up straight. "Will you go away?" My eyes dart over to the doors. Fortunately, Maksim and his friends are out of sight.

"Will you calm down?" Charlie scowls at me, putting James back down on the floor. "I'm just helping you."

"Helping me?" I squeak in shock, my hands trembling to hit him. "If you didn't provoke Maksim, James wouldn't be lying here unconscious." I'm struggling to keep my voice down. He really gets under my skin. "Why don't you go play a hand of poker? Leave the hard work to those of us who have no other choice but to do the heavy lifting."

"Why do you stay with Maksim?" he asks completely off topic, cocking his head.

I scoff. *Another stupid question.* He seems to be full of them.

"I know your friend here is fitted with a tracking device," he says, waving a hand at James, "yet, you're not and you stick around... Why is that?"

My jaw drops. He's been asking around about us? Not well enough though, it seems. I'm not fitted with a tracking device because I have my master's absolute trust. James is because Maksim isn't a silly man. He knows that if James had half the chance he'd try to leg it. It would be a foolish mistake however. Maksim has the British government in his pocket because he brings millions to the economy with his trafficked girls, so if James ever did run, he'd be picked up by the police within the day.

"Why do you address Maksim with such insolence?" I say, putting Charlie under the spotlight. "Don't you think you ought to learn some respect?"

He snorts with affront. "Because I'd speak up to someone who's below me, wouldn't I?"

I shake my head in obvious loathing, refusing to argue cat and dog style. "I don't know who you think you are..."

I grip my friend's ankles and haul him across the floor, toward the doors. Charlie takes James' wrists and lifts him off the ground, his arm muscles bulging with tension.

"Charlie," I growl his name, curling my lips against my teeth.

"Look," he says, releasing James again, "you can drag your friend out like a dead body, or you can let me help you." Though he's giving me an option, his tone doesn't really leave any room for argument. "The choice is yours." He snatches the towel off his shoulder and flings it at me. "Wipe your face. You're bleeding."

Dropping James' legs, I catch the towel with both hands, wondering why he's doing this. Why is he provoking me? And then why is he trying to help me?

Charlie nods at the towel and I don't know why, but I wipe my sweaty forehead before cleaning up my bloody mouth, wincing when I press it to my busted lip. I'm bleeding more than I thought. The white towel soaks through with claret.

Charlie walks up to me, his stride confident and unhesitant. Reaching out, he lifts my chin with a single finger, forcing us to look at each other. A rush of heat sweeps through me, making my skin flush, and then my stomach tingles with... I don't know.

I do nothing. I just stand there like a brainless statue; swallow past the restriction in my throat.

"Your eye is bleeding quite a lot," he says softly, glancing between my eyes and my mouth. With his other hand, he covers mine where I'm holding the towel to my lip and forces me to press it to my eye, dabbing there.

It stings, but that isn't what's bothering me.

I back up out of his grip to put some well needed distance between us, unable to think or speak. I just look at him, unnerved.

He observes me from a few feet away, running his tongue across the sharp of his upper teeth. I'm sure he knows how he makes me feel when he touches me. I can see it in his eyes.

He nods a few times, confirming something to himself.

"What?" I say, but he doesn't answer me.

Breaking eye contact, he crouches down, grips James around the waist and tosses him over his shoulder. Straightening, he heads for the exit with steady grace, as if carrying a shopping bag rather than a fully grown man.

For a time, I'm frozen in the middle of the ballroom, watching him leave. What is it with the way he touches me? Why does he make me feel weird?

Tossing the towel on the floor, I jog through the house to go after him. Outside, the floodlights are beaming in full force. I squint, catching up with Charlie.

He seems to know exactly where he's going because he's heading straight for the SUV James arrived in.

"Open the back door," he says, nodding at the car, so I do. He bends at the knees to put James across the back seats and tells the other two in the car to just let him rest. "If you give him water when he wakes up, make sure he takes it in small sips."

"Eh, okay," they say in union, glancing at each other, then back at Charlie.

Now James is safely in his car, I relax somewhat. I turn for the house, heading back to Maksim.

"Are you gonna answer my question?" Charlie says, walking up beside me. "I just had your back in there, so the least you could do is-"

"What question, Charlie?"

"Why'd you stay with Maksim? Why doesn't he insist you wear a tracking device?"

I roll my eyes, refusing to go there.

We jog up the porch steps together.

"Blaire?" He gently touches my arm.

"Are you stupid or just deaf?" I face him, stepping back because we're too close for comfort. "I'm not allowed to talk about Maksim. Do you want to get me fucking whipped?"

"He whips you?" Charlie says this like he's surprised, raising his eyebrows. "We'll have to remedy your situation then, won't we?"

"Fuck you." I step for him, craning my head back so I can defiantly meet his wicked gaze. "Fuck you and whatever you're up to."

He looks down on me like I'm small and harmless. "I'm not up to anything."

I laugh under my breath, jabbing a finger at my temple. "You must think me a fool, Charlie."

"Not at all. Far from it, actually."

"Yes," I huff at him, looking between his eyes as he looks between mine. "I've seen men like you my whole life. I know when one is up to no good."

"I'm not up to anything. I'm just curious as to why a pretty girl like you who has immense discipline and fighting skills, bows to a motherfucker like Maksim." His eyes pour over my body, and the lust that burns in his expression... it's back in full force. "It's crazy. I mean, look at you... how strong you are." He gestures at me with a sturdy hand. "You could choose your own path, Blaire, and you damn well know it."

I point at the ground between us. "This is all I know—it's all I've ever known."

Leaning down, putting us eye to eye, he whispers, "You can learn something new."

"Oh?" I cross my arms, stepping away from him. "Because it's that easy, is it?"

"If you had me on your side it'd be easy."

I don't for a second entertain what he's offering. I'll never be ready to abandon Maksim.

"I'm going nowhere. I'm going nowhere until Maksim orders me away. Have you got that?" The veins in my neck tick. "Now, just leave me alone."

He sidesteps me when I try to rush past him.

"Why are you doing this to me?" I ask in frustration, uncrossing my arms to squeeze my fists at my sides. "Last night you had Maksim send me home, tonight you're provoking him into making me fight, and then you almost call it off because you didn't want to see me 'half dead'," I air quote 'half dead'. I know it was him who shouted for Maksim to stop the fight. He's the only person I've ever heard address Maksim by only his first name. "And now you're trying to influence me into turning my back on Maksim?"

"I'm not doing that." The tranquil expression on his face makes my blood boil.

"Then what are you doing, Charlie?" I have to squeeze out every word through clenched teeth. "Because I can't work you out."

"Maybe I just think you are a waste as 'his little pet'." He also uses air quotations, to mock me, I think.

"That's not an explanation for all your actions," I say with anger. "Why won't you leave me alone?"

"Okay..." shrugging and nodding at once, he gives in to me, "I don't think I need to explain why I made him send you home last night—no young girl wants to watch that perverted shit—and as for the fight tonight, I wouldn't have let it go too far. If I thought you were in trouble, I would've stopped it myself." He sounds genuine, and given his actions, I think I believe him. I'm not sure.

Maybe I'm just too proud to admit to myself that I believe him.

"I can't be doing this." I push him out of the way, using both hands to move his large body. "Maksim is waiting for me." As I walk past him, he grabs my wrist, forcing me to gasp in anger.

"Don't do that, Charlie," I warn, looking down at his hand wrapped around my wrist. "I don't want to hurt you."

He yanks me into him with powerful force, causing my head to jerk back.

"I'm not afraid of you, Blaire," he whispers in my face, his brandy seasoned breath warm on my cheeks.

I glance between his blue eyes, fear and fury surging through me. "You should be."

We're like this for a moment, staring at each other in a power standoff, and then I realize...

...All of Maksim's men are surrounding us in the SUV's. They can see what's going on.

I'm going to get in trouble if Charlie doesn't back off.

"Blaire, listen to me-"

"Let me go," I say to cut him off. "Please, Charlie. All of Maksim's men are here and they're probably watching. Just let me go."

He frees me then without hesitation this time. I stumble back a step and hug my middle, letting out the breath I've been holding.

"You don't have to go back in there," he says, shoving his hands in his jeans pockets. "My car's over there. You can come and work for me if you want. You can utilize yourself in a better way, Blaire—you don't have to live like an emotionless robot."

There it is. The way the world sees me.

"You know nothing about me," I say, boldly meeting his gaze. "You know nothing about what I've been through or what I feel." There's so much more that I want to say to him, but I won't. I won't let him break me down because Maksim will only have to put me back together again. "Leave me alone, Charlie."

My eyes on the ground, I walk past him, through the welcome hall and into the snooker room where I take my position next to Maksim.

My hands are shaking like crazy. I hide them behind my back, gathering my composure.

"Do you think Charlie will attend?" Umberto says, blathering on about some party Maksim is holding next week. I don't pay attention to the rest of their conversation. It dawns on me that I didn't once attack Charlie for touching me. No one but Maksim has ever laid a finger on me without reaping my wrath.

My head is a vapor of confusion. I don't get this.

Maybe I didn't attack because Maksim said in his office that I'm not allowed to fight Charlie.

I put it down to that. It's the only thing that makes sense.

"My little pet," Maksim says, and when I look up at him, I see he's proffering my gun.

Taking it, I nod by way of respect.

Charlie returns around ten minutes later, his ink black hair a little ruffled, as if he's been running his fingers through the strands.

"Where were you?" Carl asks, examining Charlie as he takes to his seat. "We've been waiting."

"I was helping Blaire with James." He scoops up his cards from the table, focusing his attention. "We can get on with the game now."

"You helped her with James?" Maksim raises his eyebrows at Charlie, then he peers back at me with the same shocked expression on his iron face. "Ohhh, isn't that nice, my little pet?"

My bones chill from the tone of his voice. He isn't happy.

The rest of the night goes by smoothly, thankfully, and Charlie doesn't say another word to me. (Double thankfully).

The men talk business and ask Charlie to attend the next poker game. He says he will if he's in town, which pleases Carl. "But I can't guarantee anything. I've got a lot of work that needs my focus."

I'm glad to hear that he might be leaving. He's causing too much bother around me. He's fucking with my chi.

By the time the clock strikes four A.M., I'm relieved the game is over. We're all leaving to go home.

At the front doors, while Rumo is bidding us all goodbye, Charlie gives me this weird look, blatantly staring at me in front of everyone.

"We still on for tomorrow then, Charlie?" Carl repeats his question because Charlie isn't paying attention. He's just... well, he's looking at me, his hands shoved in his jeans pockets.

I disregard his scrutiny and link arms with Maksim because he's out of his mind drunk. I help him stagger across the driveway and into my car. When he's slumped in the passenger seat, I jump into the driver's seat, fire up the engine, and reverse out of the driveway.

"Here you go." He passes me a bundle of cash for fighting. He always pays me for what I do, which is sort of odd, given he doesn't pay James.

"Thank you, сэр Maksim." Leaning over him, I click open the glove compartment and shove the bundle inside.

We're quiet for a while, the only sound being the car engine rumbling as I steer out of the suburban street; the security detail on our trail.

"My friend Charlie has taken a liking to you," Maksim says eventually, and randomly. I can feel his golden eyes on my face, scanning my reaction.

"I wouldn't know," I lie for the second time tonight, my expression impassive. I'm not sure Charlie's reasons are genuine, but he's definitely pursuing me. I'm not an idiot.

"You would tell me if he tries anything with you, wouldn't you, my little pet?"

My stomach twists with disloyalty—it's almost crushing. I should tell Maksim about the things Charlie said to me, that he's curious and that I can choose my own path if I really wanted to, that he'd be on my side, but I just... I just can't. I've never kept anything from Maksim before, but this, what Charlie and I spoke about, it feels... weirdly private. And, I don't want to go over it at all, if I'm truly honest. I don't want to analyze. I just want to forget. I want Charlie to piss off back to wherever he came from so my life can go back to normal.

"After I've broken his nose for touching me," I say in response to Maksim's question, blank of emotion, "of course."

This makes him laugh, though in a lazy manner—he's tired.

"You are a good, loyal, little pet." He snuggles down in his coat and rests his eyes, and I cannot help thinking over what he just said: *Charlie has taken a liking to you.*

The man is out to cause trouble. I know it. I wish I knew why.

"Do you have anything you want to ask?" Maksim says in a sleepy voice.

There's a million things I want to ask, but only one question makes sense. I brace myself for a blow as I say, "Who is Charlie exactly?"

The blow doesn't come. Maksim doesn't move in his seat.

He's quiet for a while. I train my attention on the road so I don't look too interested.

"Remember last month?" he says in time. "Tatiana and I had you study Mexico and the Los Zetas?"

Tatiana is his boss—and more, the Russian Mafia leader. She never makes an appearance unless it's absolutely necessary, and that's only ever when she needs to cause bloody murder.

I nod when Maksim looks at me, then I turn right onto the motorway.

"Charlie... Charlie Decena is the son of the man who first deserted his army rank and created the Los Zetas." Maksim doesn't sound too comfortable speaking about this. He pauses every so often. "They are considered the most dangerous criminal organization in the world... famous for their torture techniques and power throughout Southern America."

That explains the American accent with a touch of Latin.

"Charlie in particular is known famously for his wicked torture techniques," Maksim continues. "He... he likes to break women down with pleasure and pain, always ensuring their humanity remains intact." Maksim laughs like he's proud of this, his voice a bit croaky. "Women are nothing if not weak when it comes to humanity."

I cannot relate to this, so I don't ponder over it too much.

"And the men?" I ask, swerving into the fast lane. "How does he torture men?"

Maksim stares at me with grave, golden eyes. "He will chop off their cocks inch by inch, and so slow that time feels like it no longer exists."

BLAIRE
(PART ONE)

7

After a long, emotionally grueling weekend of watching Maksim's back, I return home and try for the fifteen minutes Charlie wants to shut down London.

James texts to say he's okay, informing me that he has a few broken ribs, bruised kidneys, and a bloody, messed up face, but he'll be right as rain in a few weeks.

- You know I'm sorry, don't you? -

Though I never usually would, I text him back. I just feel so guilty about what I did—it's fucking weird. I never feel guilt for anything. I don't know what's sparking my emotions.

- I know you're sorry. Don't worry about me. I'm fine. And I hope that you are too. Text or call if you need me. -

BLAIRE
(PART ONE)

That makes me smile, a little. Hopefully by the time I see him again, he'll look as good as new and this frustrating guilty feeling will leave me the hell alone.

Putting everything and everyone out of my mind, I focus on the job at hand, working my butt off in my office.

I'm exhausted by day three.

The swelling on my left eye and lip has gone down a bit, so I'm almost back to normal—well, physically I am. Mentally, I'm fucked.

Regardless, I continue punching in codes and filling London's CCTV system with glitches so I can take over it, but by the end of the week, it's confirmed that it is impossible to grasp fifteen minutes. When the system locks me out, that's it, and it's always on eleven minutes. I can do no more, and my time to try is up.

Two hours it takes me to work up the courage to call Maksim—two bloody hours—because I know he's going to punish me for failing.

And I'm not wrong.

He isn't happy when I lie and say that I need another week, that I only have eleven minutes—I'm just trying to spare my ass some time. He curses down the phone in Russian, telling me, "Charlie will lose it if we don't give him what he needs, Blaire. Do you understand that? Do you fucking understand what he'll do to me? To us? Pizdets!" he screams with fury, 'this is the fucking end'.

I'm quiet throughout the whole ordeal, shitting bricks, and once he's finished rambling, he hangs up on me. He shows up at my apartment half an hour later, as I knew he would. Punishing me in my own home is his way of letting me know that while I don't live with him, I can't escape him.

Three loud knocks echo through my personal space. My heart is racing. My palms are sweating, and my mouth is so dry.

With a trembling hand, I open the front door to him and stand there with as much innocence as I can conjure up, sinking into my shoulders and my waist length hair.

He looks the part in a sharp gray suit paired with a crisp white shirt, but that's where his customary, docile facade ends. His eyes flair with disappointment as he looks down at me, shaking his head.

This isn't good.

Though Maksim sometimes beats me to teach me a lesson, he never looks disappointed with me.

He must be really scared of Charlie.

"You don't often let me down, my little pet," his lips curl against natural white teeth. "I'm very, very unhappy with you."

I drop my eyes to the floor so my hair curtains my face, mentally blocking out what's to come. He's an unpredictable sadist. One minute he'll whip me, and the next he'll drown me or worse... burn me.

I hope to god he'll just whip me today.

Reaching out, he grabs my wrist and drags me through the living area, into my bedroom. I stumble to keep up with him, my naked feet slapping against the marble floors.

By the floor to ceiling windows opposite my bed, he swirls me around to face him, knocking me off balance.

"You know what happens next," he warns, then he orders in Russian, "On all fours with your pants down!"

BLAIRE
(PART ONE)

When he lets go of my wrist, my thoughts go white. I scramble to obey, dropping to my hands and knees. Without shame—Maksim has seen my unclothed body more times than I care to remember—my sports trousers come down, then my pants. I have to leave them around my knees, I've always thought because the elastic in my trousers ties my knees together.

Cool air breezes through my thighs, blowing over my naked sex. A hand lifts up my t-shirt and bunches it around my waist, then a single finger runs over the scars on my back. I shiver quietly, holding myself up on all fours.

"Podgotovsja!" Maksim yells from behind for me to 'prepare', his voice resonating through the double height room.

I do. I try to relax as best as I can but it's so difficult.

The seconds tick by—I'm counting in my head.

'One. Two. Three. Four.'

I imagine he's standing there looking at my scares, at my naked ass like a hungry man starved of rage. There's nothing more in this world Maksim enjoys over inflicting pain.

He fumbles with his belt and I can tell he's using both hands. I've seen and listened to him do that for ten years.

Though I'm relieved that he's only going to belt me, the sound of metal clanging against metal makes me cringe, sends me into some dark place in my mind.

White thoughts. Focus on your white thoughts.

It's so hard. If there's ever a sound I'd love never to hear again, it's *that*. I'd notice it a mile off.

When he pulls his belt free, *woosh!* I cower to brace myself, my hair curtaining my face, the ends dripping over the floor.

The first whip whistles through the air, then a loud, powerful *SMACK* rings right through me.

I jump subconsciously, a desperate scream stuck in my throat preventing my ability to breathe for a moment.

My head rushes with the lack of oxygen. He gives me a moment, and I manage to suck in a lung full of air.

"Podgotovsja!" he yells again for me to 'prepare'.

I squeeze my eyes and my teeth shut, fisting my fingers and my toes.

Wa-tch!

I jolt in my own skin.

"Podgotovsja!"

Wa-tch!

"Podgotovsja!"

Wa-tch!

"Podgotovsja!"

Wa-tch!

My ass and the backs of my thighs are on fire, each welt throbbing...

"Podgotovsja!"

I don't move, nor do I cry out, even while tears swim in my eyes. I just take the beating, going into a numb zone.

Eleven strikes in succession, Maksim groaning after each one, and it's over.

BLAIRE
(PART ONE)

I almost pass out with relief that it's over, my head swimming with endorphins. I take deep, steady breaths now that I can, blinking away the black spots in my vision.

The belting wasn't that bad. I've suffered much, much worse. If anything, I think Maksim has been too soft on me.

"One more week, Blaire," he says, leaning over me from behind. The buttons on his suit are cold against my naked, wounded flesh. "If you do not successfully attain fifteen minutes, this-" he rubs my ass with a rough, open palm, starting with my left cheek, and then my right, making me wince, "-will be child's-play compared to how I will punish you."

The next breath I take-in shakes in my throat. He's been soft with me so the next hiding takes full effect. Now it makes sense.

"I want to see you at my house on Saturday at nine P.M.," he whispers, a Russian gargle in each of his words. "My driver will collect you from here."

Saturday is exactly one week from now. I'm petrified. I'll never have his fifteen minutes, and I know that what he says is the truth—this was child's-play compared to what he's going to do to me.

"You understand, Blaire?"

"Ye-yes, сэр Maksim."

"Good. You can pull up your clothes, my little pet."

I do. Under his tall frame because he's still towering over me, I pull down my t-shirt, then pull up my pants and trousers.

Maksim stands back when I'm fully clothed, ordering, "Get up."

BLAIRE
(PART ONE)

Pushing to my feet, I grimace, grinding my teeth because my clothes chafe against my red and sore behind. Yeah, it wasn't that harsh of a beating but it still stings.

"Here, my little pet." Maksim passes me a bottle of cream from his suit jacket pocket. Hunching down, he kisses my face, pressing his lips to the sharp of my cheekbone. "So you can focus on the job and not your pain. You know the drill—apply three times a day."

His arms wrap around me, burying my face in his warm chest, sheathing me in the smell of burnt brut. I remain as still as a rock, empty of emotion, my hands hanging by my sides. I'm used to this for this is how Maksim comes. A beating follows disobedience and tenderness follows brutality. It's always been this way.

"You know," he husks out, brushing down the back of my hair over the curves of my spine, "if you want to make me happy again, why don't you get on your knees and please me, my little pet?"

My heart leaps into my throat, but I obey. Shutting my eyes, I slide through his embrace, down to my knees, and reach for the zipper of his trousers with one hand, squeezing the bottle of cream in my other. I will myself not to think about it while he strokes the top of my head, that if I hurry up, it'll be over.

"Cэp Maksim," I hear from behind, and my heart sinks.

"Ahhh, my pet," Maksim purrs. "What a surprise."

I glance over to see James standing in the doorway, dressed in his black combat gear. In a panic I try to check out his face to see if he's okay but I'm too guilty/nervous. I know what happens next.

BLAIRE
(PART ONE)

"I'm sorry," he says, lifting a defensive hand. "I didn't know you were here. I just wanted to check in on Blaire because I haven't heard from her in a while."

"Of course you did, my pet." Maksim chuckles with dark desire, and I feel that he stares down at me when he whispers, "Always just in time, isn't he, Blaire?"

I flinch against my given name, and then he shoves my head back, forcing me to fall on my sore ass. The bottle drops out of my hand with a light thud and rolls away under my bed. I consider crawling after it but end up cuddling myself, gazing deadpan at the floor. I'm pushing filthy images of him fucking James from my mind. He often makes me watch but James says it's okay because at least I'm safe from Maksim's sexual attention.

It's quiet for a moment, bar the blood roaring in my ears. I expect they're exchanging knowing looks.

"Why don't you have Blaire make you some lunch, сэр Maksim?" James comes up to us with artificial confidence. "I'll see to you."

BLAIRE
(PART ONE)

8

A WEEK LATER

My eyes are heavy and my body is lethargic. I've not slept properly in two days. I've been studying to the ends of the earth on The Dark Web for a way to gain complete control of London's CCTV system because my hacking skills have proved useless. As I feared, there's no way, so I'm here at Maksim's house in his office to collect my punishment. Hopefully, if it's brutal, he'll knock me out cold and I won't feel anything

Hopefully.

"I can do only eleven minutes, cəp Maksim," I confess, standing with my head down. "I'm really sorry."

"Only eleven minutes?"

"Yes," I whisper, glancing up at him.

He's slouched back in his chair, behind his desk, hands clasped together in his lap.

"I'm sorry, cəp Maksim."

"Oh, I'm sure you are, my little pet."

Dropping my gaze because I can't stand that half amused, half thwarted expression on his face, I kneel before his desk so he can hit me, squeezing my eyes shut to brace myself. He warned me last week that this punishment would be brutal. I'm horrified to think about what he's going to do. The worse thing he's ever done was brand my skin. I passed out on the dining room table, only to be woken up in a bathtub full of freezing cold water.

The cold water hurt more than when he burnt me, bizarrely so.

I can't go through that again. It was torture. I can't even explain what the recovery was like, the way my skin felt stretched out every time I moved; how hot and irritated my back was.

"Stand up," Maksim says.

With my eyes still on the floor, I do, but I almost lose my balance because I'm shaking like a leaf.

"You know, my little pet," his husky voice makes me shiver, "as a child, when I failed to do what was asked of me, my parents would brutally rape me to teach me a lesson-"

Is that what he's going to do? Have sex with me?

I remember the way he looked at me when he was fucking that poor girl at the Asian Prince's party the other week. This has to be his next move—nothing else makes sense.

I'm not scared if it is time for him to have me. I've always known this day would come.

"-But I wouldn't do that to you," he tells me. "Not brutally, anyway. You mean more to me than I meant to my parents."

I pull my eyebrows together, wondering where he's going with this.

"There are other ways to teach you a lesson," he says, and then he's quiet. The creaking sound of a chair makes me flinch, then a heavy hand lands on my shoulder. "Charlie Decena will have to make the most of eleven minutes. Look at me, my little pet."

I do. I lift my lashes to find his golden gaze.

"Is there anything you need?" he asks, a peculiar, evil expression on his face. "Or any questions you wish to ask?"

"Um... I might need a few extra computers, just if I get locked out of the CCTV system."

"Of course." He leans down and says in my ear, "I'll have them set up in your apartment for when you execute the job." He kisses the side of my face with hard lips. "Now, you should go tell Charlie of your equal success and failure. He is out back."

Great.

Coming down from the rush of fear that he was going to hit me, I nod, turn on my heel, and get the hell out of his office before he changes his mind and gives me a good bloody hiding. I follow the pounding music down the hallway to the kitchen. It's packed with half naked girls dancing all over the place in a drunken state, and an assortment of men whose eyes are glazed over. They're drugged up off powdery cocaine, mountains scattered across the white worktops and the dining table by the back doors.

I continue through the kitchen in search of Charlie. One guy—I can never remember his fucking name—smirks at me as I pass him. "When is Maksim-Markov going to give it up already?" he says, watching me with glossy eyes, leaning over the kitchen worktop on elbows.

I don't even look at him. I round the dining table, shoulder barging the girls who smell sweet with perfume, and steal through the French doors.

Outside, my breath mists the cold night. A few more of Maksim's friends surround the illuminated swimming pool that's in the heart of the patio area. I also note James, who nods at me from the other side of the pool. He's dressed in his combat uniform, standing about with his work partners Oliver and Shane. I lift my hand in a small wave. A gentle smile reaches his candid, affectionate eyes. *Fuck.* His eyes are a little black. He's still bruised from our fight, dark greeny-gray patches marrying his cheeks and his nose.

I remember what he did for me last week as if it happened just moments ago—let Maksim fuck him in an attempt to spare me sexual attention.

Overwhelmed with guilt, I have to shut off my thoughts and emotions. I can't think about how bad I feel for him. I have to endure Charlie Decena soon.

To the left of the pool, Maksim's dogs—his girls—stand on all fours with leashes around their necks. They're all naked. Some of them are absolutely petrified, crying and cringing from Maksim's friends who are copping a feel. The other girls aren't bothered. They seem used to what's happening to them, staring ahead blankly.

As usual, I fight to ignore my instincts telling me to teach these perverted bastards a lesson. I'd tear them all apart single-fucking-handed.

I go over to James so I can quickly say hello; nod with respect at Oliver and Shane. They return my gesture before walking off, I assume to give James and me a moment.

"Hey." James smiles down on me, and also offers up his beer. "It's still cold."

"No. You keep it," I say softly. I can't seem to return his affectionate smile. He looks a mess. His left eye is bloodshot from the impact of my punches.

My eyes crinkle with guilt.

"Don't worry," reaching out, he gives my hand a squeeze, "it's all superficial. Are you okay?"

"Yes," I say, noticing he's got red strangle marks around his neck. "I'm fine." I look down at my feet, then back up at him. "I can't stop. I have to..." I gesture out, "you know... I just wanted to make sure-"

"I know." There's that sincere smile again. I wish he wouldn't do that. It makes me feel like shit.

Leaving James, I go off and find Charlie at the other side of the pool. He's wearing jeans over white trainers and a black round-neck t-shirt that hugs his masculine body, his hair tied back. The silvery-blue water reflects on his handsome face, lighting up his olive skin, shimmering against that perfect black hair. He's got his arm around a blonde wearing a white bikini. She has to be cold. It's freezing out here.

I know she is because her nipples are like bullets and goose pimples are racing down her arms.

Charlie is whispering something in her ear, making her giggle like a frivolous teenager. Even the other girls standing about him are giggling, indulging him.

"Jesus," I scoff to myself in Russian, continuing for him.

To think that most women are like this—giddy to the sweet nothings—makes me want to vomit. A man would have to work a lot harder than *that* to make me laugh. Mind you, no man has ever made me laugh before, so I cannot comment on how hard the endeavor would be.

When I reach him, I ask, "Can I speak to you for a moment, Charlie?" We meet each other's gaze, and I add, "In private?"

I'm surprised that I'm not anxious to see him. If anything, I'm grateful that I have to endure his disappointment as oppose to Maksim's.

The girls surrounding Charlie raise their eyebrows at me, affronted that I would even attempt to approach him. I'm fully clothed in black sports trousers, trainers, and my leather jacket, hardly dressed for the occasion.

I don't bother returning their gestures of abhorrence. Enough blood will be spilt tonight—my blood, probably.

One of the girls seems to know exactly who I am, because she tells the others to look away. "Say nothing," she urges.

"Hello, Blaire," Charlie's Latin seasoned voice is soft and inviting. Reminds me of Hannibal Lector.

He scans my appearance—just like he always does—a dirty grin twitching at the corner of his mouth.

The blonde under his arm doesn't know whether to glare at me or him, her eyes flickering between us.

I don't react to his intense, penetrating gaze—or I try not to. I cannot control my cheeks. I strive to appear impassive, my hands in my leather jacket pockets.

"Sure you can speak to me," he rasps out eventually, taking his arm from around the blonde. With his hair tied back, his features are sharper and harder. He's so handsome, and for some bizarre reason, I can't help imagining he's tanned all over.

Stop imagining, I admonish myself internally.

"Hey," the blonde grips his arm, rubbing her hip against his cock, "you're coming back, right?"

Charlie gives her a deadly stare and snatches her hand off his arm, pushes her back a step. She stumbles to find her balance, so stunned by his dominant-aggressive behavior that she just gawps at him.

I'm not stunned. Men like him are often assholes.

I lead the way into the house with cool composure, through the luminous white kitchen.

"Look at that tight little ass..." that bloody guy is still going on. "Maksim-Markov really does have to give it up."

"What'd you just say?" Charlie asks, and the kitchen pauses in silence.

I peer back on instinct. Charlie is glaring at that guy with evil authority, his eyebrows so furrowed he looks wickedly dark.

"I-I wasn't talking to you, man," that guy shakes his head, lifting self-protective hands. "S-sorry."

"Keep your fucking mouth shut." Charlie stalks up to him and points a steady finger in his face. "You understand that, boy?"

Rolling my eyes, I carry on through the kitchen and into the living room so we can be alone and undisturbed. Charlie's heavy footsteps follow me in.

"What'd you wanner speak about in private, Blaire?"

"I can do no more than eleven minutes," I say, facing him. I just want to get this over with so I can go home. "I'm sorry, Charlie, as is Maksim."

Charlie stops right in front of me—literally. We're toe to toe, my eyes level with his chest. He doesn't say anything for a moment, and my anxiety peaks because I can sense he's staring down at me. I fight for my composure, thinking about being at home reading or something. It's easier to control my mental state if I'm not spiritually near him.

Lifting a hand, he runs a thumb over my jaw line, using the sharp of his nail when he reaches my chin. I'm mentally back in the room now. His touch seems to ignite my body. Hairs raise and my blood pumps a little faster.

I don't get this, the sensation of when he touches me. No one but Maksim has ever touched me like this before. No one but Maksim is allowed to touch me.

In the moment of thinking about Maksim, I aim to slap Charlie's hand away, that black switch going off in my head, but it's Charlie's voice that stops me in my tracks.

"Maksim told you, Blaire, fifteen minutes," he whispers, his voice deeper than usual. It carries above the music coming from the kitchen.

Lifting my shoulders, I repeat, "I'm sorry, Charlie." I don't sound like myself. I sound a little... breathless, and anxious. "I can't give you what I don't have."

"Is that right?" Stepping forward, he practically puts us flush against each other.

I scowl up at him, defiantly meeting those powerful blue eyes. Why does he do this, ensure close proximity?

I step back, but he steps for me, smirking. Another step, and another, until I'm pressed against the wall. Charlie cages me in from the front, his legs slightly open as if he's readying himself for a fight.

I can feel the warmth from his body... smell the clean muskiness of his skin... It's all so inviting.

"No one is allowed to touch me," I counsel him with all the will I have, lifting my chin so I can hold his consuming gaze. He towers over me by at least eight, maybe ten inches but I'm not afraid of him.

He knows I'm not.

He smiles down on me, and I'm not sure, but he looks... excited?

"Maksim will let me touch you," he says, matter of fact.

My heart stutters. I know where he's going with this. I can see desire burning in his eyes.

To steer clear of a conflict I try to walk past him but he grabs my wrist. A black switch goes off in my mind and all I can hear are Maksim's words; *no one is allowed to touch you, ever; no one but me, my little pet.* He's told me this for years. He used to play a recorder on repeat while I slept until his words sunk into my subconscious. That's why I live to serve him.

I smirk back at Charlie. "You shouldn't have done that."

He flicks up his eyebrows to challenge me.

I twist out of his grasp so fast that I land on my knees and elbow him back in the bollocks. He gasps out, doubling over, and lands on his hands. I sprint forward and stand, turning around to face him.

He lunges at me before I can register him on his feet, grabs my throat and runs back with me while groaning in anger, slamming me against the wall.

"Ah!" I gasp on impact, closing and opening my eyes, gripping his wrist with both hands.

He laughs in my face. "I'm not your little friend James."

I choke in his grasp, my head getting dizzy, then I whack the inside of his elbow to buckle his arm.

"Neither am I." I punch him in the face, causing his nose to burst open.

He isn't bothered. He tries to grab me again but I fight him off, cross-whacking his hands away but he keeps coming at me.

I've nowhere to go, so I boot him in the stomach with lower body force and wind him.

While he's bent over, I try to dash out of the living room but he fists the back of my hair.

"Aargh!" I spin around and pound at his chest, forcing him to free me. I can't go too crazy. Maksim is going to kill me for this as it is.

When Charlie is a few feet away, forced back by my attack, I jump up on one foot to kick him in the face with my other. He catches my ankle and yanks me forward; drops me to the floor.

"Awh!" I grimace as my back slams against the hard marble floor.

I don't let my pain take over my process. I bolt upright and try to grab his hand on my ankle but right now he's quicker than I am. I'm not on par tonight. He catches my wrist, still gripping my ankle in his other hand, and manages to flip me over so my face is sliding against the cold floor.

"That's more like it," he says in my ear with humor. He gets both my arms behind my back and holds them there in one of his hands. He then grabs a hand-full of my hair again and hauls me to my feet; turns me around so I'm facing him. I have no choice but to stand here against him. If I fight while in this position and he pushes my arms up my back, they'll snap.

"You're fast..." He tugs on my hair to make me look at him, bending my neck back. His chest is hard against my breasts, crushing me to him.

I pant angrily, a little out of sorts. If only I had grabbed my gun and shot this bastard.

Through heavy eyes, he glances between my eyes and my mouth, and then he smirks like he's won. "Tell me, Blaire, why shouldn't I have done that?" He's enjoying this, I just now realize.

Is this what he wanted? To fight me?

I glare at him with wrath, at the stark perfection of his face. He's so fucking handsome it's stupid, even with his nose running red, smothering his top lip. His eyes are the most perfect shade of blue, darker under this light. His olive skin is flawless, begging to be marked.

"You really are a pretty little thing," he whispers, his expression softening as he tips his head.

What? Are we thinking the same thing, of each other's beauty?

"I've never seen a girl so pale with a million freckles who is so wildly pretty." He leans down then, putting us nose to nose.

"You need to let me go," I say in a panic, trying to shove away from him because he's going to try and kiss me.

He pushes my arms further up my back. I wince, squeezing my face in agony. My arms feel like they're going to pop out of their sockets.

"Stop fighting," he says, then his lips seal over mine, catching my pleading, *no!*

Everything goes blank. I can't see a thing, nor can I breathe. The air is caught in my throat.

Charlie is surprisingly gentle in taking my mouth, humming with pleasure, his lips soft and full.

I think about biting his tongue as it probes tenderly at my mouth, but I don't. I just keep my lips together, basking in the sensations of his smooth face on mine, his tongue doing this mind-blowing slow licking thing across my upper lip.

My veins buzz with unfamiliar sensations, every inch of my body inundated with... with... I don't fucking know. I'm so...

...In my entire life of battle and blood, I've never, ever, felt anything like this before.

"C'mon, Blaire," his breath smells like brandy, spicy and hot, "let that wrought iron guard down."

I shake, trying to keep my lips shut but it's so hard. My body wants this—everything that can be puckered, is—while my mind is screaming for me to shut down and attack.

"You'll let me kiss you." His smooth face rubs across mine as he puts his mouth to my ear, breathing heavily, making me shiver. "If you don't, I'll bend you over that sofa and fuck you right in the ass."

Fear belts through me and my eyes fly open. We look at each other for a split second, like there's nothing else in the world but us. His face is dark with lust. His eyes almost look black because his pupils are dilated.

A lure smile spreads across his face, drawing me into the darkness that is him. I gasp, horrified this is happening. I cannot help it. Maksim has never prepared me for anything like this.

Charlie takes the opportunity to invade me as I gasp. Tipping his head to the side, he dips his tongue in my mouth, moaning with satisfaction. He tastes me in endless, leisured licks, causing something hot and heavy to gather between my legs.

My toes curl in my trainers while my stomach is flipping.

His blood tastes metallic. His lips are softer than I ever imagined but demanding, making mine swell.

"You're sweet," he says in my mouth, massaging his tongue over mine. "So, fucking, sweet."

"Charlie," I squeeze out his name, but before I can say anything more, he closes his mouth completely over mine, making us airtight.

He groans with such passion. The sound vibrates through my chest.

Now, I'm throbbing between my legs—it's the most confusing feeling—and there's warm liquid in my pants. I've definitely not felt this before. Yes, Maksim has made me please him—he's made me suck his cock or milk him while he kisses me—and yes I felt a little warm at times, but this is on another level.

Divorcing everything I know, I find myself melting in Charlie's arms, almost buckling at the knees. I even think I moan. I hate that, but I can't help it.

"That's it," he rasps out. Letting go of my arms, he holds me around the waist in one arm and yanks me up so my feet aren't touching the floor, making me squeal in shock. He puts us chest to chest. His is pure, solid muscle and his heart is pounding.

So, it's not just me...

He keeps his other hand in my hair at the back of my head, holding us mouth to mouth, but right now, I don't mind. The pinching in my scalp is the only thing telling me that this is real.

I put my tiny hands on his shoulders and kiss him back, just how he's kissing me, carefully and avidly. Our lips mold as one. Our tongues dance over each others in a twisted game of seduction.

I could happily get lost in him.

Someone whistles from behind us, startling me.

"She's off limits, my friend."

It's Maksim.

My heart explodes in my chest.

Yanking up my knee, I try to knee Charlie in the kahunas but he anticipates my move, blocking my attack with his leg.

He laughs in my mouth, pressing one last peck to me, smothering me in his blood.

"I like you," he says quietly, so quiet in fact that Maksim cannot hear him.

Slowly and warily, he puts me down on wobbly legs and steps back, holding out his hands for if I might attack him again. I'm not going to. I couldn't even if Maksim ordered me to. I'm in a right old state. My body is aching for Charlie's warmth and his scent, and most of all, his touch.

What the fuck is this?

I'm confused with what he makes me feel. I know I have to obey Maksim and all his requests. I know to risk my life for Maksim. I'm wired to attack anyone who touches me—anyone but Maksim—but I didn't fight Charlie when he kissed me. I guess I let him.

My thoughts are driving me nuts! I know nothing of this... this... I don't even know what the fuck *this!* is.

"She got you good." Maksim laughs with blatant amusement. "Don't take it personally, my friend. My little pet is trained to takedown anyone who touches her without my permission."

"Why is she off limits?" Charlie prowls over to Maksim, who is standing in the doorway looking at me.

I cannot see that he's looking at me. I just know.

I wipe my lips with a single finger, relishing in the sight of Charlie's blood coating my pale skin. I can still taste him.

That kiss was nice.

I blink up at Charlie and Maksim, my head still in a desire fueled fog. They're watching each other like dangerous predators.

"Maksim," Charlie snaps, "why. Is. She. Off. Limits?"

Maksim slants his head to me, his eyes thinning. "She's innocent, and I'd like for her to stay that way."

Charlie's eyes zoom in on me and the look on his face... He wasn't expecting Maksim to say that.

"Fuck off is she innocent?" Charlie points a leveled finger at me. "Why would you have a nice girl like that and not have her?"

Silence, though I can almost hear Charlie's thoughts running through his mind.

"I have my reasons... Why don't you go and get yourself a proper drink, my little pet?" Maksim ushers for me to leave. He half smiles too, as if pleased with me. "Charlie and I have some business to discuss."

"Yeah, you bet we do."

On autopilot, feeling a little more like myself with Maksim's order filtering through my system, I nod and walk past them, eyes down, heading for the kitchen. I could do with a cold, stiff drink. It's been a crazy day.

The hallway is aglow with soft blue lights shining up the white walls, walls that boast pictures of every boxer ever to have won a world title.

Charlie is a seriously good fighter. I wonder who taught him.

I need to find out exactly who he is—knowing he's a syndicate leader isn't enough. I don't trust him or his intensions—nor his effort to bend me to his will with that damn kiss, for that matter.

Though, it was a nice kiss.

I'll not tell Maksim that. Charlie's bloody nose tells him all he needs to know, that I fought. I fought against him for touching me.

Perhaps that's why he was so relaxed about catching Charlie and I in that compromising position—he thinks I resisted.

In the kitchen, where it's still heaving in naked women, that guy says nothing to me. He moves out of the way and lets me walk through the cooking space.

Pulling out the hair tie from my bun, I let down my hair because it's a fuzzy mess. I then grab a beer out of the fridge, crack open the lid, and guzzle down a healthy mouthful, ignoring the music and the people around me. The bitter liquid is refreshing. I sigh, resting back against the counter top. The bottle is so cold that droplets of water gather under my palm. I press the bottle to my cheek, feeling hot.

I still cannot believe Charlie just kissed me. No one has ever kissed me like that before. Maksim is cruel when romantic—if I can call what he does to me *romantic*—but it's all I know. Though now, I have this. Whatever *this* is.

Over an hour passes before Maksim and Charlie enter the kitchen. I'm still standing by the fridge, looking as though barely a minute has passed.

"I guess I will see you in a week or so, Charlie," Maksim says with obvious irritation, making his way outside without looking at me.

I frown. Why isn't he coming to speak to me? He usually says goodnight at the least.

"Out!" Charlie barks, and everyone—I mean everyone—leaves through the back doors.

I aim to leave too but Charlie stops in front of me and says, "Not you."

I rest back against the countertop in resistance.

"The eleven minutes will work." He takes the beer out of my hand and pours the rest down his throat. "You all right, Blaire?"

BLAIRE
(PART ONE)

Arching my neck back, I scowl at him, noticing he's cleaned up his face of blood. "Of course I'm all right. What's Maksim doing?" I grab the edges of the kitchen counter because Charlie virtually puts himself between my legs. "What are you doing?"

With the back of his finger, he wipes my upper lip and shows me his blood is still on my mouth. Again, much to my frustration, I don't even think about hitting him for touching me. I simply get rid of the blood on my mouth by using the cold, leather sleeve of my jacket.

"Maksim's joining the party," he says softly, his blue eyes glued to my face. "We've come to a deal."

"A deal?" I whisper in mystification. Maksim hasn't told me of any deal. He usually tells me everything. "A deal about what?"

Charlie smiles lazily at me. I glower with confusion. His mood is different than before when we were in the living room. He seems very... I can't be sure. Satisfied, maybe?

"Your hair's longer than I thought it was." His eyes glance over my appearance and then he reaches out for a strand of my hair; runs his fingers down it, making my scalp tickle. "It looks nice down."

Ignoring his inane compliment and these weird vibes he's got going on, I ask, "What deal have you come to, Charlie?"

Still fondling with my hair, he stares at my mouth in total silence and my heart is suddenly pounding. I don't like that look on his face, that dark, *I won,* look.

"Maksim's got a hefty debt with me. He's been trying to pay it back but I don't want money. I've got enough of that."

"Oh'kay..." I blink at him a few times. "Well, what do you want then?"

Charlie stares up at my eyes now, gazes with wicked intent, while curling that lock of hair around his finger. "You-"

I go cold on the spot.

"-And as he knows better than to refuse me, you're now mine for three months or until I get bored." He's still speaking, still playing with my hair, but I'm not really listening.

I'm not sure how long I stand there for gawping at him until I yell, "What!?!" I push against Charlie's chest, hard enough to knock him back a step and let go of my hair. "I'm not going anywhere with you. What fucking debt are you talking about?"

I know Maksim can probably hear me shouting but right now, I don't care.

"Charlie, what debt?"

Putting the beer bottle on the side, he leans back against the fridge and crosses his arms. "We did a job together a few years back and unforeseen circumstances meant I wasn't able to collect. While I was away, Maksim spent the money without my permission, so now, I'm collecting."

Steam blows out of my ears.

"Not through me you're not," I hiss, my face tense with anger. "I'm going to speak with Maksim. He wouldn't barter me to pay off some debt."

"You're not allowed to speak to him," Charlie says in a chilled, unfazed manner. "This is part of our deal."

"Huh?" My face scrunches up. "You can't decide that."

Throwing his head back he bursts out laughing.

My eyes widen with insult. "What the hell are you laughing at?"

"Do you know how confusing you are?" he says once he's done laughing, wiping his watery eyes with one hand. "One minute I think you're so deeply conditioned to Maksim that there's no getting through to you, but then you're rebellious with your cocky attitude, and then you're thawing in my arms as I kiss you-"

A hot flush comes over me at the memory.

"-Now you have a chance to come with me, get away from this life for a while—if you can call this a life—" he casts a hand around the place, "but you don't want to leave?"

I don't know what to say right now so I just look at him.

"What ties you to Maksim?" His thinning eyes search my face, glittering in curiosity. "Tell me, I'm dying to know. I'm almost sure it's not just fear." He sounds like he's taunting me, goading me into losing my cool, and I am. My blood is boiling.

"You can shout your reasons at me if you want, Blaire. No one will stop you, and I don't mind. I like how feisty you are."

"If my reasons need explaining, you're more dense than I thought." I twist my lips, struggling to contain the bubbling explosion going off inside me. Why would I want to leave Maksim when he's all I know? Why's that so hard to understand?

"And as for *this* life," I say, unsure of what I'm about to confess, "it's mine, and I like it just the way it is." I head for the back doors with my hands fisted at my sides, certain he's talking bullshit. Maksim wouldn't barter me. He wouldn't.

"Not so fast." Charlie's large hand wraps around my upper arm and forces me to an abrupt stop.

"I'm not fucking doing this with you again!" I yank back and forth. "Let me—aargh!" Something sharp stabs me in the side of my shoulder and a cold, dopey feeling rushes through my veins.

Within seconds, my brain goes fuzzy and I fall back in Charlie's arms, my legs buckling under me.

"Wha... what have you done to me..." I say breathlessly, trying to grab my shoulder but my hands are all floppy.

"Shhh... S'all right, Blaire," he whispers in my ear from behind, stroking my hair back out of my face. "You're gonna be all right."

The world goes dark.

BLAIRE
(PART ONE)

9

"Take off your clothes, Blaire, or I will," Charlie says in a deep, low voice. He's staring at me from across the dark bedroom, around fifteen feet away. It's almost too dark to see him, but I can, his tall, broad frame blocking my way to the door. He's standing there prepared for combat, his legs slightly open. He thinks I'll try to fight him and he's right to assume that because I will.

Swaying on my feet, I clutch the bedpost with one hand. I'm trying to gain focus so I can consider if what Charlie told me about Maksim bartering me is the truth but I'm still groggy from whatever he gave me.

I'm not sure it's true—I don't need to be sober to come to that conclusion. I don't think Maksim would trade me for anything. I mean too much to him—or, I thought I did, but here I am.

Maybe I do still mean something to him because Charlie just told me in an attempt to calm me down that Maksim said he's not to ruin me. He doesn't care if they fall out or if Charlie puts a bullet in him, he wants me back alive and in one piece. Then, he insisted one of his best men transports me to this house that feels like it's in the middle of nowhere, refusing Charlie's request to take me himself. Maksim 'apparently' said he wants to know where I'll be, just if anything goes down.

Now, I'm supposed to be here with Charlie Fucking Decena for three months or until he gets bored of me. I don't know how to feel about that. I know nothing of what's going on. I'm not even sure Charlie was telling the truth about Maksim bartering me. I don't trust him.

But again, here I am.

"Go on." He comes toward me, his feet serious against the wooden floors.

My head is a mazy vapor. I'm so dazed I'm almost stupid, but I'm on my feet, which is what matters. I can fight.

When he reaches me, he tries to get me out of my leather jacket by pushing his fingers in the shoulders. That switch goes off in my head and I weakly grab his wrists but he twists out of my grasp and pins my hands at my sides.

"Just relax," he says, his breath warming my face. "You must feel light headed."

Resisting the urge to scream at him, I let my head roll to the side so I can hide in my hair. I wait a moment until his grip on me loosens.

"What did you give me?" I ask, staring into the darkness.

"Just a little something to put you down so you couldn't resist," he's still whispering. "But don't worry, it'll wear off."

When his hands over mine loosen, I slip out of his grasp and slam my fists into his chest, knocking him back a few steps. I'm strong for a small girl but just pushing him puts me out of breath. I lean into the bedpost on my shoulder. I'm not at full strength and my head is so cloudy. I can't think straight—the last twenty-four hours are like looking into a black hole—but I need my wits about me. I need to assess the situation!

Focus, Blaire, I will myself.

I remember telling Maksim that I cannot get his fifteen minutes, and I remember Charlie kissing me. I remember talking to Charlie in the kitchen and briefly waking up in the back of Maksim's SUV—I know it was Maksim's SUV because I could smell his brut scent. It was dark and the road we were driving along was bumpy. I could still taste Charlie's blood in my mouth.

My eyes widen.

"No," I breathe out, a lump forming in my throat.

"Blaire?" Charlie hunches down to look at my face hidden behind my hair. "What's wrong? Do you feel ill?"

In a moment of madness, to save my ass from whatever he has planned, I reach for my gun in my jacket pocket, hoping to fucking god he hasn't taken it.

Cold metal against my palm.

Relief sweeps through me.

I pull out my gun, and though it's heavy, I'm sure not to drop it, gripping it with both hands. I lift it high enough to aim at Charlie's head. He's standing there in mute shock.

"Where the fuck are we?" I say, clicking back the hammer, blinking rapidly.

He points a long finger at me, warning, "Put down the gun, Blaire."

"You didn't anticipate I'd have this, did you?" My voice is the wrong side of confident but I'm not confident. I have no idea what is happening. "Didn't you think to pat me down?"

His nostrils flare. He's still stunned—I can see that much. *Good.*

"Where the fuck are we!?!" I scream, tearing my throat to shreds.

He doesn't say anything, so we watch each other for a moment, the atmosphere thick with tension. I'm not sure who is the prey—inside, I feel it's me. I'm shitting myself.

Charlie walks right into the barrel of the gun, hunches down and presses it to his forehead. "Do it," he hisses out, his teeth clenched, "or give me the gun, Blaire."

I freeze, knowing I cannot actually shoot him—I'm just trying to scare him. I don't really know who he is yet, or how important he is to others, so I cannot be sure people won't come looking for him if he goes missing, and I cannot risk the blame landing on Maksim, even if he has betrayed me.

I hold Charlie's unnatural blue gaze. He's not at all afraid. I am. I'm fucking anxious because I know he's going to abuse me for the next few months. Maksim clearly cannot stop him. He took me from Maksim's house and doesn't seem to have a scratch on him.

"Go on, Blaire," he says gently this time, "shoot me."

"If I don't, you're going to do terrible things to me."

He nods, making the gun move in my grasp. "You're right. I am." There's something in his voice like vengeance. Wrapping his long fingers around the gun, he holds it in place. "Do it!" he yells, making me jump in my skin. "Fucking do it if you wanner do it!"

"Shit..." exhaling shakily, I let go of the gun and he throws it over by the door. It lands with a heavy bump that makes me flinch.

Charlie then grabs me around the arms, imprisoning me with all his strength. I stiffen in his hold, panting heavily, trying to gather my wits.

He doesn't do anything right away. He's just holding me in place, looking down on me.

"I need to speak to Maksim," I say, lifting my eyes to his.

Charlie quietly scans my face, his expression unreadable—or to me his expression is unreadable. I'm so dizzy.

"I need to ask him something. I need to speak to him!" I yell in Charlie's face and it makes me dizzier.

"What for?" he says. "Permission?"

I nod in a floppy state. He's right, I do need permission. I can't do this—whatever *this* is—without Maksim's permission.

"Are you gonna let me take off your jacket?"

Give and take... is that what this is all about?

I can let him take off my jacket if it means I can talk to Maksim. I need to talk to Maksim!

I nod again in a weak manner, and as his hands draw down my arms, he pulls off my jacket. Leaning past me, he lays it over the foot of the bed, then steps back.

He's quiet again. I can't fucking stand it. His silence seems to magnify his presence.

"Can I speak to Maksim?" I say, wavering under that powerful stare of his. "Please, Charlie?"

More silence...

I try to convince myself that I can see pity in Charlie's eyes as he studies me, but it's a lie my mind has conjured up. This man doesn't pity me.

"Charlie?" I snap, balling my hands. I'm on the verge of losing the plot.

He pulls a mobile out of his jeans back pocket, dials someone, and passes it to me. With a rickety hand, I take it and put it to my ear.

"What's the problem, my friend?" Maksim's husky Russian voice almost breaks me. "Having trouble taming-"

"Cэp Maksim," I whisper, cutting him off, squeezing the phone in my grasp.

"My little pet, are-are you okay?" he sounds worried. "What's happened? Please do not tell me you have done something to Charlie Decena..."

"No. He's-he's here." I glance up at Charlie, who is watching me intently, then I turn my back on him, holding the bedpost with one hand so I don't topple over. "Cэp Maksim, what-what am I doing here with Charlie?"

"Did he not tell you?"

"Yes," I say with hesitation. "He-he says-"

"You are to fulfill Charlie's needs without ruining your virtue, complete the job when he needs you to shut down London's CCTV system, and only that job, and return home to me alive and well in no more than three months time." Every word he says is like punching me in the chest. "Is that clear?"

"You want me to..." I blink into oblivion, swallowing past the lump in my throat. "He's allowed to touch me?"

"Yes, my little pet." There's a long pause before he elaborates, "He can do whatever he likes to you as long as he doesn't take your virginity or kill you. Also, he doesn't want you to respect him as you do me. He wants you to decide for yourself, for whatever good it will do."

I cup my face in one hand. My head is hurting. "I'm so confused."

"Don't be confused, my little pet. Do not fight him. Just do your jobs and come home to me."

His words echo while my world narrows. *He can do whatever he likes to you as long as he doesn't take your virginity or kill you.*

Charlie was telling the truth. Maksim has bartered me!

"No... No—please, I'm sorry," I squeeze out every word, gripping the phone so tight my fingers ache. "I'm sorry if I've been bad the past few years. I'm sorry for... Maybe if I come back and-and live with you at the house, it will help? I'll be good. I swear!"

There's nothing but silence.

"Сэр Maksim? Сэр Maksim, are you there?"

I check the screen, shaking so hard I almost drop the phone. It's dark. He's hung up the call.

"No..." the ability to breathe abandons me.

I'm not ready to let him go!

I try to call him back—to beg for my life—but Charlie takes the phone off me.

"No!" I scream, trying to snatch it out of his grasp but he pins me to the bedpost with one arm over my chest. "Let me go!" I grip his wrist with both hands, trying to pries him off but his body is too powerful. "I'm not finished talking to him!"

"You are." He shoves his phone in his jeans back pocket. "He just told you what you have to do."

"No. he-he didn't clarify." I'm shaking now, and Charlie is so close that I can smell the clean, sweet-musky scent of his skin. I wish he'd back the fuck up so I can think!

"Why-why didn't he tell me this in person at his house? Why did you have to drug me? I... I would have come willingly if Maksim told me too. I would have-"

"I don't want you having anything to do with him until I'm done with you, that's why he didn't tell you himself."

"But... that doesn't make any sense." I shake my head to get rid of this vertigo. "You just let me talk to him, and if... if you let him give me my orders, you-you wouldn't have had to drug me."

"I'm not gonna keep going over this, Blaire," his voice deepens with authority as he says that, determined to get off the subject. "When I decided I wanted you, I told him there and then to stay away until your time with me is up—he knows better than to go against my word. He warned me you'd resist, so I drugged you, and now you're here with me for three months," he shrugs, "get used to it."

That's hard to digest—I can't imagine not speaking to my master for three months—so I try to focus on what I have to do.

"What do you..." I start to say. "What... What can I do..." My mind is too chaotic. I don't even know what question to ask. Why did he just let me speak to Maksim if he doesn't want us to have any contact?

"Don't be frightened," Charlie whispers, cupping my face with his free hand, "I'm not gonna hurt you."

"Liar," I snap like a child, and he stands back, releasing me from the rule of his body. "You just admitted that you're going to do terrible things to me."

I'm all for a bit of sadism. I can't stop myself from thinking about when Charlie said that at the Prince's party.

Hunching down, he puts us at eye level. "If you misbehave, then yes I will hurt you."

I sink into my shoulders, shooting him a daggering glare. "What have I ever done to make you want to hurt me? What have I ever done to make you want to do this to me?"

There's a moment of visual power exchange. I don't think he likes that I just asked him that. He sighs, blinking at me, his temple ticking. It's there again, that mirage facade of pity. I wish it was real so I could use it to my advantage.

"Look," he says softly, glancing between my eyes, "I won't hurt you beyond what you can handle—you have my word on that—and if you want me to stop at any point, all you have to do is say, 'stop'. Okay?"

Stop? Is he fucking kidding me?

"You know I can't tell you to stop," I hiss in his face. "I'm not allowed to."

"Here," he points at the ground between us, "with me, you can do whatever you like. All you have to do is open your mind."

With one push, he knocks me back onto the bed and I fall with a bounce.

BLAIRE
(PART ONE)

Charlie grabs the hem of my t-shirt and tugs it up over my head, leaving me in my black sports bra and sports trousers, my dark red hair pouring around me.

I do nothing. I just sit there looking at the floor, obeying Maksim, thought after thought romping through my mind. He can't actually have sex with me, but that just makes the whole thought process worse, because I have no idea how he's planning on getting his kicks.

I imagine a beating is on the cards tonight. Men like him enjoy doing that.

When Charlie backs up a few feet, I can't help peering up at him. He smiles down on me, tossing my Tee to the side.

"What is it?" he whispers, as I stare at him.

"Maksim told me to fulfill your needs," I say, striving to gather my courage, "wha-what do you want?"

Silence, and he's just looking at me like he wants to devour my soul, diminishing my courage.

I crawl back across the bed on my elbows to put some more space between us, my heart roaring in my ears.

"Well-" says Charlie finally, tilting his head; he's not wearing a ponytail tonight, "-I wanner fuck you."

My entire body shudders with anxiety.

When my naked back touches the cold wooden headboard, I shut my eyes and hug my middle, complying with Maksim's command not to fight. What's the fucking point? Either Maksim or Charlie is going to abuse me. I might as well accept the latter.

"You're like a beautiful, wild little wolf," Charlie says.

I don't utter a word to that, and it's quiet again. I can hear Charlie's heavy breathing over the blood roaring in my ears, but nothing else. The house feels so quiet.

The minutes creep by and nothing happens. Why is nothing happening?

Eventually, I have to open my eyes to look at him standing there at the foot of the bed, mentally beckoning him to get a fucking move on.

"What are you thinking?" he says, his eyes tapering with wonder.

Is that why he's taking so long? He wants to get in my mind?

"You're not allowed to take my virginity," I warn, and I'm stunned by how even my voice comes out.

"So I'm told." His blue eyes check me out from head to toe, and he's smiling to himself. It's like he's mentally taking off the rest of my clothes.

Fuck, I hate that. It's so personal. I wish he'd just get *it* over and done with rather than longing it out and making me more uneasy than I already am.

As I blink away from Charlie, trying to center my thoughts on anything else but this, he rounds the bed, his eyes on me the entire time. I hide in my hair curtaining my small frame, hugging my middle to the point where I almost can't breathe.

He's beside me now, but he doesn't touch me yet. A flicking sound, like a lighter going off, draws my attention. The room glows with a dancing orange flame—he's lighting a candle.

"What's that for?" I ask, swallowing after. "You're-you're not going to burn me, are you?"

"What?" he says, sounding shocked. "Course I'm not gonna burn you." He wants to know why I said that—I can sense it—but he doesn't question me.

On the bedside cabinet next to me, there's a candle burner. The rim is filled with liquid. I can't see what color. Charlie puts the candle inside the burner, under the liquid, and a strong scent fills the room. It's potent and makes my head rush a little faster.

"What's that for?"

"These oils will help you relax," Charlie says. Leaning over me, he hooks his fingers into the waist of my trousers. My stomach tightens from the skin to skin contact. I instinctively go for his wrists to stop him from touching me. He pauses, and I retreat, Maksim's order swimming in my mind—*do not fight him.*

"Are you gonna fight me?" he asks. He's so close that I can feel his warm breath on my forehead.

I don't look at him. I just shake my head.

"That's a shame." Charlie tugs my trousers down my legs, yanking off my trainers one by one on his way to undress me.

I sit bare in my bra and pants now, my anxiety reaching its summit.

The only time I was ever this apprehensive was when Maksim first belted me himself—the first time I told him 'no' to sucking his cock.

What I would give to go back to him right now.

I miss what I know.

Huge hands close around my ankles and my toes curl. Charlie pulls me down so I'm lying on my back, my hair pooling around my face. I squeeze my thighs together and close my eyes. The blackness makes this seem almost like a bad dream.

Soft strands of hair tickle up my stomach, followed by a wet trail and the bed dipping around me. Charlie is licking his way up my body I realize, over my navel, through my breasts and to my throat. Tension gathers low in my stomach, and my insides tingle.

His tongue on my body feels so good. I can't deny it.

The saliva trail turns from warm to cold within seconds, and I shiver.

"You liked it when I kissed you, didn't you..." he says. It doesn't sound like he's asking. It sounds like he's telling me what I already know.

I don't bother trying to rebuff him. He knows I liked it. I hardly fought him off.

To avoid kissing him again—this is my power over him—I turn my head to the side but it only gives him the access he wants. He presses kisses up the side of my neck, inhaling on his way, his smooth face gliding across my skin like satin. He sucks on my earlobe, nips with his teeth, sending some strange vibes through my body. I'm ashamed to admit I nearly moan.

"You smell creamy," he says with puffs of breath in my ear, "like cocoa butter."

Knees try to probe my legs open but I squeeze my thighs together, hugging my breasts.

"Blaire..." he warns, his voice deepening, "if you're gonna fight me, do it with some dignity."

My blood simmers, but I reluctantly relax because I know he wants me to fight him. I remember how much pleasure he took in our first battle—the first time he won at kissing me. I won't let him have the pleasure of fighting me again.

A rough skinned hand forces me open and his heavy weight settles between my thighs, his jeans chafing my sensitive skin. I'm glad he's fully clothed. I don't think I could handle him being naked at the moment.

Fingers touch my face, my jaw, and then my cheek. He kisses me there with gentle lips.

Fuck, I can smell him, the clean, soapy/musky fragrance of his skin, and he's so warm it almost feels like a hot summer's day in here. It's all so intense, and confusing—a horrifying mixture of things. I enjoyed the way he kissed me before and the way he just sucked my ear, but I am horrified.

I don't want this.

I want to go home.

"I'm glad to learn it's true what they say about redheads. They're fiery." Charlie kisses down my neck and across my collarbones, one by one, his lips tender and nearly inviting—it has to be those oils he's burning. "But you're not fiery anymore, are you? Not with your orders firmly dished out." He sucks the pulsing vein in my neck with his lips and something surges through me. I jerk under him, unable to stop.

"What I'd give to have Maksim's control over you..."

"You're fucked up, you know that?" I spit at him, my cool slipping away—I wish he'd stop fucking talking!

I boldly meet his gaze. We're nose to nose.

"We're all a little fucked up," he says in my face, his blue eyes glowing with zeal, "it's just, some of us aren't scared to admit it."

"I don't mean like that," I say through closed teeth. "Look at you, Charlie, how handsome you are." Putting my hands on his large shoulders to keep him an inch away, I soak up his handsomeness, the stark silver blueness in his eyes—I don't think I've ever seen eyes so untamed and beautiful—the perfection of his lips; the sharpness of his features.

"You don't need to do this." I try to push him back another inch but he isn't budging. His hard body just makes me feel weaker and more helpless. "Tell me why you're doing this to me."

He tips his head to the side, lifts a hand and strokes down my face. "Why should I tell you?"

I've got a million thoughts running through my mind. Is it just that he wants to fuck me? Or is he getting his revenge on Maksim through me?

I cannot ask that. I'm afraid he'll say yes.

"Ever since I saw you walk into Maksim's office, dripping in wild beauty," he starts talking before I even answer him, "and ever since you defiantly mouthed me back at Rumo's place, I've wanted you." Running his thumb and finger down my jaw line, he pinches my chin. "And I always get what I want, Blaire. One way or the other." He isn't joking. I can see it in his eyes.

Hot lips travel back down my body, down my neck and to the arc of my breasts, making me quiver.

So, because I have a backbone and I'll tell him exactly what I think without fear, he wants me?

What a twisted motherfucker.

He sucks over the curve of my left breast, sucking my flesh into his mouth, and I don't know what happens inside me... I'm throbbing all over with heat, somewhat aroused but still anxious about what he's doing. I'm fighting not to arch into him too, using my grip on his shoulders to keep flat against the bed.

He senses how he's making me feel inside, it seems, because his teeth close around my pebbled nipple over the thin cotton material of my bra. He gently kneads, rolling his jaw from left to right, rolling my nipple in his teeth. The pain is strangely perverse and arousing; hurts at times but I... I like it.

I arch into him now—I can't stop myself. I'm losing my fucking mind!

"That's it, sweet Blaire." His tongue swirls around my nipple, soaking through the material, making my insides roll with sensations.

He goes further down my body, leaving a path of fire in his wake. He kisses and caresses me at once, kneading my body with large hands; my breasts first, tweaking my nipples with his fingers until they're standing on ends, then he massages my sides, my hips, squeezing me, having me squirm against the sureness of his large hands.

My chest is on fire. It's taking every ounce of my spirit not to groan out, not to express how good that feels.

He's kissing just above my pant line now, from left to right, over each of my sharp hipbones. My stomach quivers, and again when his hands follow his kisses down my thighs.

Letting go of his shoulders, I claw the sheets on either side of my waist, thawing under him. I know exactly where he's going. Maksim has told me that men like doing this to women. They like making women come apart with using only their mouth. It's a game of power.

When Charlie is crouched between my legs, he spreads me wide open, gripping the insides of my thighs. He leans down and licks over my black cotton pants, briefly touching my throbbing clit. I writhe against the warmth of his tongue, tightening my ass, trying to cope with the sensations. He then blows on me down there, turning everything cold. A surge of pleasure zaps right through me. I jump in my skin, letting out a small girlish moan, my senses flooding with endorphins.

"I like it when you moan like that," Charlie rasps out. "It'll forever remind me of when I first kissed you."

He does it all over again, licks and blows against my pants, teasing me with... pleasure?

I slam my teeth together, my head getting faint all over again as I struggle with the bitter sweet agonizing pleasure.

I can feel he's looking up at me from down there and it's making the whole ordeal that much more intense. I have no privacy right now.

He hooks a finger into the side of my pants and the pressure in the low of my body expands; turns to streams of desire. He strokes an invisible boundary of mine, up and then back down, just touching my sex.

"You've gotta be kidding me," he says angrily, and I wonder what the hell he's talking about. "Shaven? Fucking hell!"

The back of his dusty hand tickles my thigh as he strokes up and down my groin some more, savoring the moment. I wriggle about but I can't escape what he's making me feel.

He peels my pants to the side, then silky warmth presses to the most private part of me, my blood swollen bud, and my world blows up. I cannot hold back moaning this time, nor can I stop my toes from curling.

"Smooth, soft, and untouched." He blows on my flesh this time, sending tendrils of rapture through me, then he rips off my pants with a loud elastic snap, causing the cotton material to burn against my hips.

Nothing is said, and he buries his face between my legs.

"Ohhh!" I squeal, twisting and turning. His mouth is warm and wet and soft and... "Oh, god!"

He laughs out puffs of breath, grabbing my hips and pinning me to the bed, his hair brushing my inner thighs. He sucks my folds with his lips, gently and slowly drinking me in, then kisses me like he did my mouth. Full on, lips completely sealed over my sex.

Now he's massaging my clit with his tongue, coaxing something dark within me, making me buck forward more times than once.

I'm almost out of breath. I'm almost out of my mind with sensations.

It goes on and on... Charlie breaking me down... kissing me... sucking me... moaning like he's enjoying this more than I am.

I'm tensing so hard that I start to shake.

This is too much. Too... all over I'm hot and cold at once, my skin swamped with sweat.

"You're pretty down here, too," he says in a muffled voice, pressing a kiss to my inflamed bud.

My thoughts scatter, drifting away like balls of white light. In the back of my mind there's Maksim and what he's letting happen to me, the evilness in which he can clear a debt, then there's this: the epitome of what I think is pleasure, mindless pleasure that makes everything in the world seem like a nightmare. In all my life, I've never felt such provoking sensations.

Another kiss is pressed to my sex, making me quiver, and I don't know why, but I reach out to Charlie—I just can't deal with this. He takes my hand in one of his and holds it against my hip.

His face is soaked in my arousal, smooth and wet and adding to everything I'm enduring.

"Charlie..." I groan, trying to stop my hips from moving. I'm grinding against his tongue as it swirls around my clit, infusing the delight.

"I know, baby," he whispers, pecking my bud again. "Do you want me to stop?"

"No..." I sob in a state of dismay. I want this. It's like the first kiss all over again but on another level.

I feel him smile against my sex, then he does something that turns me inside out. He closes his lips over my clit and sucks, hard, in time with flicking his tongue against it with endless endeavor.

"Oh fucking God!" I scream out as my left legs starts trembling. I grip his hand with my nails, sure I'm drawing blood. He doesn't care. He strokes my hand with his thumb, as if to comfort me.

My veins vibrate with tension and between my legs... I'm pulsing so hard that I'm sure Charlie can feel it against his tongue, sensations rushing through me.

It's never ending, and I cannot move to deal with this—he won't let me!

I squeeze his head between my legs—it's all I can do but pass out from spiraling—but he doesn't want me to do that. Letting go of my hand, he wraps his arms around and over my hips to grip my inner thighs, and lifts my ass off the bed, practically folding me in half.

"I'm not done with you yet," he says. "Not by a long shot." His tongue parts my nether folds as he finds my clit and he makes my body blow a fuse again, manipulating me... kissing me... Or, maybe the rush never stopped. I think he's drawing it out somehow... making it go on and on and on...

He gazes down on me through heavy eyes, and I can't take anymore.

Grabbing my face in both hands, my sensory system goes into a state of epidemic as a stronger force hits me and I scream.

10

As Charlie said, he's not done with me. Not by a long shot.

He carefully puts me back down on the bed and whispers somewhere from above, "You all right?"

I'm floating in a cradle of ecstasy, my chest heavy with pants, a weird buzzing feeling radiating all over my skin.

A hand touches my face; strokes under my eye. "Blaire? You with me?"

I think I nod. I'm not sure. I'm too mindless to concentrate right now.

That was... extraordinary. I never knew such sensations existed. All I've ever felt is the lick of a belt, heat of a branding iron, or a blow from Maksim's fist. I wasn't aware there was more.

Sitting back on his knees, Charlie pulls off his t-shirt, revealing a hard chiseled stomach and broad shoulders, his chest sprinkled in rough, dark hair. The candle glowing on the bedside cabinet next to us gives an orange shine to his tanned skin.

Like that, he's more savagely handsome than ever before.

Why is he so good looking? It would be so much easier for me to resist the desire if he was ugly.

Panting still, I lie there gazing up at him, sheathed in diamonds of sweat. I cannot even hug myself because my muscles are like jelly, and I do want to hug myself.

The sound of a zipper coming down, slow and raw, and heavy movement on the bed. Then, Charlie is hovering over me, pressing into the mattress on all fours. I can feel something warm and hard just touching my pulsing sex but I don't really register what it is. I'm so hazy—I cannot even really make out his face. I've got stars in my eyes.

With a single hand, Charlie picks wet lengths of hair out of my face. "So fucking pretty," he whispers, and I can feel his eyes boring into my face.

I don't care.

After a while, my serious pants die down and the barrier that is my dizziness fades away. Charlie smiles when I really look at him, his black unruly hair dripping around his neck and face—it's a dark, exultant smile. His lips are wet, glossy against the orange candle light. My cheeks flush red. Wet from my arousal.

I try to cup my face, desperate to hide from him, but he takes my wrists and pins them to the mattress on either side of my face, supporting himself on his knees between my legs.

"Don't be embarrassed," he says huskily, reading my mind. "You're perfect." He licks his glistening lips and closes down on me, kissing my mouth. He tastes salty and smells like... a little musky. A feminine musky scent with a hint of his own.

I turn my face to the side—not because I don't want to kiss him; I just need a moment to recover—but he doesn't seem to like that. Freeing one of my hands, he grapples my jaw line and puts us nose to nose, his fingers digging into my skin.

"Don't look away from me," he says, and physically orders me to kiss him.

I do, even when he lets go of my face to hold my neck. Losing my mind all over again, I bask in that kiss, in how slow his tongue caresses mine; in how soft and alluring his lips are. I even wrap my free arm around his neck to keep him close, savoring the feeling of his smooth, shaven face on mine, his heart pounding against my chest.

Looks like we're both running on adrenaline.

My lips swell under the pressure of his, but I can't seem to stop having a taste of him. I kiss him with all I have, sucking his tongue and gasping with anxiety every time he attempts to pull away from me.

"Why are you pulling away?" I say through clatters of breath, blinking up at him. "You wanted this."

"Oh, I still want this." Releasing my neck from his hold, he braces his body up on one elbow beside my face; stares into my eyes. "I just need to loosen you up first."

My heart jumps into my throat. I know what he's going to do.

"Is it going to hurt?" My voice comes out so pathetic that I want to punch myself in the face.

He silently watches me for a second, his dazzling blue eyes flickering back and forth between mine. The orange glow of the candle makes him look so gorgeous that my heart goes a little faster.

"Might a bit at first," he tells me honestly, "but I'll go slow, and I won't go all the way in if it's too much."

Won't go all the way in!

I think he knows I'm anxious because he focuses on kissing my mouth for a while, a gentle pursuit, his hand stroking the side of my face. I'm practically purring against his touch, his kiss, rushing with heat. I shut my eyes so I can anchor my thoughts on four senses instead of five—looking at him is too overwhelming right now.

His back muscles feel extraordinary under my arm enveloped around his neck, flexing and contracting as he moves, and the weight of his body holding me down isn't so frustrating anymore. I sort of like the feeling of being under a powerful man. For the first time in my life, I feel like a girl lusted after, rather than a 'pet' ordered to please.

I'm not sure how much time passes before Charlie lets go of my other wrist. Now I'm swathed around him with both arms, putting us chest to chest, crushing my breasts between us.

I think those oils have fucked with my arousal or something because I've never felt this ravenous for anything in my entire life.

A hand slides between our bodies; finds its way to my forbidden entrance. Charlie rubs me there, making me squirm, making my core buzz with hunger. I'm so wet and juicy it's ridiculous, inundating his fingers.

"Hmmm, virgin cum," he says in my mouth, his voice full of darkness. "You taste fucking sweet, you know that?"

Pushing his fingers up through my soft, slick folds, he centers his attention on my clit again, teasing my inflamed bud. I cry out. I unhook my arms from around his neck and grab his arm. I'm too tender. It's too much.

"You want me to stop?" he asks, glancing heavily between my eyes.

"No! I just..." I blink in the sight of his flush face, not quite feeling like myself. "Please, Charlie... I just... just give me a second."

Smiling with pure wickedness, he deepens our kiss with a moan and works his tongue across mine, turning me inside out. He doesn't close his fiery blue eyes. He locks us in a period of visual bonding, possessing my fucking soul. I've never felt so vulnerable in all my life.

I begin to relax beneath him, letting go of his arm. He adds pressure to my clit then, making me whimper out loud. I claw the sheets on either side of my waist, curling my hips, wondering if this could get any more intense.

"You ready now?" he says in my mouth.

I nod a couple of times, looking desperately at him.

"Good." He pecks my mouth, then licks over my upper lip; sucks me there. "Now put your feet flat on the bed so your knees are bent."

Obeying, I spread my legs and press my feet flat on the mattress, giving him more room between my thighs. Dripping wet fingers slide down my sex, gathering more liquid, then over my virgin entrance and to my decadent entrance.

He circles me there with a single finger, softening my flesh, slowly kneading the tip in.

"Why Maksim hasn't fucked you, I'll never know." He swallows my anxious gasp as he pushes in me. "I wouldn't be able to keep my hands off you if I had you at my beck and call."

My toes bunching in the sheets, I throw my head back in the pillows, breaking away from his lips. He's halfway in, opening me up, and while it sort of stings, it's...

...I don't even get a chance to figure out how it is because he pulls out, causing a tight friction to burn my insides.

"You all right?" Charlie kisses the apple of my throat.

"I... I think so." I let out the breath I've been holding, blinking up at the dark ceiling.

"Just relax," he says, like it's that easy.

The pressure is there at my anus again and he slips inside me, loosening me up by gently twisting his hand. He doesn't stop halfway this time. He goes all the way in until I can feel his knuckles against my butt cheeks, his finger lodged so deep inside me that I feel full to the brim.

I moan through closed teeth, and I'm trying not to tense up but it is hard. It's the most particular sensation having him in there: burning and it... it's just weird.

"Breathe, Blaire," he says, reminding me to. "Don't think too much. I'm not in a rush. We'll go slowly."

"I'm just... a bit anxious," I confess, getting more and more pathetic by the minute. "I've never done anything like this before."

His entire body tenses up, and I can't help thinking what I just said has shocked him.

"Don't be anxious," he says softly, eventually. "I'm not gonna hurt you. Those oils burning help your muscles relax and I won't do anything you can't handle, all right?"

I shakily nod, telling myself that I'll just follow his guidance. He hasn't hurt me yet, not really, and for some strange reason, I don't think he is going to. Not that it really matters. He can't hurt me anymore than Maksim has.

Charlie doesn't move inside me for a while, just kisses my throat and across my collar bones, training my attention on his bizarre affections. This man just an hour ago admitted he's going to do terrible things to me, yet he's kissing me like he's in love with me or something?

I wish he'd be one or the other—good or bad. A mixture of both is too bewildering.

He's kissing over the curve of my breasts now, moaning in the deep of his throat, his hair tickling my chest. With his teeth, he kneads my nipples over the material of my bra again, left, and then the right.

"Oh, that's good," I say before I realize.

The burning and stinging in my ass easing somewhat, I relax on the bed, untying my toes because I've got cramp. He gently pulls out of my ass then and gathers some more moisture from my sex. My entire body tingles because it thinks he's going to play with my clit again, but then I feel something bigger stretching me out.

Two fingers.

I hiss through gritted teeth, squeezing my eyes shut. My muscles feel like they're being forced to work the wrong way, sharp pains shooting up my spine.

"Relax, baby," Charlie whispers, pulls out to soak his fingers in my cum and then he's gently taking my ass.

He finds a leisured rhythm that soon becomes quite satisfying, and I wonder, *is this what it feels like to have proper sex?*

If it is, I've been missing out.

I don't know why I just thought that. I want him to get rid of those oils so I can test a theory; see if they're messing with my body.

After collecting some more lubrication, three fingers press past my sphincter and it feels like he's tearing me open. His lips are on mine before I can utter a word, his tongue swirling, taking my mind to another place.

"I want you," he says harshly, lost somewhere in his mind. "I wanner fuck you." He isn't lying, but I'm convinced he won't. I can feel how much control he's exercising over himself.

Curling his fingers against a spot deep inside, he makes my core pulse. I tense my ass, clamping down on his fingers, rhapsody sizzling in my veins.

"Ah!" My eyes fly open as he pulls me up off the bed, holding me around the waist in one arm tangled in my hair. The other is hooked under my ass where his fingers are still wedged inside me.

"What are you..." I don't finish my question. Skin against skin, I can feel his stiff, warm cock touching my sex, every bulging vein.

I gulp.

Looking at me with his head slightly tilted, Charlie shifts me up his dusty legs so I'm sitting right on his lap, causing his cock to stimulate my clit with the movement. I squeeze out a moan, gazing at him in desperation, at his flush face and his blazing blue eyes. If there's ever been a look of desire, that has to be it.

"Put your feet on the bed just like I told you before," he rasps out, and I do, gaining balance with my legs open on either side of his waist.

There's a peculiar smell in the air that I'm finding hot: sweat and my arousal and Charlie's natural musky fragrance. Why do I find his body odor so appealing?

"You know, if you want me to fuck you properly," he says, making my heart pound with fear, "I will. No one orders me about. And I promise I'll be gentle."

"No," I shake out, shuddering. "Don't do that, Charlie. I can't do that."

Unable to bear that expression of desire on his face any longer, and because I'm so out of my depth, I bury my face in his dusty chest.

"No. Look at me." Grabbing a handful of my hair at my back, he tugs, forcing me to arch and meet his glowing eyes.

"That's better." His voice is softer now. He leans down to kiss my lips, warm puffs of breath coming from his nose.

I kiss him back, indulging myself, mirroring his salacious tongue actions.

His fingers begin to move in and out of my anus, slow at first but then faster and faster, creating a wet suction sound that's quite cringing, until he grinds his hips.

I swear, everything in me is boiling on the verge of erupting.

Back and forth with steady, skilled motions, he rubs his cock on my sex, rubs my swollen clit. My focus narrows. I copy his motions, curling my own hips to meet his thrusts. It's so good—so hot! Driving me nuts!

"Please," I beg in a state of aroused weakness, my voice choked with my neck trussed back.

"What'd you want, baby?" he says on my mouth, looking at me through hooded eyes.

That's a fucking good question.

"I... I don't know."

"More?"

I open to speak but nothing comes out.

He must think I mean to say yes, because it isn't long before he stops finger fucking me. His hand curved under my ass, he lifts me up, and then I feel something much bigger being pushed in me, something warm and slightly wet.

My toes fist, my finger nails digging in his hairy chest. The head of his cock is large and warm, forcing me open bit by bit.

"Relax," he whispers, gently pumping his hips to thrust past my sphincter.

"Aw!" I scream through closed teeth, my insides rolling with pain.

"Fuck, you're tight." Charlie sounds tense, like he's on the verge of erupting himself, and his expression is so powerful.

He stops when he's an inch in and I exhale, trying to sink into him for comfort but he won't let go of my hair. He's forcing me to look up at him, keeping my body arched.

Cupping his cock against my ass with an open palm, I assume so he doesn't come out, he says, "Now, we can go at your pace. If it's too much, just stop moving."

"What? No!" I blink rapidly at him, my eyes flickering all over his face with panic. "I-I don't know what I'm doing, Charlie. Please don't make me do it."

There's a moment where we gaze at each other. I know I look oddly vulnerable, but I feel like that. Charlie seems cool in his domain, like he's done this a thousand times before.

"All right." He binds both arms around me, squeezing me to him. I want this—his comfort—I need it. I turn my head to the side and rest my face against his damp, hairy torso, feeling oddly safe in his embrace.

"You'll tell me to stop if it hurts too much, won't you, Blaire? I don't wanner hurt you."

I nod, and then his hips rock back and forth, urging him in some more. It burns so bad and my muscles are aching—or stinging. I can't tell the difference right now. And I feel so full that I'm not sure how he's got any more room to move.

But he does.

Another inch, and it's too much, my insides whirling in agony.

"No more," I say in a pitiable state, and I think I'm trembling.

"Shhh," he hushes me, stroking up and down my back over my hair. "I won't go any deeper. Not unless you want me to."

He stills for a while, soothing me with his touch as he continues stroking up and down my back over my hair. It's like he's massaging me.

When I'm looser and calmer, he ripples his hips, just a few inches of his cock sliding in an out of me with ease now that I'm stretched open. There's a spot he hits every so often that makes me squeal in pleasure and agony—it's a gripping contrast of sensations. I want more now. I can't think of anything else anymore.

Pulling on my hair, Charlie seems to want my mouth again, so I give it to him, gladly soaking up his kisses. They're tender and lovely.

I stare at him in paralyzed muse, seeing again how much he's controlling himself. His temple is throbbing like he wants to go crazy with me and his eyes are scorching with something dangerous. He's moaning in the back of his throat. It's so hot! It turns me on even more.

The harder we kiss, wrapped in lust and debauchery, the deeper he goes. I want more of his cock. I ask for more, as fucked up as I am, and he gives it to me, until he's sheathed in my flesh, my clit rubbing against his hairy pubic bone.

He curses in Spanish, his fingers boring into my back.

Pressing my feet into the bed, I rondevu with his thrusts by swaying my hips, sweat trickling down my spine. Faster and faster, my heart racing out of my chest. He's really fucking me, his thighs slapping against my ass globes, body to body, only sweat between us. He hits that spot every time now, causing ecstasy to gather at my core, until it scatters.

"Aargh!" My arms fly up to hold him around the neck, clutching to him like my life depends on it. I don't know what the hell is happening to me. This is different to before—more powerful. I'm full to bursting yet liberated.

I faintly hear deep moans mixed with screaming—Charlie and myself—and then he comes to an abrupt stop, crushing me in his arms as he curses to the high heavens. Buried deep in my decadency, he curls his hips around, massaging my clit with his pubic bone. It's so intense that I buck away in a tremor of spasms, my sex pulsing while my spine is tingling. Large hands clamp down on my hips, shoving his cock right inside me again, drawing out the pleasure—it's radiating supernova.

I hide my face in the crook of his sweaty neck, scream and cry, barely handling what's happening to me.

"It's never been this good," Charlie hisses, tensing from head to toe. I can feel the tension in his body, in his hard muscles.

When it's over, when he lets go of my hips, I slump on him gasping so hard that my throat is on fire, trying to come down from whatever that was.

My ass is stinging and I can feel warm liquid dripping out of me.

A hand caresses my back over my hair, while another is holding me to Charlie because I'm sliding down his damp body. He's panting with great effort. I'm not sure if it's his heart or his chest drumming in my ear.

He says something to me but I'm not listening. The come down is scarily sobering. Reality grips me, the veil that is my lust fading away.

What the fuck have I just indulged in?

I feel sick.

"You all right?" Charlie says in puffs of breath, kissing the side of my damp face.

I don't say anything. I can't. I feel strange in my own skin.

Pressing into his chest with both hands, in time with shakily standing, I force him out of me.

"Hey," Charlie tries to stop me. "Hey, careful."

"Awh," I wince, slapping his hands away. It fucking hurts, my muscles resisting the corrupt withdrawal. I drop back onto the bed with a loud huff of relief, roll over and curl into a small ball.

No. I don't feel sick. I am sick. One sick motherfucker for enjoying that.

A hand touches my hip. "Blaire?"

"Please go away," I say, staring into nothingness. "You've got what you wanted."

Anything good I felt is gone now, and anything I could feel, I'm blocking it.

Charlie exhales a sharp breath and the room goes dark. There's a burning wax scent in the air now.

"Blaire, I'm leaving," he says, and I feel the weight of a blanket covering my body, up to my chin. "Do you want anything before I go, like a glass of water?"

Don't think. Don't think. Don't think.

Refusing to answer him, I shut my eyes, desperate for the night to take me.

BLAIRE
(PART ONE)

11

When I wake up the next morning, everything is fresh in my mind, and I'm fuming.

I untangle myself from the blanket wrapped around me like a snake and roll over onto my back, arching with a breathless moan. My ass is a little sore and my hips feel like they've been banged so hard they ache. Finger print bruises on my back where my ribs are, and parts of my neck feel like a vacuum has had its way with me.

Charlie's mouth. That sexually warped bastard.

Trying not to tense up with anger, I take deep, balanced breaths, but with every inhale I can smell cleaning polish. It's orange and citrusy. It reminds me of when my car has been cleaned.

My car...

Home...

Maksim...

James...

Just thinking about it all makes me so... I have no words.

BLAIRE
(PART ONE)

I cannot believe Maksim gave Charlie permission to do *that* to me. I cannot believe he let that motherfucker drug me when all he had to do was tell me my orders and I would have followed suit. How could he barter me in this sexually violating way? How could he do this to me... *me!* his most trusted devotee?

Seething and on the verge of pitiful tears, I stuff the blanket in my mouth and scream so hard that I can feel my throat being ripped to shreds.

I'm shaking, too.

I could kill someone.

I'm so glad Charlie isn't here because right now, I might do something I'll live to regret, especially when I think back on last night... about what he did to me... the things he made me feel...

Not only am I fuming, but I'm so embarrassed it's beyond belief.

Charlie practically had me begging for him—he even held my hand when I reached out to him and comforted me through my first orgasm.

That's humiliating.

I'm trained to kill with my own two hands—trained to punish and protect—and I wanted Charlie to hold my fucking hand?

Maybe it wasn't me, I try to convince myself for whatever good it'll do. I'm not weak. I'm tough. Charlie drugged me and he had those oils burning; said they would help me relax.

Yes, he forced my state of needy weakness. Not me.

The memory of him grabbing my hips and shoving his cock back in my ass to draw out my orgasm makes my insides tingle, and then I feel a warm gush of liquid between my legs. *Fuck.* I don't even know why I'm thinking about that but it seems to be turning me on.

I beg myself to put it out of my mind. It's too mentally consuming, and confusing, and as I've no idea when Charlie is going to show up today I need to get my shit together.

Cuddling the blanket to my chest—I'm still wearing my bra; at least one part of me is still intact—I sit up in bed, squinting through the sun flooding the room. The sun is so bright that my head pounds for a moment.

I hold my face, waiting for the pounding in my head to go away.

My eyes adjust, and I'm stone cold sober. Where the fuck has Charlie brought me?

The room is big and airy with high ceilings and dark paneled walls, a huge brass chandelier hanging over head. The parquet floors are highly buffed but old and worn. In the left corner of the room, opposite from where I'm sitting on the bed, there's a small square table housing a chessboard and a throne like chair made from redwood. An antique armoire stands next to the chair, made from the same redwood.

It's as if I've gone back in time and I'm in some medieval showdown.

I never expected Charlie to live in a place like this. It's just not him.

Through the tall sash window on the left wall that boasts no curtains, I see the sun burning low in the sky. It has to be morning. The sun isn't past noon yet.

The air breezing in is refreshing, cooling my warm skin. *He* must have opened the window for me. How fucking nice.

"Bastard," I hiss to myself, twisting my lips in anger.

I want to go outside and take in the morning's freshness. I want to feel free for a moment. I don't want to be here.

I miss home so much, my apartment, Maksim and James, and it's only been one night. How does Maksim expect me to do this for three whole months?

If James was here, I'm not sure this would be happening. I know he'd be fighting to do whatever he could to spare me. He always does.

"No," I whisper, my voice choked up. The guilt I feel for even considering letting him take my place is horrible. I wouldn't. Dealing with Maksim is one thing, but Charlie is another. None of us really know him and up until now, he's not actually hurt me. I can't be sure he wouldn't hurt James.

I hope James is okay with Maksim.

"Don't think about it all," I say, speaking to the empty room. I put last night and James in a little black box in the back of my mind and hope the thoughts will stay there.

Hooking my feet over the side of the bed, I get up on shaky legs, my muscles aching from head to toe. Something crispy and sticky draws my attention to the flesh between my thighs.

Charlie's cum and my morning's arousal.

I recoil, trying desperately not to think about it. I focus on the clothes at the foot of the bed; skinny fitting jeans, a black long sleeve jumper and a pair of knee high flat heeled boots.

These aren't mine. Where are my clothes and trainers?

BLAIRE
(PART ONE)

The clothes are all right, I guess, but the underwear isn't exactly what I'd call 'underwear'. The bra is black lace and the matching pants are just a scrap of material. I pick up the thong with my finger and thumb.

I'm not wearing this shit.

I toss the underwear back on the bed and find my way into an en-suite bathroom that leads off the bedroom. I head straight for the triple width shower. I need to get clean. I feel so dirty.

Flicking on the faucet, I snap off my bra and step under the flow to shower in ice cold water, shivering as the water sprays over my face and my body. Goose pimples race all over my skin. The water is too cold, I've got a brain-freeze headache, but I don't care. It feels clean.

I wash with a bar of lime colored soap that smells strong of mint, using my hands and fingernails. My ass stings against the soap, but the cold water is numbing. The soap dries out my hair as I lather, making the strands feel a little wiry, but there's no shampoo or conditioner in here.

I briefly wonder if Charlie pre-planned bartering me. He doesn't seem prepared—or, maybe he is. Maybe he just won't offer me luxuries like Maksim does.

That wouldn't surprise me.

When I'm done, I can only find a small hand towel in the bathroom—definitely unprepared. I dry myself as best as I can, patting my hair. There's a toothbrush and some toothpaste on the vanity sink under a long mirror, so I brush my teeth and go back into the bedroom to dress.

BLAIRE
(PART ONE)

I'm grateful for the clothes, given it's a little chilly in this big room. I don't put on the bra or the thong. They're so... trashy. They're not me. I wear sports bras and comfortable pants, not this crap. My breasts aren't that big anyhow, so going braless won't matter.

The jumper is made from cashmere. It's so soft. I hug my middle, missing home a little more. Now, if I were at home, I'd be making myself a coffee, casting my eyes out over London until Maksim calls for me or text's to say I can have the day to myself. Here, I don't know what the day has in store for me. More sexual infringement? A beating? That is what men like *him* enjoy, as far as I know.

I'll take a beating any day of the week. At least I know how to feel about that. I'm in emotional limbo when it comes to what happened last night.

My usually sleek red hair is damp and heavy around my shoulders and my waist. I notice it's frizzy, too, seeing my pale, freckly reflection in the bedroom window—I don't even recall walking over here. I'm in such a weird place mentally.

I comb out the damp kinks in my hair with my fingers.

Where is my hair tie?

I glance over the messy bed behind me but I remember; I let my hair down last night.

The bedroom door clicks open then, and closed.

I go cold on the spot.

12

Turning my head, I look at Charlie by the door. It's suddenly like there's no air in the room.

He's wearing dark blue jeans over black boots and a black jumper much like mine, his muscles clearly defined under the soft material. I remember the weight of his hard body on mine... the musky scent of his skin... the way he kissed me...

My lungs are so tight.

His eyes are striking blue against the sunshine, against his tanned skin, though they're black in the corners, I assume from taking a punch from me.

"Morning, Blaire." A sly grin tugs at the corner of his lips.

His ink black hair is a little chaotic, curling around his neck and face, but annoyingly sexy. I'd love to rip his hair out. I'd love to rip out my own hair for responding to him this way... feeling flustered at the sight of him.

I don't say anything. I'm just looking at him, trying not to think of last night. If I do, I'm not sure what I'll do to him—I don't trust myself right now. I don't trust that I won't hit him, or worse... kiss him.

I can't stomach this. I've never not trusted myself.

Charlie proffers a steaming cup, his eyes trained on mine. "I'm told you like coffee in the morning."

I wonder again, just for a split second, if he is using me to get back at Maksim. One day I'll ask him, when the time is right and I'm not terrified that he might say yes.

"I'm not really interested in coffee, Charlie."

"No?" He smiles at me, mischief flashing in his eyes. "What are you interested in then?"

I arch a brow at him, suddenly so angry I could murder him. "Are you going to do that to me every night for three fucking months?"

"Do you want me to?" He's deadly serious and a little amused.

"Eh... no, I don't want you to." My expression is hard like stone.

From being amused, he sighs and brings me the coffee. I flinch when he takes one of my wrists.

"I'm also told you like eggs for breakfast." He carefully puts the hot cup in my hand and lets me go, stepping back.

"I'm not hungry," I say, my voice weaker than I was trying for.

Coffee topples over the cup, scolding my wrist. My hand is shaking. I hate this. I never shake—not under anyone but Maksim.

Charlie doesn't say anything for a moment. He's just staring at me with a look of wonder gleaming in his eyes.

The silence is unbearable, louder than any scream or cry I've ever heard.

I can't stand it.

I need to get out of here.

Dropping my gaze to the floor, I start for the door to put some distance between us but a hand closes around my forearm.

"Where'd you think you're going?" Charlie turns me to face him.

Baffled, I search his eyes. "Outside."

"I don't think so."

"What?" My eyes widen. "You expect me to stay in this room for three whole months?"

He shrugs, like that's exactly what he expected.

"You're insane if you think I'll stay cooped up in here." I squeeze the cup in my hand, restraining myself from throwing it at him. "I need to train, Charlie. I need my own personal space."

He's quiet again, as though he's contemplating something.

It feels like hours before he says, "If I let you out, you're not gonna run screaming for the hills, are you?" He flicks up his eyebrows. "Theoretically, I mean."

I scoff at him with a smirk, on the verge of laughing my head off.

"What's so funny?" He doesn't look confused by my laughter—his expression is even and focused—but he sounds a bit confused.

"You flatter yourself."

"Oh yeah?" He's back to smirking.

"Yes," I huff. "Trust me, you're not worth screaming for."

For a second, just a split second, I think he looks insulted, but then he grins, hunches down and puts us nose to nose, making me sink into my shoulders. "You screamed pretty well last night."

My cheeks burn. I'm more embarrassed now than I was when I woke up.

I don't know where it comes from but I snatch out of his grasp and slap him around the face, *wallop!* hard enough to make his head whip back.

He slams me against the wall with his forearm over my chest.

"Ah!" I pant out on impact, dropping the coffee cup. It smashes at my feet and scatters across the floor.

"You know..." Charlie says in my face, his expression taut with darkness, "...you're the only girl I won't hit but don't think you have the advantage because there are other ways I can punish you."

I gulp, pressing my hands back against the wall.

"I'd rather you hit me," I say, my voice small.

His gaze burns into mine. My breathing accelerates. I don't know what to do. Should I fight him off?

Maksim said not to fight him.
Maksim said to indulge him.
Maksim said to please him.

"Believe me, you wouldn't want me hitting you." With his free hand, he cups my sex over the jeans.

I cower and turn my face to the side so I can hide in my long hair, my core tightening. I remember the orgasms last night, all, too, well, and I can't tolerate that I liked them.

He rubs me there with the tips of his fingers. Even with the jeans between us, it feels good. I pulse for attention, the crotch of my jeans dampening with my arousal. It makes my toes curl.

Why do our bodies react against our will?

"You like that, don't you?" he whispers, softly kissing the side of my face. "And you hate that you like it."

Can he read my fucking mind?

Looking back at him, touching his nose with mine, I make damn sure I don't break our gaze this time, even while I feel like I'm drowning. He has to know I'm strong willed if nothing else.

"Are you sore?" he asks. I'm not sure if he's mocking me or genuinely concerned.

Raising his eyebrows, he beckons me for an answer.

I nod minutely.

"I thought you might be," he whispers. Grabbing my hips in both hands, he yanks me up off the ground, making me yelp in shock. "Don't be frightened. I'm not gonna hurt you." He presses one knee against the wall between my legs and sits me there, my legs dangling freely on either side of his.

My ass feels bony against his masculine leg and a little sore with the pressure of sitting down.

I don't know what to do.

I instinctively reach out for balance and he grabs my hands; runs his fingers through mine. I lose my breath at the warm contact, trembling, desperately looking up at him.

What is he doing?

To answer my question, he puts my palms on his smooth face and makes me hold him, controlling my balance like this. His hands completely cover mine.

I can't breathe again.

Not once does he blink while staring right through my soul, his blue eyes full of desire. I feel so weak and small, at his mercy, and I know I look scared out of my mind.

I can't stand this!

"No one has ever been gentle with you before, have they?" Bowing his head, Charlie kisses my lips and fire races through my veins. "Have they?" he repeats because I don't answer him, speaking against my mouth.

I turn my face so I don't have to kiss him but he 'tuts' at me. My entire body trembles. I don't want him sodomizing me again—it gives him too much power over me—so I face him. He pecks my lips, chipping away at my will... making me want him in this fucked up endeavor of allure...

I detest that I want him. It's crazy. I should hate him—and I do hate him—but right now the desire is stronger than the hate. I can feel it in my body.

I open to say something—anything to stop this—and he takes full advantage, just like he did before. Delicately touching my tongue with his, he has me moaning and melting again, gripping his jaw in a desperate attempt to make love to his mouth.

All my anger—all my hate—it vanishes.

It seems I lose focus when he does things like this to me. I'm not myself.

He hums deeply, then he forces his sodden tongue right into my mouth and massages unholy across mine. I can taste real, bitter coffee on his tongue and Charlie's natural flavor. It's such a sexy contrast of flavors.

When he sucks the tip of my tongue, I moan again. It's such a hot moan that I forget who I am for a second. My head is buzzing with lust.

He likes that I moan. He smiles.

"Tell me the truth, Blaire, or I'll keep you in this room all day long."

"The truth about what?" I ask, blinking rapidly at him, my head swimming.

Letting go of my hands on his face, he runs his fingers into my hair and seizes my head, holding us mouth to mouth.

I don't let go of his face. If anything, I squeeze him tighter, finding the whole ordeal of us staring at each other while kissing too intimate.

"Has anyone ever been gentle with you?" he says, and then he's kissing me as though he really means it. His wet licks are unhurried, and his lips are gentle, shaping around mine, making my mouth water.

In a haze, I shake my head.

"No," he whispers in my mouth, blinking then. "I didn't think so." Wrapping his huge arms around my entire body, he forces me up his leg so we are chest to chest, crushing me to him.

Now, it feels like he's all over me, all over my mouth; all over my body, and I'm not sure I don't like it. He smells so good, like he's just had a shower.

My heart is hammering nineteen to the dozen, trying to jump out of my ribcage, and I'm so damp between my legs that I feel clammy and hot.

"Did I hurt you last night?"

I think I whimper in his mouth, anxious, struck by his question. I can't live like this for three months, wondering... drowning in anxiety... unwillingly wanting... I need to know what the days have in store for me. I need to know how bad it's going to get.

"Don't be frightened," Charlie whispers again. He grips the back of my neck with one hand and holds me there, his other arm still wrapped around my back.

"Charlie," I tremble out his name, visibly anxious, "what are you going to do to me now?"

He glances between my eyes, his alight with ardor. "Nothing. I just wanner kiss you."

I'm so relieved that I know he can feel my body going slack with relief.

"Did I hurt you?" he asks once more, taking my mouth in another deep kiss.

I want to tell him it was agony because that is after all what men like, isn't it? To inflict pain on girls?

I don't tell him that though. I shake my head, being honest. It wasn't that bad. I've suffered far, far worse.

"Good," he says softly, pecking the edge of my mouth. "I didn't wanner hurt you."

I frown at him, and he pecks my mouth again. He said he was going to do terrible things to me, didn't he?

"What did you mean by, 'I might be the only girl you won't hit'?" my courage to ask that comes from nowhere.

The way he smiles at me... My stomach flips.

"I like you," he says sincerely. "A lot more than I thought I would."

Something vibrates in his jeans pocket against my thigh. Without breaking away from me, he shifts to hold me in one arm, squashing my breasts to his hard chest. He reaches into his jeans pocket and pulls out his phone;

answers it against my mouth while still kissing me. "What?"

Now, it feels really intimate with him being on the phone, unable to stop having his fill of me.

Charlie utters a few words amid pecking me, while I'm cupping his face in both my hands, kissing him back, then I hear someone say something about arranging a meeting on Maksim's behalf.

My heart drops into my stomach.

Why would he be arranging a meeting on Maksim's behalf?

Charlie presses another kiss to my lips, then he says, "Two o'clock is fine." And he hangs up, shoving his phone away.

"Why are you talking about Maksim?" I pull away from him but I don't get far because his arm is still around my waist.

I grip his shoulders, wishing he'd put me down.

"I'm paying the Albanians a visit." He doesn't teeter about telling me, which surprises me.

"The Albanians?" That girl who got fucked at the Prince's party springs to mind.

"Yeah," Charlie says. Using his free hand, he tucks my hair back over my shoulder, really looking at me through heavy blue eyes. "Maksim is having a few issues with them, so I agreed to sort it."

"Maksim is having problems... and he...he went to *you!* instead of me?" I'm affronted. I cannot believe this!

I push against Charlie's chest, forcing him to drop me on my feet, and craning my neck all the way back, I look up at him.

"Why has he come to you and not me?"

"They're a little outa your league." Pressing one hand against the wall beside my face, he cages me in, towering over me.

"Out of my league?" I ask, glowering, my body getting hot because he's doing this weird primal proximity thing. "What does that mean?"

Glancing between my eyes, he smiles at me. It's such a gorgeous smile that I can't stop my heart from going a little faster.

"They're quite dangerous-" he wipes across my upper lip with his thumb, as if he doesn't give a shit about what we're talking about, then he kisses me once more. He seems solely focused on me. "-Too dangerous for one small girl."

I laugh sarcastically, folding my arms over my chest. "You actually believe that you best me with ease, don't you, Charlie?"

He doesn't answer me, but he thinks just that. It's in his meditated stare; in his cunning, lax smile.

"Well, understand this: I put up a little bit of a fight in moments because my heart is in warfare with my head," I put a finger to my temple, "not because I'm weaker than you. So when you have your way with me, know it's because I let you under Maksim's wishes. Nothing more."

"Is that right?"

"You bet it is," I speak through clenched teeth. "I do whatever Maksim says—I'm only here because he wants me to be here."

Charlie hunches down, putting us face to face. "And if Maksim told you to come home right now?"

I point at the space between us, feeling like myself again. "I'd kick your ass if you didn't let me go, then I'd leave."

"You really do think you could beat me in a fight, don't you?"

"Oh, I don't think. I know."

He chuckles, standing back and crossing his arms. "Maybe one day-" he cocks his head, "-we'll get in the ring and battle it out."

"Name the time and the place." I'm so sure I'll beat him that I want him to say, 'right here, right now'. He doesn't, of course. He's just looking at me like he's gently taking off my clothes. My cheeks get hot, so I stare down at the floor. "I'll come with you to meet with the Albanians if you don't mind. You might find me useful."

He scoffs, insulted. "Maksim might have no shame in having a tiny girl on his security detail, but I do."

"Shame?" Glaring up at him, I cross my arms again, mimicking his pose. "I took you on—and almost vanquished you, might I add."

He flashes the filthiest smirk, reaches out and gently pinches my chin. "Almost."

I pull my chin out of his grasp. He starts chuckling again, his cheekbones clearly defined with that large smile.

"I'm not surprised Maksim sees you as his trophy. That lucky motherfucker has had you for far too long."

"Charlie," I say softly, thinking about Maksim, "I want to avoid any intimate conversations with you, if you don't mind."

"I do mind, actually," he says, his voice taking a dark edge. "Over the next three months, I plan on knowing you inside out."

My chest tightens because I have a horrible feeling he isn't going to tire of me.

He inhales, like he's sighing. "If you have some breakfast, you can come with me."

"What?" I'm so astonished he just gave in like that, I gawp at him.

He nods. "And on one condition."

"What condition?"

"You have to stay behind me if any trouble breaks out."

I scowl at him, confused.

"I don't want you getting hurt on my watch, little Blaire." He's mocking me. He lowers his tone when he says, 'little Blaire'.

I snort at him. "Maybe I'll kick the Albanians' asses before kicking yours. That ought to shut you up."

Before we leave for the Albanians, Charlie brings me a plate of warm scrambled eggs and a glass of orange juice on a silver tray. I'm so pissed off by how easily he makes me enjoy what he does to me that I hesitate to take it from him. He raises his eyebrows, but I continue looking at him in wrath, wanting to punch him again. Maybe if I fuck up his face I won't find him so attractive, because that has to be the reason why I respond to him so easily, right? It's physical?

"You can always stay here," he says, reminding me of his ultimatum—eat, or stay here. "It's no bother to me either way."

Simmering inside, I snatch the tray from him. The orange juice almost spills over but he's quick to grab the glass, steadying it on the tray. He tells me to take it easy but I'm not really listening to him. Glancing over the tray, I wonder how he knows I like eggs for breakfast, and scrambled eggs for that matter. Did Maksim tell him?

"What's wrong?" he asks.

I don't like to assume *they've* spoken about me, that's what's wrong. It's too... weird, given what Charlie wants me for.

Holding the tray in both hands, I push past him. He sighs but I don't let it affect me—hopefully, if I keep on like this and refuse to indulge him, he'll tire of me. I can't live like this for three months. He's going to ruin me. How Maksim thinks I'll go back intact, I don't know. He knows Charlie and what Charlie is capable of. Hell, Charlie has managed to tap into me and my desires, and I'm like a fucking ice queen.

Sitting on the foot of the bed, I shift to get comfortable in these jeans while Charlie gets all domesticated and cleans up the broken coffee cup, using a dustpan and brush to sweep up the splinters. Now I wish I threw it across the room to really put him to work.

I'm laughing before I can stop myself. Charlie glances up at me, pulling his thick eyebrows together. Avoiding his stare and trying to stop laughing, I grab the glass of orange juice. It's sweet and refreshing, cool as it pours down my throat. I then dig into my breakfast. The eggs are nice, fluffy and seasoned right.

Did he cook this?

That makes me feel a bit weird. I can't recall a time when anyone ever made me food. Maksim used to feed me bread and water when he was conditioning me as a kid but I wouldn't exactly call that making food.

Charlie mops up the spilt coffee and disappears with the bucket for about five minutes, then he returns and sits beside me, making the bed dip.

I'm so aware of his closeness that my skin pricks, and my nipples... they're like fucking bullets. I'm not sure that I don't like being so close to him. How bizarre is that?

I try to focus on eating but I can't shift this personal feeling of him watching me. It's so strong.

I peek up at him, a question in my eyes.

"What is it?" He's glancing between all my features. It's quite flattering the way he looks at me, as if he sees only me.

"Where are my clothes and trainers, Charlie?" I put down the fork and pinch the jeans I'm wearing. "I don't like wearing jeans."

He half smiles, gently pushing my hair back over my shoulder with one hand. "I'll get your things if you want them."

I look down at the food on my lap and pick at the toast with my fingers. He's got those weird dark vibes going on. I've noticed how his aura changes when he wants to kiss me, or worse...

"What else do you like other than eggs, Blaire?"

I lift my shoulders. "I'm not fussy. I'll eat anything."

BLAIRE
(PART ONE)

"I didn't ask if you're fussy. I said what do you like other than eggs. What would you usually eat at home?"

I definitely want to punch him, especially when he speaks to me like this. I'm not a fucking child.

I don't find his gaze again. I eat the rest of my eggs, keeping my eyes down. "I don't know... chicken... vegetables... potatoes..."

Nothing more is said about what food I like. Charlie sits with me until I finish off my breakfast, then he stands and takes the tray from my lap. I look up at him, and of course he's staring at me. He's always staring at me, intrigued or something.

"Meet me downstairs in ten minutes," he gestures with the tray, "I'll clean this up and then we'll head off."

I nod, glad that he's taking me with him. Someone has to look out for Maksim because I doubt Charlie is. He has other intentions. I know it.

BLAIRE
(PART ONE)

13

Charlie and I shrug into our jackets by the double front doors. He's wearing a brown leather jacket, and I have to admit, he looks good in it, especially with his black hair curling around his features. He looks dangerous and rugged.

"Here, let me get that." He helps me into my jacket, slipping it up my arms.

I want to stop him but why bother? Unless I want him making my life hell for the next three months, I need to find some common ground with him.

He pulls out my hair and drapes it down my back.

"I want my gun before we leave," I say, zipping up my jacket and facing him.

"Yeah, all right." He chuckles, grabbing a set of car keys from a cupboard on the wall by the doors.

"I'm serious." I stare at him without blinking. "I want my gun."

He's quietly looking at me, his eyes flittering between mine, then he snaps, "You're mad if you actually believe I'll let you loose around me with a pistol."

It seems he wants to control everything about me—even my safety.

"Charlie," I sigh out his name, running my fingers through my hair, "I can't live like this for three months. You're too intense-"

His eyebrows shoot up.

"-There has to be some kind of mutual respect between us, otherwise, I'd rather you and Maksim fall out and I go back to my old life." I shrug. "It's your choice."

"You can't decide that."

Slowly and softly, I say, "I can. I'll just pay for it."

He grinds his jaw, and now he's glaring at me. "You'll put a bullet in my head while I sleep if I give you back your gun—why'd you think I took it from you in the first place, hm? I don't trust you."

Like I give a shit if he trusts me or not.

I reach past him for the door handle. "I don't need you to be asleep to shoot you." I tug the door open, allowing in a rush of cold air. "I'll be waiting outside. Bring my gun. I don't feel safe without it."

When I walk past him, I barge him with my shoulder. He huffs, as if he wants to say something, but he doesn't.

Exiting the house, I jog down the porch steps, immediately noticing Charlie has a fetish—for cars I mean. There's a black Mercedes, a red Ferrari, two Range Rovers—one in black and the other in white—and an old red sports car. They're all parked on the right side of the stony driveway, under a wall of climbing white flowers.

Who needs this many cars?

"I must be crazy giving this back to you," Charlie says from behind.

Pivoting, I take my gun from him. It's cold and heavy. It's my safety blanket.

"Blaire," he says my name gravely, giving me his hardest stare, "I'm only gonna warn you this once; if you ever pull that gun on me again," he points a finger in my face, "I'll put you down. Is that clear?"

I nod, unbothered. I don't plan on using my gun on him. I only used the fantasy of it last night to scare him, which failed immensely.

Closing his eyes, he lets out a deep breath. He's uneasy about me having a weapon. *Good.*

"Let's go," he says. "We have to be in West Sussex by two."

The black Range Rover flashes to signal it's open, so I head for it, my feet crumpling against the driveway.

"Do you want me to drive?" I tuck my gun away in my inside jacket pocket and zip myself up again.

Charlie throws me the keys without question and I catch them in steady hands.

"I suppose this mutual respect has to start somewhere." He winks at me—actually winks at me. It makes my cheeks warm up.

What is it with him and that dark alluring thing he's got going on? Even Maksim doesn't affect me on this level.

I jump into the driver's seat and press the button to fire up the vibrating engine, and for a moment, just a quick moment, I wonder if Charlie has spoken to Maksim; if he's told him that I pulled a gun on him.

I'm petrified that he has. Maksim will beat me half to death for provoking Charlie—the man he clearly fears.

"Blaire?" Charlie says from beside me. I haven't even noticed him getting into the car. "What's wrong?"

I realize I'm frozen, squeezing the wheel of the car so hard that my knuckles are white.

"Have you spoken to Maksim today?"

He shakes his head, pulling on his seatbelt. "I'll be seeing him next weekend. And don't worry, I won't tell him you tried to shoot me."

The relief of hearing him say that is comforting. I sag in my seat, letting out a breath.

"Is that what you're worried about?" he asks, touching my arm to attain my attention.

I shrug. It's obvious I was worried.

"Blaire, listen..." he gives my arm a gentle squeeze, "I know this isn't exactly conventional, the way I've taken you from Maksim, and I know you're having a hard time, but soon you'll see that you can trust me. Whatever happens between us is our business. Not Maksim's."

"I'll have to tell him when I see him, you know?" I twist at the waist to face him, holding the steering wheel in one hand. "He'll ask what we've been up to."

"That's on you." Turning up his lips, he shrugs. "As far as I'm concerned, this is our private business."

"It's not that private when Maksim gave you permission to drug and abuse me." I sound bitter, but I am. He's twisting my mind... making me take pleasure in things I shouldn't... kissing me like he's in love with me or something...

I don't even know why I'm talking to him like this—as if I know him on a personal level. It pisses me off royally.

"Blaire, oh, Blaire," reaching over, Charlie grabs the back of my seat, giving me his full attention, "whether Maksim gave me permission to take you or not, I'd have taken you, because I wanted you-"

I frown at him, fighting not to react to that consuming look in his eyes.

"-He isn't the boss of me, as I'm sure you've noticed."

I huff at him, glancing away.

"Anyway," he says, lightly tugging on a strand of my hair, making me look back at him, "regardless of all that, as far as my intimacy with you goes, it's our business."

I don't reply to that.

In silence, we gaze at each other, Charlie's blue eyes pacing back and forth between mine, and I don't know what happens inside me, I feel a sense of privacy between us. I actually believe he won't tell anyone about what he's doing to me. It isn't like Maksim can force information out of him—it's Charlie who has all the power.

"All right?" He raises his eyebrows at me.

After a while of thinking, and holding back a million questions, I nod, trusting him like the fucking idiot I am. It's not even forced trust, I just... do.

"Can I ask you one more thing, Charlie?"

He tips his head; seems a little surprised. "Sure you can."

"Why did you let me talk to... *him*, on the phone last night?" I have to know this at the least. "You said you didn't want us having any contact until you're done with me, so why-"

"You looked too nervous for my liking—more nervous than I anticipated you'd be—and I knew that if you spoke to him, you'd be okay." He gestures out the window screen like he's averting from my question. "C'mon. We need to get a move on."

I want to tell him that I was nervous, that he didn't need to drug me because if Maksim said so, I would have come with him, but I won't get any more out of him. So I put the car in gear and pull out of the wide driveway, between tall electric gates that open on command.

I fleetingly wonder if he is using me to get back at Maksim. It doesn't feel like he is. The way he looks at me and kisses me... I feel like he genuinely likes me. But perhaps I'm just green to men of his standards.

I don't know.

He really confuses me.

We don't talk much on the drive to West Sussex, bar Charlie telling me to "Take a left; get off on that motorway; turn right." We just watch the city landscape change to farming fields and acres of flourishing green land packed with sheep. I suppose there isn't much to say, really. *He* got what he wanted last night and I'm safe from his sexual desires for a while.

It takes about two hours for us to arrive at our destination, but we arrive when the Albanians expect us—two o'clock on the dot.

"Let me do all the talking," Charlie says, tucking a gun into the back of his jeans.

"Do you think I'm stupid?" He should know by now that I don't usually speak unless spoken to. I only talk back to him. I just now ponder over why I have the guts to do that.

"What is it?" he asks.

"Nothing." I shake it off.

"Blaire..." he elongates, "if I ask you a question I expect you to answer me... please?"

I sigh, blinking down, then back up at him. "I'm just wondering why I talk back to you when I wouldn't dream of doing it to anyone else."

Sitting back, he grips the handbrake, watching me in quiet muse.

"Maybe because I don't order your silence. Maybe you feel comfortable around me."

I laugh mordantly. "Comfortable? Really?"

"Well, as you said," he shrugs with one shoulder, "apart from me, you've not dreamed of speaking before being spoken to, yet, you've never questioned yourself with me."

The idea isn't lost on me. Staring at him staring at me, I mull it over, annoyed that he might be right. Even at Rumo's poker game, I indulged Charlie... spoke to him... I lied to Maksim when he asked what Charlie and I had talked about after I bested James. I've never lied to Maksim before. I've never spoken to anyone like I do Charlie before, and I don't even know him.

"Don't think about it too much," Charlie's raspy voice breaks through the silence. "I like that you prefer this rather than the obedient dog Maksim has trained you to be."

"How do you know I prefer this?"

"Don't you?" He raises his eyebrows, locking us in a moment.

I can't tell if he's manipulating me or not. I just can't read Charlie.

"You're trying to get in my head," I say through gritted teeth.

"No, Blaire," he says softly, looking between my eyes. "I just wanner know you, that's all."

"Why though?" I ask with clear frustration. "Why do you even want me? You could have any woman you want—a woman who doesn't resist you," I add with sarcasm.

"You'll soon give into wanting me too. It's the law of attraction."

It's like he just slapped me around the face. I will admit, I do fancy him. I just hate how he makes me feel.

"That doesn't explain why you're doing this to me." I peer down at myself, mystified, then back up at him. "I'm not your type—not like those girls at Maksim's party. I'm not what you want, not really..." I go on and on. Don't ask where my audacity has come from, but I just can't seem to stop the verbal diarrhea. I need to know why.

Reaching over, Charlie flicks down the sun visor and opens the mirror.

I scowl between him and my haunting reflection.

"What?" I say, still scowling.

He looks at me in mocking fondness, as if he knows I don't get his point, then climbs out of the car before I have a chance to ask anything more.

"Charlie, for goodness sake..." I huff out, tensing my fists.

He rounds the car and opens my door for me, just as he did the first night I met him. I don't think about the gesture. I slide out of the car, wishing he'd give me a straight fucking answer.

Of course, he won't. Charlie is nothing if not calculating. I feel he wants me to work out everything on my own.

Seven black SUV's with heavily tinted windows pull up around us. I grab Charlie's arm to keep him near and reach for my gun, thinking this is a setup.

"Relax." Charlie closes his hand over mine. "They're my men."

"You have a security detail?"

"Yeah." He strokes over my knuckles with his thumb, warming me from the outside in. "I don't go anywhere without backup."

I snatch my hand back, trying to evade the way he makes me feel.

"C'mon," he says, nodding at the mansion before us—it's all smooth white walls and tall sash windows.

I walk with Charlie towards the house, peering up at him from the side—I can't seem to help having a nose at him. He carries himself with pure confidence, strolling onward like he owns the world and everything in it, his handsome face as impassive as ever.

We reach the bottom of the porch, and he catches me staring. A huge smile spreads across his face.

BLAIRE
(PART ONE)

"Ready?" he says.

In a bit of a fluster with being caught ogling, I blink away and focus on the stone steps in front of us. "Yeah, I'm ready."

Charlie's hand hovering on the low of my back, we pace up the porch steps together.

"If anything goes down," he says, something untrusting flashing through his eyes, "make sure you don't fucking shoot me."

"I know how to use a gun, Charlie," I sound offended, because I am. He gives me no credit for my skills. "Believe me, I've never shot anyone I didn't mean to."

"Just make sure." He knocks on the door and an unfamiliar face greets us.

14

Charlie shakes hands with a guy he addresses as Robert. He's as tall as he is wide, standing there in the doorway draped in a long black coat.

Remaining in the background, I observe the situation, listening to every word they exchange with extra awareness. I need to know why the Albanians have beef with Maksim, and then I can find a clean solution to how we can avoid a war.

Tatiana doesn't like unnecessary conflicts.

"I appreciate you agreeing to see me," Charlie says, withdrawing his hand. "I understand the situation is tense."

"No. Thank you for coming on Maksim's behalf." Robert's accent is thick and cold, like his eerie brown eyes. "I'm not sure we would have been able to resist killing him otherwise."

Killing him!

My defensive instincts buzz in my veins.

No one is killing Maksim on my watch.

I glance between Charlie and Robert with careful scrutiny, my hand twitching for my gun.

"Do you have a picture of her?" Charlie says, and I frown, trying to read between the lines. "I see no point in pissing around."

A picture of *her*...

Her... I rake through my mind for who this *her* could be. The only conclusion I come to is she must be the Albanian girl Maksim and his friends fucked at the Prince's party. It's too much of a coincidence.

"No. I agree," Robert says. Peeling open his coat, he pulls out a tiny photo and passes it to Charlie. "She was very beautiful. As you can imagine, my anger is quite justified."

Charlie doesn't bother studying the photo. He proffers it to me, of all people. I don't take it. I don't even look at it. I scowl up at Charlie, wondering why he's trying to show it to me.

"Do you recognize her?" He raises his eyebrows at me, gesturing with the photo. "The girl in the picture..."

"Why are you showing that to me?" I ask softly, beyond confused. If it is the girl I'm thinking of, then he knows what she looks like.

"Just answer the question, Blaire," he whispers, though I can feel the urgency under his voice.

He pushes my hair back over my shoulder, trying to create intimacy between us. My eyes flicker to Robert, then back to Charlie, who is watching me like a hawk.

"So, you're Blaire," Robert interrupts us, gaining Charlie's attention. "She's the fighter, is that right?"

Charlie faces Robert and tells him that I am, shoving one hand in his jeans pocket. "And she's good. I've seen her in action."

"Oh, I don't doubt that," Robert drawls, his cold gaze journeying up and down my small frame. "I've heard great things about you, girl."

Quiet, I analyze him as he analyzes me. He's got blood on his hands. I can tell from his icy, gangster-like exterior; that puffed out chest; that hard-life wearing expression on his face.

He doesn't scare me. I've ended men greater and more dangerous than him.

"I've also heard of your silence." He laughs, giving Charlie this sultry look, flashing coffee stained teeth. "Is she on offer in exchange for the girl who was taken from me? Because I'd be more than happy to forget about all the bad blood for her." Smiling down at me, he adds, "She's pretty."

I don't react to his smuttiness. I remain as impassive as ever.

"Blaire isn't on offer," Charlie's tone leaves no room for negotiations, nor does his body language as he steps in front of me. "As we agreed, if Blaire confirms that this is the girl Maksim and his friends fucked-up, you'll tell me how much she was worth and I'll ensure she's paid for in full."

"What!?!" I shout without thinking, and now I'm nervous. This can't be right. I had to bargain with Charlie so he'd let me come to this meeting, and now I'm to identify someone? And, he fucking knows what that girl looks like, so why does he need me to identify her?

Charlie glances over his shoulder at me. It takes every ounce of will I have not to attack him.

How dare he put me in a situation of dropping Maksim in it!

"Her name was Arjana-" Robert confirms that it is the girl from the party, "-she was worth half a million euro's for she was a virgin with Palestinian blood."

"That's fair enough," Charlie says, nodding a few times. He then pivots to me, holding up the photo again. "Do you recognize her?"

I don't look at the photo. I give him this wolfish glare, on the verge of ripping his head off.

"Blaire?" he says my name gravely, walking into me, lifting the photo so I can't avoid seeing it. "Do. You. Recognize. Her?"

My jaw ticks. Arjana is wearing a green Oxford college uniform, her dark hair pinned back. She looks very content in this image, hugging what looks like a bunch of school folders. Her big brown eyes are innocent and her smile is wide and pretty; carefree.

My throat is so tight that I can barely breathe.

"If you don't answer me," Charlie says under his breath, his eyes flittering between mine, "I can't sort this."

I swallow, standing my ground of silence. I won't do this to Maksim. I won't betray him.

Briefly shutting his eyes, Charlie sighs, then he turns to Robert. "She won't answer. Trust me on that."

"Thing is," Robert shrugs, "we can't take Blaire's silence as a yes or a no. Everyone is aware of her loyalty to Maksim. Everyone is aware that she won't talk without his permission. And I need to know who took

Arjana from me. I need to know who has her so I can get her back."

So, Robert doesn't know Charlie took her.

I don't know what to do. In any normal situation, I'd end Robert and be done with the bother, but I'm not sure Maksim wants that to happen.

Charlie pulls out his phone and tells me to call Maksim, to ask for permission to speak to Robert. "Make it concise," he says.

I refrain from taking the phone, clenching my fists. I can't speak to Maksim in front of these two. They could overhear.

"I'll pay you the half a million," I blurt out to Robert. "I'm not saying I know that girl or that I don't. I'm just agreeing to pay the debt."

Silence.

Robert is surveying me with curious eyes. I can feel them on my face.

"Why would you pay a debt that doesn't belong to you, girl?" Robert comes out of the house and prowls toward me.

"I won't have this looming over Maksim," I say, wary that he's still coming at me.

One more step... if he takes one more step, I'll tear him to pieces, and then Charlie for lying his way out of knowing Arjana.

Before I can say or do anything, Charlie meets Robert chest to chest, acting as a barrier between us both. "Not another step."

Smelling war in the air, I pull out my gun and hold it beside my leg. I then glance around the front garden, rapidly tucking my hair behind my ears so I can scan our situation. Charlie's flock of men dressed in black combat outfits are standing outside their cars. Their attention is focused on us here by the front doors, emotionless eyes studying the state of affairs, hands clasping machine guns.

That makes me feel a little better to know that we have backup if need be.

I focus back on Charlie and Robert.

"I need to speak to Blaire," Robert says eventually, his eyes narrowed in on Charlie. "I need to look into her eyes and find the truth."

"She won't say anything more than offering to pay the debt."

Robert tries to walk up to me but Charlie sidesteps him, and then again.

"Leave her alone or we're gonna have a problem," Charlie says, his voice oddly calm. "That's not a warning."

"I can't leave this alone-" Robert presses his hands together, like he's praying or something, "-I want to see the girl's eyes when I ask if she knows Arjana."

Charlie grabs his gun from the back of his jeans and slips back the top hammer. Robert reaches in his coat.

"I wouldn't-" Charlie says, gesturing out, "-there's over thirty of my men and one of you."

"That's because you warned me there would be consequences if I had my security detail!" Robert is red with fury. "I only came alone because I know you are a man of your word—you said there would be no trouble!"

My heart is in my throat. I'm not scared, just nervous—I don't know what to do. Yeah, I'm not

Charlie's greatest fan, but I won't stand back and watch him get shot, not after he's clearly watching out for me.

Robert is visibly conflicted, a thoughtful expression on his face as he stares at Charlie. He's not sure whether to press Charlie or not. In all honesty, I'm not sure if I ever should, either.

"You need to stop this, Robert," Charlie says coolly. "Don't start something I'll have to finish. Just take the money and let this be over with."

"I need to know who's got Arjana," Robert snaps, the veins in his neck contracting. "I can't just let this go. I had her for barely two hours before someone came into my house and stole her. Someone invaded my personal space! I can't just let that go, Charlie."

"That's irrelevant to me," Charlie says, and he warns, "If you start a conflict with Maksim, I'll be on his side."

"What!?!" Robert's face lights up with shock. "Why would you side with that scumbag? He's the reason you did a stretch in a Russian jail!"

My mouth drops open. Charlie went to jail because of Maksim? *What the fuck...* Why?

Charlie cocks his head. "Let's just say, I've got other interests when it comes to Maksim now."

Robert pulls his eyebrows together and looks down at me, then back at Charlie.

Charlie nods, and I sense he's grinning.

It all ends pretty quickly from there, which baffles me completely. Charlie says that Maksim will pay within the month. "Any longer, and I'll call you."

Robert lets out a steely breath, obviously pissed off with the outcome. "Looks like I have no other choice but to accept that offer then, does it?"

I hide my gun away before anyone sees it, wondering how the hell I'm going to tell Maksim about what's happened here today. He needs to know.

"Trust that I'll find out what happened to your girl," Charlie says, shoving his gun in the back of his jeans before fixing his t-shirt to cover it. "And anyone who was involved will suffer my wrath, as a favor to you for trusting I'll deal with the situation." Reaching back, he grabs one of my hands and entwines our fingers together. My stomach flips, mostly with anxiety for touching him, but also with a dollop of embarrassment that he's holding my hand like this in front of Robert. His grip is firm yet gentle, his hand completely covering mine.

"We'll be off now, Robert. Take care and I'll speak to you very soon." Forcing me down the porch steps, Charlie leads me back to his car.

Robert says a curt goodbye from a distance and then I hear the front doors close with a loud thud.

I cannot believe how easily people back down from Charlie. I don't know why. He isn't any different from all the other underworld elites—or is he? Maybe Maksim didn't tell me the full story about him. Charlie does refuse to address Maksim in the proper manner and gets no reprove from anyone.

Charlie puts his lips on my ear and whispers, "You did well, Blaire."

"Huh?" I say, screwing up my face.

Opening the car door for me, he puts me in the passenger seat and plugs in my seatbelt. I briefly wonder why he isn't letting me drive us back to his house, but I don't really care.

"What do you mean, 'I did well'?"

He smiles sneakily at me and my eyes enlarge.

Did he just use my loyalty to Maksim to his advantage?

He clicks my door shut, jogs around the car, and jumps into the driver's seat, firing up the engine. I vaguely see all his men piling into their cars but I'm not really paying attention.

I turn to face Charlie, gripping the edge of my chair. "Did you just use me?" I say louder than necessary, but I can't help myself. I'm fuming.

"Not exactly," Charlie says, a stupid, naive expression on his face. "I knew you wouldn't say anything about Maksim without his consent—actually, I was banking on it."

I'm stunned, and I know I look it. Yes I'm glad he's taken care of Maksim's problem with the Albanians but I can't say I'm happy about the way he's used me. He could have told me what the plan was. I'm not an idiot. I would have followed suit.

Putting the car in gear, Charlie pulls off the driveway, between the arsenal of SUV's that follow us out.

"Why did you just pretend you've never seen that girl Arjana before?" I ask, striving to keep my cool so I can get the answers I need.

"Because I've got her," he steers down a country lane, "and I won't be able to keep her if Robert knows that now, will I?"

"What the... You can't be... Are you kidding me!?!" I yell, feeling sick. "Who the fuck are you, a female kleptomaniac?"

He bursts out laughing. "I can't believe you know what that means."

BLAIRE
(PART ONE)

"This isn't funny, Charlie. Why the hell do you have her?" My eyes are blazing, and my guts are turning over with guilt because I can't help thinking he's mistreating her, too. "You're abusing her, aren't you?" I have to ask, then I add in anger, "You're all the fucking same!"

"Jesus, calm down, Blaire," he lifts a wary, defensive hand at me, "I'm not abusing her."

"Then why do you have her?" I speak through clenched teeth.

"I sent her to Mexico because she said she didn't wanner stay in Europe." He shrugs with one shoulder, withdrawing his hand. "I've sorted her out with a place to live and enough money to keep her comfortable until she can work."

I'm gawping, absolutely baffled. "But... why? Why would you do that?"

He looks at me from the corner of his eye. "Because I can."

What a smug motherfucker. Yeah he's done a good deed but why does he have to season it in arrogance?

"Aren't you worried Robert will discover it was you who took her?" I say. "He only has to ask around, you know, anyone who is anyone was at that party."

Charlie laughs with mockery. "Everyone who was there that night has been briefed and know that if they say anything about my presence, they'll not only have the Albanians on their asses, but me."

I don't know what to say anymore, or how to feel about what he's just done—using me, and the fact that he's clearly saved that girl—so I don't say anything at all.

"You all right?" He side-glances me.

BLAIRE
(PART ONE)

I refuse to look at him, holding my tongue. He's the most confusing man I've ever met.

He steers onto the motorway that is chock-a-block with bumper to bumper traffic.

He reaches over and cups my hand, giving me a squeeze. "Are you ignoring me?"

I snatch away from him, staring out of the side window.

"Oh, don't sulk, Blaire." He gently pushes my hair back over my shoulder. "I know I used you but it worked in our favor, and as for the girl, I've no desire for her—I just wanted to help her."

I don't utter a word. In silence, I fester in my own thoughts.

"Okay then," he says softly, flicking on the radio. "Silence it is."

I'm quiet throughout the entire journey back to his house, which is three fucking hours long given the traffic.

Lately, it feels like someone *up there* really hates me.

We pull up on Charlie's driveway at just shy of six in the evening. I'm thirsty, hungry where I haven't eaten for over six hours, and I'm still simmering over the fact that Charlie just used me to his advantage. But, most of all, I want to get the fuck away from him for a while before I explode. I can't take how many different personalities he has.

I step out of the car, slam my door shut with noticeable anger, and head straight for the house.

"Blaire..." Charlie calls out, sighing, "c'mon... You can't really be that mad at me?" He jogs up beside me and stops in front of me so I can't go inside the house without forcefully moving him. "If Robert found out Maksim definitely had a hand in fucking that girl, I cannot say what might've happened. It's better this way."

I cross my arms, looking at his chest, my aggravation like a living thing in the air between us.

"I have to say, I never imagined you'd sulk." Charlie hooks a finger under my chin, forcing our eyes to line up. His are glowing with fond amusement, I guess because he feels like he's breaking me down... revealing my layers...

"S'all right, though," he smirks at me, "I think it's kinda cute."

CUTE!

"I need a car," I say in a blank manner, "and a phone so I can call Maksim to arrange a plane."

Dropping his hand to his side, he glowers at me. I knew that would get him.

"Why?" he asks.

I tell him that I need to go to the Cayman Islands. "As soon as possible."

"What?" He runs a hand through his black hair, frowning. "Why?"

"All my money is in an offshore account there," I tighten my arms over my chest, "and the only way to access it is to take it out in person."

He still looks confused, though he's trying to save face, giving me this awkward smile that doesn't quite reach his eyes. "You don't need any money, Blaire. Maksim can sort his debt."

I shake my head. "He'll have to go to his boss for that much money, who will want to know what's going on."

A pulse near Charlie's temple starts throbbing. "Then he'll have to explain."

"Maksim won't do that," my voice comes out deceivingly smooth. "His boss will be fuming that he almost started a war with the Albanians over a girl. He won't risk that." Though I have more to say, I stop talking, watching Charlie's cool facade slowly dissolve.

"Then I guess he'll have to reap Tatiana's wrath."

I shake my head once. "I won't let Maksim suffer her wrath."

"Why not?" he sounds like he's gradually losing it, his eyes a little wider. "It's not your job to protect him from his dense hobby of raping girls. Maybe he deserves a comeuppance."

I cock my head. "It is my job to protect him, actually."

Charlie minces his teeth together. "How'd you have that much money? And how the fuck do you have access to more money than Maksim does?"

"That's none of your business."

As if I'd tell him Tatiana vetoed Maksim's finances for five years due to his overspending? Any money that goes through him goes straight to her.

Charlie raises his eyebrows like he usually does to summon an answer, but I say nothing. I don't have to give him the ins and outs of my life. The deal he made with Maksim was for my body, nothing else.

"Why'd you bow to Maksim when you've got money, physical and intellectual skills, and beauty? Shouldn't it be the other way around?"

"I don't expect you or anyone else to understand me, Charlie," I say. "Are you going to lend me your car or what? I need to go as soon as possible, as I just said."

"You..." he points at my feet, his eyes flashing with clear loss of control, "...are to be here with me for three months. I shouldn't even be letting you come on jobs with me, let alone fly to another fucking country!"

"Oh, don't even go there," I say with bold conceit. "We both know you tricked me into believing you were doing me a favor by letting me come today, so you can stop taking the moral high ground."

"Moral high-" he doesn't finish with whatever he's trying to say, just glares at me, his nostrils flaring.

"Calm down, Charlie, before you have a stroke." I smirk at him. It's quite entertaining seeing him on the verge of boiling over for once. "Don't worry, while I'm gone you won't be alone. I'll get you a nice girl to keep you company for a few days—a nice Russian girl who won't mind being sodomized," I sound bitter as I say that but I am.

It seems I've hit a nerve because Charlie shuts his mouth, the muscles under his jaw contracting.

We're quiet for a few seconds, staring at each other, the atmosphere thick with tension. I'm not going to break the silence. *He* can. It's his fault.

"I'm not doing this with you, Blaire," his tone comes out ice cold. "If it's an apology you want for last night, then fine. I'm sorry. If I hurt you I never meant it—I told you this morning that I didn't wanner hurt you."

"You could've fooled me with your pathetic attempt at scaring me."

He scowls at me. "Attempt at scaring you?"

"Yeah," I step up to him, "you know, when you agreed that you were going to do terrible things to me." I've no idea where my daring has come from, but I'm not backing down.

"I said that to put you in your place."

"And drugging me? Was that okay *'because you could'*?" I mockingly repeat what he said about his reasons for saving Arjana.

"No, course it's not," he says through clenched teeth. It's like he's sucking on a lemon—men like him don't apologize, but I will admit it's good to hear.

"I realize now I went too far with you, all right?" He lifts both his hands in a shrug. "What else can I say, Blaire? You tell me and I'll say it."

"There's nothing for you to say," my voice comes out in a whisper, as I stare down at the ground.

"Well," he whispers back at me, dropping his hands to his sides, "if it's any consolation, I'm not normally so soft with girls," he looks very honest saying this, like it matters. "You pulled a gun on me and I let you get away with it. Believe me, I've killed others for less."

I scoff. Is that his silver lining?

"As for The Cayman Islands," he narrows a firm finger at me, "you can forget that. I'll lend you the money so you can pay Robert—I'll pay him within the month. You can give it back to me when your time here is up."

"You're just going to lend me half a million pounds?" I say with a gawp, my voice higher than it's ever been. "Just like that?"

"Yeah." He nods, his eyes glittering with some strange emotion. "I want us to get along. I don't want you loathing me for three months."

I twist up my face. "Why do you care if I like you or not?"

He shrugs. "I dunno. I just do."

The reality of the situation really starts to sink in. "You're not going to tire of me, are you?"

He doesn't answer me right away, just looks at me with... I don't know. I've never seen that expression on his face.

"Probably not, no," he says eventually, his tone softer now. "How could I?"

This is just fucking great.

I want to scream.

"In spite of how you feel about me right now," he says, "you're better off with me than with Maksim. I wouldn't dare let you take a bullet for me."

"That's good then, because I wouldn't."

He rolls his eyes. "I'm not gonna keep arguing with you, Blaire, so why don't you lose that stinking redhead attitude for one damn night and let's go have something to eat and drink; overlook all this bullshit."

I give him my hardest stare yet, knowing my eyes are balls of blue fire. As if I'm just going to forget about all of what's happened since he bought me from Maksim?

"Will you give me a break?" he waves out a hand in frustration. "I'm trying to level with you here."

I don't believe him. He's playing me—I know it. He has to be. He's being nice to get me on side. It's classic emotional bonding. Maksim used it on me, I know because I've researched it.

Charlie sighs, then he steps up to me. I instinctively step back, holding out my hands to defend myself. I can't tell what he's thinking. He doesn't have that dark alluring thing going on, but... I just can't tell what he's thinking.

"I'm not gonna hurt you." Taking one of my hands in his, he strokes over my knuckles with his thumb, turning my bones to jelly. "Just kiss you."

Heat spreads across my cheeks.

I look down and pull my hand free, holding it to my chest.

"Blaire-"

"We should go have that dinner you're so hungry for," I say, and I don't hang around for his kiss. I walk past him, half expecting him to stop me and force his tongue down my throat.

He doesn't. He lets me leave.

He is seriously doing my head in. One minute he's arrogant and dominating, then twisted and sexually infringing, and then he's... he's... well, he's like this.

I'm still not sure of his agenda with me—I've never met a man like him before. I can't figure him out. I'm not even sure if I hate him or if I'm taking a liking to him. I fancy him for sure, but I... I just don't know.

I don't know anything anymore.

In the entrance hall, I try two sets of doors before I find the kitchen, which is all rough sandstone floors and high ceilings with crisscrossing dark wooden beams. The walls are an uneven pallid yellow.

Hiding my hands in the sleeves of my jacket, I wander in. It smells like lemon zest, and when I find two readymade chicken salads in the American style fridge, I notice why. Grabbing one out, I pick at the leaves with my fingers. It's seasoned in lemon juice, and on the side there's a bowl of grated lemon zest.

I think Charlie has a thing for cooking. I haven't seen a housekeeper or a cook here, so I'm assuming he made this.

I pull open a few drawers in the alcove cooking area, searching for some cutlery, then I take my salad over to the dining table. It seats ten, resting before French style doors that are set between a collection of windows on either side. The garden is enormous, perfectly cut grass that seems to go on for miles. I hover above my chair to peer out the windows: a patio area with a bistro set, then a large swimming pool that's sparkling under the evening's sun. I can see myself training out there in the garden. It's big enough to get lost in.

Surrounding the garden, far in the horizon, tall, thick trees hide the house, the majority of them blooming in white flowers.

I'm an outdoorsy person, so I'm glad Charlie has ample space.

Lowering onto my chair, I fork the salad. It's fresh, crunchy and sour with that lemon juice. It's not an overpowering flavor. It works well with the oily, grated garlic.

A faint clanging noise makes me jump. I glance about on alert, hoping Charlie doesn't join me for dinner. I'm not sure I'll be able to stomach the food with him watching me. It's been such an intense day already.

There's no one in here but me, I see, scanning every corner.

It doesn't take me long to polish off the salad—I'm too anxious to sit back and enjoy how yummy it is.

I wash up my bowl and cutlery in the sink before drying them, leaving the kitchen as I found it, then I sneak upstairs to my room, kicking off my boots on the way in and shutting the door.

I'm almost sure Charlie is going to come and take me again, so I crawl into bed fully clothed, leaving the lights on for when it gets dark. I'm not scared—or I don't think I'm scared—just a little anxious. I don't understand what he makes me feel when he... you know...

I force myself not to think about any of that. I don't want to think about being intimate with Charlie, and I don't want to think about today. I just want to switch off.

After a while of peace and quiet, listening to the birds chirping outside the window, I start to relax, counting the rose moldings on the ceiling so I can put myself to sleep. I'd usually wear headphones so I can learn in my sleep, the voice of a stranger teaching my subconscious, but I don't have any headphones here, and I quickly find out it's hard to nod-off without them.

Rolling onto my side, I give in and reflect on today, and only today, hoping the fact that it's over can put me out of my misery.

It's been okay, really, which surprises me given how our time together began yesterday. I think I might be all right here for three months, if he really is sorry that is, and we stick to business as usual.

Somehow, I don't think that's going to happen. Charlie might have been kind enough to offer me an apology but he's still a man, a powerful, needy man. I'm still here for a reason.

"Two months, three weeks, and six days," I tell myself, closing my eyes.

BLAIRE
(PART ONE)

15

The next day welcomes rain. I love the sound lashing against the window. I find it serene.

I'm snug in bed, warm and sleepy, staring out the window for over an hour before I strip out of my clothes to take a shower.

I'm surprised to find there's a white body towel hanging on the heating rack by the frosted window, and things other than soap. My bra is gone from the floor too. Charlie must have stocked the bathroom while I slept. I'm not sure how I feel about that. How long was he in here? And how the hell didn't I hear him? I'm trained to be aware of my surroundings even in an unconscious state of sleep.

I shower under warm water this time, washing with some kind of soft body cream rather than soap, though I don't wash my hair. I curl it around my fist and knot it up without a hair-tie.

I feel a bit better today. I'm not so anxious. I slept well and woke peacefully, just like I usually do at home.

In the towel, dripping in water, I brush my teeth and wander into the bedroom, noticing for the first time a stack of books under the window: Shakespeare's collection and Oscar Wild's The Picture of Dorian Gray, amongst other reads. I've got those books at home.

That's odd.

Charlie hasn't left out any clean clothes like he did yesterday, so I pull open the creaking doors for the armoire. My clothes—they're here! My sports trousers and jumpers hanging up, a few pairs of my trainers lined up on the bottom shelf. Even my combat outfit is here.

Is this why he didn't join me for dinner last night? Did he leave to go get my things?

My underwear isn't here, I see, rustling through the drawers with one hand, holding the towel to my body with my other. There's a collection of lace bras and thongs and some other risqué garments that I've seen women wear before; risqué garments that I'll not be wearing, for sure.

I smile to myself nonetheless of the underwear. Charlie said he'd get my things for me and he has—I'm assuming those books are mine. I still can't stomach the fact that I didn't hear him enter my room last night but I will admit, I'm grateful to have some of my things.

Ignoring the chosen underwear, I dress in my combat gear and trainers, feeling like myself again. I find jeans so uncomfortable. I can't fight properly in them. They restrict my movements. Yes my sports trousers are tight too but they're made of stretchy material.

Exiting the bedroom, I wander down the landing, then the sweeping staircase, and into the kitchen. Charlie isn't here. It's so... quiet, bar the rain spitting wildly against the windows.

I wonder where he is...

Pulling open the back doors, I go outside in the rain, shivering as it spits across my face.

The sky is a fortress of angry gray, breaking with heavy black clouds. The back garden is just as breathtaking as I remember, flourishing in lush green grass. I jog down the patio steps, around the titanic swimming pool, and to the end of the garden until I'm under the trees. The cold air chills my lungs, and my now damp clothes cling to my skin, but there is nothing like testing yourself in bad temperatures.

When my muscles feel loose and relaxed, I stop by a flowering rosebush. The petals are so red, like blood, each one more perfect than the other, sheathed in thorns.

I step out of my trainers, wiggle my toes in the soggy grass, and then I train with meditating Tai Chi, punching and kicking in slow motion, soaking up the way the earth feels right now. My feet become sodden and muddy but I don't mind. I love this feeling of being free.

The memory of Charlie taking me flows in and out of my thoughts, as does his apology and the way my body desires him when he touches and kisses me. It's like my subconscious is sorting the conflict for me, rather than me having to sit down and seriously mull over what he makes me feel.

This is why I delight in meditating. It's so peaceful.

My hair tied back in a slack, man-made bun, the rain falls freely over my pale, freckly face, drenching through my clothes. It's refreshing.

BLAIRE
(PART ONE)

I can sense eyes watching me from the house. I suspect it's Charlie. I don't stop my meditation. I go at it for two hours, lashing out lengthy, focused kicks and breathing steadily but softly.

When the rain dies down, I pick up my trainers and jog back across the garden, inside the house. I'm dripping water everywhere but the kitchen has stone flooring, so I don't worry over it too much.

Dropping my trainers by the dining table, I go into the kitchen area. The coffee machine is steaming. I pour myself a cup, lift it to my nose, and breathe in with delight. The smell of coffee in the morning is like home to me—the bitterness of real Columbian beans.

Roaming back across the kitchen, I stand by the back doors and hold the cup to my chest, taking in the last of the gray morning.

"Morning, Blaire."

I flinch at the sound of Charlie's raspy voice, my stomach whirling with anxiety. It's a new kind of anxiety now. Worry yes, but also because I know I fancy him. It's so strange but I can feel it in the way my body responds to his presence. Since he turned me on, I seem to notice everything he makes me feel with extra effect.

He wanders over with heavy footsteps and stops behind me, his large body warm against my back. He's wearing jeans and a gray round-neck t-shirt with his hair pulled back, I see in his mirror image in the French doors, and he smells like he's fresh out of the shower, a mixture of male musk and clean body wash.

"Do you do that every day?" he says softly, and we make eye contact then.

BLAIRE
(PART ONE)

So, he was watching me, probably like he is now, staring over my head at my reflection like he's hypnotized on something, and he's smiling at me. It's his unholy alluring smile.

Wordless, I nod to answer his question and take a sip of my coffee, breaking eye contact. My heart is going crazy. Every time I see him it's like the first.

"You look beautiful when training..." he leans closer and whispers in my ear, "...so focused."

Little hairs on the back of my neck prick. There's something in his voice. Something fervor.

Reaching around my waist from behind, he presses a large hand onto my stomach and forces me back against his front, forcing me to emit a rough breath. He's hard in his jeans, pushing into my lower back.

My toes curl against the cold stone floors.

"Are you going to fuck me in the ass again, Charlie?" I ask blankly, peering up at his reflection. I have to ask. I need to know so I can mentally prepare to lose my mind.

He stiffens behind me, his hand like a rock on my stomach. He's not breathing, either.

Somehow, I've gotten to him. He's not the type of man to stop in his pursuits, but he has today.

How have I got to him?

I wish I knew so I could use it to my advantage.

Charlie takes my coffee cup and puts it down on a nearby side table, then he grips my hips and makes me turn into him, my eyes level with his chest.

I don't know what to say or do, so I just stare at his chest, wondering... filtering these vibes coming off him in electric waves.

Lifting my chin with a single finger, he orders me to look up at him, then he grips my hip again.

"I want you," he says sensitively, glancing all over my face, promise and restrain in his expression. "You know I do."

I drop my eyes to the floor between us, everything in my body tightening with anxiety. I reluctantly want him too when he's touching me—it's so fucked up—and it makes me sick. I should hate him. Just because he's handsome it doesn't make what he's doing to me okay.

We're silent for a while. He's watching me—I can feel it. I can feel every-fucking-thing now.

"Stop making me feel guilty, Blaire," he says, his voice now void of emotion. "You're my plaything, nothing more."

"I'm not making you feel-"

A hand fists the back of my hair, causing me to yelp, and Charlie pushes me down to my knees. "Suck my cock and I won't fuck you."

My heart leaps into my throat.

It's an ultimatum, and one that I'm going to take if it prevents him from having my ass, but I can't admit I'm happy. He started to show kindness yesterday... we found our mutual ground... he apologized...

Maybe he's regretting his apology.

I don't know why, but that hurts, and I feel like such a fool for trying to make myself believe him.

Shutting off, I don't even think. I let my thoughts escape me.

BLAIRE
(PART ONE)

I fumble to unzip Charlie's jeans, careful not to make a sound when opening his belt. The sound of a belt reminds me of Maksim and I can't think of him right now.

I pull down his black boxer briefs in time with lifting up his Tee. His length juts free, long, thick, and hard, swollen with veins. A mixture of sensations trickle through me. He's so robust and hairy all over, his pubic hair meeting with a thin line of black dusty hair below his navel. His stomach is a work of art, not like those athletic men who have ironing board stomachs. Charlie is buff, made of raw chiseled abs.

Something in me clenches and warm liquid surges through me, gathering between my legs. I recognize it as arousal now, but I don't know what the fuck it's all about. He isn't even... you know... teasing me down there.

I glance up at him, at the taut look of desire on his face. He's waiting.

Not using my hands—my master taught me to suck his cock with no hands—I shut my eyes and run my tongue down the length of Charlie's cock, swallowing a few inches of him in my mouth. He tastes like body wash where he hasn't long showered, but he smells all manly and musky, his skin soft yet broad with solid veins. I find it all so bizarrely appealing that my sex throbs, making me conscious of how tight my trousers are.

I try to ignore the desire thriving inside me, focusing on satisfying Charlie, but it's so hard. I've never felt this power of desire for a man before him.

I pull back, then I take another few inches of Charlie, wrapping my lips completely around him, causing my cheeks to ache because he's so thick. He moans with zeal, his grip in my hair tightening. It makes my scalp tear, though I try not to tense up too much so I don't end up biting him or something.

Back, and then I gulp him right down this time, his crown hitting the back of my throat.

"Fuck," he emits a curse, gasping out, and the sensations in me are no longer trickling. They're erupting, burning all over my body. I'm not completely sure, but I think I like this, having Charlie under my spell for once.

I fold my hands behind my back, curl my lips against my teeth, and suck back and forth, settling in to a leveled, satisfying rhythm, his cock smoothly gliding against my lips because it's inundated in my saliva.

Charlie mutters another violent curse under his breath. I can't resist peering up at him. Our eyes meet. His are heavy, a dark shade of blue because his pupils are expanding. He's so fucking gorgeous when intoxicated, lips slightly parted to accommodate faster breaths.

He cups my cheek with his free hand and strokes under my eye, his other hand still in my hair. He's back to being soft with me. I bask in his tenderness, sighing however I can as I mouth-fuck him.

Another deep suck, then his cock throbs and pre-cum melts in my mouth. He's salty, on the verge of reaching his summit. I swallow before pushing him to the apex of my throat, blocking my air passage, but then he slips down my throat opening, causing me to gag. My lips now against his pubic hair, Charlie's entire body trembles with lust fueled anger and want.

BLAIRE
(PART ONE)

I choke with watery eyes and pull back, saliva coating my chin, but he doesn't seem to like that. Holding my cheek in one hand, my hair in his other, he starts fucking my throat, rippling his hips back and forth, making me retch over and over. He's losing control. I can feel it in him.

Using my hands, I press against his hips because I cannot breathe for long periods of time. I gasp for air in a dizzy state, then he's right inside my throat again, swelling in my air passage.

"You're so..." he groans out, his face tight, teeth clenched. "I'm not sure I'll ever be able to give you back to—Fuck!" he spasms, his cock pulsing warm, thick liquid down my throat.

My eyes are watering like crazy, tears streaming down my face, and my throat is on fire, but I swallow every inch of his orgasm, heaving at times. He's overflowing.

When he's done, panting through his nose, I fall back on my ass and try to catch a breath but he doesn't give me a chance to sort myself out. Making me yelp again, he yanks me up by my arms and pushes me down on the dining table, face up. I grab onto the edges, looking up at him, a bit anxious.

I don't know where he is in his mind but he looks like he's losing it.

He hooks his fingers into the waist of my trousers and pulls them down my legs, tugging in places because they're damp and sticking to my skin. I'm not wearing any pants. I feel exposed in the daylight.

"Charlie," I lick my lips, squeezing my legs together, "what-what are you doing?"

"I'm gonna make you cum so fucking hard. That's what I'm doing." He tugs off my trousers, then runs his large hands up my legs, up the insides of my thighs to wrench me open. His palms are rough on my skin.

I quiver under him, a sharp pain shooting through my thighs because I'm open so wide.

"Don't worry. I'm not gonna fuck you, and I'm not gonna hurt you." Now, he sounds like he's here, but I'm still panicking, digging my nails into the table, unsure of what to do.

He presses delicate yet hungry kisses up the insides of my legs after his hands. I moan against each peck, my body on fire, my head flooding with this overwhelming dizzy feeling.

I know he's going to kiss me down there again and I'm not sure I want to stop him.

I let my head drop back on the table and grab my face.

He nibbles up each side of my groin with his teeth, and I writhe, squirming, unable to deal.

I can't do this. I'm too anxious.

"Charlie, please, don't do this to me," I beg him. For the first time, I actually ask him to stop. I can't help it. I'm not sure I like feeling so at his mercy.

He freezes, a bit out of breath.

"You want me to stop?" he rasps out.

This is so embarrassing.

Of course I don't want him to stop. I want him to make me feel good again but I don't at the same time.

I cover my eyes with one arm and nod. This is my control. Since his apology, he seems to be giving me a semblance of control—or, I thought he was before he made me suck his cock; before he gave a warning for making him feel guilty.

Oh, I don't fucking know. I'm so confused.

"Blaire, look at me," he demands, though his voice is soft. Fingers close around my wrist and Charlie gently moves my arm off of my face.

I peer down at him, finding his dilated blue eyes. He looks so hot. Why can't I just let go and be with him like this? Why can't I shut off mentally?

"Do you want me to stop?" He raises his eyebrows at me, stroking the inside of my wrist with his thumb.

I nod again, trying to close my legs but I can't because he's between them.

Our gaze united, he's not sure what to do. I imagine his instincts are telling him to just do whatever the fuck he likes but I think he's working on this whole mutual respect thing, and he did tell me that if I want him to stop, all I have to do is say.

This is his chance to prove I can trust him.

I hope he doesn't fail.

When he steps back, scoops my trousers up from the floor and puts my feet into the legs, I feel a little gutted. I like the way he turns me on and makes me cum, but at the same time, I just don't want him doing that to me again. I'm the architect of my own confusion, I know, but I'm just not sure what *this* is between us.

I'm torn.

I pull up my trousers and stand on jelly-like legs, drawing into my shoulders. My hair is a static mess, flowing around my shoulders and waist. Must be an endorphin reaction.

Charlie is frowning down on me. He doesn't know what to make of this either.

"Do you have a gym where I can work out?" I ask, hugging myself.

His frown deepens. "You wanner work out again?"

I nod. I feel so vulnerable knowing I just sucked his cock and he's just seen me splayed out in front of him there on the dining table. He said I was pretty down there. That makes me blush and I never blush.

"Are you all right?" he whispers.

I nod again, though I'm not all right. He's fucking with my head.

After a while of staring me down, Charlie nods left and heads out of the kitchen, his masculine back flexing under his Tee.

Though my feet are dirty, I slip into my trainers and go after him.

In silence, we walk down a long hallway just off the entrance hall. At the end, there are a set of steel double doors. Charlie pushes them open and pale blue double height walls fill my gaze.

Wow. It's not just a gym. It's a bloody sports arena fully loaded with a boxing ring in the center, surrounded by blue exercise mats, and a collection of treadmills and other exercise equipment stretching across the left wall; chin up bars and boxing bags...

The right wall boasts rock climbing.

"Wow," I whisper under my breath, in my element.

"Wait here," Charlie says, pointing down. "I'll be five minutes." He exits the way we came, so I do as I'm told.

Still hugging myself, I glance up at the ceiling. Monkey climbing bars. How the hell can anyone get up there? I scan the space and find in each corner of the gym there are ladders.

No wonder Charlie is so fit.

"Here," he says softly from behind.

Turning around, I find he's passing me a bottle of water, and he's changed out of his jeans, into gray joggers and trainers—why?

I take the bottle of water from him, twist off the cap and have a mouthful. It's so cold that my brain aches for a moment.

"I'll make you a deal," Charlie says, nodding like it's already set in stone. "You and me," he gestures between us with a large, steady hand, "we'll have a friendly fight, and if you can put me on my ass in fifteen minutes, I won't touch you ever again—not unless you ask me to or want me to."

I stare vacantly at him. That's why he's changed...

"But, if I win," he continues, his voice full of promise, "you'll let me make you cum right here and whenever I want to—and you'll enjoy it."

Oh, I fucking like this.

Putting the cap back on the bottle, I shrug and nod at once. This could be fun. I've wanted to kick his ass for weeks now.

"And you promise not to touch me ever again once I put you on your ass?" I raise my eyebrows. "You swear?" I don't know why I'm trusting his word but something inside me is convinced Charlie wouldn't make a misleading deal. He's too cool for that.

Charlie leans down and presses his lips to mine like it's the last time. I lose my breath, my blood warming with fire.

"If..." he elongates, whispering against my mouth, "if you put me on my ass."

I have no idea what comes over me but I arch into Charlie and kiss him back. I grip his t-shirt with my nails and let out a girlish, moany sigh, delighting in this humid rush of sensations that always come over me when we kiss.

"Don't do that..." he warns, his tone taking a dark edge.

I step back, breaking away from the kiss, my head a little faint. "Do what?"

"Kiss me like that and whine as if you're enjoying it when we have this deal on the table."

Crossing my arms, I flick up my eyebrows. "You're worried I'm going to win?"

He takes in a long, steely breath, his blue gaze flickering all over my face. "A little... but this is why I like you." He steps closer to me and I step back. Again and again. "You're different to any girl I've met before. Stronger, smarter, ominously alluring, and I like your nasty attitude." Raising a hand, he strokes down a length of my dark red hair. "Girls like you don't come around often."

He keeps playing with my hair as if fixated, still walking into me.

"I have to admit," he says, "I'm having a hard time even thinking about giving you back to Maksim."

My brain switches from hot and lusty to robotic, and my expression goes flat.

"I don't want to talk about Maksim." I blink down, searching for the words, then back up at Charlie. "I know you said you plan on knowing me inside out, but talking about Maksim, it... it bothers me."

He doesn't argue about my request. He simply says, "All right," lifting his hands in defense, "All right."

He's doing it. He's working on our mutual respect. Why is that making me like him a little more?

He tugs out his hair tie and combs his hair back with one hand, the strands sleek and shiny under the downlighters. "Here," he says, "tie your hair back."

Putting down the bottle of water, I take the tie from him, grateful—I've needed a hair tie all morning.

I walk past him, putting up my hair in a bun, then I slip under the ropes and into the ring.

This is going to be epic. I'll put him on his ass in five minutes, let alone fifteen, and it's that much sweeter knowing I'm going to win the rights to my body.

"What are the rules?" I say softly.

In one swift motion, he grabs the back of his t-shirt and whips it off; drops it on the floor. My eyes are having a hard time adjusting because I just don't know which part of his body I should focus on. He's so fit it's actually stupid.

Thank god he doesn't have stubble.

"I won't punch you," he says. He bows under the ropes and steps into the ring, every muscle in his body contracting. "Anything else, I can't be held responsible for." He winks at me.

I feel my cheeks warm up, and I hope to god he doesn't notice.

"Okay." I step back, rolling my shoulders. "Let's do this."

"Fifteen minutes," he warns, pointing at me. "After that, I'll have you cumming in my mouth."

Charlie tries to slap my face but I catch his wrist and boot him in the stomach with a loud, "Aargh!" making him groan.

"Fucking hell!" He folds over, winded.

I don't even think about my next move. I grab behind his left knee and Karate chop him in the throat with my other hand, slamming him back on his ass. He's so heavy that it takes all my lower body strength to put him down, but I do. He lands with a profound thud. I bolt forward to escape him, kneading out my hand because it hurts—it's like he's made from bricks rather than muscle.

Safely in the corner of the ring, I face him, my chest heavy with adrenaline. He's lying on his back with his knees pulled up, and he looks a little stunned, blinking up at the ceiling.

Well that's a sight for sore eyes, Charlie bested.

"I reckon that's thirty seconds," I say, the smuggest smirk plastered across my face.

He chuckles under his breath, shaking his head. "You're fucking quick."

I wander across the ring and crouch down to him, leaning on my knees with my elbows. He lets his head roll to the side, catching us in a moment, making my chest squeeze with anxiety. Our eyes flicker between each other's, and I'm surprised to find he doesn't look bested anymore. He looks... glad? smiling at me.

"I hope your ego isn't too bruised," I say, my goal being to rile him—I want to go again, though longer this time if he can handle it. "I hear it hurts getting beaten by a girl."

He isn't bothered by my arrogance. He says in a low, raspy voice, "Didn't you wanner stretch that out to show me how good you are?"

"You already know how good I am." I don't look away from him. "My objective in a fight is to win, not to pussy foot around."

He hums in agreement, glancing down at my mouth, then back up at my eyes. "Where'd you learn to fight?"

"Somewhere you didn't." I stare down the length of his tall, muscular frame, at the defined muscles in his stomach. "Do you want to go again? Whoa!" I squeal as Charlie grabs my legs and yanks them out from under me, dropping me to the bouncy surface.

He's on top of me, seizing my wild, combatant hands in both of his.

"You're like a feral little cat," he says through laughing, struggling to get me under control.

Growling and straining, I kick the ring surface, giving myself the strength I need to turn us over, the veins in my eyes almost popping. He's under me now, so I jump to my feet, my thigh muscles burning from the abrupt movement.

Charlie catches me—I didn't even notice him getting up. He wraps his big arms around me from behind, squeezing me against his powerful chest.

I tighten my fists, readying to elbow back, but he whispers in my ear, "You win," making me shiver because his breath is so warm. "Stop, Blaire. You win."

I swallow down a mouthful of air. His cock is hard in his joggers, pressing into my spine. My stomach rolls with liquid desire, the memory of having him in my mouth taking over all thoughts. Why do I find it so hot when he dominates me?

"And... and you won't..." I start to say, but I can't concentrate on my vocabulary. I wish he didn't affect me on this level.

"And I won't, what?" he says softly.

"You won't..." I swallow a second time, gripping his hand over my chest, "...touch me like *that* anymore?"

He doesn't say or do anything for a moment, just holds me, closing his fingers over my grip on his hand. I relax against his body, his touch melting my will.

"Not if you don't want me to," he says on my neck, his hot lips making me squirm in his grasp.

"No," I say, though I hardly sound convincing—my voice comes out too girlish and husky. "I-I don't want you to."

Silence.

It's not awkward silence. It's... I don't know, and I'm not sure if it's the adrenaline or desire running through my veins but I have a sudden urge to kiss him. How fucked up is that?

"You gave me your word," I say, peering up at him from over my shoulder, finding his expression is tight with control. His lips aren't far away. I stare at his mouth.

"Yeah, I did." Charlie lets me go then and jumps out of the boxing ring, his motions fluent and gracefully masculine. He pivots to me, his black hair dripping around his handsome face, framing those stark blue eyes. "You can trust that I'll keep it," he says, and while I'm weak in my pose, we look at each other.

BLAIRE
(PART ONE)

The silence becomes a living thing; unspoken words and tension—*you can trust me on that.*

I feel a little lightheaded, falling under his spell, unable to look away from him.

He's the one to break the moment, and I realize I've been holding my breath—that's why I'm lightheaded.

Reaching down, Charlie scoops up his t-shirt from the floor and flings it over his shoulder, nodding at me. He then turns to exit the gym, his back contracting with his movements.

I lean back against the ropes, trying to gather my wits, my chest rising and falling with heaviness.

I'm not too sure how I feel right now. That fight just changed the dynamics of our situation.

BLAIRE
(PART ONE)

16

Night falls while I'm meditating outside in the cold, the dark sky glowing silver with a full moon. I've been meditating since besting Charlie earlier today because my thoughts have been whirling over what the next few months are going to be like. Now I know—or assume—he won't touch me in a sexual manner, I can't help but wonder.

Will he start beating me now? Is that how he plans on getting his kicks? - Because I can't imagine he'd make a deal like this without a backup plan to ensure his appetite is satisfied.

I'm not sure, so I let the energy that is my thoughts course in and out of me with each breath I inhale and exhale; every slow movement I execute.

I go at it for hours, until my stomach howls for food. I haven't eaten all day. I didn't even have breakfast, which isn't me. Breakfast is the most important meal to me—to anyone, really.

Gathering my trainers in my arms, I patter barefoot up to my room where I take a quick shower, washing away the saltiness on my skin. I dress in my usual—black sports trousers and a black long sleeve sweater—still appreciative that Charlie went and got my clothes for me. They make me feel like me, not some cheap whore he bartered.

Tying my damp hair back with the tie Charlie gave me, I head downstairs to the kitchen.

"Evening, Blaire," he says from the cooking space, wearing only a pair of gray joggers, his ink black hair curling loosely around that gorgeous face.

I stop on the threshold, startled that he's here, then I carry on toward the table, ignoring my intentions for the fridge—I'll fix myself something to eat when he's gone.

"Hi, Charlie," my voice comes out softer than I was trying for. It's because I'm looking at him from the corner of my eye, at his tanned, powerful body, sprinkles of black hair across his chest and under his navel. He's one of the most exquisite men I've ever seen—I can't deny it.

"You must be starving," he says, and grabbing a plate out of the oven with a kitchen towel, he proffers it to me.

He's cooked dinner?

I nod, slipping behind the dining table, my cheeks a little hot. There's a jug of water in the middle of the table and two glasses. I fill a glass, glad the water is at room temperature. It's easy to guzzle down and quench my thirst.

"You all right?" Charlie says.

He rounds the kitchen and puts the plate down in front of me: chicken and potatoes with green vegetables, exactly what I said I eat at home.

"You look a little flushed."

"I've just had a shower," I say softly, putting down the glass of water.

"Hm," he hums, his eyes following my tongue as I lick my lips dry. "Do you mind if I eat with you?"

I raise my eyebrows, and it seems to pull his attention from my lips to my eyes.

"Or do you wanner eat alone?"

Extending a hand, I urge him to sit across from me. I don't mind having dinner with him, I suppose. There isn't anyone else to talk to. At home, if I got lonely, I'd give James a call. Here, there's only Charlie to speak to because I don't have my phone.

He smiles down at me before sauntering back across the kitchen. I feel warmed from that smile.

He grabs another plate from the oven and comes back to the table. He's not wearing any shoes, and I can't help noticing that even his feet are masculine.

"Do you realize you've been meditating all day?" he says, passing me some cutlery over the table.

"How do you know that?"

"I was watching you." He gestures with the cutlery.

I take the knife and fork from him in a state of dismay, barely registering the way he runs his thumb over my fingers.

Is he constantly watching me?

"You need to be careful you don't burn yourself out," he sits opposite, in my line of vision, "especially if you don't eat properly."

"There's nothing else to do here but train."

Resting his elbows on the table, he cups his square chin. "Well, what would you normally do to fill your days? Bar serving Maksim," he adds with bitterness.

My stomach is in knots. It's the way he's looking at me, utterly focused on my face, curiosity and zeal glittering in his eyes.

"I guess I'd train in my gym at home." I cut off a piece of chicken. It's tender and juicy. I think he's cooked it in some kind of butter.

"Yeah, I saw that you've got a gym in your apartment. You train with Wing Chun, don't you?"

"You've been in my apartment?" I almost spit out my food, so I cover my mouth with an open palm. That's a personal thing for him to do, mooch through my home.

"Yeah," he says candidly. "I got your things for you, remember? I brought some of your books too so you could read when in your room here."

"Oh." I blink at him, that feeling of appreciation all too real—he didn't have to fetch my things. "How do you know what style of fighting I do?"

"You've got wooden dummies... balancing tackle..." a long list of my gym equipment rolls off his tongue in that Latin accent. "You're a beautifully controlled fighter..." He shrugs. "Call it a hunch."

I realize I've just been staring at him, at his lush mouth, listening to him flannel on about my equipment, so I drop my gaze to focus on my food.

What made him go upstairs in my apartment? It's an open balcony top and anyone at the front door can see that it's a gym up there. Also, I'm sure I left my bedroom doors open the last time I was home, so he would have noticed my room as soon as he walked through the front door. He's not stupid. He knows my clothes would be in my bedroom.

"Your place is incredibly clinical," he says.

"I bought it like that." I reach for my glass and have another mouthful of water.

"So, *you* bought it?" he asks, cocking his head.

I swallow down the water before saying, "Well, yeah."

He nods, like he's confirming something to himself. "How long have you lived there?"

"Two years."

I don't think Maksim will mind me saying that—it's hardly a secret. Two years ago, he told me that if I wanted to, I could have my own place. As anyone could imagine, I jumped at the opportunity. Not because I didn't want to be around Maksim. I just wanted my own mental space. I've always suspected his boss Tatiana had something to do with the decision but I have never asked.

"Wow, that young..." Charlie glances away from me, his jaw ticking, and when he looks back at me, his expression goes flat. "What else do you do, Blaire, other than train physically?"

"I study a lot," I whisper.

"What'd you study?"

I lift my shoulders, trying to avoid the blueness in his eyes. "Whatever Maksim wants me to study, really." A light goes off in my head. "My last project was Mexico."

"Mexico?"

I nod, forking some vegetables.

"What about Mexico?"

"The culture and the geography. I came across a newspaper article about the economy and decided to study the country," I flat out lie.

"So, you studied it off your own accord?"

I nod. I shouldn't say what I'm about to but I want to see Charlie's reaction. "I've learnt a lot about the Los Zetas, amongst other things."

He sits back then, keeping his hands on the table. "Is that right?"

I nod.

He watches me for a moment in total silence.

"What did you learn about the Los Zetas?"

"Nothing special, really. They're a criminal syndicate much like any other." I'm trying to mock his organization, to rile him into saying something. Sure I know he's the leader but I want more Intel.

"What else does Maksim have you study?" he says, unbothered by my mockery. Picking up his cutlery, he cuts up his food.

"This and that." I slice into the fluffy potatoes. "I tend to focus on technology."

Charlie turns up his lips and shrugs in agreement. "Makes sense, given your talent."

I smile with arrogance. *Yeah, I'm not just a fuck toy.*

"You know," he says, "you were recommended to me by three different leaders to execute the job."

I frown at him.

"To shut down London," he adds.

I don't react to that. I know I'm good at what I do, as do a lot of others. I could spend years without so much as touching a computer and still do what is asked of me. Studying and hacking are my forte, even before my fighting skills.

"What's happening with the job?" I ask between bites. "I assumed that by rushing me to attain your fifteen minutes you needed it done ASAP."

"It'll happen when it happens," he says. "I just needed you to be ready." He doesn't give me any more than that. He begins telling me about himself, that he doesn't usually spend a lot of time in England. "I'm almost always in Mexico." He talks about this for quite a while amid eating his dinner, saying he doesn't typically deal with Westerners because they're chauvinistic pigs.

What does he think he is then?

"But sometimes," he says, "it's inevitable."

I think I know where he's going with this. He wants me to verbally connect the dots between him and the Los Zetas, who are based in Mexico, but he's doing it in a coy manner.

"Why are you here now then?" I ask, pushing against my plate. I cannot eat anymore.

Smirking, Charlie flicks up his eyebrows. *Me.* He's here because of me.

"Don't let me get in the way of your work."

He tips his head, chewing on a piece of chicken. "I never said I work in Mexico."

"I just assumed." I straighten up in my seat. "You just told me that you're almost always in Mexico, that you don't usually deal with Westerners..."

He hums in concurrence, also pushing against his plate. He hasn't had any trouble with his dinner. He's polished off everything with gusto.

"Do you know how Maksim and I met?" he asks, sparking my interest.

I shake my head minutely.

"Well, Blaire," he puts his elbows on the table and winds his fingers together, "when I chopped off my father's cock for trafficking little girls and watched him slowly bleed to death, I obtained a list of his associates-"

My stomach bottoms out of me.

"-Maksim was on the top of that list."

Silence... and we're just looking at each other.

"And yet, you-you let Maksim live?" I ask bravely, immediately wishing I didn't. I don't want to piss him off, not now I know he cut off his own father's dick.

He nods, resting his chin on his hands. "I had details to a job in Russia, and given Maksim's influence over there with Tatiana, I thought I could use him."

He knows Tatiana?

Now I've gone white.

"I pardoned Maksim for his word that he'll stay away from children, and brought him in on the job." Charlie goes quiet, and his eyes seem closer than they really are.

"Why..." I start to say, but I just can't find the courage to finish.

"What?"

"Nothing," I say.

"Blaire..." his voice deepens as he says my name in a summoning manner.

"I just..." I gulp, and he sees, his eyes dropping to my throat. "Why did you kill your father?"

It's a while before he answers me. He's assessing the situation, as I would, wondering if telling me is of any benefit to him.

"I had a sister once," his voice is soft as he says this, grief flashing through his blue eyes, "and now I don't."

"Oh..." there is a semblance of emotion in my voice, which is strange, given I don't give a shit about Charlie or his sister. "What happened to her?"

"Can't you guess?" he says, giving me his hardest stare.

I look away from him, a niggling feeling telling me that Maksim might have had something to do with Charlie's sister not being around anymore. Maybe that's Charlie's real agenda with me. Maybe *this* isn't about Maksim double crossing him after all. Maybe his agenda is about getting some justified payback for his sister.

"Tell me, Blaire, you've known Maksim since you were... what... seven/eight years old?"

"Why would you think that?" I screw up my features. "I never told you how long I've known him."

"I've asked around about you, and one person told me that he stole you ten years ago."

Stole me? That's news to me. Maksim said I was sold to him.

Another long pause. The silence between us is stifling, and my thoughts are rambling.

"Why would you ask around about me?" I say eventually.

A smile plays on Charlie's lips. "Curiosity."

I scoff again, though in irritation. I don't like his prying.

"Is it true?" he says, looking between my eyes. "Have you known him since you were that young?"

"I think so," I whisper, swallowing and nodding in union. I don't want to talk about this. I want to know why he thinks Maksim stole me.

"You think you were that young?" Charlie says, putting his hands back on the table, looking solemn in his pose. "What does that mean?"

"I don't remember much of being young, Charlie," I tell him honestly. "I don't even remember meeting Maksim." I shouldn't be indulging him but I'm hoping that if I let him in on a little of my past, he'll tell me more about Maksim apparently stealing me.

Why would Maksim tell me he bought me when he stole me? It doesn't make sense. If he stole me, he should have just told me. It wouldn't change things either way.

Charlie doesn't elaborate on what he knows. It seems he's got other things on his mind, like, "Did he sexually abuse you when you were younger?"

On autopilot, I jump to my feet. "Why would you think that?"

With a sardonic expression on his face, he arches a brow at me.

"Don't you look at me like that. You know I'm a..." *Fuck,* I can't even bring myself to say that innocent word. "You know I've not had sex before."

He looks me up and down in irony. "There are other ways to toy with girls, as I'm sure you know."

A cold drop of sweat slides down the side of my face.

"I can't be speaking about this. I can't be speaking about Maksim to you." Yes, I want to know what happened to me, but not that much.

I fiddle to tuck a strand of hair behind my ear.

I never get anxious when it comes to a confrontation, but he—after that revelation about his father—he makes me anxious.

"It's getting late," I say, wiping my face with the back of my hand. "I should probably-"

"Sit back down, Blaire—that's not a request." He extends a steady hand, motioning for me to take to my seat. "I was just asking. I'm concerned, is all."

Concerned? Yeah, right.

I need to watch what I say around him. He's charming and it's easy to get lost in conversation with him.

"Blaire..." he nods at my chair and I sit on command, fisting my hands in my lap. "Forget about all the heavy stuff."

That's fucking easy for him to say. I'm sweating in my seat.

"Do you wanner train daily with me?"

"Huh?"

"In the gym," he elaborates. "Do you wanner train daily? I find you quite challenging and I don't find anyone challenging, usually." He smirks, his sly amusement back in full force.

"If you think you can keep up with the pace, then sure." I shrug. "Why not?"

"Okay then," he says, wiping his lips with a napkin before tossing it on the table. "I'll see you in the gym bright and early."

"Any time specifically?" I watch him gather the dishes on the table.

"Six thirty, if you can manage that." He stands, and my eyes zero in on his body. "I have to train early because I make a lot of business calls during the day."

"I can work around your schedule." I force myself to look up at him, and my next line comes out thick with sarcasm, "It's what I'm here for, isn't it?"

He chuckles, glancing between my eyes and mouth, then he takes the dishes to the sink. "Do you want anything else to eat?"

"No."

With raised eyebrows, he looks back at me. "No 'thank you'."

I snort. I barely say please and thank you to my master, so as if I'd be courteous to *him*.

"Can I go now?" I say. "Or do you want to grill me some more?"

Shaking his head, he pulls open the fridge for a bottle of beer. "You can go if you wanner go."

I'm out of my seat before he barely finishes speaking, and the sarcastic me says, "Thank you."

BLAIRE
(PART ONE)

17

The next morning, I eat a scrambled egg breakfast courtesy of Charlie, wash up the plate and cutlery in the sink, and then I wander inside the gym, ready to put him on his ass again. I'm wearing my trainers, a black long sleeve sweater and sports trousers, my hair rolled back in a bun.

Charlie is on the treadmill already, a little sweaty but lean and running like an athlete. He looks good in gray sports shorts with trainers, no top, his lean legs tanned and dusted in dark hair.

Trying to ignore how gorgeous he is—he's got a better body than Maksim—I pursue for the boxing ring. He stops running as soon as he sees me, pushing a button to slow the pace.

"Morning, Blaire," he pants out, so I look at him. His lips are curved in a sinfully alluring smile.

I wish he wouldn't smile at me like that. It makes me feel all funny inside.

"You ready?" Tying up his hair, he rolls back off the treadmill. He's only a little breathless but I'm not surprised. He's fit.

"Sure." Pulling the ropes apart, I climb into the ring and hold them open for him.

"I wanner teach you something," he says, straightening and stepping up to me, towering over me.

"What?" I walk backward, wondering why he's walking into me like this... prowling... "You're not going to start questioning me over Maksim again, are you?" The thought just popped into my head. After that intense conversation with him over dinner yesterday, I want to avoid the topic of Maksim like the plague.

"No," Charlie says, circling me.

I pivot to his stride, my eyes trained on his. "Okay. So, what do you want to teach me then?"

"Mental control." He attacks me without warning but I block his punch with my forearm.

"Bloody hell, Charlie! Give me a chance to prepare." I step back, blinking at him. "Why do you want to teach me mental control?"

He tries to slap my face but I swerve his effort.

"Because," he says, his gaze dark and focused, "I don't want you listening to anyone else around you when you're fighting."

He snatches for my throat but I punch his hand away, keeping my legs slightly open for balance. I need my wits about me today, clearly.

"You don't want me listening to anyone?" I say, baffled.

"I noticed how quickly you stopped fighting when Maksim told you to kill James." Charlie follows me around the ring, trying to dominate me with his presence, his neck a little hunched. "If James was out for blood that day, you'd be dead."

Is he fucking kidding me? James would have needed more than that stupid moment of distraction to end me.

I'm insulted and getting pissed off.

Charlie swings for me with a straight front-jab. I catch his punch in one hand and clout him in the face with my other, adrenaline spiking in me.

He laughs, wiping a drizzle of blood from his mouth with the back of his hand. "That was vicious."

"Vicious?" I yell, shaking out my hand, pain simmering in my bones. "You're trying to punch me! You said you wouldn't-"

Charlie ambushes me then and grabs the back of my neck with both hands. He forces me to bend over and tries to knee me in the face, letting out a deep groan with each assail. Growling in anger, I beat away his attacks with the heels of my palms, then I tackle him with my shoulder, putting him on his ass.

He's so fucking heavy to move it's physically taxing.

Dashing to my feet, I jump about and roll my shoulders, trying to warm up. I should have stretched out before fighting him today but I didn't anticipate this.

Charlie gets up and runs at me like a bull in a china shop. On instinct, I bob and weave, using up all the boxing ring space, escaping his strikes and booting away his kicks.

"What are you doing?" I yell, slapping his face with a loud, *WALLOP!*

"Training you." He laughs, catching my next slap and bending my arm back.

"Ouch!" I sidekick behind his knee, knocking him over. He pulls me down with him. We fall with a bounce.

Rolling away, I leap to my feet, fisting and flexing my hands. Charlie merely takes his time getting up, still chuckling.

"What the hell are you laughing at?"

He gestures up and down my body with a steady hand, the smuggest grin on his face.

"I don't need any training from you, Charlie." I point at him in anger. "I could keep up with you in my sleep."

"Yeah, maybe you're right, but you're not focused when it comes to Maksim."

I'm fuming.

"If Maksim says something-aargh!" I whack away his next punch. "I stop on instinct!" I don't mean to yell this so passionately, but I do.

We go back and forth like this for ages, Charlie really trying to put me down, chasing me around the ring. I'm dripping in sweat, and I'm glad that he is too, though he looks in his element.

I'm not.

This is supposed to be a friendly, right?

He swipes for my face with brutal force.

"Aargh!" I seize his arm, yank him forward, and shove his face into the boxing ring, my knee between his shoulder blades. "I thought you said you wouldn't punch me?" I say angrily in his ear. "Are you trying to make me really hurt you?"

He flips over and manages to pin me under him, putting us face to face. "I assumed you'd want me to keep up with the pace."

My heart picks up a beat. I can smell him... the sweaty, soapy fragrance of his skin... and the way he's looking at me... It's raw.

"Yeah, I do want you to keep up with the pace." I knee him where it hurts because I need to put some space between us.

"Awh!" He doubles over, cupping his crotch with both hands, pressing his face into the floor. "Fuck, Blaire!"

I roll away from him and stand, panting so hard that my chest is on fire. No one has ever put me so out of breath.

His ripped back is glistening in sweat, his muscles bunching as he tenses in agony. I lick my lips, imagining what his skin tastes like, feeling that heavy desire form in the pit of my core.

"You can't just do that in a friendly," Charlie hisses.

Putting my hands on my hips, I say, "Stop trying to talk me under your influence then."

I know what he's doing. He's trying to mentally bond us. I'm not stupid.

He shakes his head, taking in easy, controlled breaths. I actually start to feel a little guilty. Did I go too far with hitting him in the balls?

"Are you all right?" I kneel down beside him and softly touch his side. "Charlie?"

Making me squeak, he grabs my arm and yanks me under him again, settling between my legs with heavy force.

I cannot stop myself from gasping out. He's only wearing sports shorts and the thin material doesn't exactly hide how big he is.

"Charlie..." I husk out his name, gripping his solid forearms.

His eyes are level with mine, dark blue because his pupils are large. "Now, how would you escape me? You can't kick me in the nuts this time."

I dig my nails into the insides of his elbows but he twists out of my catty grasp. He grabs my wrists and heaves them up above my head, stretching me out.

"And now?" he says in my face.

We're nose to nose, watching each other, and he's smirking, his eyes glittering like blue crystals.

"I'd head-butt you," I whisper, slowly blinking at him.

He doesn't say anything for a while, just keeps me pinned under him, making me feel vulnerable and small. The expression on his face is tight with control but burning with want.

"And now?" he says eventually, pressing his damp forehead to mine.

Oh, shit-it.

I tense my stomach, trying to manage this rage inside me. I'm not sure if it's anger or desire or both. They seem to be blurring into one.

"What would you do now, Blaire?"

I kiss him.

Out of the blue—and I'm sure I've lost my damn mind—I push my chin forward and I kiss his soft lips.

The kiss moves through my body like waves of electricity, making me throb like crazy between my legs.

With a deep moan, Charlie thaws against me, closing his eyes. His grip on my wrists loosens, so I use the heel of my left foot to turn us over, putting him under me.

"That's what I'd do, Charlie." Straddling him with my thighs, I gently slap his face, feeling uncharacteristically playful. "I think I win this round too."

He sits up faster than lightning and slams his lips to mine. I squeal, trying to push him away with my hands on his damp, hairy chest—I only wanted to distract him so I could prevail, I think.

He catches my hands and bends them behind my back, having me whimper in pain.

"Ouch, Charlie!" I screw up my face. "My arms!"

He doesn't care.

Moaning, he licks across my tongue, massaging mine with slow seduction, crushing my breasts to his chest. I groan unwillingly, sinking into him, losing all focus. I think I even close my eyes.

We're not supposed to be doing this!

"You're a little fucking tease," he says harshly.

"And you're a cheat," I say too softly, making him laugh.

Tilting his head and curving his lips around mine, he takes me in an extremely passionate kiss, our mouths shaping as one, inundated with saliva and sweat and the metallic flavor of his blood.

I know I should keep fighting him off, but I don't. I can't. The kiss is satisfying.

He kneads the inside of my wrists with his thumbs and an odd sense of relief washes over me, like he's tapping into my pressure points or something. I sob in his mouth with fervor, and the more he kneads my inner wrists, the quicker my anger and my worry about the way he was attacking me vanishes. All I can think about is having him.

BLAIRE
(PART ONE)

The way I'm sitting on his lap is provoking too, his hard cock just touching my throbbing clit, only scraps of material between us. I cannot move out of the way he's holding me, yet I can move my hips, and if I shift forward just an inch, I'll be sitting in the hot zone.

I fight not to fulfill my desire to rub against him. I fight with all the will that I have left, which isn't much—Charlie is slowly but surely making sure of that. He's making me spiral out of control.

A phone starts ringing from across the gym, causing me to jump in my skin. My eyes flutter open. I try to yank back from Charlie, but he snaps, "Ignore it," his grip on my arms at my back tightening.

"I need to go have a shower," I say over our kiss, going all funny inside when he pushes his tongue in my mouth again.

"Ignore it," he whispers, softer now, pecking a kiss to my lips before consuming me again.

I whine, my will now evaporated, and I indulge him for one more kiss—it's not like I can stop this, is it?

Charlie lets go of my arms, I assume because he can sense that I'm into this, and before he can do anything, I'm swathed around his neck, trapped in an erratic, lusty haze. I've no idea what the fuck I'm doing. I'm just doing it.

The kiss turns wild now, his lips becoming more urgent and aggressive, making mine swell. He cradles the back of my head in one hand and the curve of my ass in his other, shifting me up his lap so we're flush against each other, sitting me right on top of his erection. It's all heady... the flavor of his blood... his sweaty fragrance... His sweat seems to have magnified his scent. It's all I can think about, until he moves under me, rolling his hips, rubbing his bulging cock against my sex.

My veins charge with fire and I cling to him so desperately, raking my nails down his back, moaning like I'm in pain or something.

The phone is ceaseless, ringing over and over again, all but shattering the moment.

Charlie curses. I can feel his anger on the surface of his skin.

"Go... go answer it," I say in puffs of breath, panting in his mouth.

He's not sure for a moment, his face taut with deliberation, then he bites out, "Fuck..."

Gripping my hips in large hands, he stands with effortlessness and puts me on shaky legs. I'm dizzy and flush, blinking through my haze. When I tilt my head back, I see Charlie's cheeks are flush too, his eyes unfocused and glowing with arousal.

"You all right?" He scans my face, his eyes dancing between my eyes and my swollen mouth.

A little embarrassed, I nod, dropping my gaze to the floor between us. Even unfocused, his burning blue eyes are too intense.

"Good." He shocks me with another gentle kiss, leaning down and pecking my lips. "Wait here."

I nod again, but when he turns his back on me, it breaks the spell.

My lungs fill with hot air and I realize what I've just done...

...After I fought to have the power over my body, I just kissed him?

Fuck.

BLAIRE
(PART ONE)

This is so fucked up.

He stole me away from my life—from Maksim. He used me to satisfy his own perverse needs without any regard for what I wanted...

Holding my face in both hands, I duck out of the boxing ring and sprint across the gym for the exit doors. One second I can hear Charlie yelling, "Who the fuck helped her leave The Site?" And the next he's calling my name, telling me to wait.

I ignore him with all the will I have and rush upstairs to my room, baffled with myself.

Why did I do that?

I pace my bedroom, stewing over what the hell has come about me.

Three days I've been here with Charlie. Just three fucking days, and I've gone from being a strong, mentally disciplined combatant, to a slut? The only person I should ever want like this is Maksim, but I don't.

It makes me sick. I don't get it. I just don't understand how this can happen, and so quickly.

I once read somewhere, 'the only way to get rid of temptation is to yield to it. I can resist everything but temptation'. Is that true? Is that what I need to do? If I give in to wanting Charlie, will it fix me?

I'm not sure. I know nothing of what's happening here.

I wish Maksim had prepared me for things like this, because if he did, I wouldn't be so mystified.

I bury myself in a book to take my mind off things and when it's mid afternoon, the sun hovering between high and low in the sky, I go downstairs, hungry from working out. I'm hoping to avoid Charlie but of course, there's no avoiding him. He's in the kitchen, on the phone by the back doors, wearing jeans and a black round neck t-shirt, his hair tied back. He's almost as tall as the back doors, his shoulders broad and his waist narrow, blocking the view over the garden.

"So she's in Europe then?" he says in Spanish, and I stand there on the threshold with a familiar tightness in the low of my stomach.

I shake my head, frustrated with myself. His presence alone fucks with my chi and he hasn't even looked at me yet.

Trying to keep my shit together, I open the fridge. There are pork medallions and fresh chilled asparagus, and on the kitchen countertop there's a bowl of potatoes.

Busying myself, I rummage through the cupboards to gather the utensils I need. I peel and cut up the potatoes so I can boil them for mash. I then fill a stainless steel saucepan with water and set the stove ring on medium, gently dropping in the potatoes.

"Why did you rush off this morning?" Charlie says from beside me, glancing over everything.

My chest constricts.

"I called for you to wait."

Swallowing down my anxiety, I keep my eyes trained on the task at hand. "I had to have a shower."

"You smelt all right to me." He pinches a stick of asparagus from the side and nips off the end. "You're cooking..." he says between bites

"Yeah." I rinse off my hands. "Are you hungry? I can make some for you too?" The least I can offer is to cook for him. It is after all his house and his ingredients, and he could just as easily not feed me properly.

He leans back against the kitchen units. "This, is something I never expected to see."

"What?" I dry my hands and hang the towel back over the sink.

"You, cooking." Charlie smirks at me, mischief glittering in his eyes.

"I'm not an idiot. Of course I can cook."

"I never said you were an idiot," he says, popping the rest of the asparagus into his mouth. He then says something about me being into sports and... I don't know. I'm not paying attention. I'm watching him eat, my eyes focused on his mouth as he chews that piece of asparagus. He's so mesmerizing. Everything he does is executed with surety, not an ounce of hesitation in his movements.

The longer I look at his mouth, the quicker my thoughts divert. I remember our kiss this morning all too vividly; the way he groaned in my mouth; the way he crushed me against his hard body as though he couldn't get me close enough.

Charlie raises his eyebrows at me and I blink away in a fluster. Why the fuck do I fancy him so much? Is this normal?

Using a colander, and trying to ignore Charlie standing there, I set the asparagus to boil, then I oil a frying pan for the medallions.

"Here, I'll do that." He takes the frying pan handle, grabbing it over my hand.

I snatch away from him, determined not to go there again.

He smiles coolly at me before seasoning the pork with salt and pepper and some herbs, his motions smooth and confident.

"I don't mind cooking if you're busy, Charlie."

"No. You're my guest," he says. "I don't want you cooking."

Guest?

Resisting the urge to point out that I'm not a guest, more of a prisoner—now, a half willing prisoner who might want him—I try to walk past him so I can get out of his ozone.

"Not so fast." He catches my wrist and urges me back a step, then nods at the fridge. "Get two beers out."

Tugging out of his grasp, I grab one bottle of beer out of the fridge, twist off the cap, and put it on the side by Charlie.

"You're not having a drink?"

I shake my head, stepping away to put some distance between us. I don't need anything impairing my mind right now. Charlie does that alone.

"Ohhh, go on." He gestures at the fridge, his blue eyes shining with amusement. "Live a little. It might help you relax."

"I don't need a beer to relax." Crossing my arms, I rest against the sink in resistance.

"You sure?"

"Absolutely."

He chuckles, his cheekbones sharp with that large smile. He then peppers me in questions, first asking if I learnt anything from our sparring session this morning.

"Nope," I lie. I learnt that, if one is going to kiss another as a distraction, do it quickly and without adding desire to the mix.

I won't tell him that.

More questions; he's still intrigued by my fighting skills. "Are you gonna tell me who taught you yet?"

"Nope," I say again, my expression flat of emotion. It's better this way. If I can steer clear of that lusty zone he puts me in, I can maintain control over us. I won't end up kissing him again.

Charlie smirks at me. "Okay then, if curt is how you wanner play it." He turns down the heat to put the potatoes on simmer, then he steps in front of me, mimicking my pose by crossing his arms. "If you don't want me to touch you, why did you kiss me earlier?"

My stomach rolls with embarrassment. I don't for a single moment want to talk about *that*, but I won't keep letting him chip away at me. He has to know that I'm strong minded and more perceptive than he gives me credit for.

"I took advantage of you."

He flicks up his eyebrows. "Smart girl."

I huff. That has to be the most modest compliment he's ever given me.

"You know, Blaire, I think you like it when I kiss you," he stares down the span of my body, then back up, "you just won't admit it because what I make you feel confuses you."

Could he be anymore arrogant—or right?

"I think it's the other way around, Charlie." I'm being brave, trying to take him down a peg, but on the inside

I'm so embarrassed it's stupid. My stomach is in knots. "I think it's you who likes kissing me."

"Sure I do." He glances between my eyes. "You're a nice looking girl. I wouldn't kick you outa bed for love nor money."

I look away from him, my cheeks burning. How can he say things like that to a girl with such cool composure? I'd never have the guts to tell him how I feel.

"I give you one week before you're revoking our little deal," he says softly, with a hint of sarcasm.

I swallow, keeping my eyes down. "I think you'll be sourly surprised when I don't."

"You're right," he whispers, leaning into me, "I will be."

BLAIRE
(PART ONE)

18

The next week passes slowly.

Charlie wakes me up the morning after pledging I'll revoke our 'little deal' with a cup of coffee and I'm so startled to see him in my room before the sun has even risen that I just lie here leaning up on one elbow; stare at him in the doorway. He saunters in to put the coffee down on the bedside cabinet and as soon as he looks down on me, my stomach twists with knots. There's this familiar pressure in the pit of my core too. Sexual anxiety. I think he's come to do something to me. To satisfy his appetite—or mine.

"What-what are you doing in here, Charlie?"

"Don't look so nervous. I'm just bringing you a coffee because I know you like it. You all right?" he says this sounding concerned. Though it's quite dark in here with only a burning pink sky peeking in through the window, I can see he's frowning.

"Yeah," I croak out because my throat is a bit sore, "why wouldn't I be?"

Standing there at my bedside, he watches me for a moment in total silence. I don't know where to look—I feel as if I'm naked and on trial when he looks at me like that—so I sit up against the headboard and reach for the steaming cup of coffee.

"Be ready in half an hour for the gym," he says eventually in a low, soft voice, "I've made you some breakfast. It's in the oven."

"Um... okay."

"If you ever wanner eat breakfast with me, let me know and I'll wake you up earlier."

Eat breakfast with him? Why would I want to eat breakfast with him? I barely make it through dinner mentally unscathed.

Hugging the blanket to my chest, I nod to answer him, and then he leaves.

That was really weird, but it doesn't end up being so. This becomes a pattern and I'm less and less nervous by the day. Six A.M. wake up calls with a coffee and Charlie asking if I'm all right, then breakfast alone in the kitchen. We fight in the gym after, our sweaty bodies often rolling around the boxing ring in a battle of power, then I spend the deaden part of the days reading in my room. We have dinner together every evening where he teases me about apparently fancying him; wants to know why I don't come down for lunch during the day. He hasn't clocked on to the fact that I need that time alone to mentally come down from whatever he makes me feel. Conversation starts to flow more freely and I gradually ease into spending time with him. Might even look forward to spending time with him. I'm not totally sure yet.

Though he was sold on the idea that I would revoke our deal, I don't. As much as I want to because our sparring sessions are almost unbearable with this sexual tension that's now constantly between us, and at dinner he talks me under a charm that I start to enjoy, I don't revoke.

Not that it really matters though because with every day between us, the old me is drifting further and further away like a soul being swept by the wind. I find myself getting weak to Charlie's charming seduction, holding conversations with him rather than letting him take the lead. I'm awake before he even comes into my room in the mornings now. I'm desiring him more and more... sneakily looking at him... enjoying the way his body flexes when he moves about... basking in his attention when he talks to me... Hell, I'm even dreaming about him in the most risqué manner—that's what wakes me up before sunrise—and I never usually remember my dreams.

Everything in my mind is narrowed in on him now.

I don't know how this happened. I should fucking hate him—he stole me away from everything I know—but I don't.

The line has gone blurry.

"It seems I'm gonna have to work a little harder," he says, wrapping up my knuckles with stretchy medical bandages. I've been going at it with the punch bag this morning, trying to relieve some of this sexual tension that's in me, and my knuckles are bloody. Charlie took one look at me and said I'm not to fight with naked hands anymore. Not while I'm living here with him. I tried to resist letting him touch me but it was fruitless. By the time his fingers were on mine, I folded.

I cock a brow at him, assuming what he's talking about. The deal. It's the only thing on his mind lately, other than teasing me. He's always teasing me about something; usually over the fact that he knows I fancy him. Or, assumes. I haven't told him the truth.

"I'm sure you will," I say.

Chuckling to himself, he works on my left hand. I watch him with careful meditation, nodding and shaking when he asks if the bandages are too tight; too loose. He's got his hair tied back today and while this is my favorite look on him, all I can think about doing is yanking out his ponytail and raking my fingers through the strands, steering him to my satisfaction. I want to touch him. I want to run my hands over every bulging muscle under the t-shirt he's wearing... feel the power in his body... I dreamed about touching him last night; felt the callousness of his body hair under my palms—maybe that's why my mind is twisted this morning?

Charlie glances up at me from my hands and holds my burning hot gaze for a few seconds. "You shouldn't stare at people like that, Blaire."

I give him a funny look, drawing in my eyebrows. Does he know I'm thinking about him being naked?

"Your eyes are haunting..." he says softly, his blue stare flickering all over my features, "possessing..."

I glance away from him then. When he says things like that it's as if he's an incubus talking to my unconscious soul.

BLAIRE
(PART ONE)

"You don't even realize what you're doing, do you?" he whispers, pinching my chin between a finger and a thumb, forcing our gaze to align once more.

"I don't even know what you're talking about." I tug out of his grasp to break the spell.

"No," he says under his breath. "I know you don't." He finishes bandaging me up, then he gives my hand a squeeze, nearly making me moan. "Before we spar, I wanner do something with you."

I back up, my stomach contracting with frustrating wishful anxiety.

"Nothing like that." He laughs, a wide smile dominating his face. "I wanner see how high you can kick."

"Oh..." I blink at him, coming down from that rush of anxiety. I've come to like that rush. I like everything about the way he makes me feel now. "Okay," I say. "Sure."

He nods left, so I follow him across the gym, fisting and unfisting my hands to loosen up the bandages. Charlie rustles through the cupboards on the back wall for something, saying that once he's satisfied with seeing how high I can kick, I can show him a few tricks.

"Tricks?" I say in a distracted fashion because he's got a Wing Chun ring on one of the shelves in the cupboard.

"Yeah," he sounds like he's trying not to laugh, "I'm sure you have many."

"Why do you have that?" I ask. Picking up the Wing Chun ring, I run my fingers over the smooth bamboo outlay.

239

He smiles at me. It's his deathly handsome smile that makes me feel all warm and tingly. "I got you some Wing Chun equipment so you can train. Don't want you getting bored now, do we?"

"I was going to say," I glance up at him, putting the ring back in the cupboard, "you're into boxing, right?"

He nods, smirking at me like he's got a hidden secret.

"You know, you're going to have to learn a different style of fighting if you want to beat me."

He doesn't look offended by my arrogance. If anything, he looks amused. "Yeah, I'm well aware."

Grabbing a remote control out of the cupboard, he uses it to move a punch bag up the wall. The bracket hums with electricity as it ascends, until Charlie clicks the stop button, leaving the bag hanging just above my head.

"Is that too high?" he asks, ushering me back across the gym with his hand on the low of my back.

I shake my head, walking with him, training my attention on the bag. I can high-kick around eight feet in the air if I run up to a target.

"All right then," he says. "But if you want it lowered, just tell me." Wandering past me, he checks the bag over, grabbing it with both hands and shaking it so vigorously that the wall shudders. I assume he's making sure it's safe to use. He then crosses his arms and moves back to give me the space I need, telling me, "Go on then."

He's curious to see me do this, I can tell by that fire in his eyes.

I bend over to stretch out, ensuring I have no knots in my muscles. There's nothing worse than getting cramp mid-fight. Charlie is watching me—I can feel his eyes on my ass—but I knew they would be. In fact, I'm taking great pleasure in winding him up, especially when he clears his throat.

My muscles now loose, I jog back for some distance, getting in position by slightly bending my knees. Then, to gain the strength and speed I need, I run up to the punch bag, my muscles easing into my motions. Two feet away, I leap into the air and kick the bottom of the bag. A warm surge of adrenaline shoots through me as I softly land on my feet, my interest centering on my training. I've missed this—the relaxed routine of training in this manner. It reminds me of home.

"Yeah, you're quick," Charlie says, seeming to be confirming his own thoughts.

I glance at him, smirking with conceit.

"Go again," he says, gesturing for the bag, his arms still folded over his chest.

Backing up, I pull in a large breath and run up to the punch bag, jumping into the air with an athletic kick when I'm within range. Again and again I attack, each kick executed more brilliantly than the last. I spend the next forty minutes doing this, flashing Charlie the odd smile as he tells me that he could watch me do this all day. "I don't think I've seen a girl so disciplined."

I know there's an ulterior meaning to what he's just said, but I'm having such a good time that I don't want to spoil it by being snarky.

I keep going at the bag, and when I'm a little puffed out, sweat dripping down my back, I have a go at teaching Charlie. I don't know why. I just fancy it.

"Everyone can learn, but you should lower the bag a bit," I say, estimating that it's got to be six feet in the air. "That's quite a fall if you miss and drop on your ass."

He arches a brow at me. "Are you sure you don't want me to make it higher then?"

Pursing my lips, I hum in a musing fashion. "Second thought, you should make it higher."

"I knew you'd say that." He playfully pinches my side, making me squirm.

I kick his feet out from under him and he drops with a heavy thud. I burst out laughing, grabbing my stomach because it aches, hardly containing myself. This is the oddest thing. I've never laughed like this in my life.

Charlie shakes his head at me, and I think he's trying not to laugh too.

"Go on," I say amid laughing, gesturing out, "form position. You can't kick the punch bag from down there."

Grinning, he gets up from the floor and stands before the punch bag, rolling back his shoulders. I love watching him do that. Every muscle in his back waves and flexes beneath his t-shirt.

I tell him to warm up with a few axe kicks, that he doesn't need to jump up and kick the bag until he's ready, but he's terrible at taking advice.

"Do as you please then." I shrug, walking back and forth with crossed arms, observing him.

My face drops when he strikes the bag with a high-air-kick, landing perfectly on his feet. Another kick, and another, every one achieved with focus and refinement.

My mouth hanging open, I glance between him and the punch bag.

"Didn't expect that, did you, little Blaire?" he says, triumphant plastered across his face. He walks into me, playfully slapping my face.

I flick away his hand but he catches my wrist. We start fighting then and we're not even in the ring. We are all legs, trying to knock each other over—I guess because we've been practicing our kicks. I put Charlie down more times than he does me but I have to admit, I underestimated him a little. He's not as good as me, though he's not as bad as I thought either, and he's definitely into more than boxing.

Sweating, Charlie yanks off his t-shirt and flings it at me. The smell that hits me in the face is overwhelming—his clean-sweaty, musky scent.

Jesus...

Before I can toss his t-shirt aside, he runs at me and hooks one arm between my legs, gripping my ass.

"Charlie!" I squeal, grabbing his shoulders, the feeling of him between my legs all too familiar.

He fists the back of my hair with his other hand, yanks me up off the ground, and slams me down on a training mat.

"Aargh!" I groan out, arching.

"Shit!" He crouches over me on all fours, his knees pressing into the mat on either side of my body. "Are you all right?"

"The mats aren't that soft." I roll onto my side, my face taut with pain.

"Ohhh, Blaire, I'm sorry, baby." He runs a large hand down my spine, over every curve, kneading out the pain. "I didn't mean to hurt you. The mats are supposed to be quite thick."

BLAIRE
(PART ONE)

I start to say, "Well they're not," but then I find myself leaning into his touch like a dog getting petted, my stomach coiling with sinister desire.

Why the fuck is this happening to me? Why can't I go one day without desiring him? What's his poison?

While I'm bathing in his touch, practically humming in delight, he whispers in my ear, "Are you gonna kiss me again so you can beat me? Because I really don't mind."

I smirk up at him from the side, and I can't help thinking, *does he want me as much as I want him?* I sense that he does but I can't be one-hundred percent sure that this isn't his agenda—to have me utterly under his spell.

Charlie looks like he's going to kiss me, his face dripping in want as he comes closer to me, his eyes flickering between mine.

I playfully tell him to piss off, pushing his mouth to the side. One more kiss and I'm not sure I'll be able to stop.

Taking my hands, he helps me to my feet. "You all right?" he asks with genuine concern, giving me the once over, his eyes sweeping up and down my body. "Does your back still hurt?"

"No." I roll my shoulders, trying to iron out the tension in me. "I'm fine."

"Here," he says, circling with a single finger, "turn around."

"Why?" I can feel my heart hammering in my chest. "What are you going to do?"

The way he smiles at me...

BLAIRE
(PART ONE)

"Turn around," he still circling his finger; flicks up his eyebrows, "you'll be glad you did."

A bit wary, I do, and just to really fuck with me, he puts his large hands on my shoulders. He massages me there with gentle fingers, getting into knots and kinks that I didn't even know existed. It feels so good that I sigh and let my head fall back. I can't resist closing my eyes for a moment either, imagining that he's doing this to me while I'm naked and withered after an orgasm.

"Feels good," Charlie whispers in my ear from over my shoulder, "doesn't it?"

I'm living in my own sexually repressed hell and it feels like things are just getting started.

BLAIRE
(PART ONE)

19

Over the coming weeks, I adjust to living with Charlie.

After the way he dropped me in the gym the other day, he's a little delicate with me when we spar now, but it's all right. I don't want to get too physical with him anyway. I'm trying to control my hormones and given they don't regulate until at least ten o'clock in the morning, his guilt for 'hurting me' has worked in my favor.

I also don't hide away in my room during the day anymore, reading the books he brought me. I come down for lunch as well as breakfast and dinner, though we never eat breakfast or lunch together—I always get up too late to share breakfast with him and he's always 'working' at lunchtime.

Today however, he isn't working, so I'm indulging myself in his company, making us both a sandwich before he disappears again. We eat standing in the kitchen space, Charlie leaning against the countertop next to me, topless. I'm not sure if he owns a bloody top anymore.

"You know you've been down for lunch every day this week?" he says, flicking crumbs off his chest.

"Yeah, so?" I have a sip of orange juice but it barely quenches my thirst. "Is that all right?"

"Course it is," he says softly. "You can do whatever you want here, Blaire." He reaches for my glass so I give it to him, and he finishes off every last drop of orange juice. I watch the Adams apple in his throat bob up and down, captivated—everything he does captivates me.

"Why have you only just started coming down in the daytime?" he says, leaning past me to put the empty glass in the sink. "You've been here for over a month now."

"Maybe because I didn't like you before," the words are out of my mouth before I can stop them. "Not that... you know... I don't mean..." I blink at him, internally cringing.

Why did I just say that?

"So..." he says amused, licking his lips, "you like me now?"

I exhale under my breath. He isn't offended.

"Hm?" he hums, flicking up his eyebrows for an answer. "Yes? No? Maybe?" His eyes thin. "Maybe a little?"

"You're all right, I suppose." I shrug, and trying not to laugh at him, I bite a chunk out of my sandwich. He is all right. Nothing like I thought he'd be.

He laughs at me, his eyes glittering, trapping me in his spell—I could stare at his wicked blue eyes all day long.

"Well, that's better than you hating me, I guess," he says, having another deep bite of his sandwich.

"Why don't you have a girlfriend?" I blurt out. I'm not ashamed to ask. I've been wondering for weeks now, wondering that if he does have a girlfriend, who she might be; what she looks like.

He coughs, almost spitting out his sandwich.

"I mean, you probably have got a girlfriend. I just assumed..." I put down the last of my sandwich and hide my hands in the sleeves of my sweater, looking up at him innocently. "Sorry. I'm not prying. I just wondered, is all."

"No..." he laughs, wiping his lips with his fingers, smirking down at me. "You haven't gotta be sorry." He's still laughing, trying to swallow down his sandwich. "I've had plenty of women," he explains, but says he couldn't be bothered to make the effort with them. "I work all the time so I don't have time to fuck about with women."

I incline a brow at him.

"Except from you, but you're different." He winks at me, polishing off the rest of his sandwich by popping it in his mouth.

I look away from him, my cheeks warming up.

Gathering the dirty dishes, I drop them into the sink, then I wipe down the sides.

His words are like a mantra in my head: *I don't have time to fuck about with women—except from you.* Why am I so flattered by that?

"Blaire..." he says my name after a while of silence, and when I peer up at him, I find he's giving me an unusually cautious stare.

"What?" I shove the butter and the salad bits away in the fridge.

"I wanner ask you something-" he says, then he pauses for a moment, chewing the inside of his mouth, "-but if you don't wanner talk about it, then that's okay. Just say."

Crossing my arms, I rest back against the kitchen counter.

He crosses his arms too. "You said you don't remember meeting Maksim, nor do you have any memories of being young-"

My eyebrows draw together.

"-What's your earliest memory?"

My frown intensifies. "That's a bit random, Charlie."

For the past few weeks, he's not so much as mentioned my past, and now he wants to know what my earliest memory is?

He lifts his shoulders in a shrug. "I've been meaning to ask you for a while now but I don't wanner make you feel uncomfortable. You seem relaxed with me now."

He's noticed... Fuck, that's so humiliating. I don't want him to know that I'm comfortable around him. It gives him all the power.

"Do you mind telling me?" he asks, holding my gaze with trained enthusiasm. "I'd like to know."

"Um..." I run my teeth across my top lip. "I guess."

I don't answer his question right away. I'm not shying away from it, which is bizarre to my nature. I'm actually digging into my thoughts so I can explain myself to him. I want to explain myself to him. I want him to know me—or, I want him to know what Maksim will be okay with him knowing.

BLAIRE
(PART ONE)

What I recall isn't a memory, per se. It's more of a feeling. A feeling of coldness and total darkness—claustrophobia—and absolute quietness for long periods of time. There's also this damp smell that I can never escape in my dreams. I tell Charlie this, laughing uneasily. "I don't really remember much before I was thirteen, and what I do isn't exactly clear enough to say it's a memory."

Silence. He looks puzzled with my answer.

"What isn't clear?" he asks, tipping his head.

I glance down, then back up at him. "I can't tell you that."

He nods a few times, understanding my unspoken words. "Are those memories like the feelings you remember? You don't have to tell me if you don't want to."

I take a moment so I can find the words, but all I come up with is, "They're sort of like those feelings, though fuzzier." I won't elaborate more than that because all those unsure 'memories' have something to do with Maksim and how he conditioned me. From what I can gather, I was drugged up and forced to endure sleep deprivation for extensive stretches of time—the objective was to ensure my mind was open. During these times, images and videos would flash through my mind, images of a girl protecting her lover, slaying man after man and woman after woman. The first time I saw those things I was petrified. They never stopped filtering through my mind's eye until I could control my heart rate, as Maksim's voice would tell me. When I could control my heart rate and my fears, I was allowed to sleep, but only to Maksim's voice... to his promises and the promises he made me commit to... the constant reminder that I fear nothing but Maksim's safety; that I live to worship and protect him.

Then there was the pain. Most of all the aches and pain. The stretched out feeling of hanging from my arms. Being drowned in cold water while my hands and feet were in scorching hot water. Electric shocks that made my entire body spasm with agony. Beltings.

It all sounds so sadistic, even to myself as I recall the... 'memories', but it's not. It made me who I am now; a fearless combatant.

"Don't you think that's strange?" Charlie says softly, glowering with confusion. "How you can't remember much?"

I shrug with indifference. "What isn't strange about how I grew up?"

His eyes swim with something I've not seen before... sympathy?

My chest does this odd squeezy thing.

It's definitely sympathy.

"Don't feel sorry for me, Charlie." I turn away from him and busy myself with washing up, barely registering how hot the water is. "I'm not worth it."

"That's subjective to think you're not worth feeling sorry for," he says. "Regardless of what you've done, you're just a kid, really."

A kid?

"Don't you know who I am, Charlie?" I leisurely peer over my shoulder and scowl at him. "Don't you know how many people I've killed? How many lives I've ripped apart?"

"Yeah, I'm quite aware." He doesn't react with disgust, as I thought he would, but that just annoys me. He should find me repulsive and evil. He shouldn't want me as he does. The only reason I've never questioned Maksim's fascination with me is because we're as deeply as sick as each other.

"You know," I snatch the towel off the sink so I can dry my hands, "just because I'm... well, innocent or whatever, it doesn't mean I'm some sweet, blameless girl." I give him this hard, wolfish look. "I don't deserve your pity. The only thing I deserve is a guaranteed ticket to hell, and you'd do well to remember that."

"I didn't realize you regard yourself with such high esteem."

"What's that supposed to mean?" I ask, flinging the towel on the countertop.

"Well, ever since I met you you've been emotionally constipated, and now you're..." he shrugs, his arms still folded over his chest. "I never knew you felt guilt for the things you've done."

I snort, affronted. "I don't."

"I think you do, you just execute a great job of blocking your emotions out," his eyes taper as he says that, like he knows how I feel deep down at times. "You should ease up on yourself, Blaire. Half the people you've killed probably deserved it."

"And the other half?" I remind him that some were innocent; remind myself what real guilt feels like. I once killed a man who worked at the club for stealing a hundred pounds off Maksim, even after he told me it was to put the gas on and get some food for his kids. It was a cold English winter at the time. He had a nasty cough,

BLAIRE
(PART ONE)

was constantly spluttering up phlegm because he was ill. While I felt pity for him, it didn't stop me from slitting his throat to make a point of him. And then came the guilt. For days I couldn't sleep. I kept seeing his face in my closed eyes, the photo he showed me of his kids who were barely five years old. He said they all had the flu and because they were illegal immigrants, he couldn't take them to a doctor.

Now, they have no father and that's because of me.

"Collateral damage," Charlie says frankly, and there isn't an ounce of pity in his eyes now. "It happens in the best of wars."

Silence wraps around us as we stare at each other in a moment of reflection.

I have no idea why I'm even talking to him like this. For weeks we've been teasing each other, falling under a spell of desire, and now...

Why did he have to ruin things? Why does he want to know what darkness I've suffered? Is that how he's getting his kicks now?

"Let us get a few things straight," I snap, pointing at the ground between us, guilt trickling through my frosty heart, "I don't feel culpable for anything I've done," I try to convince myself, "I don't care about who I've killed or who I've tortured, and I don't give a shit about your stupid, curious questions, either." I want to keep going at him, but I can't stand the way he's looking at me—outright unbothered by my ominous confession.

I try to leave the kitchen but Charlie sidesteps me, blocking my exit with his tall, muscular body.

"Blaire, calm down," he says, "I told you if you didn't wanner talk about it all you had to do was say."

My teeth grind, and I fist my hands. "Is this what you're trying to do? Splay open my emotions?"

He doesn't answer me, just stands there in a deadpan fashion.

"Good luck with that," I say, huffing at him, "it'll take more than sly humdrum conversation to achieve that."

Barging him with my shoulder, I head out of the kitchen and go up to my room. I don't come down for dinner, not even when Charlie knocks on my door and asks if I'm hungry. I curl up in the middle of my bed and shut off mentally, trying to forget this afternoon ever happened; try to forget that man's face.

I'm quite stupid really, to think I could live in a world with Charlie where only peace and desire exists side by side until I go home. Of course he's going to want to know who I am inside—that's his objective, isn't it?

BLAIRE
(PART ONE)

20

The next morning, my erratic period comes.

If there's anything I'd like to avoid right now, it's this time of the month because I am never myself when my period comes. I'm withdrawn and morose and so uncomfortable it's beyond belief. I always try to keep it together and remain as Blaire as I can, for Maksim wouldn't take too kindly to me being in a mood—he'd whip me to death until I learnt to control my mood—but here, however, Maksim isn't about, so I'm not quite sure how I'll cope with my period and that bothers me. Charlie has been all right up until now—minus yesterday afternoon with his prying—and I don't want to rock the boat by being overly rude. I've enough emotions to deal with, let alone his wrath.

Feeling like bugs are crawling under my skin, I wake in the middle of the night and go to the bathroom, knowing exactly why I feel the way I do. My throat is a bit sore, as if I've been screaming my head off in agony. I hand feed myself some cold water from the sink to soothe my throat, then I search through the vanity cupboards for some toiletries. All of what I need is in here, surprisingly—it seems Charlie has thought of everything.

I sort myself out and get back into bed where I lie staring through the window for hours, the blanket draped over my waist. The sun hasn't risen yet—the sky is like a sheet of black silk, slipping down the horizon that's half alight.

I toss and turn for a while, hoping for the sun, but I just can't relax. I'm too tense and itching to do something... anything...

Slugging it out of bed, feeling bloated and heavy, I dress in the usual and patter downstairs to the kitchen barefoot.

It's quiet in the kitchen and it feels empty without Charlie around. I've come to like him being around. It's so weird.

I make some toast and take it to the dining table, where I watch the sun rise through the back doors with burning pink rays.

"Blaire?" Charlie says, entering the kitchen. "I wondered where you were."

I turn in my chair to look at him in the doorway. He's on the phone, wearing jeans over black boots and a white t-shirt that boasts all his muscles. His fucking hair is pulled back, too.

Great.

A warm feeling travels right through me, making my skin flush. I'm suddenly aware of how tight my black jumper is across my swollen breasts... aware of how tight my trousers are against my sex... aware of how cold the stone flooring is against the soles of my feet.

BLAIRE
(PART ONE)

It seems my desire for him has magnified.

This can't be happening to me—not now. Not while I'm already uncomfortable in my own skin.

"Morning, Charlie." I drop my gaze to the now empty plate, too pissed off with everything that's going on inside me. I wish my car was here so I could go for a drive or something. I feel like I've been stuck in this damn house for years rather than weeks, lusting after *him!*

"I'll call you back." Charlie hangs up the phone and then I hear him wandering over to me, his feet heavy against the kitchen floors. "What's wrong?"

I keep my eyes trained on the plate, clasping my hands together in my lap. "Nothing."

He pulls out the chair to my right, making it scrape against the floor, and sits down. He's showered. I can smell the clean soapy aroma of his skin.

"I know there's something wrong." Gently touching my hand under the table, he grasps my attention for a split second, but then I look away.

"Did I cross a line with asking you those questions yesterday?" he says softly. "Have I upset you?"

"What?" I frown up at him. "No, Charlie. I don't hold onto irritation for very long, as I'm sure you've noticed." I have to look away again. I can't stand that intense blueness in his eyes—not this morning—and I can't stand it when he wears his hair back. He's too handsome.

"So, I did irritate you then?"

"For all of an evening," I whisper.

"Okay... Well, if it's not me, then what's wrong? Has something else pissed you off?"

I try to avoid telling him but he goes on and on and on, demanding an answer. "I won't relent, Blaire. I wanner know what's wrong."

"It's my period, all right?"

"Oh!" He's lost for what to say for a moment, blinking at me as if I just admitted to something dreadful. "Have you got a stomach ache?"

Shutting my eyes, I shake my head. "But I can't be bothered to train today, if you don't mind?"

"Course I don't mind. Do you need anything? I put all the necessary toiletries in your bathroom."

"I'm fine."

Another long pause, then he rises from his chair. He saunters across the kitchen, rustles through the cupboards and the draws, and then returns with two cups of coffee. "Here." He passes one to me.

I take it from him and hold it on the table, training my eyes there. The cup is warm against my palms and smells deliciously of the morning—bitter coffee beans.

"Do you want anything in particular to eat?" he asks.

I scowl up at him. "Are you being funny?"

He snaps his thick eyebrows together.

"Why would I want anything in particular to eat?" I say.

"Don't women have cravings when it's this time of the month?" I think he's trying not to smirk as he sits back against his chair, looking as cool as ever.

My scowl hardens. I have cravings every fucking second of every fucking day, but not for food.

"Chocolate?" He raises his eyebrows at me.

"I don't eat chocolate."

"You should." He sips his coffee with steady movements. "It's supposed to have natural pain relief chemicals known to be effective on women. And it's supposed to help with bad moods," he adds with sarcasm.

I don't answer him. I'm worried I'll say something I'll live to regret and end up unleashing the evil within him, because it has to be there somewhere. He can't be like this with everyone, surely?

Guzzling down the rest of his coffee, Charlie gets up and leaves the kitchen without saying goodbye.

I close my eyes with a harsh sigh, simmering over the possibility that I've pissed him off. I know I don't say much as it is, but I'm not usually this blank and rude to him—or I don't think I am.

Half an hour passes, and then he's back with a flimsy blue shopping bag in hand.

"Chocolate." He drops the bag in front of me on the table, shoving car keys away in his jeans pocket. "Eat, and cheer up."

Shit, he is pissed off.

"Sorry," I say, looking down, squeezing the cup in my grasp. "I don't know what's wrong with me. I should know better than to be rude to you."

"S'all right." He winks at me when I peer up at him. "Do you wanner sit with me while I make my phone calls?" He takes a seat next to me again, the wooden frame creaking under his weight. "Tis' gotta be better than being cooped up in your room."

I'm confused. Is he pissed off with me?

I try not to frown at him, keeping my expression ironed out.

BLAIRE
(PART ONE)

I can't really tell what mood he's in.

"I... sure, if you want me to?" I shrug, feeling a bit weird with today's situation. Is it just me, or does he seem different?

"Course I want you to." Charlie empties out the contents of the rustling bag and peels open a few bars of Galaxy Caramel. He tucks into the chocolate with gusto, popping a few cubes into his mouth amid dialing someone.

I don't think he is pissed off. He seems to be taking my bad mood in his stride.

Strange.

He starts speaking in Spanish to his caller. I make out something about prices, and I feel like I'm intruding.

"Charlie," I whisper, pointing out, "I can go up to my room if you-"

He shakes his head, giving my shoulder a gentle squeeze. I tense up, wishing he wouldn't touch me. I can't deal with his intensity today. All I want to do is pounce on him or hit him.

Still speaking on the phone, he nods at the chocolate, I assume for me to have some.

I grab a square and nip off the corner with my front teeth, and the sensations that rush through me are stimulating. It's like nothing I've tasted before. It's fucking delicious, sugary and creamy and mouth-watering and... I can't find the right words to explain what chocolate is like for me.

By the time Charlie has finished with his call—which I think lasts for over an hour, I'm not too sure—we've eaten the entire contents of the bag.

"Told you you'd like chocolate." He smirks at me, putting his phone down on the table.

I stare at him in total silence, deliberating on asking him a question.

"What?" Stretching out his large body, he reaches back and holds the top of my chair.

Fuck it. It's not like I've got anything to lose.

"What's with you today?" I hug my middle, giving him this wolfish look.

"What's with me?" He seems confused, screwing up his face. "What'd you mean?"

"Why are you being so nice?"

Now, he looks insulted. "Am I not normally nice to you?"

"I... well..." I try to speak but I'm suddenly stuck, too.

Yes, he is always nice to me, though he's usually oozing with dark sexual intensity. Today, he isn't. Yes he's still intense, but he's... I don't know... I don't even know why I'm pondering over this.

I hate being on my period. It makes me think too much.

Breaking eye contact, and needing some space, I say, "I'm going to go lie down for a bit."

I try to stand but he rapidly catches my arm. "This isn't just your period. I have upset you, haven't I?"

I peer back at him, finding his eyes are full of apprehension.

"No, Charlie. You haven't done anything to upset me."

He nods at my chair, so I sit back down.

"Then what's wrong? Why can't you look at me properly?" His fingers slide down my arm to my hand where he holds me, running his fingers through mine, sending waves through my body.

"Nothing is wrong." I lick my lips because they're dry, fisting my hand in his.

"Blaire... don't lie to me."

My stomach cramps with anxiety.

"I was just wondering why you're being... I don't know..." I look away from him, my cheeks burning. Why is he doing this now?

He tugs on my hand, making me face him.

"You're not usually like this," I snap, and then with my free hand, I flick one of the chocolate wrappers. "You don't usually sit with me in the mornings or speak to people in front of me. You usually leave me alone during the day."

He stares me down, his gaze full of marvel. This has to be his most confusing expression. It doesn't suit him.

"Duly noted." He nods at me and gives my hand a squeeze, making my bones melt.

This is so messed up. He seems to understand me when I don't even understand myself. I have no idea where I was going with that.

The following morning Charlie is just as weird and confusing—no, worse. He wakes me up by gently giving my shoulder a shake and tells me to join him for breakfast.

"Why?" I throw back the blankets and sit up in bed. "Has something happened?"

It's almost pitch black in my room but I can still see his tall frame at my bedside.

"No, nothing's happened." He goes over to the armoire and pulls open the doors, gathers some of my clothes and passes them to me. "Everything's fine."

On alert, I slip out of bed in my pajamas—a gray spaghetti strap top with shorts. I rub my eyes in an attempt to gather my wits and then I see the time. I sigh with frustration. Who the fuck gets up at four thirty A.M. unless it's work related?

"If everything's okay, why do you want me up so early, Charlie?"

"Because I wanner have breakfast with you and this is the time I eat in the mornings."

Puzzled, I reach for the clothes in his arms, carefully studying him. He doesn't seem uneasy or fidgety, so I'm almost certain nothing has happened. He gives me his best smile as I stare at him, one that makes me feel warm all over.

"Chop, chop," he says in a playful manner, gesturing for the bathroom.

I'm not sure what to make of his intensions but I go with the flow. I'm too tired to do anything else right now.

While he's pacing around my bedroom in black joggers and a black v-neck t-shirt, reading a message on his mobile, I get dressed. I brush my teeth in the bathroom and change my sanitary towel, and when I'm ready, follow him through the house.

It's dark in the entrance hall and so quiet I could hear a pin drop. I glance out the windows on either side of the front doors. The sky is presidential blue with a glowing pink moon—or the sun.

BLAIRE
(PART ONE)

What is with this man and early mornings?

In the kitchen, I'm greeted with an arsenal of chocolate scattered across the dining table, a few newspapers and a pen for the crosswords.

"To keep you occupied," Charlie says, tapping a finger against the table where the newspapers are. He then pulls out a chair and as I sit, he pushes me against the table.

"You didn't have to go out of your way to buy me more chocolate." I feel at fault just looking at it all.

"I know," he whispers from behind, "but I want you happy and well."

I don't really know what to say about that, so I don't say anything at all.

He wanders into the kitchen's alcove cooking space and whips up some scrambled eggs on toast with warm maple syrup, and then we eat sitting opposite each other like we usually do. I'm a little on edge about his behavior/mood but he seems to be as happy as a clam at high water. He asks how I'm feeling this morning, if I've got a stomach ache. I tell him I'm fine, spreading butter across my toast. "I don't really get stomach aches."

"That's good then," he says, his eyes glittering with something as he looks at me from over his coffee cup, having a mouthful. "I think this time of the month suits you. You've got a nice pink tint to your cheeks."

Wrinkling my nose, I focus on my breakfast, striving to ignore his weird mood but it's very hard. This is a new side to Charlie I've not met before.

Once we've finished with breakfast, he clears up. I aim to get up from the table so I can go back to my room for a few more hours of sleep but he orders me to stay put. "I want you to sit with me again today while I work."

My face screws up with bafflement. "Why? Surely you don't want me-"

"Sit down, Blaire," he points at my chair, "I want you down here with me, not locked away in your room until lunch comes."

His tone of voice is clipped and demanding, so I do as I'm told right then, lower onto the chair without questioning him further.

After he's cleaned up the kitchen, he returns to the table with a coffee for us both and begins 'working'. Keeping a chary eye on him, I execute the crossword puzzles in the newspapers and read the headline stories. He makes over a dozen calls and leaves the kitchen for a few that I assume he doesn't want me prying in on, but I still learn a lot about him today. I'm not sneakily listening in on his conversations but I can't exactly avoid hearing what he says—he's sitting right next to me now. Charlie sells human army details—well, the army details are for hire—and he charges a fortune. For ten men to execute a job it's ten-million English pounds and whoever is buying doesn't bat an eyelid because there are no negotiations. I think Charlie even sells himself as a soldier but I'm not too sure. That part of the conversation isn't so clear cut because I zone out when he touches my hand, asking if I want another coffee.

"Yeah, sure." I forcefully smile at him as he begins across the kitchen, a question niggling away at me. "Charlie?" his name is out of my mouth before I can stop myself—I'm blaming everything on my period.

From the kitchen space, he faces me.

"Aren't you worried I'll hear something I shouldn't? You know, with you speaking in front of me?"

He laughs at me. "Who you gonna tell, Blaire?" He pours out the coffees with steady motions. "Maksim?"

"I wouldn't tell Maksim any of your business," I spit out, illogically affronted, "even if he asks me." And that's the utter truth. I know Maksim will ask about what's been going on with Charlie, but for some reason, deep down, I know I won't tell him about Charlie's business. It's not mine to tell.

Charlie is stunned by my snappy retort. He looks right at me, wonder flashing in his eyes. The atmosphere freezes between us. I don't break eye contact. Sitting tensely in my chair, I hold his executed stare.

Still watching me, he saunters back across the kitchen and puts down two cups on the table with heavy thuds. He grabs the back of my chair, towering over me, causing me to crane my head back so I can maintain eye contact. We silently watch each other like this, and for the first time ever, I don't feel like shying away from that powerful stare of his. I feel strong in standing my ground.

"You know," he half smiles at me, reaching out and gently pinching my chin, "I actually believe you."

I scoff at him, tugging out of his grasp. So he fucking should believe me. I'm not a liar.

We reach a turning point after I tell Charlie I won't speak of his business. I don't know what changes between us precisely but something does. I can feel it in the air in the coming days, the way he looks at me with more than desire in his eyes... the way he speaks to me now... There's no holding back on his behalf anymore—he's not once left the kitchen to have private conversations on his phone. And I find I'm more comfortable around him now than ever before. I want to open up to him on a level. Connect with him.

Over breakfast on Wednesday morning, I boldly confess, "I know you lead the Los Zetas."

He smirks at me, sprinkling crumbs of toast from his fingers onto his plate. "I gathered that when you told me you studied them."

"Oh." I glance away, feeling like I've betrayed him or something. "I have been meaning to tell you that I know. I just-"

"S'all right." He shrugs as if he doesn't much care. "I haven't exactly hidden the fact from you, have I? You've been listening in on my phone calls for days now."

"Yeah, I guess..." I don't feel bad for too long, partly because, as he just said, 's'all right', and partly because I have other things on my mind.

"Are your services for sale too?" I ask, thinning my eyes with curiosity. "Or do you just hire out your men?" He's not long gotten off the phone to someone and I'm almost certain he said he's available in a few months' time.

"No, people can hire my skills," he says between sipping his coffee. He explains that he charges double for himself to personally commit to a job.

"You're obviously good at what you do then?"

"Yeah. My mother ensured my skills by putting me into a secret military camp when I turned thirteen, so of course I'm good at what I do. Guns and physical combat is all I've ever known. I trained all my top ranked men, who now train their own details."

"What do you do though, exactly?" I want to imagine what he's like in action.

He tells me that he and his men sometimes commit terrorist attacks so the American government can blame other religious communities in pursuit of oil and gas. "But my men and I typically carry out search and rescue missions... political correctness—in our own fashion." He laughs when saying this.

"Political correctness?"

He nods. "We want Mexico returned to us—others out there don't realize how kind my people are, Blaire. We don't want Mexico overpowered by the puppeteer Americans. So, when the Americans try to implement New World Order rules in our country that ensure us no economic equality, we retaliate in ways we know will force them to back off, mostly fiddle with the stocks and shares. American cares about nothing more than money."

Cupping my chin, I soak up everything, falling further and further down the rabbit hole that is Charlie, a good image of him in my head wearing army gear. I even conjure up the courage to ask about his sister. She's been on my mind the past few days—I've no idea why—and with things being light and intense free between Charlie and me, I feel comfortable enough to ask.

"You don't have to tell me if you don't want to," I say softly.

"My, you're a curious little cat this morning." He smiles at me with indulgence. His phone buzzes on the table with an incoming call but he cancels it, pressing the 'end call' red button.

"I'm not prying," I say. "As I said, you don't have to tell me if you don't want to."

"No," he puts down his cup, "it's fine. I like talking to you." His face softens as he speaks of his sister, Gina, telling me that I remind him of her in so many ways. "But you're evidently a lot stronger and more perceptive than she was."

"What happened to her, Charlie?"

He gestures for the chocolate on the table so I pass it to him, and he cancels another call.

"My father was a conceited, greedy French pig," he says, peeling open a bar of Galaxy Caramel.

"Your father was French?" I give him a surprised look, widening my eyes.

"Yeah, but when he married my mother, he became an American citizen and took her name." He tells me that his mother was a Latin American who fell deeply in love with his father. They had nothing, so his father joined the American army, though he abandoned them to create the Los Zetas when he saw that if he had enough soldiers, he could take over Mexico. "The organization he created grew stronger and my father thirsted for money and the wrong kinda power."

I learn that his father started trafficking young girls to fund his men because back then the Los Zetas didn't have any connections with the American government. "I was the one who solidified a political connection and other ways to earn money. As you know, I won't deal in sexually exploiting children."

"Yeah," I whisper. "I've heard you mention that." I want to ask why he associates with men who do abuse young kids if he's so against it, but I hold my tongue for a while as he continues talking to me about his sister; telling me of a dark story.

"One evening, my father took my little sister and my mother to a fancy party in Columbia," he says, "but when they returned home, the only thing my parents brought back was a bag full of money."

So that's why he has issues with men abusing young girls—it's because of his sister.

My heart sinks. I have no idea why. I've never felt guilt for anyone before. No one but James and most of all, Maksim, and that's only when he tells me stories of how his parents abused him.

"I looked for Gina, but what I found wasn't her," Charlie says, focusing on the chocolate. "You know the rest."

"You chopped off your father's... you know..."

Side-glancing at me, he nods. "Then I cut out my mother's heart and burnt it."

I huff in agreement, crossing my arms. "I don't blame you for doing that. If anything, you should have made her death as slow and as painful as you made your father's."

He snaps his eyebrows together. "It doesn't bother you that I massacred my own parents?"

"No," I say honestly, confused as to why he'd think it would bother me. "Why would it bother me?"

We're quiet after I say this, the conversation lingering, and Charlie is just looking at me with some strange emotion in his eyes.

I'm glad it wasn't Maksim who ended Charlie's sister, but that doesn't make me feel any better about what I now know. I've never lost anyone before, so I can't comment on what it feels like. I only know what Maksim's told me, and that is simply this: "Loss is like living in a black hole that's too deep to climb out of. Only time can make it smaller."

"Things are different in Mexico now," Charlie says, breaking the silence, "none of my men deal in the underage sex trafficking industry—they know I'll cut off their nuts if they do."

"And what about girls who are of age? Why do you associate with men who force their prostitution?" There, I said it.

Charlie gives me a sympathetic look. "I can't save the world, Blaire-"

My chest aches as he says that, because he sounds like he really wishes he could.

"-As much as I'd like to, I'm still a criminal who has to take care of thousands of freed men, so I have to draw a line between what darkness I will and will not accept. That's just the way it is for people in my line of work. You know that." He continues talking about his men, how he pays for each of them to have a home, an education for their children, and hobbies for the wives while their husbands are away working. "Sometimes, we're gone for months, so I like to know that everyone back home is happy and looked after."

"That's really nice of you, Charlie," I say, getting lost in him. "Do you handle things on your own? Your organization, I mean."

BLAIRE
(PART ONE)

"No." He smirks at me, slyness glowing in his eyes. "I've got two brothers."

I raise my eyebrows, stunned and impressed at once. Imagine that, three of Charlie?

"Nicolas—or Nic, as everyone calls him—and Andres," he says.

"How old are you all?"

"Andres is twenty-five and Nic is thirty-two."

I arch a brow at him.

"I'm twenty-eight."

Twenty-eight... Wow.

I study Charlie's face now. He looks about twenty-eight, though his features are flawless—if you can overlook how wickedly intense and full of wisdom his eyes are, that is.

"What are your brothers like?" I say, blinking at him, still studying how handsome he is. I'm really interested in his brothers. I'm interested about how similar they all are.

A large, devious smile spreads across Charlie's face. "Andres is like me. Nic is an egotistical, smutty bastard, though loyal to the bone."

"Are they both Los Zetas too?"

"Yeah," he whispers, looking right at me. "They trained with the military from thirteen, as I did, and were more than ready for the world's war when I took over the Los Zetas."

For hours he tells me stories about how he and his brothers grew up in Mexico, how they were all happy until his father left the army, how even after he ended his parents at just seventeen, he is as close as ever with his siblings.

Night falls.

Charlie gets up to make dinner and I decide to help him: peel and cut the carrots while he seasons the meat. We continue talking, standing side by side in the cooking space. He asks a few questions about me and how I grew up with Maksim. "You can carry on from the feelings you were telling me about if you want to?"

I tell him that I can't talk about it. "I'm sorry, Charlie." But he's understanding. No, more than understanding. As if he never asked me anything at all, he returns to telling me more stories of his childhood.

I can't ever remember a time where I felt so relaxed in someone's company. I'm not sure why I feel so at ease with Charlie, but I do, and I'm glad that I do. Things are better this way.

BLAIRE
(PART ONE)

21

Four days of pure mental connection with Charlie, and my period ends.

I'm so fucking glad that I could die of relief. My desire for him and my overly curious mind are back to a more manageable state, and I'm me again.

We fall back into our routine of sparring at the crack of dawn and eating dinner at sunset, however, now, we have breakfast and lunch together. I pretty much spend all my time with Charlie. I have no idea how he ever makes time for 'work' because he's always with me. Yes, he conducts calls during the daytime—or he does now that I'm done asking questions—but that's where his 'work' seems to end. It's like his life revolves around me. Fuck knows why. I'll be gone in around six week's time.

I try not to think about that—*this* ending—because I've come to like living with Charlie. I've grown comfortable around him... used to him... I'm not sure how he's achieved making me feel like this, but he has, and I'm thankful. When he first took me from Maksim, my life was turned upside down. There wasn't a single moment of peace in my days. I was always anxious about him and what he might do to me. Now, I look forward to seeing him. I'm at peace all the time. I wake feeling refreshed and rested, and I spend my days in what I can only describe as contentment. There's no carnage with Charlie. There's no brutality. There's no walking on egg shells. There's just... *this*...

Even in the gym, like now, we're sparring and I'm not focusing on all my natural combatant senses. I don't feel the need to with him anymore, and he knows. He tells me that he knows and asks why. "What's changed?"

I shrug at him, my chest rising and falling with heavy pants because we've been going at it for over an hour straight.

"Here." He passes me a towel so I can wipe my sweaty face. I do. The soft material is cold because it's been lying over our bottles of water, and it smells like Charlie.

"Do you know what I reckon?" he says, helping me out of the ring by holding my hands.

Standing up to him, I say with a smirk, "What do you reckon, Charlie?" passing back the towel.

He drapes it over the ring ropes and puts an arm around my shoulders, pulling me into his side where he's warm and damp. He's never done this before. It makes my stomach... *flutter?*

"I reckon you like me now," he says in my ear, walking me toward the exit doors, "and not just a little bit."

"Well, sure I do." Tipping my neck back, I frown up at him—that's hardly rocket science.

As if he's accomplished a great goal, he grins, then he squeezes me against his side.

"It took long enough," he says, laughter lingering under his tone. "But you're worth the wait."

Now my stomach is going like crazy. Does he really mean that?

Reaching the doors, he pushes them open with his other hand and urges me onward with him. It's a little awkward to walk with him like this, under his arm, but I don't mind. I enjoy his affections.

"I've gotta go away this weekend for business," he says. "You wanner come with me?"

Today is the day I discover that he does things other than phone calls, it seems, and I will confess, I'm glad he's offered me the chance to go with him—I want to be around him all the time since that change happened between us. He's not at all like Maksim. He talks to me, spends time with me for things other than jobs, and he's never physically hurt me for being rude and/or insulting.

The fact that he's never hurt me has sealed the deal for me taking a liking to him. He could have conditioned me with brutality, but he hasn't. I think that was his initial plan, to beat me into being loyal to him, but somewhere along the way he's changed his mind. I don't understand why. I don't care to want to understand why. All I do understand is—all I do know is—I like Charlie, and I doubt anything could sway my mind from that now.

"If you want me to go with you," I say softly, as we reach the bottom of the staircase, "then sure."

"Don't you get tired of that?"

I turn out from under his arm and walk up a few steps, putting us at eye level.

"Of what?" I grip the banister rail, mentally holding his blue gaze.

"People pleasing," he says, folding his arms over his chest and leaning against the wall on one shoulder. "Don't you ever just wanner do what you want to do?"

I screw up my features.

"Well, for example," he stares at my mouth as I lick my lips, "don't you wanner eat what you fancy rather than what people tell you to eat? Don't you have taste preferences for food?"

I still don't get him, and he seems to know.

"Okay... how about this: do you wanner come with me this weekend or stay here?" He lifts a steady hand to cut me off from interrupting him. "It's a simple question. And don't ask what I want. I'm only interested in what you want."

"Well, yeah, I guess I'd like to come." I focus on my fingers stroking over the glossy banister outlay. "I've been stuck in this house for nearly two months."

"I know you have," he sounds almost sorry, reaches out and gives my other hand a squeeze, causing everything in me to tighten. "That's partly why I want you to come with me. I also need to get some food, so you can come shopping with me and tell me what *you* wanner eat. You can have whatever you want."

The penny drops and I can't help this horrid sinking feeling that washes over me.

He's only interested in what I want. I can have whatever I want. That's bullshit. Men like him don't put women before themselves.

I give Charlie this look, silently telling him that I know what he's up to—the emotional bonding. I haven't really noticed it much before today—I've been too focused on fancying him and connecting with him—but now, I know. I don't know how I've suddenly realized his agenda, but I know. Him spending time with me, telling me about his sister and his brothers, letting me listen in on his phone calls, the sweet gestures, the way he looks at me...

"What?" he says, pulling his eyebrows together.

"I know what you're doing, Charlie." I school my attention on my fingers again so I don't chicken out of telling him what I think. "I know you're trying to emotionally bond me to you."

He scoffs, but not out of anger. He sounds conquered. "I think we're both a bit past that now, don't you?"

I don't answer Charlie. Not even when he cocks his head to the side and says, "Are you ever gonna open up to me about how you feel?"

Turning on my heel, I go upstairs and spend the rest of the morning alone, a little pissed off but more confused if anything.

I try to focus on mentally preparing for London—it's been so long since I was in the city and it reminds me of Maksim in so many ways—but I can't focus. I can't stop deliberating over how Charlie responded to my opinion about the emotional bonding. What did he mean by, 'I think we're both a bit past that now, don't you?' I'm almost certain he means he's accomplished his goal with me but I just... I'm not sure. Or maybe I don't want to believe that's the answer.

I wrack my brain for hours, amid taking a shower and dressing, but I don't come up with a better explanation than his agenda, and that hurts in a way I've never felt before.

I consider asking him what he meant, hoping he'll tell me the truth, but when he comes into my room, dressed in jeans and a long sleeve red sweater, my thoughts blank.

"You've had a shower?" he says, opening the armoire. He's holding a duffle bag in one hand.

I nod at him, then climb into the middle of my bed and cross my legs, watching him with caution.

"We'll be gone for a few days," he's speaking to the armoire, "but just in case business drags, I'll pack you some extra clothes."

"What business do you have to sort out in London?"

He gathers around four days' worth of clothes for me and folds them in the duffle bag. "First, I need to see Maksim."

"Maksim?" I say, my eyes widening. "You-you want me to come with you while you see Maksim?"

"No," he glances back and laughs fondly at me. "You can stay at the hotel while I pay him a visit." He then says something about meeting up with his men but I'm not really paying attention. I'm too fucking nervous about running into Maksim while with Charlie. How uncomfortable will that be?

Strolling across my room, Charlie puts the bag on my bed. "Once everything is taken care of, we can go out for dinner if you want? Then we can go dancing or go see a movie..."

BLAIRE
(PART ONE)

I don't think about the whole 'dinner and dancing/movie' thing. I couldn't even if I wanted to.

"What is it, Blaire?" Holding my questioning gaze, Charlie gives me his full attention.

"Why haven't you seen... *him,* already?" I hide my hands in the sleeves of my sweater. "I thought you were meeting up with him a week after you took me?"

I remember Maksim saying on the night Charlie took me, 'I'll see you in a week or so, Charlie'.

"I've been enjoying my time with you," Charlie says. He sits next to me, causing me to sink into his side because the bed dips. He looks down at me, his eyes too blue. "I've not wanted to leave."

My chest does that odd squeezy thing as he says that. How strange that we both feel the same?

Or do we, really?

"Do you wanner come with me for the weekend?" he asks, his eyes flickering between mine.

I don't answer his question. I'm searching for the right words to pose my own niggling question at him.

"Blaire?" He glowers at me, and he seems on edge.

"What did you mean by, 'you think we're a bit past that now'?" There, I asked him, and I feel better for it.

There's a moment where we stare at each other. I'm beckoning him to just tell me the fucking truth. He's very deadpan.

"I've got feelings for you," he says in time, sounding really sincere. "What'd you think I meant?"

"Oh." I blink at him all cross-eyed, my cheeks blazing. I never expected him to say that. "I don't know what I thought you meant. I guess I just..." Shaking my head, I stop this conversation with, "Never mind."

"Oh'kay," he says, skeptical. He then touches a length of hair on my shoulder; runs his fingers down it. "Do you wanner come to London with me then?"

I shake my head minutely, dropping my gaze. I don't want to be anywhere near Maksim while living with Charlie. It's too weird. What if Maksim calls me over or something? Would I need to ask Charlie for permission?

Fuck, this is so uncomfortable.

"S'all right, Blaire." He gives my foot a squeeze, making my toes curl against his hand. "If you wanner stay here, then you can—I've told you many of times, you can do whatever you want to do while living with me."

Closing my eyes, I breathe out with relief. That was easier than I thought it would be.

"Do you want me to bring anything back for you?" he says softly. "Do you need anything?"

I try to focus on my needs but I can't—my head is swimming—so I shrug.

"All right," he whispers.

"Will you be okay going on your own?" I ask, a sickening feeling of worry coming over me. What if something happens to him and I'm not there to protect him?

He flashes me his most doting smile. "I'll be fine, Blaire. All my men will be around."

"At the hotel too?"

He nods.

That eases my worry a little, though I'm still nervous something might happen to him. Maybe I should just go with him? But what if we bump into Maksim?

I frown to myself, conflicted.

Though I'm clearly acting awkward, Charlie isn't. He gets up, leans over and kisses me on the head, sending some strange feelings through my chest.

"Here's the key for the white Range Rover." He pulls it out of his jeans pocket and puts it on the bed beside me. "There's money under the driver's seat, so if you need to go out for anything or if you wanner get a takeaway... There's a few takeaway menu's in the drawer under the coffee machine. To leave, the gate code is four sevens, two ones and nine."

I smile at him, mentally bidding him goodbye.

He leaves for two days—I count every minute.

BLAIRE
(PART ONE)

22

Day one alone: I wake feeling relatively normal, I guess because I'm subconsciously expecting breakfast to be made and waiting for me in the oven. It isn't of course, so I thoroughly beat a few eggs, season in salt and pepper, melted butter and double cream, and scramble them in a hot frying pan with a drizzle of olive oil. It feels peculiar to be cooking again, but over the days, it all comes back to me.

After pouring a coffee, I take my breakfast to the table where I find a military style laptop and a note. Holding my plate in one hand, I put down the coffee and lift the note to my eyes.

> **Thought I'd leave this out for you. The password is Decena-in-numbers, literally.**
> **X**

A warm feeling spreads through my chest at the sight of Charlie's note. Yes, it's brief, but it feels like he's here as I read it.

BLAIRE
(PART ONE)

I run my thumb over that X, wondering what it means. I soon learn it's not part of the password because I type it in and get a warning.

Parking up at the table under the warm sunshine beaming in through the windows, heating up my back, I eat my breakfast while reading over the note a few times, chewing slowly because I'm concentrating. He's left this out to keep me occupied, just like he did with the newspapers. I smile for so long that my cheeks ache, but then I roll my eyes. I've officially lost it—become a hormonal female statistic—and I suddenly feel like I've been too judgmental on women. I've always mocked their weakness when it comes to men, the whole 'deer in headlights' stare and stuttering over words... But now I get it. Even while I'm not actually that silly yet, I get it.

To take my mind off my own inanity, I fire up the laptop but end up spending my morning reading up on French/Spanish guys, of all things. I don't know where the need to research Charlie's culture has come from but I find it all very calming.

The French don't waste time, Google says when I do a more thorough search, while Spanish men apparently like to draw things out, soak up every moment. I laugh to myself, thinking that's what Charlie is like to a T. He's quick to force intimacy but then takes his time once he has a woman in a state of desire.

Next, I look up what a capital X on the end of a message means. I'm itching to know what it means.

It denotes a kiss, Google says.

A strange sensation moves through my body, like a sinking/fluttering sensation but it makes me feel happy.

He must know what an X means on the end of a message. He isn't thick.

Lunchtime comes, though I'm not hungry—I'm too hocked up on this weird fluttering sensation in my stomach—so I shut off the laptop, clean up my breakfast, and head for the gym to train.

A dark cloud comes over me in here. It's a lonely feeling, given I've always trained in here with Charlie. The space feels bigger and colder, and I jump every time I hear the slightest of sounds—like the drains in the walls clanging. I've never heard that in here before. It's so eerie.

I shower after working out, then I go downstairs and make myself something to eat for dinner, which isn't much—chicken and bacon pasta. The chicken doesn't taste half as good as when Charlie cooks it.

Stop thinking about him, I scold myself, but I can't. It's been a really odd day; odder than the first day I spent with Charlie. I've never been completely on my own before—I've always had my phone at least, in case Maksim needed to give me orders—but today... I don't know. I feel a bit lost and mentally white.

The sun setting on the horizon, I go outside and strive to center myself in meditating, reaching high above my head and putting my hands together to stretch out.

I wonder where Charlie is now... if he's safe.

I admonish myself again for thinking about him but it's no use. I can't meditate either. The longer I try, the more mentally swamped I become. For the first time in my life, my thoughts aren't flowing freely—they're just overflowing, every emotion I've ever felt for and against Charlie romping-

BLAIRE
(PART ONE)

Fierce protection over Maksim.

Anxiety when I first met Charlie.

Anxiety mixed with a dollop of fear when Charlie told me in Maksim's kitchen that he'd bought me.

Lust.

Frustration with Charlie's prying.

Enchantment.

Desire.

Now, I am sure I'm fond of him. I maybe even care about him. I find that the most disturbing thing because I'm not allowed to care about anyone other than...

Giving up in the garden, I go up to my room and take a cold shower, then I sink into bed.

I don't sleep much this night—I'm flooded with dirty dreams: Charlie's mouth all over my body, his hands exploring every corner of my soul—then it's another ferocious day full of routine.

Day two alone: I have breakfast where I'm again reading this stupid note, then I clean up the kitchen and venture into the gym. I feel really isolated in here, just like I did yesterday. I find myself wondering about the gym equipment, unsure of what kind of training I fancy. I start out on the treadmill but give up halfway through a session. I then wrap up my hands for the boxing bag, hopeful it'll stimulate my mind, but even that loses my interest. I stop for a moment, stand about in a conflicted manner. I then lift my fists in another attempt and hold them there under my chin but I'm just not into this.

BLAIRE
(PART ONE)

I skip lunch and have an even harder time at meditating, my thoughts scattering.

I feel very lost in my days, like I don't belong anywhere or something. It's this droning style of living, I think. I'm not used to it. It's driving me nuts.

At dinner time, because I'm sick of being in this house all by myself, I decide to go out and grab something from a fast food place. Probably McDonalds. I like McDonalds.

I pull on my jacket, swipe the car key from the bedside cabinet and jog down the staircase, outside to where the Range Rover is parked.

"You're her, aren't you?" a Spanish peppered voice says from behind. "Blaire Markov?"

Before I turn around, I pull my heavy gun out of my jacket pocket, hold it against my leg, and then I face her...

...She's extraordinarily beautiful, standing there under the burning orange sunset, in front of a beaten up old Mercedes. Wearing a thigh length red dress that hugs a curvaceous body—large breasts and coke bottle hips.

Remaining deadpan in my pose, I search her face to analyze what her deal is. Oval shaped with large, deep brown eyes and facade blushed cheeks. Her full lips are coated in something glossy and her dark, chocolate brown hair is pulled back so tight her eyes are elongated.

How did she get through the gates? Does she know the code?

She slowly comes up to me with a walk that would make men bow at her feet, swaying her hips, her black heels crunching against the driveway. The way she's looking at me... curious and damn right pissed off.

She's something to do with Charlie. I'm certain.

"You can't be her." Stopping a foot away, she stares me up and down with pure hatred, twisting her lips. "You're barely a woman and you're... you're not exactly pretty, are you? You're not even Latino."

Raising my eyebrows, I blink at her, stunned by her audacity to insult me. Definitely something to do with Charlie.

"Are you her or not?" she demands an answer, pointing a red-nailed finger at me.

"Yes, I'm Blaire," I say, keeping my tone level. "What do you want?"

"You're actually Russian?" Grimacing, she flashes gleaming white teeth. "He hates Russians..." she sounds like she's talking to herself, clarifying something. "I want to know why Charlie Decena would prefer *you!* to me."

"Huh?" Why would she think that?

"Yes." She swallows down what looks like a heave. "He told me earlier tonight."

He told her that he wants me over her? That's not right.

"I traveled five and a half thousand miles to see him because he's been gone for months now and he told me that he doesn't want me anymore." She scoffs with disgust, shaking her head. "It didn't take much to find out why."

She must be a jealous ex-girlfriend. *Great.*

"Look, I don't know what's going on between the two of you," I tuck my gun away, sure I don't need to use it on her, "but it's none of my business. If you've got beef with Charlie, call him."

BLAIRE
(PART ONE)

Turning on my heel, I try to walk away but toothpick fingers close around my wrist, urging me to stop.

"I'm not done talking," she hisses from behind. "I want to know what's going on with you two. Are you his girlfriend?"

"What?" I look back, screwing up my face, on the verge of laughing. "No. I'm not Charlie's girlfriend."

"Don't you fucking lie to me, little girl!" the anger in her voice... I can feel it coming off her in waves.

"Why ask me that question if you're not going to believe my answer?" I tug out of her pathetic grasp and face her properly. I really can't be dealing with this shit. "I'm not Charlie's girlfriend, and whether you believe that or not is your problem, not mine."

"If that is the case, then why is he at a gangster's party making a show of how much he likes you?"

My stomach rolls with nerves because I can't help thinking Maksim is at that party.

She gives me the once over again, revolted and livid at once. "How can a *girl!* like you—a filthy Russian—entertain a man like him?" She gets in my face now, putting us nose to nose, smelling sweet like strawberries. "That man is a sadist junkie, so how the fuck can you keep up with the pace?"

I grind my jaw, feeling an irrational need to defend Charlie. "Not that I have to explain myself to you," I walk into her, causing her to step back with caution, "but Charlie hasn't been sadistic toward me. I've no idea what the hell has happened between you two, but leave me out of it."

I turn to walk away again, but she says, "Ohhh, come on. You'll be telling me he's a tender puppy next.

Cuddles and kisses on the couch while you watch movies, is it?" She laughs out loud with clear sarcasm. "Do me a favor, little girl... I know that man like the back of my hand—I've been fucking him for two years!"

"Good for you," I say, feeling a pang of something in my stomach. "Now, if you don't mind, I have to go." I really, really want to hit her but know I shouldn't. I've never in my life used my physical abilities to hit a woman—not unless Maksim tells me to—and I'm not about to start now.

Using the key to unlock the car, I pull open the driver's door but notice she's writing a message on her phone, so I wait by the car, wondering what she's doing.

Her phone blows up with an incoming call, and as soon as she answers, I know who it is.

"You don't want me because of this Russian little girl?" she says in Spanish, shaking her pretty head at me. "What the fuck is wrong with you?"

I can hear Charlie yelling down the phone in Spanish and then she puts it on loud speaker, flashing me an evil smile.

"How fucking dare you go to my house and confront Blaire, you bitch!" he shouts so loud the speaker cracks. "When I get my hands on you, Celine, I'll knock the life outa you before putting a bullet in your fucking head! You hear me!?!"

"This is what Charlie is like," she says with obvious amusement, unveiling her agenda of putting him on loudspeaker. "He's not a very nice man."

He doesn't sound it at the moment, spitting out every curse word in his own language, but I know he's just lost his cool. I've seen every square angle of Charlie. I know he can be nice.

"Then what's your problem?" I go over to her. "If you think he's not a very nice man, why are you here?"

"Because he's mine, you little whore!" Her body literally shakes. I think she wants to hit me as I do her.

"Fuck off before I lose my patience with you," I say in an odd, tranquil tone. "This isn't anything to do with me, so why don't you go find him and sort it out?"

"Yeah, you know where I am, Celine," Charlie says down the phone in his own language, "come here and we'll have it out."

There's a long pause of silence between us all, the energy in the garden stark with fury.

"Does he strangle you to enhance an orgasm?" she says, as if to rile me, and Charlie is going nuts down the phone now. "Belt you so hard that you can't walk for days? Order you to remain in one place on your hands and knees until he says otherwise? He's fucked up like that, Blaire," she says my name with such abhorrence. "He derives pleasure from hurting women, and do you know why?"

My stomach twists with... I can't even explain.

"Celine, if you don't shut the fuck up...!" he yells in Spanish down the phone, "I'm gonna kill her—get my car," he yells at someone else, still speaking in Spanish. "You listening, Celine? If you're there when I get back, I'll fucking strangle you to death—how'd you like that, hm?"

"You know I won't mind, my love," she says with lust, tipping her head to me. "That's the difference between you and I, Blaire; I'll do whatever to keep him satisfied."

My cheeks are pale and I feel sick to my stomach with anger, barely containing myself. I don't give two shits about what Charlie fancies, but I don't want to stand here listening to some beautiful woman who's clearly in love with him, tell me about their sexual encounters.

In a low, deceivingly calm voice, I warn, "You've got two minutes to leave before I rip your head off."

She steps back instinctively, and I can see her heart must be racing with nerves.

"Yeah," I say, prowling toward her, "I'm not sure if you know me, but I reckon I can break your neck in three seconds, and it doesn't look like Charlie will give a shit now, does it?" I gesture at her phone, which is now silent. "Get in your car and leave, before you can't."

She stands there staring at me, I imagine questioning if I'm telling the truth.

Fuck this.

I grab for her long, sleek ponytail and drag her kicking and screaming to her car. There, I drop her on the graveled driveway, warning, "This is your last chance to go or I'll keep you here for when Charlie gets back."

She scrambles to her feet, dropping the mobile. She fumbles to pick it up and yanks open the driver's door; jumps into the driver's seat before struggling to put the key in the ignition.

I watch her to make sure she leaves, the uncontrolled way her hands are shaking. Even after three attempts she still hasn't got the key in the hole. I feel a little bad for her. She's obviously in love with Charlie and is just here fighting to get him back. I understand. He's a gorgeous man. Most women would kill for someone like him.

I lean into the car, snatch the key out of her bony hand and fire up the engine.

"Don't come back here, Celine," I say in her face, holding her watery brown gaze, "because I really don't want to hurt you."

"I love him," she whimpers, her lips wobbling, and a single tear drops down her cheek. "I just want him back—don't you understand that?"

There's a moment between us. I pity her, and I sigh to show that I do. I know she loves him.

"Sometimes we love what we shouldn't," I say, then I slam the door shut and walk back across the driveway, debating between the house and the Range Rover. I won't be able to endure food now—not after this—so I go back inside the house.

On autopilot, I make a cup of coffee, desperately trying to switch off mentally, but I soon realize coffee is a bad idea. I won't be able to sleep if I drink coffee now. So, I pour it away down the sink and take the laptop from the kitchen table up to bed; study into the small hours as a distraction. I try to put what happened out of my mind by focusing on Russia and what's going on in the news, and because I can't—that woman keeps popping into my head, the things she said, how random her arrival was—I search for a book that I love to read. It's working, my idea of a distraction. I manage to get lost in the story of a queen consumed with guilt, my eyes racing back and forth reading the novel on the glowing laptop screen.

"Does he strangle you to enhance an orgasm?"

BLAIRE
(PART ONE)

"Belt you so hard that you can't walk for days?"

I must've fallen asleep because the next thing I know, a hand pushes my hair back out of my face. On alert, I lean away from that hand, and when I look over the edge of my bed, culpable blue eyes smile at me.

"You're back?" I say to Charlie under my breath. Putting the laptop aside, I sit up on one elbow.

Charlie nods, crouched down beside me with his elbows on his knees, all gorgeous in jeans and a black round-neck t-shirt, his black hair a little longer and unruly. "Thought I'd come check you're still here."

"Of course I'd still be here." I rake my hair back over my head, squinting through the sunrise. I've been out for hours but it feels like I've had barely an hour's sleep. "Why have you come back early? I thought you were leaving for the entire weekend?"

His eyebrows shoot up. "After what happened, you wanner know why I've come back early?"

What happened... *"Does he strangle you to enhance an orgasm?"* I hate knowing this. It doesn't bother me that he obviously has sadist tendencies—it's not like I'm unfamiliar with men who are like this. I just hate the idea that I've met someone he's shared this with. It's the most fucked up, annoying emotion, bubbling under the surface. I don't get it.

"Don't worry about it, Charlie." I force a sleepy smile at him, endeavoring not to let this come between us. "Did... did everything go okay?" I want to know if he saw Maksim but I'm not quite sure how to ask.

"Like clockwork," Charlie says softly, winking at me, and then there's an odd moment between us.

Silence.

He's hesitating to tell me something, I can sense it.

"What's wrong?"

"What she said..." he studies my eyes, pausing again, "I would never do anything like that to you. You know that, don't you?"

A weird tightness forms across my chest.

"You don't have to explain yourself to me," I say, sounding oddly cold, "I'm not your girlfriend."

He sighs, tipping his head to me. "I just want you to know, Blaire, that's all." He sounds very sincere, like he really wants me to know this. "I knew she was in Europe but I never anticipated she'd come to my fucking house and confront you. I wouldn't have left you otherwise."

The phone calls... I remember him on the phone a while back, wanting to know who helped 'her' leave The Site.

Maybe her visit isn't so random. *Just have to take better note of what's going on around you, Blaire,* I tell myself.

"I thought you said you didn't have a girlfriend?" I say, wanting to know the facts. "I asked you and you said-"

"She's not my goddamn girlfriend," he seems illogically insulted. "I've fucked her a few times and that's it. She's always known the score."

"Perhaps you didn't make your relationship status with her clear enough." I scoff, lying back in bed, confused for why I even give a shit. Maybe it's because I'm tired; wired from the night's events.

Charlie gains height on his feet and sits on the edge of my bed, looking down on me. "Is this gonna cause a rift between us?"

I turn my head to him, glowering. "No. Why would it?"

He doesn't answer my question. He wants to know what she said to me before he called her back.

"Why did you call her back if you want nothing to do with her, Charlie?"

"She texted saying that she was with you—my guess because she knew I'd avoid her call otherwise, like the other thousand she's left on my phone over the last month. Obviously I'm gonna call back. I won't have my bullshit problems confront you.

"What'd she say to you, Blaire?"

Letting out a breath, I roll my eyes and then close them, feeling hidden in the darkness of my mind. "She seems to think we're together or something; asked why you'd want me over her. I put her straight but of course she didn't believe me. She's just bunny boiling." I open my eyes to look at him, to see his reaction as I ask, "How did she know I was here?"

"She must've overheard me talking about you tonight and because you weren't with me, assumed you were here at my house."

I huff. "Makes sense."

Twisting at the waist, he leans over me and presses a hand against the mattress at my side. "I don't want that woman, Blaire."

"What?" I scowl at him. "Why are you telling me that?"

"Because I don't want this to cause a problem between us," he says, giving me this hard, honest look. "I've no designs on that woman whatsoever, all right?"

My chest squeezes with relief. I don't know why I'm relieved, but I am.

I nod minutely.

"Good." He winks at me, and then we stare at each other for a while in connecting silence. I'm almost certain he wants to say more but doesn't. Just smiles at me, his eyes glittering with some emotion.

Kiss me... I mentally implore, gripping the sheets in my hands while my stomach clenches in sweet anticipation. I don't know where the abrupt urge has come from but I need him to kiss me.

He doesn't.

After a while of looking at me, he reaches up to touch my face for a split second, making my heart race, and then gets up to leave my room, quietly clicking my door shut.

BLAIRE
(PART ONE)

23

Morning welcomes sunshine in its irony. It's pouring in through the window, making my eyes sting as I blink myself awake.

My throat is sore like it is most mornings but I put the raw sensation down to needing a drink of water.

I get up out of bed and stretch out, moaning because it feels so good as my muscles unwind. Yesterday briefly flashes through my mind, reminding me of that irritating sentiment that I've put down to jealousy, but then I notice a few bags on the chair in the corner of my room. I wander over and rustle through them: shampoo and conditioner, cocoa butter moisturizer and a group of hair ties. I also notice the car key and the laptop are gone. I'm not really bothered about the car key, but I'd like to keep the laptop—I enjoy studying and reading. It helps take my mind off things when I can't meditate.

I search around my room for the laptop, under the bed and under the pillows, but it's definitely gone. Charlie must have taken it when he came back into my room last

BLAIRE
(PART ONE)

night with those bags. That's the only plausible explanation.

Giving up on searching, I strip out of my nightclothes and take a shower with my new products, giving my hair a good scrub. I then relish in moisturizing my skin, lathering the cream between both hands before spreading it all over my body. My legs are a bit bristly because I haven't visited a salon in two months.

I pause then, staring blankly at my freckly reflection in the steamed up bathroom mirror.

Two months... It's been two months since Charlie bought me. That means I have four weeks left until I go home.

My heart sinks as I think of this, so I distract myself by getting dressed and going downstairs to find Charlie, leaving my hair down so it can dry naturally.

There's a note in the kitchen by the stove.

Breakfast is in the oven.
X

Smiling to myself about that stupid X/kiss, I take out the plate using a towel and eat scrambled eggs on toast at the kitchen countertop. Charlie wanders in then, dressed in black joggers and trainers, nothing else, his powerful, tanned body contracting in muscles. He's on the phone like he usually is, saying something in Spanish about returning to Mexico soon; that he isn't coming home empty handed.

Our eyes align and he gives me this sly smile—it's sharp and savage because his hair is pulled back.

BLAIRE
(PART ONE)

My stomach fills with this weird fluttering stir and I'm almost sure I'm going to be sick, so I stop eating; put down my fork.

"Yeah, just over a month," he says, still smiling slyly as he comes up to me.

He stops beside me, leaning against the fridge on his shoulder. I can smell that he's just showered, the fresh, musky scent of his skin clouding my ozone.

Jesus... It's too early for this.

"Morning," he says in a chirpy manner, hanging up his call. He gives me the once over, leisurely gazing down my body. "You're up late. It's past ten."

"I've been sleeping in late," I whisper, trying to control the rage in my stomach.

"You all right?" he asks, gently tapping my arm. "After yesterday, I mean."

I feel that pang of jealousy again but will it away. "Of course I am."

He hums like he doesn't believe me, his eyes tapering as they glance between mine. "How was it being here on your own?"

I lift my shoulders. "Fine."

"Yeah?" He raises his eyebrows.

I nod.

"Did you miss me?" I think he's teasing me. He looks like he is, flicking up his eyebrows.

"Like a hole in the head," I say playfully, trying not to grin at him. Though he's been gone for a few days, and his—well, that woman showed up, nothing between us has changed. I like that. It cuts through all the bullshit.

Crossing my arms, I rest back against the countertop and ask again, "How was London?"

"Same shit. Different day." He shrugs, folding his arms over his hard, dusty chest. "You've used the cocoa butter I bought you then?"

I snap my eyebrows together. "How'd you know that?"

Dark desire flashes through his eyes, and he hunches at the neck to come closer. "Because I can smell it on you."

I glance away from him, reaching for my fork to busy myself.

"You ready to hit the gym?" he says. "Once you've eaten..."

"Actually, Charlie," I say between bites, "I was going to ask if I could go to a salon today." I tilt my head back so I can see his face. "I can drive myself but the car key is gone from my room."

"*You!* go to a salon?" he says, his expression lighting up with pure amusement. "Why can I not picture that in my head?"

"Believe me, I don't enjoy going," I say, having another mouthful of eggs.

I know the joke is on me, but this is a ritual Maksim has me indulge in—going to a salon once a month—for he says that he always wants me clean and hair free. I initially hated the idea but I'm used to it now, and as I'll be going home soon, I need to freshen up.

"You know, I think I remember you saying you've been to a salon before... when I first met you." Charlie is smirking at me, amusement still gleaming in his eyes. "What do you have done?"

"At the salon?"

He nods; looks like he's trying his best not to laugh.

"The usual," I say, giving him a funny look. I don't get why he finds this so funny—don't most girls go to a salon? "Can I go?"

"Course you can. I'll take you." He digs into his pocket and pulls out a set of car keys. "I just need to grab a t-shirt. When you've finished with your breakfast, meet me outside."

He leaves the kitchen then, glancing back at me when he's at the door, smirking.

I shake off his humorous mood and eat the rest of my eggs, then I jog upstairs to grab my leather jacket, double checking to see I've got my gun. I don't like going anywhere without it.

Outside, Charlie is resting against his Range Rover, wearing a black round-neck t-shirt over his black joggers. How is it that even in sportswear he looks exquisite?

No wonder that woman is going nuts over him.

"Do you wanner drive?" he asks, dangling the keys in the air.

I roll my hair around my hand so I can tie it back in a bun. "You can drive if you want. I don't know where we're going."

Tilting his head, he gives me this look.

"What?" I tug open the passenger door.

"You're not cutting your hair, are you?"

I instinctively touch my bun. "I'll get a trim, but I won't have it all cut off."

He nods, beginning for the driver's door. "Just keep it long."

I pull a puzzled face at him, wondering why on earth he cares about whether my hair is long or not.

BLAIRE
(PART ONE)

I jump into the car and pull on my seatbelt, breathing in that strong smell of lemon polish. It reminds me so much of when my car has been cleaned.

My car...

Home...

It all seems so far away now, like my old life could never have happened.

Charlie takes to the driver's seat, fires up the engine, and we drive into a local town, chatting about his stay in London. He says he didn't do anything but eat, work, and sleep. I don't buy that, not for a second. That woman said he was at a gangster's party.

"I thought you said you wanted to go out dancing... or whatever?"

He side-glances me. "Yeah, with you."

I blink at him all cross eyed. Why the fuck would he want to go dancing with me? The only knowledge I have of dancing is dancing someone around a boxing ring.

We're quiet when his phone pings with a text message, so I flick on the radio and take in the view of Tunbridge Wells—that's where Charlie's house is, just on the outskirts. It's very old English and lush with greenery, the streets lined with trees; the people seeming middle-class in their suits.

"Blaire," Charlie says my name, rounding a corner, "why don't you wear underwear?"

"What?" I burst out laughing to the point where my stomach aches. "Where'd that come from?"

We glance at each other, but then he looks ahead and pulls into a small car park. He stops in a double space and switches off the purring engine, facing me.

I try to avoid his question but he raises his eyebrows at me.

"I do wear underwear," I say between laughing, "just not the ones you want me to wear."

"What underwear do you wear then?" he says coolly, like this topic of conversation is okay and not awkward.

"I wear sports bras and comfortable pants. Not scraps of lace." I roll my eyes, not getting these weird questions he's asking today. First he's interested in my hair, and now my underwear? "I need some money, Charlie, so I can buy an appointment because I haven't-"

Grabbing my hand, he puts a few hundred in my palm. "The salon is over there." He nods forward. "I'll wait here for you—unless you want me to come in?" He's dying for me to say 'yes'. I can see the hilarity glowing in his eyes.

"Eh, no," I say with sarcasm, "I think I'm okay." I climb out of the car and wander across the car park, into the salon. It reeks of toxic peroxide, I notice as soon as I push open the heavy glass front door. I've always hated this smell.

"Good afternoon," a blonde greets me, giving me a curt look.

I drop all the cash on the white reception desk and tell her that I need a full body wax, a haircut, and my nails filed down.

"You must be Blaire?" she says, and that curt look is gone.

An iron shield comes up and I step back. "How do you know my name?"

She leans into her desk, her eyes streaming from left to right like she's reading something. "A Mr. Decena called about an hour ago and booked you an appointment." She peers up at me from whatever she's reading.

"Oh, yeah," I say, relaxing in my pose, "I'm Blaire."

"Of course. We have a room ready for you. Please follow me." Clicking her fingers, she assembles a team of beauticians to accommodate me, and I spend the next few hours trying not to scream my head off because my skin is on fire from being waxed.

The appointment costs me—no, Charlie, a tidy three-hundred and fifty pounds, but it's worth every penny. My hair is trimmed, my nails are filed down and no longer like cat claws, and I'm smooth to the touch.

When I get back in the car, dripping in smooth, dark red hair, Charlie is on the phone, talking about coming to a political agreement. He addresses his caller as, 'Congressman'. *The American Congressman?*

He gestures over his shoulder with his thumb, so I look in the back seats. There are a few shopping bags. I grab one, pull it open, and my expression drops when I see a whole bunch of lingerie sets—sports bras and normal pants.

The most natural smile spreads across my face as I peer over at Charlie. He winks at me, puts the car in gear, and we head back to the house. He's on the phone the entire time, and I learn it's definitely the American Congressman he's conferring with. I'm not that surprised—he has told me that he deals directly with the American government.

"Blaire, in the glove compartment-" Charlie says, pulling onto his driveway; he's still on the phone, "-there's a small red book. Can you get it out?"

BLAIRE
(PART ONE)

Leaning forward, I click open the glove compartment and rustle through a pile of papers but I can't find a red book.

Charlie leans over and tries to help me find it, saying something to his caller about 'payments'.

"There," he points out, so I grab the red leather book and give it to him.

As I sit back, my face brushes against his. I freeze, the sensation of my skin touching his surging right through me like a zap of electricity. He looks at me then, still leaning over. We're eye to eye and I can't breathe.

He isn't saying anything on the phone now. He's just staring at me, a million emotions flickering through his blue eyes.

I feel like I want to kiss him or something—I almost do, and I'm sure he's expecting me to because he moves closer to me.

In a fluster I break eye contact and try to get out of the car but Charlie snatches my arm. "Stay put."

"I was going-" I start to say, but he shakes his head at me.

Shutting my mouth, I sit back and wait patiently for Charlie to end his call, my toes curling in my trainers.

Why does he want me to wait?

Five minutes I remain in the car listening to Charlie cut his call short. He's still holding my arm hostage, and I'm sweating bullets.

He finally hangs up the phone and let's go of me, and my heart is roaring in my ears.

"Why do you do that, Blaire?" he says, shifting in his seat to face me.

I blink at him, silent—I just don't know what to tell him.

His eyes widen for an answer.

"Do what?" I say naively, and I'm surprised to hear my voice comes out normal.

"You know what... Don't be coy with me."

I stare down and pick at my nails, wishing the moment away. Why does he have to make a meal out of everything?

Charlie runs his fingers into my hair and tugs my head back, forcing me to look up at him.

"I'm sorry," I say in a sudden panic, thinking I'm in trouble, but then his lips are on mine. He pecks me with a brief, full kiss, making my head spin, and the panic I just felt... it evaporates. I melt into him and put my hands on his chest, moaning, wanting more, but he breaks away from me within seconds and smiles. It's a dark devil smile, sending another rush of hunger through me.

"Don't ever be frightened of me, Blaire," he says, still holding my head craned back so we're eye to eye. "I'd never hurt you."

We stare at each other like this, mere inches apart, his promise lingering in the air. I don't think he'd ever hurt me but he's so unpredictable sometimes that it makes me uneasy.

"All right?" he says, his blue eyes flickering back and forth between mine.

I nod, licking my lips. His dazzling gaze follows my tongue, his pupils dilating.

BLAIRE
(PART ONE)

"You like salmon, right?" he says, gently pushing my hair back over my shoulder to fix it in place. "Because I've got us some for dinner."

"Sure," I say breathlessly, wondering if I just imagined him kissing me.

He reaches into the back seats and grabs the bags. I try to take a few from him but he won't let me. "I've got them."

"I can manage a few bags, Char-"

He gives me this prompting look, cutting me off, so I climb out of the car, feeling in a bit of a daze.

He did just kiss me, right?

I go in pursuit of the house, my feet crunching against the stony driveway.

"If you don't," Charlie walks up beside me, "I can make something else."

I peer up at him. "If I don't, what?"

He laughs with sly amusement—yeah, he did just kiss me, and he knows exactly what he's accomplished by doing that.

"If you don't like salmon, Blaire."

"Oh. No, honestly, I like salmon."

His eyes journey down my body, blazing with zeal, and my heart speeds up. It's so intimate when he looks at me like that.

I pick up the pace to put some distance between us and enter the house, baffled to see the front doors are unlocked. Isn't he worried someone could break in?

Inside, the house smells like lemon and fish and... Is that boiled potatoes?

I head for the kitchen, struck to find the table is already laid, our plates set up side by side. On a huge silver platter, the fish is steaming in the middle of the table, surrounded by an assortment of dishes.

"Who cooked, Charlie?" I also notice a few fancy boxes of chocolate laid out beyond the food.

"I had someone cook for us because we were out." Wandering in past me, he puts the shopping bags down on the countertops and pulls open the fridge, grabs out a beer, and twists off the lid. He has a deep mouthful, sighing like he's been waiting for that all day long.

"A housekeeper?" I ask, rounding the table to look over everything.

"Something like that." Charlie crosses the kitchen space and puts his beer down on the table. "Here, let me get you outa your jacket." He helps me out of my jacket before shrugging out of his own, laying them both over the back of a chair.

I settle at the table. Charlie sits to my right, having another mouthful of beer.

"I got these for you," he says, and putting down his beer again, he leans over to grab the chocolate boxes. 'Dark Sugars' is written on the sides and the lids are clear, so I can see what's in them. One is full of colorful looking biscuits—or I think they're biscuits. The other houses small blocks of chocolate, which I can't wait to scoff. I've had a fancy for chocolate ever since he introduced me to it.

The third box... I'm not sure what that is. It doesn't look like chocolate.

"These are truffles," Charlie says, apparently reading my confusion. He opens the lid and shows me the contents. "I bought you an assortment of flavors because I didn't know what you'd like. These ones," he focuses on the colorful biscuits for a second, "are macaroons. And that," he shows me the last box, "is the best cocoa chocolate money can buy."

I don't really know what to say—I can't actually believe he's bought all this for me—so I just smile at him, my heart going a little faster. He smiles back, puts the boxes over there on the table behind the food, and reaches for my plate.

"Was it all right at the salon?" he asks, filling my plate up with fish, vegetables, and new potatoes.

"It was fine," I say softly. "I can do that, Charlie." I try to take my plate from him but it's too late—it is loaded with a healthy portion of everything.

He puts it down in front of me, squeezes a drizzle of lemon on my fish, then he dishes up his own dinner.

We're eating much earlier than we usually do. It's just past two thirty in the afternoon.

Maybe it's because he knows I'm going to pig out on sweets.

"Your hair looks pretty," Charlie says, glancing at me.
Pretty?

I give him a funny look, noticing there's something crafty glittering in his eyes. I'm not sure, but I feel like he's up to no good. It's the way he's acting today.

Picking up my cutlery, I dig into the salmon. It's lovely. It melts in my mouth and tastes tangy with lemon.

I eat in silence, paying acute attention to Charlie, trying to figure out if he's up to something or if I'm going mad.

"You okay?" he asks in time, chewing on a piece of salmon. "You're really quiet."

"I'm fine," I say, swallowing down my food.

Though he doesn't for a second believe me, he doesn't press on. He starts telling me about the phone call he had earlier in the car. "There's a gang crisis going on in North Mexico and the Congressman wants me to deal with it." He looks between me and his plate, speaking after every mouthful. "I need to send funds for more weapons so my men can get rid of the problem before it gets out of hand."

I don't say anything. I listen intently to him, opening my eyes in astonishment when he explains how he took over three cities, so this little issue isn't a problem.

He's achieved more than Maksim

"Have you ever been to Mexico, Blaire?" He has some more of his beer, and that crafty gleam in his eyes is still there—he's definitely up to no good.

"Yeah." I finish off my food and push against the empty plate.

"Did you like it there?"

I shrug. "It's hot."

"Yeah, it is hot." He laughs fondly, then he wants to know where in Mexico I've visited; if I'd ever live there. It's like *that* moment earlier in the car—the kiss—didn't happen.

"I'm not sure I'd be able to deal with the heat," I say, looking directly at him, studying him and his odd behavior. He's finished his food too, and now he's leaning against the table on one elbow, bestowing me his full attention.

"People climatise..." he says softly.

I gesture at my hair. "I'm a pale redhead—not sure I'm meant for the sun."

He gazes over my hair, utterly fixated. It's streaming down my back in sleek locks. I haven't tied it up since visiting the salon.

"If you had to, would you give it a try?"

"What?" I wipe my mouth clean with a napkin and drop it on my empty plate.

"Try living in Mexico."

"Oh. Well, sure, if I had to—I doubt Maksim would ever live in Mexico though." I laugh awkwardly, not sure where he's going with this.

He reaches for my hair and strokes down a length, making my scalp tickle. I don't really know what to say again, so I remain quiet, clasping my hands together in my lap.

"I reckon you'd like it in Mexico," he says, lifting my hair to his nose. "Where I live, it's a big estate boarded by a village with only the trusted..." he goes right into saying what sort of people live there; how many people live there, which sounds like thousands. "It's completely secluded from the world—you can't even see it on Google maps."

"Does that woman live there too?" I ask, holding my breath for his answer.

"What woman?" he says, still playing with my hair.

"Celine?"

I nod a couple of times.

"Not anymore she doesn't." He stares right at me then, into my eyes with raw sincerity. "You don't have to be curious about her, Blaire. She's not like you. She's nothing special. Mexico is flooded in women like her."

I break eye contact with him, feeling my cheeks heating up. I've no idea why I even wanted to know if she lives near him. It's not my business.

"What sort of things do you enjoy?" he says, going in a different direction of conversation, "other than sports, I mean. I really wanner know."

"Other than sports *and* food, you mean," I say, making him laugh. It seems to lighten the mood between us.

"Yeah, other than sports *and* food," he teases, winking at me.

I tell him about my silly desire to travel to strange places, that I like being around normal people. "I know it's weird, but things are always so dark and intense with... Maksim," I gulp out his name, "so I guess I just like being around the ordinary every now and again."

"That's not weird. It makes sense."

"You think?" I ask, genuinely interested in his opinion.

He nods, completely absorbed in me. "We all have our own ways of escaping life as it is."

"Yes, we do." I glance down, then back up at him. "I'm not allowed to visit strange places anymore though. You know, since Maksim said-"

"I know what he said." Charlie pulls the car keys from his pocket and puts them down in front of me on the table. "You can do whatever you want with me. If you wanner go out, go out. I won't stop you."

I really believe him, and in this moment, I don't think I've ever felt closer to him.

"What's it like where you live?" I say.

BLAIRE
(PART ONE)

"There's no bloodshed, Blaire—or we try to make sure there isn't," Charlie's eyes glisten with possibilities as he says that. "We all live peacefully and spend as much time together as possible, having barbeques... celebrating each other's birthdays... that kinda thing." He talks about this over a few hours, while we dig into the chocolate he bought me, and I don't know why, but I feel like he's trying to sell living in Mexico to me.

BLAIRE
(PART ONE)

24

I wake early the next morning to a dream I'm not sure doesn't disturb me.

I bolt upright in bed, diamonds of sweat dripping down my face and chest. The moon is glowing low in the curtaining black sky, set between a collection of dazzling silver stars.

Is it morning yet?

The dream... *Fuck...* Charlie broke my virginity without permission from Maksim, and I didn't stop him—didn't even try!

I grip my throat, recalling every moment, every phantom image of Charlie's muscular body rippling against mine. It didn't hurt when he thrust inside me, stretching me open. It didn't hurt when he fucked me with gentle rhythm, whispering sweet nothings in my ear, kneading my body with his large hands. I came so hard that I actually had an orgasm—that's what has woken me up.

I feel between my legs, sliding my fingers over my soft folds. I'm warm and damp but there is no blood when I look at my fingers. It was definitely a dream I just had.

Why am I wishing it was real? If Charlie ruined me, Maksim wouldn't want me anymore... but then again, Maksim would put a bullet in my head and it will all have been for nothing.

I scoff, rationally disgusted with myself. Why the fuck am I thinking about this shit—betraying Maksim's orders? What's happening to me?

Putting my face in my hands, I take a moment to adjust to the real world.

I have to stop this, what's going on with Charlie, but how? How can I stop myself from wanting something when I'm around it twenty-four seven?

I wish I came with an off switch. I've never mulled over so many things in all my life, and I've certainly never remembered my dreams.

Climbing out of bed, I get dressed and brush my teeth, then I head straight for the gym to relieve some of this tension/confusion inside me before Charlie gets up.

Like hell is that going to happen—someone *up there* is fucking with me.

Charlie is already on the treadmill in the gym. I cannot resist watching him from the doorway. I hold the frame, tipping my head. His body is exquisite, tanned and broad, dusted in hair in all the right places. I can see everything I want to see because he's only wearing gray shorts and trainers, his back muscles bunching with every step he takes. His black hair is damp and curling around his neck and face, making him look like a savage, handsome brute.

The orgasm I just had is all too real.

"What you doing, standing in the doorway?" he asks, grabbing a towel to dry his sweaty face.

"Watching you," I say softly and without shame, then I wander over to him. "You're up early. It's not even four yet."

He grins, his blue eyes dancing with amusement. "Got a lot of tension in me that needs releasing, hence no sleep and working my ass off in here."

I smirk at him, crossing my arms. "A lot of tension, huh?"

"You bet." He sounds like he wants to laugh but doesn't. He's as cool as ever.

While he finishes off his session on the treadmill, I lean back against the wall beside him so we can look at each other.

"Why you up so early?" he says, giving me a curious stare. "You don't usually roll out of bed until at least six unless I wake you up."

My cheeks flush.

"Couldn't sleep," I say awkwardly, uncrossing and crossing my arms.

"Hm..." he hums like he knows, his eyes thinning at me.

I glance away from him, down at his phone on the floor beside the treadmill. It's flashing with a text message and though I'm not one to pry, I can't help reading what the message says.

- Just fuck the redhead with or without permission. She'll thank you for it later. -

Crouching down, I pick up his phone and double check what it says. My eyes haven't deceived me. Someone called Rico sent him that.

"Blaire?" Pressing a button, Charlie rolls back off the treadmill. "What's wrong?"

I read the message once more, growing angry.

"You've been talking about me?" I look up at him, throwing wolfish glares.

"What?" He snaps his eyebrows together, drapes the towel over his shoulder, and tries to take his phone.

I don't give it to him.

"Just fuck the redhead with or without permission," I say, showing him the message. "She'll thank you for it later."

Charlie's face goes flat. "That's not what it looks like."

"No?" I raise my eyebrows. "Well, it sort of looks like you've been telling your 'friend' that I won't fuck you, and it sort of seems like you're bothered."

"No." He grinds his jaw. "If you read the rest of the messages, you'll see how the conversation started. Rumors are flying around that I've got a redhead living with me, and before people started assuming the worst of you—which they will when Celine can talk again—I told Rico that it's not like that."

"Like what?" my voice comes out cold and hard.

"That you're not some piece of ass I'm hooking up with to pass the time while I'm here."

"I don't believe you," I say, my anger bubbling on the surface.

He gestures at the phone. "Read the messages then."

I can't. I'm nervous I'll see something I won't be able to erase from my memory.

"I don't need to read them." I step up to Charlie. "Your friend's response is all I need. Why would he say that?"

"Give me my phone, Blaire." He holds out a hand, and I have no idea where it comes from, but I fling his phone at the wall, shattering the glass screen.

"Fuck you." I narrow a finger at him, looking right up into his eyes with pure wrath. "That's the last time I trust your word." Turning my back on him, I storm toward the gym exit.

"Blaire!" he yells my name so loud I feel it shake the atmosphere. "Come back here, right now!"

I don't listen to him. I go up to my room and grab my jacket, then I jog back down the stairs, heading for the front door.

Before I even grab the handle, Charlie is in front of me. "Where are you going?" he says, blocking my way to the door.

"Out," I snap, avoiding his eyes. "Move, Charlie."

"You haven't even had breakfast."

"I'll get something while I'm out."

"You don't have any money."

I defiantly meet his blue stare. "Give me some money then."

His temples tick. "You're not going out." He walks into me, hunching at the neck to look at me. "We're not done here."

"You said I can go out if I want to. You said you won't stop me."

"Not like this, Blaire."

I try to sidestep him but he mirrors my movements.

"Charlie, get out of the way," my tone is low but violent, "or I'll move you myself."

Grabbing the collar of my jacket, he throws me back against a wall, causing me to gasp on impact.

"If you didn't just smash up my phone you'd see that I wasn't mocking you," he says harshly in my face, making me feel claustrophobic.

I slap him so hard that his head turns, using the full force of my body.

Wallop!

"What the fuck!" He lets me go then, his entire body contracting with anger. His right cheek is red and I imagine it's throbbing. "Don't you dare slap me," he warns, his nostrils flaring. "I've let you get away with too much but if you slap me again..."

I huff at him, not in the slightest bit worried about his warning. I'm not scared of him.

I slip past him but he catches my wrist, hauls me around and into his chest. Thrusting up my knee, I try to hit him in the bollocks but he anticipates my move, blocking it with his thigh.

"Let me go!" I scream, pushing against his chest.

"What the fuck is wrong with you?" he says, catching my free hand. He then wraps both his arms around my body and imprisons me, my face in his chest. "Whether I said something about you or not is irrelevant—you're mine! I've paid a fucking fortune for you!"

My heart twists and crumbles.

Betrayal. All I feel right now is betrayal for falling for him... trusting him... caring about him...

I'm so livid that I could rip his head off.

Yanking out of his hold with sheer force, I slap him again, harder this time.

WALLOP!

"Is that how you see me?" I say, clenching my fist even though my palm is pulsing with pain. "As something you bought yourself? Is that why you're slagging me off to your friend?"

"No..." he says, breathing heavily, striving to control his rage. "I didn't mean to say it like that."

"Ohhh, of course you did," I hiss through gritted teeth. "I bet you're regretting the deal you made with me too, aren't you? Because if you didn't give me 'your word'," I air quote this in a sarcastic manner, "you'd be able to sodomize me whenever you want, until your thirst is quenched."

His eyes burst into flames, and then he's yelling at me, "I've not touched you since that night! Not unless you've wanted me to!"

"And what? Now you're angry because I won't let you fuck me?"

The veins in his neck throb.

"Why don't you go out and find someone else to fuck!" I scream so hard that the veins under my eyes pop. "Stop talking me under your spell and find someone else, like that fucking woman Celine!" I go into a full blown screaming rage, and I end up slapping him again. I've no idea what the hell has gotten into me.

What he just said hurts. *You're mine! I've paid a fucking fortune for you!*

He doesn't stop me from slapping him, which surprises me, given his warning. He's just looking at me, his left eye red from my blows.

BLAIRE
(PART ONE)

I stop going wild eventually, panting like a feral lioness boiling with fury.

"Are you done?" he says, his voice deceptively soft.

My hands shake to punch him.

"Stop being a little bitch and listen to me, Blaire." He leans into my face, his harsh breaths burning my cheeks. "I didn't say anything bad about you. Rico messaged asking, 'who's the redhead', and I told him you're a friend, that it's not like that. I don't want people thinking you're some whore." Though he's trying to calm me down, I know he's fuming. I can see it in his eyes. "No one but you, me, and Maksim, knows I paid for you."

I don't say anything. I'm too agitated to speak, wondering why I even care if he's speaking about me behind my back. I shouldn't care—I don't have the mentality to care about such bullshit—but I do.

Blood pulsing in my ears, we stare at each other in a power standoff, the atmosphere between us on fire, and I can't even explain how this happens, but we pounce at each other and kiss so hard that all I can taste is blood. I'm not sure whose blood it is but it's thick and metallic. It's heady.

I push my fingers into Charlie's damp hair and cling to him, standing on my tippy toes. I taste his tongue with hungry licks, how supple and wet it is... how salty his skin is... Charlie's holding my small face in both his hands, devouring me, moaning so hard that his voice vibrates in my body.

I'm so mad with emotions that all I want to do is take off my clothes, and his, and make my dream come true—I want to fuck him until my brains fall out—but I know I can't. I hate that I can't.

"I would never, ever badmouth you," he says between kisses. "You have to believe me, or all this means nothing."

"I do believe you." I bind my arms around his neck to pull him closer. "I'm sorry."

We stop kissing but only so Charlie can turn me around and hold me, my back to his front. He's caging my arms to my chest in one of his, and I'm panting so hard trying to catch a breath.

"I've wanted you since the moment I laid eyes on you," he whispers in my ear from behind, "but I won't ever take you again without *your* full permission." He's kissing my neck now, making me tingle all over. "I respect you too much for that."

My eyes are unfocused and my head is swimming, every nerve ending in my body buzzing.

"I want you," I say in a foreign voice, and I'm not lying. "I'm sorry for going crazy... I'm sorry I've wasted so much time denying-"

"Shhh," he whispers, stroking over my fingers in my chest with his thumb. "S'all right."

He slips into the front of my trousers with his free hand, still embracing me in his other arm. My ass tightens with nerves as he fingers his way into my pants, the elastic of my trousers pressing his dusty arm into my pelvis. It enhances my arousal for him; makes me throb with zest.

I can't believe I'm letting this happen, and after how hard I fought...

I don't feel like myself anymore.

Charlie scissors my throbbing clit and holds me with callous fingers, his huge hand covering my sex. I whine out loud, the feeling of skin against skin sending me into a lust fallen meltdown.

"He doesn't make you feel like this, does he?" Charlie massages me then, teasing my swollen clit. Around and around he makes my body tingle. "He doesn't make you feel good."

He's right. Maksim doesn't make me feel this good.

"No..." I breathe out.

One more kiss to the neck and I cave at the knees, my head rushing with endorphins. Charlie holds me up with his arm still wrapped around my chest.

"I've got you," he says softly, raining kisses down the beating vein in my neck.

I let my head fall back against his hard chest, my eyes rolling.

He changes motion, rubs me gently in a different rhythm. "I'll always make you feel good, Blaire. I promise."

"Charlie," I sob his name, my toes fisting in my trainers as his motions become harder and faster, more demanding.

He slows down when my leg starts to shake. I can't believe how quickly he can make me cum. Is this normal?

Sneaking through my damp folds, he dips the tip of his fingers in my virgin entrance. I try to close my legs to stop him but he whispers, "I'm not gonna break your virginity. Trust me."

I do trust him—I've trusted him for weeks now.

I open my legs for him, standing on tippy toes again. He relentlessly flicks my clit with his thumb, making me jerk forward in his arm, while he torments me from the inside. He's not deep enough to spoil my innocence.

"I do trust you," I say in a voice so lost to me, closing my eyes.

Carefully pulling his finger out of me, he smothers my clit in my own succulent arousal. It's hedonistic and wet and...

"Fuck..." I whimper, digging my nails into his arm over my chest, arching forward.

The more he kneads me, the quicker the build climbs. It's an all new high. My left leg is shaking uncontrollably. I have no idea why my leg does this when I cum, or when I'm about to cum, but it does, and I cannot stop it. It's a tremor in my body.

"Relax," he says softly, rubbing his smooth cheek against mine so he can speak in my ear. "Just relax, baby."

"I can't," I whimper, tightening my face. "I just..." Turning my head to the side, I kiss him with hope that I can focus on something other than what I'm enduring, but I can't.

The kiss turns me inside out.

"Ohhh!" I whine, trembling all over.

I'm pulsing so hard... cumming so hard... It's like every sensation in my body is being sucked into one place, then radiating outward...

...He's never made me orgasm like this before. He's never made me feel so mad and wanted and hot all at once.

He wrings me dry, and when he finally stops rub-fucking me, I'm absolutely wasted, my heart hammering in my chest. I let my head fall forward, trying to catch a breath.

"Charlie..." I pant, holding his arm with my nails. "Charlie, I... We..."

"Shhh..." he takes his hand out of my trousers and I hear him sucking his fingers. "Kick off your trainers so I can take your trousers off."

I do. My legs are wobbly like jelly but I toe the backs of my trainers and kick them off one by one. I manage to say his name again, and what I'm feeling like inside—I have to tell him. "This is so wrong. This shouldn't be-"

"Hush, baby." He hides his face in the back of my hair, holding me tighter in his arm in an effort to cuddle me or something. "Everything that's wrong in the world always feels right."

BLAIRE
(PART ONE)

25

Life with Charlie turns into a bit of a lusty blur after my outburst. He's twisting my mind—it's like a battle field—and I'm letting him. I don't even think about Maksim anymore. I just want Charlie, whether it's for a fight or for an orgasm or for company—most of all his company.

He makes me cum more times than I can count—in the boxing ring, on the kitchen table, on the staircase when he catches me coming down one morning—and I never stop him. I couldn't even if I wanted to. I'm lost to myself—lost in him.

He kisses me down there like a starving man, sucking my folds and kissing my bud with gentle pecks, turning me on so badly that my leg vibrates, until I fall apart, begging... sobbing with wild desire...

I suck his cock at least three times a day because I want to. I crave the taste of him. Revel in having him under my power for a time. I need to please him as he does me, to show him how much I desire him because I can't say the words.

BLAIRE
(PART ONE)

He never gets aggressive with me or loses control like he did before. He never forces himself down my throat and makes me gag as he did when I first took him in my mouth. Sometimes, he doesn't even let me finish him off. He's in too much of a hurry to satisfy me, and always with his mouth.

I'm falling deeper and deeper down his rabbit hole with every day that passes; emotionally spiraling out of control when he first cuddles me.

We're sitting at the dining table, having just eaten an early breakfast. He's staring at me for a while—I can sense it—until he tries to pull me onto his lap. I'm so caught off guard because I'm absorbed in doing a crossword that I actually ask, "What are you doing?" stopping him with an uplifted hand.

Grinning, and ignoring my warning stare, he pinches the pen out of my hand and flings it on the table. He then grabs my hips and effortlessly lifts me up over his lap so we're face to face, my legs dangling on either side of his waist. His hard cock is pressed against my sex, stirring my arousal, and I can't help letting out a heavy moan.

His pupils expand when I moan like that, the blueness turning black with ardor.

We look right at each other, as I put my hands on his tough chest to control the rage within me. He reaches over my shoulder to let out my hair; breathes in the smell as it falls around my body like a dark red cape.

"I want you to always wear your hair down," he says. Tipping his head, he gazes at me with stark concentration. "Unless we're in the ring sparring."

Swallowing past the tightness in my throat, I nod. He leans down to kiss my mouth then with a raspy groan, taking me in a dark, ardent kiss.

I watch him, hypnotized by the blue-blackness in his eyes.

The sun rising behind us, the kitchen is burning in orange rays, making this moment that much more beautiful. Now, every moment with him is beautiful to me.

Charlie cups my face, covering my cheeks in his large, callous hands. He massages his tongue across mine, slowly, hungrily, and sucks the tilt, making my stomach whirl in sensations. He then runs his fingers into my hair to wrap his arms around me and holds me to him, body to body.

I break away from our kiss because I have a sudden need to huddle in his chest; to rest my head under his chin, so I do. I shut my eyes and exhale a sigh of contentment. I'm not sure why but in this moment, I feel... whole. Safe and whole. I don't ever want to leave him. Whenever I think about going home, it brings me to the verge of tears.

He strokes up and down my back for a while in silence, and I'm sinking into him—like I used to sink into Maksim—listening to his heart beating at a steady pace. Breathing in his scent.

I've never felt, cherished? before, if I can even use that word, but I do when Charlie holds me like this. It tells me that this isn't just sexual. He wouldn't waste time cuddling me if it was.

"Blaire," he whispers after a while, "have you given living in Mexico a second thought?"

He's asked me this a few times now, though in a less obvious manner.

Lifting my eyes to his, I say, "Do you know something I don't?"

"What'd you mean?" He stares at me as if I'm the only person in the world, his eyes glued to mine.

"Well..." I tuck a length of hair behind my ear, "you keep asking me about Mexico. Is Maksim moving there or something?" The thought has crossed my mind more than once but I've never said anything up until now. "Did he tell you when you visited him?"

Charlie doesn't answer my question—he doesn't even attempt to—he just gives me this look that's filled with zealous obsession.

I know he wants something from me—I can feel the sexual energy coming off him in waves—so I give it to him, and with pleasure.

Crawling back off his lap, I get down on my knees so I can satisfy him, crouching between his legs. I reach for the waist of his joggers but he stops me.

"No, baby," he husks out, brushing my hair back out of my face. "I don't want that."

I gaze up at him from between his legs, pleading with my eyes for him to elaborate because I don't have the courage to ask, 'what do you want then?'

Gripping my forearm, Charlie guides me to my feet and tells me to take off my trainers. I do, and I also peel off my socks. He tugs down my sports trousers and pants with one hand, his eyes with mine the entire time.

"You're so pretty," he whispers. Pulling me forward with still holding my arm, he makes me straddle him. He feels so masculine under me, like a fortress of man, and I feel so vulnerable.

"I could stare at you all, day, long." Inclining forward, he kisses my lips once. "I can't imagine a day without seeing you anymore."

My stomach knots. I'm still not used to *this,* his sexual attention or the way he freely confesses what he's thinking.

Shifting me on his lap, he pulls down the waist of his joggers, freeing his hard cock.

"Charlie?" I say, worried. He's never done this before.

"Don't be scared." He grips the small of my back and pulls me closer, putting us chest to chest, squashing my breasts.

I stare right at him, at the lust burning in his eyes, my lungs rising and falling with harsh intakes of breath.

"I'm not gonna fuck you," he whispers, then he arches his hips and touches my sex with his cock, causing heat to sprint through my body.

I put my hands on his shoulders, desperately trying to keep it together. I've felt nothing like this before—sex against sex. It's so intimate.

"Rub your pussy against my cock until you cum," he says, his eyes hooded, dazzling with lust.

I look away from him, my cheeks flushing red. I've heard men say things like that many times before, but never to me. It's so... personal and lewd.

He knows I'm embarrassed, and I'm glad that he doesn't pressure me with words. He grips my hips in both hands and tells me to kiss him, so I do. I close my eyes and kiss him hungrily, though I find his tongue and mouth are more demanding than mine. He devours me with powerful, leisured licks, breaking away the barrier that is my anxiety. The maple syrup we just had on our breakfast tastes sweet and delicious on Charlie.

"Do you trust me?" he whispers in my mouth.

I open my heavy eyes, squeezing his hard shoulders with my nails.

"Do you?" he says again, staring right through my soul. "I wanner know that you do, Blaire."

I nod, consumed by that fixated expression on his face.

He forces me to grind against him, sliding me up and down his vein swollen cock.

My stomach rolls with sensations.

"That's it," he groans, closing his eyes. He curls my hips back and forth with his, making me wave harder and faster. My flesh wet, I move up and down him with slick ease, sobbing when my inflamed clit touches him.

I'm too shaky to just hold his shoulders, so I tie my arms around his neck and cling to him, deepening the kiss as I tilt my head, my heart rate hitting a dangerous speed. He blinks at me, and we watch each other like this with desperate yearning, Charlie's eyes flickering between mine.

"So beautiful..." he whispers, taking my mouth again. He places one hand on the curve of my back and forces me to arch into him, ensuring my clit is constantly massaged by his cock.

I whimper his name, a familiar pressure brewing low in my stomach.

"Fuck, I want you, Blaire..." he moans, the sound so loud it vibrates through us.

My leg goes into a wild spasm, his words slaying me open. I want him too.

I can't kiss him anymore—it's too intense—so I press my forehead against his, putting us eye to eye, rub-fucking him with all I have.

"Charlie..." I sob his name. I'm almost there but I just can't.

"Don't think, baby." He blinks in a haze, grabbing my outer thigh to calm my shaking. "Just don't think. Close your eyes."

I do close my eyes, and I let my thoughts escape me like a river running free. It hits me then, like lightning. The head of Charlie's cock slides through my folds, over my bud, and I cry out so hard that my throat hurts, ecstasy bursting out of me.

Charlie finds his peak with me, groaning as if he's in pain, heat searing off his body. Warm, thick liquid inundates my sex, his cock still stimulating my clit. I cum again—or I think I cum again. I'm not sure I ever stopped. It's a never ending spiral of sensations starting at my center and radiating supernova.

He binds his arms around me, crushing me to his muscular body, and when I can't take anymore, I fall wilted, gasping for my life, my limbs lifeless and aching beyond words.

I'm panting. The smells that consume me... hot, sweaty, sensual smells.

My head is spinning.

Charlie relaxes with me. He holds me in his arms, putting my head in the crook of his damp neck so he can kiss my forehead.

BLAIRE
(PART ONE)

I come down slowly and in stages, and then what just happened really starts to sink in.

This is the part that embarrasses me most, the aftermath of intimacy. I get so lost in the moment that I forget what I've said... how I've looked at him...

Charlie isn't embarrassed one bit—he never is. Careful not to crush me again, he stands and puts me down on his chair, tucking his cock back in his joggers. I pull my knees up to my chest, trying to hide my innocent value. I block out what happens next because it's too personal—how he cleans me up with soft tissue paper and puts me back together by dressing me.

Our initial plan today was to spar in the gym after breakfast but I'm not in the right zone to play fight with Charlie. I'm stuck in a strange, sensual place. I have been since I let go of myself.

Charlie crouches down in front of me, elbows on his knees, and he just looks at me in utter silence. I can't hold his gaze—he looks like he's ready for round two. I reach for a glass of orange juice on the table to wet my dry throat, then I ask, "Do you mind if I go up to my room for a while?"

A soft smile, then he rises and pecks me on the mouth, making my body crave him all over again.

"No, baby," he says softly, straightening, "course I don't mind."

It's like this all the time now. When we spar in the gym, I can't even begin to explain how erotic it is. Imagine fancying someone on this level who you're almost sure fancies you back, and time is of the essence, so you're both trying to make every moment count...

BLAIRE
(PART ONE)

...Charlie and me never talk about how long we have left together. We just do. We spend every second of every day together. Eventually, he even ends up sleeping in my bed with me.

The first night is when I fall asleep at the dining table. He's cleaning up the dishes after dinner and I rest my head on the table in my crossed arms, having had so many orgasms that my body is exhausted with them. I stir in Charlie's arms as he's carrying me up the stairs, into my bedroom. In the darkness, he pulls back the blankets to lay me down, and when I'm safely sinking into the mattress, half dazed with sleep, he tugs off my trousers, undressing me for bed. Smiling at me as though I'm his most prized possession, he stands back, his head slightly tipped to one side. I'll never get enough of when he looks at me like that. I always want him to look at me like that. It makes me feel important to him.

He turns away from me and I reach out to catch his hand, wanting to thank him for everything he's done for me but I can't find the words. My throat is thick with words, my eyes glittering with *thank you for respecting me, caring for me, and most of all, for showing me a moment of happiness.*

I know I'll never feel happiness like this again. No matter how much money I have in that offshore bank account, it cannot buy me happiness, and as long as Maksim is looming over me, my life will always exist in the shadows.

Charlie seems to think I'm saying something else in my gaze because he strips down to his black boxer briefs and slips into bed beside me, gathering me in his arms; his chest.

BLAIRE
(PART ONE)

"Do you mind if I stay with you?" he says, and I sense he's staring down at me.

I snuggle into his warmth, breathing in the clean scent of his skin, and while I don't answer him, my actions tell him all he needs to hear.

I want—no, need to be right here.

He kisses my forehead; embraces me like he's never going to let go.

Over the days, I convince myself that even when *this* is over, it's okay, because I'll always have my memories.

BLAIRE
(PART ONE)

26

Today, things change, and not for the good.

Everything starts out very normal. I wake up tangled under Charlie's muscular body, to sensations of kisses being pressed all over my face, mixed with soft strands of hair tickling my cheeks.

"Well, good morning," I say, smiling sleepily as I stretch out beneath him.

"Morning, baby," his voice comes out low and raspy—distracted. He's moaning with zeal, and so am I when he sucks the throbbing vein in my neck; cups my sex over my night shorts. Arching into him, I purr like a cat getting petted, thrusting my fingers into his hair and gripping him tightly.

Those kisses journey down my body, over my chest where only a thin night top separates us. At the waist of my night shorts, Charlie licks across my hipbones, starting with my right, and then my left, making my stomach quiver like crazy. In time, he takes off my night shorts, gently slides them down my legs, tugs them off my ankles and tosses them on the floor. He spreads my legs wide open by gripping my inner thighs with large hands and touches my clit with his tongue; makes mouth-love to my pussy, driving me nuts before I've even opened my eyes properly.

Restless from cumming, and hungry for more, I try to return the favor but he won't let me. He orders me to get dressed while climbing out of bed and shrugging on his joggers. "I've got a busy day planned but I wanner spend the morning with you first."

"Oh..." I stare at him with bashful embarrassment—I never understand it when he says 'no' to a blowjob. So I ask him.

"Delayed gratification," he's smirking from ear to ear as he says that. "It's new to me too. Get dressed, baby."

"Um... Oh'kay." Doing as I'm told, and wary of what he's up to, I pull on my usual apparel. He wanders into my en-suite and I follow. We brush our teeth one after the other, both using my toothbrush, and then we go down to have breakfast in the kitchen.

I'm flush from the overwhelming orgasm that's still lingering on my skin, and he's bright eyed, teasing me about kicking my ass in the gym. He doesn't though. He's as soft as ever with me, catching me from behind every time I try to strike, and like the lust sick cat I am, I let him.

"If you notice a few Mexican guys wandering about the place today," he says, panting in my ear from over my shoulder, "don't be alarmed. They're my men."

My spine pricking with nerves, I turn out of his arms to look at him. "Your men?"

"Yeah." He picks up a towel from the ropes and pats his damp face. "I need to pop out so they're gonna be here to keep an eye on the place. Celine is still MIA and I don't want her coming back here confronting you again."

"I can handle the likes of her," I say, momentarily offended, but then I'm gutted because he hasn't asked me to go with him.

"I know you can handle her but I won't have you dealing with my shit, Blaire."

"Do you... do you need my help with anything?" I say, unaware that I'm pulling an evil face until Charlie tells me.

"There's nothing to worry about." Reaching out he pinches my chin and then playfully slaps my cheek, setting off my desire to play fight with him.

He does this a lot when I come across worried, I've noticed over the months.

When we're done play fighting in the ring, I go back up to my room for a shower before relaxing in bed with a book. I don't go down for lunch because I know he's not here.

As I said, bar Charlie's odd behavior, the day starts out very normal. No. Perfect. I couldn't ask for anything more.

At half past four, it's time for dinner, and I'm itching to ask what's going on—I know something is—but I don't get a chance to go downstairs because Charlie strolls into my room with a fancy shopping bag in hand. He puts it on the foot of my bed and remains quiet in my presence, watching me.

"What's that?" I frown up at him, studying his clothes. He's dressed in well fitted jeans and a tailored royal blue shirt tucked in at the waist, the sleeves rolled up, revealing a big silver watch on his left wrist. His hair is pulled back, and I can smell he's wearing some sweet/musky cologne.

Charlie never wears cologne.

"A present," he says, waving a hand at the bag—that's where he's been. Shopping. He smirks at me, his blue eyes flashing with amusement.

Leaning over, I put down my book on the bedside cabinet and sit up with crossed legs, my eyes thinning with wonder. "What's going on?"

"We're going out for dinner-"

My stomach knots as he says that.

"-I've bought you some nice clothes and shoes, so if you get dressed, we can leave."

"Leave to go where?" I can feel the color draining from my cheeks as I think about the last time he said he wanted to take me to dinner. I'm staring at the bag now, dreading what's inside. If that's a dress, I'll kill him. No. I'll make him fucking wear it. "You're not going to make me dance, are you?"

Charlie throws his head back and bursts out laughing, though in a fond manner. "Not if you don't want to."

Well, that's a relief, I think.

When he's done laughing, he rustles through the bag and pulls out a green strappy top, light blue jeans and a pair of *heels!*

Worse than a dress.

"I am not wearing them," I say before I realize, unsure of what face I'm pulling. Shock, probably.

"You're not wearing what?" he says, demurely pretending he cannot see my expression. Putting everything down on the bed, he comes around to me, his stride slow and confident. "The shoes?"

I focus on the shoes, one toppled over on the jeans. Nude and strappy. They're not very high but I've never in my life worn heels, and I'm not about to.

"What's wrong with my clothes?" I look up at him standing beside me, at his face glowing in shrewd hilarity.

"Well," he crosses his arms, still smirking, and licks across his lips like he fancies something, "I'm a very big fan of your tight sports trousers, but where we're going, they're not the right attire."

"So, where are we going?"

"It's a surprise."

My heart is hammering in my chest, and my mouth is so dry that I'm surprised my voice comes out even when I say, "I'll wear the clothes, but I'm not wearing those shoes." I don't really want to wear the clothes either but I'm used to the whole give and take thing that's between us now.

"All right then," he says, shocking the hell out of me. "Get dressed and I'll meet you downstairs." He saunters off, leaving me in a state of dumfound.

I expected him to put up more of a fight about the shoes. He obviously wants me to wear them, otherwise why would he have bought them?

I climb out of bed and pick up the clothes, twisting my face. They're so... girly. Where on earth is he taking me that requires me to wear shit like this?

Perhaps I should have asked him. I always leave it too late to ask him things.

BLAIRE
(PART ONE)

I strip down to my underwear and dress in the jeans, which are so tight they might as well be painted on. I shake off how much I dislike them, pulling the strappy top over my head. It's made of silk, the green material shimmering under the lights in the room, the straps crisscrossing my back.

I feel odd, like I could be a different person. Maybe that's what he wants.

I have to shun the thought because it's like being punched in the stomach.

I slip on my trainers, tie the laces, and go downstairs to meet Charlie, fighting to keep my anxiety level. He said we're going out for dinner, so it shouldn't be so bad, but I've never been out for dinner like this before. I usually man-watch Maksim while he dines.

Coming down the staircase, I find Charlie is wandering back and forth across the entrance hall like a caged tiger, and when he gazes up at me, a huge smile spreads across his handsome face. He nods a few times. "Yeah, you look lovely in green."

I scowl with bafflement—he's in one of those funny moods—walk past him and reach for the front door.

"Not just yet," he says, taking my hand in a feather light grip. He turns me away from the door.

"Huh? I thought you said we were going-"

Entwining our fingers together, setting my blood on fire, he leads me into a room I've not seen before, left from the staircase. It's really warm, humidity hitting me like an Indian heat wave as soon as we cross the threshold. A long, wide room and high ceilings, aglow with fancy brass lamps on side tables. Dark rosewood paneled walls and brown leather couches in the heart of the space, the parquet flooring covered in huge expensive rugs.

"Sit here," Charlie says, helping me lower onto the biggest couch that faces the window. The sky is crystal clear, the sun burning low in the horizon.

When I look up at Charlie, I'm not sure which is more beautiful—that strange expression on his face or the sun.

He smirks at me, his eyes flickering between mine, then pivots and disappears into the entrance hall. I pull my eyebrows together, wondering where he's going.

It smells strongly of lemon polish in here, which is strange, given I've not seen a cleaner here at the house and I can't imagine Charlie polishing this big old room. Yes, he has a knack for cooking and the odd bit of cleaning, but this room is much too big for one person to clean.

Charlie comes back a few minutes later and passes me a small black box with gold detailing, BVLGARI written in gold across the lid.

"What is it?" I ask, taking it from him.

He's still smirking. He gestures at the box. "Open it and you'll see."

I hesitate for a moment, tied up with anxiety, then I click open the lid. I find a silver bracelet inside with BVLGARI written across the side. There's a row of sparkly crystals in the center.

"If you want my opinion on jewelry, you're out of luck." I laugh awkwardly, peering up at him. "I know nothing about jewelry, Charlie."

"I don't want your opinion." He's trying not to laugh, biting his lips closed.

I screw up my face. "Then, what?"

BLAIRE
(PART ONE)

"What'd you think?"

"About this?"

He nods.

I shrug, glancing between him and the bracelet. "I guess it's... nice-looking?"

Where is he going with this?

Something switches on in my mind—the clothes he just gave me—and I point at myself. "Is this for me?"

"Yeah. It's for you." He's still trying not to laugh. Inclining toward me, he takes the bracelet out and puts it on my left wrist, clicking it shut.

The metal is cold against my skin. It's a hard band, not something delicate.

"Do you like it?" Charlie squats down in front of me with elbows on his knees, eyes dazzling like blue diamonds.

I blink at him, feeling like he's putting me on the spot. "Yeah... eh... sure."

Now he laughs, fond of something, his eyes crinkling in the corners. He takes the box from me and puts it down on the coffee table, grabs my hand and holds it in his, covering mine completely.

"Why would you buy me a bracelet?" I just don't get this. First he says he's taking me out to dinner, and now he's giving me a bracelet?

"Why not?" He looks me dead in the eyes, his steady and observing.

His question lingers while we stare at each other, and the moment is so intense that I think I stop breathing, especially when he reaches out and pulls my hair forward, so it hangs over one shoulder, down my front.

I can't help feeling a little... I don't know.

Why would he buy me a damn bracelet? And why's he looking at me like that?

"I'd like to give you a lot more than just a bracelet, Blaire," he says. "Anything you want, I wanner give it to you."

My chest does that weird squeezy thing and I find myself gripping the bracelet on my wrist with my free hand.

"You don't have to buy me things, Charlie," I say softly, "I've got my own money."

His eyes... *Fuck.* He looks raw with passion and promise, making my chest squeeze even tighter.

"I'm not just talking about things," he whispers, his words coming out slow and hypnotic. "I'm talking about you and me."

Now, not only is my chest squeezing, but my heart is in knots.

There's something about Charlie tonight, something about his mood. I can't tell if it's sexually fueled or what.

"Can I use the toilet before we go?" I ask, to stop whatever is going on with him—hopefully by the time I come back, he'll be his normal self.

Letting go of my hand, he stands. "You don't have to ask for permission, baby. You know that."

I sink into my shoulders, push to my feet, and begin to leave the room.

Really, why would he buy me a bracelet? It has no real use to me. It can't protect me or feed me.

"Blaire-"

Stopping on the threshold, I peer back at Charlie, anxious beyond words—I just want the moment to be over with already.

"-What's that on your back?" he says, glowering at me.

"Huh?" I push my hair aside, trying to see what he sees. "What?"

He's behind me now, pulling the strap down my shoulder. "Those marks."

I scowl at him, baffled, then I feel him run a finger over one of my scars.

"They're whip marks." I don't sound too bothered telling him this, because I'm not. Maksim gave them to me, as a gift and a way to remember him, he said.

Charlie stands back and practically gapes at me. He doesn't say anything for a moment. He looks a bit... I don't know... angry? Confused or angry?

"Charlie?"

"Did he..." his voice is so low that I can barely hear him. "Did Maksim do that to you?"

"Do what?" I cannot fathom what he's talking about for a moment. "The marks on my back?"

He nods, swallowing, the large apple in his throat bopping up and down. I'm having a hard time trying to process the look on his face.

"Well, yeah. Why?" I pull up the strap and fix it on my shoulder.

Charlie is still quiet, looking at me like I'm a stranger.

"Are you okay?" I ask, then I realize he must not have seen my scars before. When he first took me on that horrible night—the first night—I was lying down on my back, and when he pulled me onto his lap, my hair must've curtained my ugliness. Any other time we've been intimate, we've not had a chance to fully undress because our moments are just that... moments, wild and unthought-of.

"Don't look at me like that, Charlie," I playfully nudge him in the arm. "They're just marks." For a second, just a brief second, I think he might find them hideous—the women he's had are probably perfect in every way. Celine certainly looked it. "Do you want me to put on a jumper or something? Do they make you feel... ill?"

"No! No!" He reaches out to me, but then retreats. "Course I don't want you to cover up. And they don't make me feel ill, Blaire... I just..." he doesn't finish. He cups his forehead and scratches restlessly. "I can't believe he's whipped you that hard."

I gulp, wrapping my arms around my middle. I remember Charlie saying that he's all for a bit of sadism, and Celine confirmed his dark desires. Does he feel like he's missed out now he knows I can take a beating?

I don't know why I just thought that. It's ridiculous. Charlie would never hit me. Or, I don't think he would.

"I'm just going to the toilet," I say, and I'm out of the living room before he can utter another word.

I don't use the downstairs toilet. I dash up to my room and shut the door, giving him a chance to come down from whatever mood he's in.

I'm dreading the next moment I see him—which is now.

———

BLAIRE
(PART ONE)

"Open the door, Blaire." Charlie knocks on my bedroom door with three heavy taps that echo through my room. "I wanner talk to you."

My throat restricts, and I don't know why, but I'm scared shitless.

With a shaky hand, I pull open the door. He marches in past me and kicks the door shut with his foot, makes me flinch as it bangs.

"When did Maksim do that to you?" He towers over me, his temples ticking.

I step back, not liking that darkness in his eyes.

"Blaire..." He raises his eyebrows at me.

I look down, knotting my fingers together over my lap. "You know I can't talk about Maksim."

We're quiet after I say that, but the tension in the room is like blow horns going off.

"Can I see them?" Charlie says eventually.

I keep my eyes down.

"I guess," I whisper, shrugging minutely. "If you want to."

"Do you mind if I see them?"

"I'd rather you didn't." I descend into my shoulders. "I know they're making you uncomfortable."

"They're not making me uncomfortable at all." His voice darkens as he yells, "They make me wanner rip Maksim's fucking head off! When did he do that to you?"

I cringe against his yelling. I've never seen Charlie this mad before.

"I wanner know when he did that to you, Blaire. Does he still hit you? When was the last time he hit you?" He goes on and on, baffled that he's never seen the marks on my back before. "Why haven't you told me the extent of his abuse?" He's practically spitting fire as he yells, "Answer me!"

I take a step back and look up at him with tears in my eyes, putting up a mental wall between us.

"Why are you doing that?" he says, glaring as he studies my eyes. "Why are you moving away from me?"

"If I don't answer you, are you going to hit me?"

"What!?!" He backs away from me now, his face draining of color. "No... I would never... I'd never lay a finger on you! Why would you even ask me that, Blaire?"

I drop my gaze to the floor, fighting to shut off.

"I'm sorry..." he says, trying to reign himself in. "I'm not angry with you. I'm just... angry." He steps up to me but I step back again. "Baby, don't do that. Don't back away from me. I'd never hurt you, I swear it."

My skin is pricking with anxiety. How can I escape this situation?

"Talk to me, Blaire, please? Tell me what's going on with those marks. Are they all over your back?"

"Can we drop this?" I sound like I'm on the verge of tears, because I am. "I don't want to talk about it."

"I can't just leave this alone—I won't!"

I glance up at him. He still looks angry as hell, his eyes like blue balls of fire.

"How would Maksim feel if I whipped him like that, hm? Maybe I will, just to show him how much it fucking hurts."

I don't feel any instincts over Maksim as Charlie says that.

I stare at my feet, shaking a little.

"You know that you're supposed to go back to him soon, don't you? We've only got a week left together."

Lifting my eyes, I glower at Charlie. "Of course I know that."

Why does he have to point that out now?

"Do you wanner go back to him?" He reaches for one of my hands but I don't feel his touch.

His question echoes.

Do I want to go back to Maksim?

I'm not sure it's a matter of *wanting* to go back to him. It's a matter of knowing I have to. Regardless of how much I want to stay with Charlie, my subconscious works on another level. I'd probably end up returning to Maksim in my sleep if I didn't willingly go in my conscious state.

'Just do your jobs and come home to me', Maksim said. Recalling his order seems to put me back two and a half months. I'm Blaire, my little pet, again.

There's this weird ringing in my ears and it won't go away.

"Blaire?" Charlie gently tugs my hand, trying to grasp my attention.

I nervously scratch the side of my leg with my free hand.

"Do you wanner go back to him?"

"Yes," I say, though I don't let on that I might miss Charlie. What's the point?

"I don't believe you," he says softly.

"Why not?" I peer up at him, then I look past him because I cannot stand that intense blue stare of his.

"Because I think you're lying."

"I'm not," I say innocently. "I've really come to... I don't know... enjoy being around you, but I've known Maksim longer than I've known myself. My life is with him. It's all I know—it's all I'm allowed to know."

"He treats you like a dog. You can't possibly wanner go back to that?"

"Yeah, you're right, he does." For some unknown reason, I get lost in my explanation, in trying to make Charlie understand me. "He beats me for his own pleasure and pets me for mine. I protect him. I work for him. I study, execute jobs, and that is it. I'm not meant for another life—I won't be able to function properly in another life."

Charlie takes my other hand and runs his thumbs over my knuckles, but still, his touch doesn't affect me.

"You can have a different life if you want one, Blaire," he says, his eyes glowing with desperation. "If you wanner stay with me, you can, and you won't ever, *EVER!* have to fight or kill to please Maksim again."

The ringing in my ears intensifies. I start blinking really fast, trying to get rid of that annoying sound.

"Blaire?" Charlie whispers. "Blaire, what is it?"

Snatching out of his grasps, I pace my room, raking my fingers through my waist length hair.

If you wanner stay with me, you can, Charlie just said, like he's god or something.

Maksim told me to complete my jobs and come home. That's what I have to do. I know it. Deep down, I know it. But, why is something in the back of my mind telling me to choose Charlie?

I feel all jumbled up inside, my ears ringing and my head is pounding.

"Blaire," Charlie says, "stay with me. Don't go back to-"

"You think you can offer to keep me and I'll leap into your arms?" I say through gritted teeth, cutting him off. "You think you can take me away from Maksim?"

"You've enjoyed being here," he says with caution, "being able to live... being able to feel... feel alive... Why wouldn't you want that?"

"Yes, I have enjoyed the past weeks," I say hopelessly, "but I cannot stay with you in this soap commercial life."

"Why can't you?"

"Because I'm wired wrong!" I yell, pointing at my head. "And I can't do anything to change it. I-I want to please Maksim—he's my master. He's all I know."

"You've barely mentioned him over the past two months," Charlie says frankly. "He can't mean that much to you."

"It's you!" I pull my hair, needing to feel pain, pacing faster now. "I did forget, but now... now you've put him in my head with just saying his name... I can't... Fuck!" I stop dead in the middle of my bedroom. "I can't think about anything but him!"

"You can learn to be different." Charlie closes the space between us. "You can change the way you think."

"Ohhh, because it's so easy, isn't it?" I cannot keep the sarcasm out of my voice. I go around the room again, holding my head. "I wish you didn't bring him up. I wish you wouldn't talk about him. You make me think of my orders."

"I'm trying to help you."

"That's a lofty goal," I scoff.

"Don't you dare be snarky with me." His eyes narrow. "Not now."

"Ugh... Charlie," I sigh his name, rubbing my temples. "You just don't get it."

"Tell me then." He reaches out to me like he's praying or something. "Make me understand. I'm here... I'm listening..."

A while passes where I don't know what to say, then it spills out of me. I ramble on about who I was and who I am now. "I've never even spoken to someone the way I speak to you—and I probably won't ever again. I wouldn't dream of it. But you... you make me feel... Everything goes out the window with you!" I wave out angrily. "You're going to get me in trouble because when I go back to Maksim, I won't be the same and he'll torture me for it."

"Then don't go back to him," Charlie says. "Come and live with me in Mexico."

"What?" My face screws up. "I can't decide that." The penny drops, and I stop pacing again. "Is this why you keep asking me questions about living in Mexico? Are you trying to take me from Maksim?"

"No. I want you to decide for yourself."

"You know I can't do that." I clench my teeth, trying to keep it together but I can feel my cool slowly slipping away. "I do care about you, Charlie, that's obvious, but the fact is, I belong to Maksim, and nothing you say or do can change that."

"You can decide for yourself," Charlie says. "I don't give a shit about how ruthless and brainwashing Maksim is, you'd rip him apart and you damn well know it."

"I can't hit him."

BLAIRE
(PART ONE)

Hunching down, Charlie meets me at eye level. "Why not?"

I frown. "What do you mean?"

"Why can't you hit him?"

"You know why."

He shakes his head. "I know you think you can't, but believe me, you can." He scans my face, going quiet for a few seconds. "All you have to do is raise this-" grabbing my hand, he makes me ball my fist, "-and swing."

I don't know what happens to me, but I explode.

"Aargh!" I punch him in the chest, hating the way he's gotten in my head. "Why have you done this to me? Why did you buy me and make me feel things I don't want to feel?" Charlie doesn't fight back when I punch his chest again, just stands there looking down at me. I hit him over and over, pounding viciously. "Why!?! Charlie? Fucking tell me why!" Because he isn't answering me, I really lose it. I grab my jacket hanging by the bedroom door, pull out my gun, and put it to my head. "Is all this because Maksim wronged you!?!" I scream. It's like shards of glass ripping through my throat. "Are you breaking me down to get some payback!?!"

Silence. I can almost hear Charlie's heart pounding through the tension.

"Tell me," I click back the hammer, "or I'll fucking shoot myself."

Then, Charlie sprints at me and snatches the gun out of my hand. I hear a loud thud—I think he's tossed the gun somewhere—and then he uses his full strength to put me down. I fight against him, scratching to get free, but

I'm not in my right mind. Fisting the back of my hair, Charlie drags me across the room and folds me over the bed. He presses a forearm across the back of my shoulders, burying my face in the mattress.

"Calm down," he says.

"You're a twisted bastard," I spit out weakly, turning my head to the side so I can breathe. "I'm a cold blooded murderer. I've taken hundreds of lives—some by my own two hands," I taunt him, my endeavor to make him hate me, "and you want me? You want to take me out on stupid dinner dates? You want me to come and live with you—be with you? Do you know what sick things I've done?"

"I don't care," he says under his breath.

"I once butchered a man, Charlie," I moan beneath the pressure of his weight, "I cut off each of his body parts while he scream/cried for me to stop, and I bathed in his blood for Maksim. I've blown away entire families... killed people before they were barely out of their teenage years... I've watched girls get raped and done nothing—NOTHING! Do you still want me now?"

Pressing me further into the mattress, he puts his mouth on my ear and whispers, "No matter what you tell me, I'll still want you. You're worth saving, and do you know why?"

A huge lump forms in my throat.

"Because you feel guilt for the things you've done."

"I don't," I say with pity, barely convincing myself.

"You do. I know you do. I've heard your screams in the middle of the night... You beg for someone to stop the torment—and don't tell me you beg for someone to stop Maksim from hitting you because you say names, and none of them were ever Maksim's.

"Nothing you say can change the way I feel about you, Blaire, because regardless of all you've done, you're innocent. You wanner be guilt free."

"Stop! Please... Just stop..." I beg, unable to take this.

"No. I won't stop. You need to know that I really, really care about you. You need to know that I won't let you suffer because of what Maksim's turned you into."

I'm shaking now, tears leaking out the corner of my eyes.

"You're lying," I say naively. "You don't care about me. You care about your objective."

"No, baby, you've got that all wrong. I fucking care about you, and I won't sit back and watch you sell your soul to the devil before you've barely become a woman."

I burst into tears then, unable to stop, my entire body wracked with emotions that I just don't understand.

"I-I won't come with you, Charlie. I won't come and live with you in Mexico. No matter what you say or do, I'll-I'll go back to Maksim."

He doesn't say anything to that, so I just cry away my pain.

"Shhh, baby..." he strokes down the side of my face, catching my tears. "S'all right."

"It's not all right," I sob each word. "I'm not all right." *I'm lost.*

More tears. I'm inundated in them, sobbing like a child, soaking the blanket under me.

When my body goes flaccid, Charlie pulls me down to the floor with him and gathers me in his lap. He rocks me back and forth, telling me again, "Everything's gonna be all right. I promise."

I bury my face in his chest and cry so hard that my belly hurts, often squeezing out hiccupping whimpers. I don't even really know why I'm crying. Am I sad because whatever is happening between Charlie and me will be over soon? Do I miss Maksim? Am I just angry? Have Charlie's words cut too deep?

I just don't know.

"I'm sorry," Charlie whispers against the top of my head. "This was never supposed to happen."

BLAIRE
(PART ONE)

27

I wake alone in bed the next day, and cold, but I'm okay. I feel no anger, no confusion, or a sense of being lost. Having a little cry seems to have helped because I actually feel okay.

Once I've showered and dressed in the usual, I go downstairs. Charlie isn't in the kitchen, and he hasn't made breakfast, I notice, checking inside the oven, so I wander into the living room on a hunch. He's in here, amongst piles of clothes and handbags and shoes. He doesn't greet me with the usual, 'morning Blaire'. He doesn't even look at me—it's as if he can't. He just stands there at the other end of the room, by the huge window, wearing gray joggers—no top. His glossy black hair is freely curling around his neck and face, and his broad, masculine body looks exquisite under the morning's sunshine coming in through the window.

"Morning," I say, smiling at him.

He doesn't answer me, and I feel my heart sink a little.

"Did you rob a clothes store?" I laugh warily, grabbing a pair of trainers from the coffee table. They're nice. I turn them over. And my size.

"It's all from a truck robbery." He glances over everything, his expression dark and almost empty. "I'm holding it all here for a friend." There's something tense in his voice.

When I peer up at him again, I see two Mexican looking guys by the open doors that lead off the living room, onto the garden. "Hello, Miss Blaire," the taller of the two says.

I force a smile to say 'hi' back. Charlie tells them to give us a minute, and they do, head bowing respectfully to him, and then me.

"How are you feeling this morning, Blaire?" Charlie says, crossing his arms. He stays the other side of the living room, behind the couches, and I see it's true—he can't look me in the eyes.

"I'm fine," I dismiss him because I don't want to go over last night. I lift the trainers to show him. "I like these."

He frowns, staring at the trainers in my hands. "Have them if you like them. Have whatever you want."

Sitting down on the leather couch, I kick off my trainers and put on the new ones, twisting and turning my ankles to get a good look at them.

"Take them up to the bedroom so they don't get taken," Charlie says. He still doesn't sound like himself. His tone is flat, a million miles away from here.

"What's wrong?" Putting my old trainers in the box, I get up and roam over to him, pulling the sleeves of my sweater over my hands. "Why do you sound like that?"

He turns his back on me and gazes out of the window, his broad shoulders rising and falling with long, drawn out breaths.

My stomach twists with rejection.

"Charlie?" I touch his shoulder, desperate for his attention.

"You put a fucking gun to your head last night," he's speaking to the window, "that's what's wrong."

I'm stunned, and I know I look it. I revealed to him an inkling of what sick, twisted things I've done in my life, and he's upset because I put a gun to my head?

I should have pulled the trigger. The world would be a better, safer place without me in it.

"I'm hungry, Charlie." I decide not to answer him—not that he asked me a question, but I know he's expecting me to say something.

"Tojo!" he calls out, making me jump, and a dark-haired guy—the taller of the two who were in here a moment ago—pops his head in through the open back doors.

"Have the housekeeper whip up some eggs for Blaire," Charlie says.

Tojo nods and leaves immediately.

"The housekeeper?"

"Yeah." Charlie sighs, running his fingers through his hair. "I sent her away when I brought you here. She's back now."

"Oh..." I linger by Charlie, picking at my nails. I don't really know what to say.

After a while of silence, he faces me, his arms still folded over his chest. I don't look up at him, but I can sense he's staring at me. He stares for so long that I burn under his gaze.

What is he thinking? Does he think I'm crazy?

I am, so I wouldn't damn him if he did.

"The job is happening tomorrow-" he breaks the silence.

Finally, I lift my eyes to his, immediately wishing I didn't. He still cannot hold my focus.

"-We need you to shut London down," he glances away, and then back at me but only for a second, grinding his jaw, "and then... and then you can go home."

WHAT?

But we still have a week left... And he wanted to go out for dinner...

"We'll leave first thing in the morning," he says.

Out of nowhere, while I'm staring at his face, tears well-up in my eyes.

"You got that, Blaire?"

I nod at him a few times, trying to study his deadpan expression.

He says nothing, and I can't stomach the way he's struggling to look at me, so I walk past him for the garden. I need some space.

Home. I'll be going home tomorrow and all this will be over.

Why the hell do I feel so sad?

"Blaire, I'm sorry," Charlie says, following after me. "Wait."

I stop on cue, as if his orders affect me like Maksim's do.

"I don't want you to go," he whispers from behind. I can feel the warmth from his body at my back. It makes me think about how I woke up this morning without him in my bed.

"I want you to stay with me," he says. "I'll make Maksim give you to me, even if I have to pay him to tell you you're free."

I swallow down the lump in my throat. That's not ever going to happen. Maksim will die before giving me up indefinitely. I'm his. I know I'm his, and even while he's clearly scared of Charlie... I just know he won't give me up. I don't even want to choose Charlie over Maksim, because when all is said and done, Maksim and I are the same—we're both as fucked up as each other.

"Blaire, I want you—I dunno how many different ways I can tell you," he sounds frustrated, his tone of voice sharp and demanding. "I want you to come and live with me in Mexico. I wanner be with you."

I remain quiet, staring down the garden, my throat swelling up even more. I just don't know what to tell him.

"All right," he says, clutching at straws, "if Mexico is the problem... You can't stay here—Maksim knows where the house is—so I'll buy you a place in England, or wherever you wanner be, set you up with an allowance so you'll never be without, and I'll come see you as often as I can. No one will know where you are..." he goes right into selling a new life to me.

Does he really think Mexico is the problem?

He touches my arm from behind, trying to grasp my attention. "Why aren't you saying anything?"

BLAIRE
(PART ONE)

I scratch my face, searching for the words. "I... I just... Thanks for treating me well, Charlie. It's been... different." That's all I have, and I say it knowing my fairytale has come to an end.

"Thanks?" he questions, scoffing like he can't quite believe I just said that. "I don't want you to thank me. I want you to say you'll stay with me. Please, Blaire... Or tell me what I have to do?"

I remain staring down the garden. "There's nothing you can do, Charlie. I'm sorry."

I wander off into the garden then, and I'm surprised that he doesn't stop me. I wish he would stop me. I wish he would stop me and tell me that we can have this last week together.

Trying hard to shut off mentally, I lose myself in the day. It's a little chilly. I haven't got a coat on. I don't care.

Tomorrow... *this... we...* Charlie and me... it'll be over.

I'm not sure how I feel about that. I'm not even sure I can block the fact out.

I want to cry.

I do cry.

I huddle by the back fence that feels miles away from the house, hug my knees to my chest, and I bawl my eyes out.

I wring myself dry of tears and wander back to the house, feeling very disconnected, stuck between the idealism of the past two and a half months and the reality of what I have to go back to tomorrow. As much as I try to shut off mentally, I can't.

BLAIRE
(PART ONE)

Charlie has treated me so well—it's almost been like a dream. He's fed me and clothed me, trained with me for whatever reason, and he's ensured me some happiness. He's spoken to me on a platonic level, comforted me, and he's never hurt me. He wouldn't ever hurt me. I know that deep down. I trust him.

Maksim hasn't treated me very well, but he gave me a life when I didn't have one, and I can't help feeling grateful for that. Though, I now know he might've stolen me... Thinking of this confuses me a bit—I start to wonder if I had a family, parents that might have loved me—so I put it out of my mind.

It's too painful.

I round the swimming pool and make my way up the patio steps, and the more I think about what-is and what-could-be, the more I realize it doesn't really matter what I want or need. I can't stay with Charlie unless Maksim says I can—subconsciously, I don't want to stay with Charlie unless Maksim says I can—but he won't ever say that. He'll kill me before letting me go, as he's always promised. Up until now, that threat has never bothered me, I guess because I thought a life without Maksim wasn't a life at all. Then I met Charlie.

I'm not sure if I'd rather die than live in an unemotional world again. Ever since Charlie tapped into my emotions, all I want is to feel good things. I don't want anyone to hurt me anymore. I need the scars on my back to remind me of how strong I can be; not how strong I have to be.

I'm in thought mayhem, and I hate it.

Reaching the back doors that lead into the living room, I overhear someone speaking about me in a Latin brogue, telling Charlie to just take me. "She'll be happier and safer in Mexico with us rather than staying here with that dirty Russian pig."

Stepping back, I plaster myself against the wall and listen in, wondering if that's Rico. It sounds like something that Rico guy would say—*just take her.* I'd like to rip him apart, the smarmy ass bastard.

"I can't take her," Charlie says, his voice full of uncertainty.

"Why not? Nothing's ever stopped you before... Have you gone soft?"

I smile with fondness at his observation. Charlie has gone a bit soft on me.

"It's not about going soft," Charlie snaps. "She's too conditioned for Maksim."

Someone's pacing about in brooding silence, footsteps heavy. I'm almost certain it's Charlie. I know the way he walks in anger and solace; either way, he has heavy footsteps.

"It's as simple as this," Charlie says eventually, sounding calmer now, "if she doesn't make the decision to come with me for herself, she'll never feel comfortable and at home with me; with us. She'll run back to Maksim the first chance she gets because deep in her subconscious, she thinks she has to go back to him."

He's right about that. It's tormenting how well he knows me.

"How has he conditioned her?"

"You don't wanner know." Charlie doesn't give the Latin guy any more than that. I smile again, though with something else this time. He's always said I can trust him, and along our journey, slowly but surely, he's ensured that.

"What I can tell you is," Charlie says in his own time, "Maksim apparently outbid a government agency for her, but I dunno if that's true, and I dunno what government."

That's news to me.

"Why would a government want her?"

"She's smart," Charlie says. "Knows technology and numbers like a second nature, so everyone keeps saying."

I don't think it's true—that Maksim outbid a government agency for me—not for a second. I think he made it up to stop others from prying about the fact that he bought or stole me.

But, then again, Maksim did know about my skills before I even told him, and he's cashed in on them, big time.

Maybe it is true.

"Cutting the story short," Charlie says, drawing my attention; I hold my breath to listen in, "Maksim took Blaire and locked her up for years—conditioned her to evoke loyalty and worship, and it's worked a treat. She only has to hear that someone's gonna hurt him and she'll make hell rain on earth."

"Jesucristo," that guy says, and I imagine he's raking his fingers through his hair—it's the tone of his voice. "Who told you all this?"

"Carl."

"Is it true what they say about her fighting talent?"

Charlie chuckles under his breath. "Yeah, she's as dangerous as hell. I've been full on sparring with her and while I suspect she thinks I've been holding back, I haven't. She's just like Nic told us."

Nic? His brother Nicolas?

"Doesn't Carl know where she comes from or what government wanted her? Because if this is true, the bodying government will have a paper trail that we can get access to. All we have to do is contact them and we'll get the information you want."

"Carl doesn't know where she comes from," Charlie says. "Believe me I've asked. I've also asked Maksim and Tatiana but they're playing their cards close to their chests."

They talk for a while about what I'm like; how I word things; how I analyze things. I don't get why they're discussing me like this. What's their objective?

"She's got a slight Russian accent," Charlie says, "so I started my search based on that, but I know she doesn't come from Russia or Ukraine, nor England or America for that matter. I've checked every country."

"Don't take this the wrong way," that guy says, sounding wary, "but, have you bothered to ask her where she originates from?"

Charlie scoffs, and the floor just inside the doors near to where I am creaks. "She's as likely to fight me as to speak to me about herself. Trust me, she doesn't say anything without Maksim's permission."

I take a step back to stay hidden.

"Okay... Do you know her last name?"

Silence between them. The creaking moves further and further away.

I assume Charlie has shrugged at his friend, because his friend says, "She has to have a last name. Put her photo through every government system. Search the missing person's database. Have her fingerprint checked."

"I have had her fingerprint checked," Charlie says, "and nothing. How'd you think I searched the government ID database for her?"

I'm numb to the touch, mentally digesting what he's saying about me.

"All I know is, she drives illegally in a Porsche that would cost the average person four years of wages, doesn't own a real passport, and she's got no friends. I've searched every inch of her apartment for information and ID but found nothing."

How the hell has he gotten a hold of my fingerprint?

My mind whirls from every cup I've touched to every piece of cutlery.

And what the fuck is he doing snooping through my things?

"Maksim lets her drive a Porsche?"

"Kinda." Charlie tells him that I've got my own money. "Piles of it in her apartment and in the glove compartment of her car, and she's got an offshore account with a few million in it."

My jaw drops. He knows how much money I have in my bank account?

"Huh?" that guy says, absolutely confused. "So, if she's minted, why does she live under Maksim?"

"I asked myself that very question when I first learnt how much money she's got-"

I'm on edge listening to Charlie psychoanalyze me.

"-I rang the shrink at The Site..." he says. "I was so confused that I could barely get my words out. She told me that I have to look at Blaire's conditioning as I'd look at a child who loves its parent's no matter what they do."

"No," that guy says. "That's not right. A lot of kids turn their backs on their parents because of cruelty and abuse."

"Yeah, I agree, but in Blaire's case, she apparently works on an emotional bonding level, like most kids do. She'll love and worship Maksim no matter what he does to her, because when all's said and done, she knows nothing else."

"That's so fucked up, Charlie."

I shudder a little as his friend says that. Yeah, I am fucked up. Tell me something I don't know.

They discuss all of what the psychologist said, which isn't much: how I've never had a normal life, and how it'll be hard for me to adjust to anything different to what I know, blah, blah, blah.

"Do you know her date of birth?" that guy says. "How old is she?"

There's a long pause before Charlie admits reluctantly, "She's young."

"How young?"

"Told me she was eighteen."

"Eighteen!" that guy practically yells.

Charlie laughs. "Don't look at me like that, Andres."

Andres? He's talking to his brother!

I think I've gone white.

"She's a pretty girl," Charlie says, praising me to the high heavens, "smart, witty, strong; keeps me on my feet because she's feisty as fuck."

They laugh together like men do, pompous and proud.

BLAIRE
(PART ONE)

"Well... shit," Andres says when he's done laughing, "the only time you ever want to be with someone, she's barely a woman, mentally warped, and comes with a bent Russian military force."

Charlie laughs again, sounding as smug as ever.

"Look, you obviously want her," Andres says in a reasoning tone, "and you sound sure that she won't come with you, so how about I have a chat with her? You know how persuasive I can be. Maybe I can find out where she comes from. I might be able to save you the trouble."

That's what this is all about—Charlie wants to know where I come from? I want to ask why; what does it matter?

"No," Charlie cuts him off from saying anything more about talking to me. "You don't know Blaire. She won't speak to you unless Maksim says she can. It took me weeks just to find some common ground with her, and she actually had permission to speak to me."

"Maksim gave her permission to talk to you?" Andres sounds confused again. "Why? And, why's she here with you anyway? You never said."

So, whatever Charlie's agenda is, he's kept it to himself.

That makes me nervous.

Charlie doesn't say anything for a moment, but he soon brushes his brother off with saying, "It's a long-ass story, and I promised Blaire that it's our business, so I can't tell you."

"That bad, huh?"

Charlie's voice is dark, almost filled with shame, as he says, "I reckon you'd think I'm a callous motherfucker if I told you how I came to having her."

For some reason, the first night I spend with Charlie whips through my mind.

The leather couch creaks under someone's weight and hairs all over my body narrow. I take another step back to keep hidden.

"Charlie... you don't think you want her because you can't have her, do you? I know what you're like. You desire things people say you can't have."

"No," Charlie doesn't hesitate. "I can take her if I really want too—and trust me, you don't understand the irony of me saying that—but I won't just take her. I respect her too much then to just lock her up like an animal. I want her to feel freedom and peace with me."

Peace...

He catches my emotions with one, single word.

I have felt peace with Charlie. The idea of never feeling it again cuts deep.

My eyes sting with tears.

"She sounds like a slow burning project," Andres says.

"She is, but she's... Oh, I dunno..." Charlie sighs, and my lips wobble because there's something moving in his voice, "if you ever get to know her, you'll see why I like her." His tone softens even more as he says, "She's so eerie and intense with eyes that take you straight to the dark side, and she's gotta stinking redhead attitude, but she's... she's the loveliest little thing. All I wanner do is look after her but she won't let me."

My heart goes. If only he knew how much I care about him... I wish I had the stomach to tell him.

Andres asks about me on a personal level: wants to know how Charlie and I have spent the past few months. "I know you said she's a bit feral, but have you taken her out or anything? Girls like that kind of shit."

Feral? I nearly laugh, even through my depressive mood.

"Blaire doesn't want dinner dates," Charlie laughs mordantly at his brother. "Trust me, I already tried that one and she looked at me like I was speaking a dead language."

"Okay... Well, I know you said she's very into sports-"

"Yeah, she loves sports, *and* food," Charlie's voice is thick with amusement. "I'd love to see her on The Site, executing the training course."

"Yeah, that'd be pretty cool," Andres says. "I like women who are into sports... What was it like having her here with you?" Andres goes off in a different direction, studying his brother. "I mean, I know you like your own space."

Charlie tells his brother everything about our time together, minus any sexual intimate details. "Life sort of became routine once she opened up to me: breakfast, a sparring session, dinner, free thinking conversation... I even told her about our parents and Gina."

"What?" Andres is lost for words. "But... you-you don't talk to anyone about that."

"I trust her on another level, brother."

"Why though, Charlie? She's just a girl."

"She's not just a girl. You won't understand what it's like to be under Blaire's spell until you've experienced it," he sounds lost in deep thought, "she draws me in with her undivided attention and keeps me there in an odd state of trust, consuming my fucking soul with the way she looks at me. It's like a therapy session talking to her." Charlie laughs under his breath, as if he's recalling a memory or something.

I can't actually believe how he sees me. It's baffling. I'm nothing special. I'm just... well, I'm me.

"What'd you say to her about our parents exactly?"

Silence, then Charlie says, "She knows what I did."

"What!?! And she doesn't think you're..." I don't hear what he says, so I shift a little closer to the door. I can just see a large figure dressed in black clothes sitting on the couch. It's not Charlie.

"No. She actually understood—said I should've tortured our mother."

"Fuck..." Andres says, and I see he lifts a hand to his head. "You can't just send her back to Maksim. You obviously have feelings for her."

"Course I do," Charlie says with a hint of anger. "Nothing makes sense without her anymore. I can't imagine a single day without her."

"Then take her, you idiot-"

Panic races through me and I step back again, clamming up.

"-We'll keep her locked up for a while if need be, then we'll put a tranquilizer tracking bracelet on her and introduce her to The Site and our people. She'll learn a new way of living, Charlie—we've all had to do it."

Charlie doesn't utter a word. I'm not sure if he's ignoring his brother or being slowly influenced by him. Either way, I'm anxious. I won't let him take me. I can't.

"Look, I get why you're forcing her hand by sending her back early, but what if she doesn't change her mind and stay with you? What if she leaves?"

"That's a chance I have to take. I love that girl—I won't make decisions for her. I won't treat her like my property."

The world closes in on me, and I have to grab my chest because it's... It aches.

No one has ever said they love me before.

Someone sighs—I think Andres. "You're mad for not taking advantage of this last week with her. You'll regret it, Charlie, trust me."

"I probably will, but last night something happened that scared the shit outa me, and I won't risk it happening again."

I flush with embarrassment, and as Andres badgers Charlie for what happened, I'm unable to listen in anymore. The last thing I need to hear is Charlie telling his brother that I'm fucking crazy and explaining the reasons why.

Pushing away from the wall, I sneak around the house, click open the front doors, and peer through a crack to make sure I don't run in to anyone.

I hope Andres can talk Charlie around to letting me stay for the last week—I'm not ready to go home yet. I'm not ready to go until I tell Charlie that I care about him.

There isn't anyone in the welcome hall, so I sneak upstairs to my room and sink into bed fully clothed, trying not to wish the day away because I know it's the last day of peace I have left. It's the last day with Charlie I have left.

It amazes me that I've just overheard Maksim outbid a government agency for me and I'm more concerned about my time with Charlie. I don't even remember how I got like this. I'd usually focus on the imperative, boycotting anything less. Now, I'm emotionally selfish.

"Blaire, baby," Charlie says, startling me.

Peering over the duvet at him, I see he's standing there in the open doorway, dressed in dark jeans over black boots and a red polo shirt under his brown leather jacket. He looks like he's going out. Nervous, I find his blue gaze but he still cannot look me in the eyes.

That hurts.

"The job has been moved forward," he says in a deep tone.

I frown, studying the carrier bag he's holding in one hand.

"Why?"

He scratches his head, blinking at the floor. "We've been waiting for a map of the bank vault, and Maksim got it a few hours ago, so we need to do the job now."

Why do I feel like he's lying to me? Why do I feel like the whole 'waiting for a map of the vault' has been an excuse to lengthen my stay? He was in such a rush for me to grasp control of London for fifteen minutes, yet he's only mentioned the job once in the entire time I've been here with him. And, to add to my suspicion, he confessed to his brother that he's trying to force my hand by sending me home early...

I think about all this for a moment, but then what's about to happen hits me like a ton of bricks.

"We are... we're going back to London today?" I push the blankets aside to stand, and suddenly, nothing else matters to me. I have to do the job in my apartment. My computers are the only computers set up and equip for the job.

Charlie nods, the muscles in his temples ticking.

I glance down at the floor, then back up at him, my throat burning to cry. "I... Charlie... I..." I have a million things I want to say. *I don't want to go!*

"We need to get a move on." He waves me onward, and still cannot look at me. "We have to be at your apartment in two hours."

"But, I-"

"C'mon, Blaire," he says, stopping me from speaking

This is happening too quickly—my anxiety is through the roof. I thought we had tonight at least. I have so much that I want to ask him. So many questions about what he's found out about me, but most of all, I want to tell him that I care about him. He has to know.

Raising his eyebrows, he urges me onward. I drop my eyes to the floor and go over to him on mental command. He exits the room before me and leads the way downstairs in absolute silence. There by the front doors, he puts the carrier bag down on the floor and grabs my leather jacket. I snap my eyebrows together, remembering having it upstairs.

"Don't bother trying to find your gun-" he pushes my jacket up my arms, walks around to in front of me and fixes my collar.

I'm just staring up at him... panicking.

"-I've got it," he says, his eyes flickering up to mine, and then back down to his hands where he's still playing with my collar. "You can have it back when... when I drop you off at home."

I don't give a fuck about my gun right now. I can't get my head around the fact that *this* is over

His hand hovering over the hollow of my back, he picks up the carrier bag and leads me out of the house, to his car.

I peer over my shoulder at his house, at the stately aspect of it, feeling it drift further and further away. I really, really don't want to go.

"Charlie," I whisper his name in a broken voice, but when he looks down at me, blue eyes full of conspiracy, I can't speak. I glance away, feeling like the biggest coward in the world. I care about him so much but have no courage to tell him.

Reaching his car, he opens the passenger door and helps me inside, putting the bag he's holding on my lap. He even buckles me up. I guess he can read my dismay.

"I made you something to eat," he says, gesturing at the bag.

"I'm not hungry," I say softly, blinking at him.

"You'll eat, Blaire." Shutting my door as a way to suggest there's no room for discussion, he rounds the car and jumps into the driver's seat. He opens the bag and tells me to eat at least half the sandwich. "I won't be around anymore and I'll be damned if I'll leave you unfed."

"Okay," I whisper, every hair on my body spiking.

The sandwich doesn't get past my lips. I fiddle with crumbs of bread to make it look like I'm eating, but I'm just not hungry.

We make the drive to London in total silence. Charlie has the radio on low. I'm grateful for the music cutting through the tension that is us, though it's doing nothing for my panic.

I can't believe this is probably our last few moments together and we're like this. It's heartbreaking.

"Eat some of that sandwich, Blaire," Charlie orders, making me flinch.

I do this time. It tastes of nothing, and it's so hard to swallow, clogging up my air passage because my throat is so dry and tight.

As soon as we enter London, my panic turns to dread. I have to say something. I have to sway him into taking me back with him after I've done the job so I can spend this last week with him. I miss him already and he's not left me yet.

We pull into my underground car park, pull up beside my Porsche, and Charlie turns off the car. He's quiet for a while, staring forward. I watch him from the corner of my eye, unsure of what to say. I have so much that I want to say but no capacity to speak!

Charlie leans down for the glove compartment, digs out a mobile—my mobile—a set of keys, and my gun. He passes it all to me.

"I've put my number in your phone. It's under Decena." He looks me right in the eyes now, causing mine to water. "If you ever need me, no matter the reason why—no matter what time of day it is—call me, and I'll come."

I can't even nod at him. I'm cold to the bone.

"Are you sure you don't wanner come with me?" Twisting at the waist, he grabs the back of my headrest and looks down on me, putting us mere inches from each other. "Because I can turn the car around and we'll leave. You can come and live with me in Mexico or I'll set you up here in England. I'll take care of you. I'll do whatever you want."

I stare down at everything in my lap. "I can't go with you, Charlie," my voice is so small. "Maksim said I have to come back." *But I can stay with you for this last week...* Why can't I tell him that?

He doesn't question me further. I can feel that he wants to, but he doesn't. Staring at me with powerful intensity, he reaches over, grabs my left hand, and shows me the bracelet he bought me.

"Don't take this off," he says, stroking over my palm with his thumb, turning my need to cry into a full blown stream of tears. "It's got a tracking device in it-"

My heart contracts.

"-I can't let you go without knowing where you are, Blaire," his eyes pace between mine, "I'll not be able to live with myself if something happened to you."

Oh, fuck... It's over. I cannot get my head around how we've gone from being madly in lust with each other, to this.

I'm not sure I'll ever see him again, not unless I call him, as he just said, which I won't. I won't be allowed to call him.

I don't know how, but we seem to be on the same page, because in a moment of desperation, we lean over and hug each other. He squeezes me to his chest, burying his face in my neck; in my hair. I wrap my arms around his waist and hold him like it's the last time, breathing in his scent; taking in the warmth of his body.

"Goodbye, Charlie."

BLAIRE
(PART ONE)

28

I step inside my apartment and stare at everything, frozen, remembering when Charlie said my place is incredibly clinical. It is. I've never really noticed before. The double height ceilings and the vast curving walls are gleaming white with no imperfections, cold to the eye. The arc staircase beyond the kitchen consists of smooth brushed steel, the floating steps wrapped in white veneer. The furnishings are white and ultra-modern with sharp edges. Even the air smells clinical with bleach.

It feels like forever since I've been here.

Shutting the front door, I wander around the dining table and through the kitchen area, where I put down my keys and my gun. I flinch at the sound of the keys clanging against the countertop.

It's so quiet in here.

Charlie's house is quiet too but it's so full of things... so full of personality. I miss his house already, the way it smells of him, the homely feel to it...

Stopping in my lounge area, I gaze deadpan out of the windows. The sky is dark gray and almost breaking with rain, the clouds twisting and churning to the tune of the wind. It was sunny this morning. Now, it's gloomy.

I lower onto the middle of the leather couch, holding my phone in my hands, trying to remember a time when I felt comfortable here.

I can't.

It doesn't feel like home. It never has.

Warm tears spill down my cheeks, spitting over my hands in my lap.

I cannot believe Charlie just left me here. We still have a week and he just left me?

Hunching over, I break into mute sobs, my chest aching so badly.

In one day I've discovered that my entire life might have been a lie, that Maksim might've outbid a government agency for me, but none of that bothers me. I don't give a shit about anything before Charlie anymore.

He said he loves me and that he wants me to choose to leave Maksim and go with him for myself. No one has ever given a shit about what I want. No one has even thought to give a shit about what I want.

I cry harder and louder, to the point where I can't really breathe, hoping it'll make the pain in my chest go away. It doesn't. If anything, crying makes *this* seem more real.

Why has Charlie played Devil's Advocate by forcing my hand like this? He knows me. He knows I can't make such a massive decision for myself.

A part of me wishes he'd listened to his brother and just taken me—I can't bear to think of a life without him in it, a life where only Maksim matters.

Panic rolls in my stomach as I think of Maksim and I start trembling, my mind whirling.

He might be here soon, and then... and then everything goes back to the way it was before *him*. Before Charlie.

Maksim might want to hit me—the satisfaction he derives from causing me pain might be stronger than ever before because we've never been separated for so long.

I'm scared.

I think about the first time I saw Charlie in Maksim's office, how crafty and careless he was, and how wicked he looked. He's changed so much over the past few months. He's not the man I first met.

He said he loves me.

Why does that hurt so fucking much to know?

My phone vibrates in my hand with an incoming call from Maksim and my stomach coils with dread.

I haven't spoken to him in so long that he almost feels like a stranger. I don't want to speak to him. I want to go back to Charlie, but I can't.

"Hello?" I say softly, putting the phone to my ear with a shuddering hand. I have to answer Maksim's call. If I don't, he'll definitely come over and belt me, and it's been so long since anyone has hit me... I don't want him to hurt me.

"My little pet..." he croons, his voice bizarrely warming me from within. It's an unanticipated, relieving feeling. "How are you?" he says huskily, his Russian accent like home to me.

Combing my hair back over my shoulder, I blink ahead, filtering the familiar sensation of his voice.

I still have Maksim, I remind myself, breathing in and out steadily to stow my tears. I still have him, so it's going to be okay. If I had neither Charlie nor Maksim, I'd really feel lost.

"I'm okay," I say, a little nervous.

"Good. I'm glad." He sounds very relaxed, nothing like I was expecting. "Are you ready to shut down London, my little pet? Everyone is waiting on you."

Everyone? Does that mean Charlie as well?

I try to push him out of my mind because I can't think about him right now, not while I'm on the phone with Maksim, and not while I've got a job to do. I can cry over him tonight if need be.

From the couch, I roam into my dark computer room, sliding open the paneled door. I'm stunned to see my computers are all turned on. The room is aglow with white light.

Maksim has already been here today, it seems.

Did Charlie tell Maksim that he was going to leave me here today? That he's relinquishing his last week with me?

Don't think of him.

I sit in the large office chair and set my mobile on loud speaker, putting it on the desk.

"I'm just setting up," I lie softly to steal a moment. I take in a deep breath and let it out, allowing my emotions to flow freely as if I'm meditating. I need to get a grip. I can't function in a state of emotional turmoil.

Blanking, I say, "I'm ready, cэp Maksim."

"She's ready," he tells someone. "Right, my little pet, first, I want you to shut down a mile radius around Canary Warf."

Putting my fingers on the keyboard keys, I lock in a few codes and a decent percentage of London goes down, giving me full control. I scan the CCTV screens to be sure it's worked. Cars skid to a stop at blind traffic lights, causing a few minor accidents. Shop owners dart outside and glance about in a panic because their electricity is now nonexistent.

Perfect.

The next code I enter turns every traffic light red, causing mayhem.

"She's done it," I hear someone say; I don't recognize his voice.

"Good girl," Maksim says, which is strange because he never calls me a 'good girl'. "Now, the black truck parked outside of Canary Warf Barclays bank, the one with a number plate reading, 'Zeta', do you see it?"

Looking up at the top left computer screen, I zoom in using the computer mouse.

"Yes, I see it." My chest aches. That's something to do with Charlie.

Please, stop thinking about him!

"You are to guide that truck through London to a private underground car park with no mistakes. Do you understand?"

"Sure," I say softly. "I understand."

He tells me the underground car park address, then he snaps, "Podgotovsja!"

Sharp hairs cascade down my arms at the sound of Maksim telling me to prepare, my entire body coming to attention.

I train my attention, and so it begins. While I bash at the keyboard keys like a robot, locking in some more codes to keep control of London's traffic system, I listen to all of Maksim's instructions: "Make these traffic lights red. Make those green."

The truck is on target, speeding through every green light I summon.

On the screens, I notice the police are going crazy, lighting up London with their blues and reds, the sirens howling through the streets. I shut them off by the Museum of London Docklands, ensuring the traffic is so wild that they cannot get through. I then focus back on the truck, on getting it to point B with no hiccups.

The job is done within ten minutes. I delete my codes to hand back control of London's Closed Circuit System and sit back, clasping my hands together in my lap.

I listen to a commotion in the background on the phone, an array of voices saying, "We need to go. You get the money. I'll burn the truck. Tell Charlie I'll drop the money off to Andres."

Charlie...

"You did well, my little pet," Maksim says, pulling me from my crushing thoughts, "but I never for a second doubted you." He goes quiet for a moment, and I suspect he's covering the phone speaker because I cannot hear a thing. Then, his voice fills my ears, "I want you at my house in an hour. I'll be here waiting for you."

"Of course, cəp Maksim," I whisper. "See you soon."

We bid each other goodbye and I hang up the phone, wondering what he has in store for me. I've done everything he's asked of me, so he has to be happy with me. He has to be. If he isn't, I'm not sure I can handle his wrath right now. I'm not in the right frame of mind.

"Don't think of that, Blaire," I beg myself.

BLAIRE
(PART ONE)

———

Pushing to my feet, I make my way out of my apartment, grabbing my keys and my gun off the kitchen countertop on my way out. I shove my gun in my inside jacket pocket, just as my mobile pings with a text message.

Checking the screen, I see it's from Decena.

My heart drops through me like a boulder. Why's he texting?

Eyes glued to my phone, I subconsciously press for the elevator and step inside, torn for whether I should read the message—*itching to read it.*

I shouldn't. I need to let go of Charlie. I need to let go of the past two months if I'm to get back to normal. Maksim will appreciate me getting back to normal, and even more so if I suffer no problems. He won't hurt me if I behave.

My heart splitting in two, I delete the message without reading it and exit the elevator when the steel brushed doors slide open.

The lobby is dead quiet, like my apartment.

I carry on through the building, pushing open the underground car park doors with effort because they're so heavy.

In the car park, it's cold and dark, the ceiling lights flickering on and off; buzzing with electricity.

I reach my car and click the keys to unlock it, making it beep and flash. I remember Charlie asking me stupid questions about this car. Why does my chest ache when I think about him?

BLAIRE
(PART ONE)

Sinking into the driver's seat, I press the button to beckon the purring engine, and while my car warms up, I scroll through my other unread messages on my mobile.

James has been going nuts. I've got over thirty messages from him, asking if I'm okay; where am I.

- Blaire where are you? I'm in Maksim's house looking for you. People are saying that Charlie Decena just shouted at everyone to leave the kitchen, though not you. Are you okay? I need a favor. Text me back ASAP. -

- Is it true that you had a fight with Charlie yesterday because he tried to kiss you? I've just overheard Maksim telling Rumo. -

- Blaire I'm worried. It's been over a week since anyone has seen or heard from you. Text me back to let me know you're still alive. -

- I've been to your apartment and taken some of your money. I'm hiring someone to find you. I have to know you're okay. You've been missing for three weeks now. -

- Blaire things are getting strange. MI5 have been to see Maksim. Your image and your fingerprint have been processed through the British system without Maksim's knowledge. What the fuck is going on? -

BLAIRE
(PART ONE)

- Maksim has tried to pay off MI5 so they stop your search but they won't. They say the order has come from above. Where the fuck are you? -

- Some Latin American guy called Nicolas is in Maksim's office with him. He's trying to find out where you come from, asking questions about your parents. Please, I'm begging you Blaire if you can, message me back. -

- Blaire I'm fucking nervous. Charlie is at one of Maksim's parties and he's making a show of his feelings for you, saying how lovely you are; that he'd like to have you for himself. What's going on? I'm losing the plot here! -

- If you're getting my messages, here's an update. Tatiana has just flown in. She's going crazy at Maksim for supposedly bartering you. Why haven't you texted me back to tell me what's going on? Are you staying with Charlie? -

- Is it true that Charlie pardoned Maksim a debt of thirty-five million Euro's for three months with you? Tatiana is screaming at Maksim as I write this text, saying that he should've gone to her for the money, not sold you. Maksim is fighting his corner, telling her that Charlie wouldn't take any amount of money. He wanted you as payment. Is this all true? -

BLAIRE
(PART ONE)

- Blaire Tatiana has warned Maksim that if Charlie doesn't give you back, he's not allowed to come after you. She won't start a war with the Los Zetas. Everyone is shit scared of the Los Zetas, and when I say everyone, I mean everyone! The Albanians say not to fuck with them; the Turks; the Columbians... Who are the Los Zetas? -

- I know you haven't messaged me back, but it doesn't matter. I know what's going on now. Tatiana has been questioning me, and in exchange for my answers, she's told me where you are and that you're okay. Apparently, she wants to talk to you also, but Charlie refuses to let her. I'm glad he won't let her.
I just want to say, if you can, you should stay with Charlie and try to find some peace Blaire.
I'll never forget you. -

I read a small portion of his text messages, stunned. I'm so stunned that I can't really process anything. It feels like so much has gone on in my absence—it's almost like everyone has been going crazy over another girl and I'm reading about it from afar.

Feeling numb, I shove my car into reverse, straighten up, and then I steer out of the underground, into the gray day.

Charlie wasn't lying when he told his brother that he's run a check on me. I don't know why this thought creeps into my mind, but it does, and I can't will it away.

Turning right, I cross The London Bridge, barely registering the city bustling before me.

BLAIRE
(PART ONE)

How did he get my fingerprint? I subconsciously watched him wash up everything after our meals, and when I ate alone, I cleared up my own mess. There wasn't any surface he could have gotten my fingerprint from...

...Maybe he obtained it from my apartment?

I stop at a roundabout as the lights signal red to wait, amid bumper to bumper traffic.

And, how did he get my photo? Maksim doesn't even have a photo of me.

The light flashes green, so I maneuver through the traffic. I take the third exit off the roundabout and reach the motorway junction for Dartford, and I don't know what comes over me. Hitting the break, I come to a screeching stop in the middle of the road, all those messages hitting me like lightening.

MI5.

Tatiana.

Tatiana telling Maksim he's not to come after me if Charlie decides to keep me. *Fuck,* if Charlie didn't send me home, I'd still be with him.

A flock of people surround my car, and I vaguely hear them yelling to see if I'm okay, am I hurt.

I stare at the sign that will take me back to Tonbridge Wells—to Charlie.

A part of me—my heart—wants me to turn toward Tonbridge Wells. I want to go back to Charlie.

The other part of me—my head—tells me to veer for Dartford. I know I have to go back to Maksim. I've always known. But there's something else at play now.

I don't know what to do, so pushing the car in gear, I do the only thing that feels right.

BLAIRE
(PART ONE)

29

I find Maksim at his house in his office, sitting behind his desk with cool composure.

My heart drums at the sight of him. He's wearing a white shirt with the sleeves rolled up and his brown hair tied back, his golden eyes trained on me here in the doorway.

The life that I've spent with him coils in my mind, his voice on repeat while I slept, whispering, *"We'll kill for each other. We are each other's."* The hidings, the darkness and the dampness...

Half an hour ago when I was in my car, conflicted between my heart and my head, I chose this path. I chose this path because it's the only path I am allowed to walk. Of course I'd greedily take a life with Charlie over a life with Maksim, but I'll only do that with my master's permission. I *can* only do that with my master's permission.

So, here I am.

Holding the doorframe, I smile awkwardly at Maksim. He extends a hand for me to sit in the chair opposite his desk, so I do, keeping a wary eye on him.

"You are wearing your hair down?" he asks in Russian—the whole conversation is in Russian—and then he tips his head, his eyes thinning at me.

"Oh... sorry." I grip a length that's hanging over my shoulder. "I-I didn't get a chance to tie it back. Shall I-"

"No." He lifts a hand to stop me. "Leave it down. It looks nice." He sits forward, cupping his—*clean shaven chin?*

I try to stay focused but I can't help screwing up my face. Why has he shaved? Maksim always has stubble dress his oval chin. And since when did he tie his hair back?

"You look different, my little pet. Nervous."

That's because I am nervous.

I'm surprised to find I'm not upset with him for bartering me to Charlie. If anything, I'm grateful for the time of peace and happiness he's given me.

"It's been an odd few months, cэр Maksim," I say vacantly.

"Yes," he drawls. "Charlie told me earlier today that he isn't taking you back with him. Is he bored?"

I shrug because I don't want to tell him about what happened yesterday, or today.

He cocks a brow at me. "You don't know if he's bored of you?"

"No, cэр Maksim."

"Hmmm," he hums. "I see... How was your time with him?"

I don't even blink when I say, "It was okay."

BLAIRE
(PART ONE)

"And your health?"

I frown, not following.

"Your virginity." Every word he says is executed with slow purpose. I almost forgot how intense he is.

I swallow. "Still intact."

"Good." He grins at me. "I imagine Charlie wanted so badly to take it."

I don't know what to say, so I just look at him. I imagine Charlie did too.

"Before you give me a thorough account of your time with him, I want to know something." He runs his thumb across his lower lip. "Did you overhear any of his business dealings? Is he speaking with The American Congressman?"

My eyes widen. How the fuck does he know Charlie deals with The American Congressman?

"No. I never heard anything," I flat out lie, but it weirdly comes naturally to me.

"He *never!* spoke in front of you?"

I shake my head, desperate to ask why he wants to know if Charlie spoke to The American Congressman. What's that to him? None of the Russians deal with the Americans.

"Huh... strange..." he brushes this off, believing me—Maksim thinks I'd never lie to him, and I wouldn't have lied to him before meeting Charlie, but Charlie has changed me.

"So tell me, my little pet," he's still musing, pinching his bottom lip now, "what did Charlie do to you exactly?" He says that he wants intimate details—when and where—and he wants them now. "What did he do to you sexually? How did he make you feel?"

I have to start right from the beginning, so I bashfully tell him about the first night. "I woke up in a strange bed with... with Charlie sitting next to me, playing with my hair. He told me what was going on... I attacked him with feeble effort because I was drugged but it was enough to put some distance between us. Then, once I calmed down, he told me to take off my clothes but of course, I-I refused... I wanted to speak to you."

"Of course you did, my little pet. Of course." His eyes glow with mockery. "Carry on. I'd like every detail."

"Well, after I spoke to you," I blink at Maksim, "I did what I was told; I let him take off my clothes." I tell him all of what I remember. It's internal torture when I get to the part where Charlie first went down on me... how he splayed me out and forced me to orgasm over and over; the sensation of his cock sliding in me. I want to cup my face and hideaway in my hands. Everything feels too private to speak of—this is *our* private business, as Charlie once said. I now understand what he meant.

I stop and pause a few times but Maksim yells at me to give him, "Every bloody detail! How did he make you feel? Did he go down on you more than once? Masturbate you with his hands? Did he fuck your pussy with his tongue? Tell me everything, Blaire."

Cringing, I do tell him everything. My cheeks heat under my pale skin as I speak of my emotions. "I felt... broken and whole at once when he had sex with me anally. The sensations made me feel a bit head-drunk...

"...The next day, Char-Charlie kissed me on the mouth like he was in love with me or something. I-I was terrified, cəp Maksim. I didn't know whether to fight him off or not. You told me not too, so I-"

"What next?" he urges me to get to the good parts.

I'm almost green with embarrassment when I say Charlie had me please him with my mouth, that he would use his hands to stimulate me when he didn't go down on me.

I don't tell him about the deal we made—the deal where, if I put Charlie on his ass, he won't touch me—because that feels more private than the sexual intimacy between us.

"Did you like it when he made you orgasm?" Maksim says, his eyes tapering with wonder.

Silence, and I nod.

Maksim grinds his teeth. I can see his mind working overtime.

"How were your days when Charlie wasn't abusing you?" he says, running his tongue along his upper teeth. "Were you kept in one room? Did he let you out?"

"No. He didn't keep me locked up." My voice softens when I speak of our friendly fights; when I explain how he took care of me. "He cooked me food—breakfast, lunch and dinner—and he ate with me. He always made sure I was okay." I shrug. "Charlie was nice to me."

There is another long pause where we look at each other, blue eyes to golden brown.

"You care about him," Maksim says eventually. He's not asking. He knows.

I nod.

His expression drops, his eyes flashing with some emotion I've not seen on him before, and I'm not sure, but he almost looks... frightened? No... can't be. Why would he be frightened that I care about Charlie? If anything, he should be angry—ready and willing to belt me.

He doesn't.

Fondling with the collar of his shirt, he tries to straighten up in his chair, plastering on that iron stare he executes so well.

"Do you care about *him!* more than you do me?" he asks.

I don't know why, but I hesitate. All I can think about right now is how Charlie cuddled me, touched me, and kissed me.

I know I have to say something, so I tell Maksim, "No. I don't."

My words don't affect him. I suspect he knows I'm lying. It's only a half lie. I care about Charlie in a different way compared to how I care about Maksim.

"What he did to you, Blaire, did it hurt?"

I visibly flinch as he uses my given name.

"Did it hurt more than anything I've ever done to you?" he says.

"No." I look down at my hands in my lap. "Nothing hurt."

"Not even when he fucked your ass? I find that hard to believe. You were a virgin there."

"Um..." My stomach tightens with nerves. "I'm not sure. He... he prepared me."

"How? How did he prepare you?" He's back on par, taking no prisoners. He wants to know every fucking factor. "You left those details out, didn't you?"

"He..." I gulp, blinking in the sight of my trainers—the trainers Charlie gave me this morning. "He used my orgasm for lubricant and fingered me for a while, starting with one finger, and then two..."

"How long until he took you?"

I'm tomato red. I can't look Maksim in the eyes. *When is this going to be over?*

"A while... maybe an hour... I'm not too sure. I was dizzy because he drugged me and he was using these strange oils that he said would help me relax."

"Isopropyl Nitrite..." His chair creaks as he sits back. "So, when he penetrated you-"

Oh, god... *STOP!*

"-It didn't hurt?"

"It hurt a little at first but he took his time—said he wasn't in a rush."

"Do you miss him, Blaire?"

Maksim's abrupt question causes me to look up at him. There's no expression on his face.

I nod innocently. I cannot lie about this—it's written all over my face. I know it.

His eyes enlarge, and there's that look again; that look of fear. I've never seen Maksim look frightened before.

"Does that hurt?" he says with caution. "Missing him, I mean? Does it hurt, Blaire?"

My lips wobble because that ache in my chest... it consumes me.

I nod.

"So, he has hurt you," he sounds relieved, taking in a few purifying breaths.

My hands start to shake in my lap.

"I guess so," my voice comes out all small, peppered in tears. "But that's the only pain he's caused me. He's never hurt me like you do, сэр Maksim."

"And do you like that he didn't physically hurt you?"

Swallowing, I nod.

I'm expecting Maksim to lay into me—to give me a good bloody hiding. I can feel his anger on the surface of my skin—but he doesn't. He's acting carefully, and utterly confusing me when he diverts with telling me about his time over the past two and a half months, that he went to Russia to visit Tatiana, that he missed me more than he thought he would.

"I visited my parents' graves and laid burnt roses," he says, giving me this heartless look. He burns the roses to take the beauty out of them. In his mind, anything burnt and damaged represents his parents.

"Red roses?" I ask softly, feeling sorry for him. He hates his parents. He has a hard time visiting their graves—usually takes his anger and hurt out on me after visiting them, or James.

I suddenly wonder where James is but I'm too nervous to ask.

"Of course red roses, my little pet." Maksim glances between my features, his strangely soft and inviting. "Whenever I'm there, I think of you, of your loyalty and your passion to defend me. It gives me strength." He touches his chest, then he goes right in to how he feels about me, that while he doesn't always show it, "I do love you, Blaire."

My heart is in my throat. He's never said that before. He never explains himself to me or tells me that he loves me, and just too really fuck with my head, he offers me a week off duty.

"I-I don't need any time off, сэр Maksim. I don't..." I pause, lost for words. The last thing I need is ample of time to think about the last few months. "If you need me, I'm here."

He smiles wickedly at me. "I know, my little pet. I know."

We talk a while longer about his time in Russia, how cold it is there and how Tatiana is colder. "She isn't happy that I bartered you, but in all honesty, I'm not glad I did, either. I shouldn't have used you as a bargaining tool. You were mine and mine alone, and I've failed you."

I don't know what to say—I'm wavering under his golden eyes—so I say nothing.

When he's done pouring out his emotions to me, he tells me that I can go home now. "I'll call you when I need you, my little pet."

I rise to my feet, feeling a bit awkward. I'm not sure if I should say goodbye or just leave—it's been so long since I was under Maksim's power.

Maksim decides for me.

He rounds his desk, walking tall and gracefully masculine, and he ushers me to the front door, where he kisses the side of my face. "I'm glad you're back, my little pet. So, so glad."

I smile at him, and just when I think it's over, he grabs my wrist.

"Where did you get this?" He lifts my hand to eyesight—the bracelet.

I hesitate to speak but he narrows his eyes at me, making me feel small and feeble

"Charlie gave it to me."

It's like I just slapped him. His face drops again, and he blinks at me, flabbergasted.

"So, he's tried to spoil you with twenty-thousand dollar bracelets, has he?" His fingers dig into my flesh. "Give it to me."

My entire body sinks with panic.

"No. I-he... he said... I can't, сэр Maksim."

"You can't?" His hand wrapped around my wrist shakes with fury. "Are you taking orders from him now too?"

"I... He said I-" I don't know what to tell him. *Just give him the fucking bracelet!*

He laughs under his breath, and it's like the last hour didn't happen. Old Maksim is back, and he means business.

"Okay, my little pet, then I guess you'll earn that bracelet."

Fisting the back of my hair, Maksim drags me through his house and up the stairs, tearing my scalp. I don't stumble. I'm gracefully poise as he hauls me along with him.

Outside his bedroom, he stops to kick the door open and yanks me inside, yelling in Russian as he does. The curtains are drawn and it's almost too dark to see anything. Almost. Surrounding the edges of the ceiling, blue lights beam down, illuminating an assortment of gadgets meant to inflict pain. The Saint Andrew's Cross with leather handcuffs standing in the tall bay window—it looks like hell warmed up, old scratch marks crisscrossing the wooden surface where someone has tried to escape. Whips and leather floggers are lined up around the huge wooden four poster bed, like ornaments. A cattle prod hangs on the wall above the dull fireplace next to the bed.

My blood runs cold. I'm absolutely terrified, my eyes glazing over with tears. He used to sting me with that cattle prod until I could stomach the pain.

"Get out, now!" Maksim yells, and I cower, his voice sharp enough to raise hairs.

I wonder who he's talking to, thinking it might be James, until I see a little blonde girl in his bed. She's wearing a black leather leash, nothing else. She flicks the duvet back, scrambles to her feet with her lush parts jiggling about, and dashes out of the bedroom; slams the door shut with a loud *bang*.

I don't cringe. I'm trying to stay mentally balanced— *block it out, Blaire.*

There's a strange smell in the air; strawberries or something, a sweet, fruity aroma. I don't know why. Maksim usually burns brut candles.

He pulls on my hair and forces me around to face him, bends my neck back and glares down on me with fiery golden eyes. "You will forget about the last three months, my little pet," his hand in my hair twists and tightens to the point where I moan in pain, "because I'll beat the memories out of you. And if I can't beat the memories out of you, I'll medicate them out of you."

WALLOP! He slaps me around the face, knocking me onto the bed. Tangled in my own hair, I land with a heavy bounce, my knees hitting the carpeted floor. My cheek throbs and my head... fuck it hurts. I cup my face, frightened shitless, suddenly thinking about Charlie. He never once hurt me. I remember when he said, 'You might be the only girl I won't hit...'

Why the fuck am I thinking about that?

"Last chance to give me that bracelet, my little pet."

I sob in my closed mouth, not wanting to give it to him. It's mine. It's the only thing I have of Charlie.

Trembling violently, I shake my head to say 'no'.

"Okay then. As you wish." Maksim tears me out of my jacket, then my t-shirt, his nails scratching my skin because he can't undress me quick enough. I sink to the floor in my sports bra and trousers, desperately looking up at him; looking up at my master, the one I shouldn't ever refuse.

"You look scared, my little pet," he sounds pleased as he says this, smiling evilly at me with crinkled eyes.

He points out, and I know what he's gesturing at—I've been trussed up in this room many times before. Unfolding myself from the floor, I get up and walk across the room, stopping in the corner. *Breathe. Focus.* Closing my eyes and shakily reaching up, I grab two sets of chains that are fixed to the ceiling. The metal is cold in my palms, but the room is too warm, creating a mist of sweat down my spine. I feel like I can't breathe.

A rustling sound by the bed draws my attention, wood clanging against wood. I peer back through scraps of hair, immediately wishing I didn't—he's choosing his weapon.

"Podgotovsja!" Maksim yells for me to prepare once he's behind me, like he usually does.

I cower, bracing myself, then he whips me senseless with a sjambok, an African cattle whip, *Wa-tch!* Each assault blazes through my mind like red flashes of light.

BLAIRE
(PART ONE)

Screams get caught in my throat, my body jerking back and forth against his attack.

Wa-tch!

Wa-tch!

It goes on for what feels like hours.

My back arches and my flesh splits open, hot blood slithering down my spine and soaking the waist of my trousers.

Wa-tch!

Wa-tch!

By the time he's finished, I'm in such a strange zone in my mind that I can't really see anything. I feel like a shell of a person, the old Blaire—the Blaire before Charlie.

Charlie... Fuck! Why does thinking about him make me want to cry?

I break into sobs, and Maksim punches me. Holding my neck in one hand, swinging with his other, **THUMP** he knocks my head back; blacks my left eye. Blood trickles down my cheek, over the throbbing where he slapped me.

No pain, I tell myself, *you can't feel anything.*

While I'm a messy, lifeless pile on the floor—I don't even know how I got here—he cuts me out of my trousers and my pants.

"Awh!" I wince in agony as he snaps my bra open and hauls it down my arms, tossing it across the room.

"On the bed," he commands, panting with anger, "head down. Ass in the air."

Not registering what's going to happen, I crawl to my master's command like a cat, from the floor, up the side of the bed, until I'm in the middle with my hands and knees sinking into the mattress.

The night gets so dark with punishments, Maksim doing fucking awful things to me. Things I can't even bring myself to think about.

The sound of buttons clanging against the wooden floors. He's undressing, dropping his shirt, and then his trousers. The bed dips at my feet, almost knocking me off balance. Large, cold hands on my hips; nails digging into my flesh with hungry pursuit.

"Open your legs," Maksim says. He's breathing so hard I know he's excited, warm air blowing up my back.

Shivering, I do as I'm told, my ankles twisted inward because I'm nervous. He pushes against the low of my back, forcing me to arch, shoving my face in the sheets. They smell like musky man sweat.

I squeeze my eyes shut.

Don't think.

It's so hard not to. Nausea rises through me when I feel he's parting my ass cheeks with callous hands, saying, "That Latin fuck is lucky, testing my goods before I have."

A dripping, spitting sound. It makes me retch. The head of his cock is wet, I feel as he smears it against my anus, urging the tip in. My insides churn and now I'm silently crying my heart out, struggling to mentally will away what's happening.

He's going to fuck my ass and he's not even preparing me. How can I block that out?

A powerful thrust, he's roaring with dark passion, and then he's wedged right inside me, causing me to spew up all over the pillows and all over my hands.

The smell is vile; acidic and...

I heave again, my insides burning: my throat, my ass muscles. It's too much. I feel too full.

"Show me your bracelet, my little pet," Maksim's voice is stark and enraged, evil lust coming off him in waves. "Show it to me!"

I whimper, terrified out of my mind, then I brace myself up on one elbow and reach back to show him my bracelet.

Long fingers curl around my wrist and pull my arm back some more.

"Aargh!" I scream so hard as he bites me, his teeth sinking into my wrist.

He kisses the bite mark after—I hiss. It's so sore—and then he licks over each puncture with the tilt of his tongue. "Every time you look at this bracelet, you will think of me—this scar will make you."

Letting go of my wrist, he shifts on his knees, causing his cock to shift inside my ass. My stomach rolls. I vomit again, retching so hard that my belly pangs in pain.

I think I mentally pass out from here. It's just too much.

I vaguely hear Maksim ask if I want him to stop, and I tell him with weak effort, "No, сэр Maksim." I wouldn't dare say anything else.

"Now that your mind is frail and open," he lies over my back, crushing me, and says against my ear in a head drunk voice, "you will succumb to my orders." Pulling out halfway, he tells me to prepare, and then plunges back in me, balls deep, tearing me apart. "You will not think about Charlie anymore, my little pet."

Out, and back in with viciousness, he stretches me open.

I'm crying in agony through closed teeth. He's groaning with rawness, the sound pulsing through my chest.

"You will not speak to *him!* or anyone else without my permission. You'll not look at another man..." the rules are never ending, as is his cruelty. "I am the only man you want."

Grabbing a hand full of my hair, he yanks my head back as he sits on his knees and fucks me with all he has, skin slapping against skin, him pounding my ass.

My body is shaking uncontrollably with cold sweat. I scream in agony every time he practically hits my stomach, until he cums violently, his cock getting longer and thicker, emptying inside me.

He doesn't beckon my arousal, not once—there's nothing hot about this. I'm as dry as a bone, disgusted with what he's doing to me, whimpering in pity for myself.

"That was good," he drawls, "worth the wait."

Curling his fingers around his cock, he slowly pulls all the way out of me. Warm juices slither down my inner thighs, over my knees, dripping on the bed.

Gasping with relief that it's over, I drop on the bed, but I only get a moment's rest before he continues his torture.

He climbs off the bed, causing me to bounce up and down on the mattress, and picks up a different whip from the floor-

Wa-tch!

-He beats me into a numb state, yelling with zeal that I'm his. "You will always be mine, my little pet!"

BLAIRE
(PART ONE)

I don't even know how many times he sodomizes me. It's a pattern. He cums, stops for a while to whip me on the bed, then he fucks me again.

By morning, I'm empty that when he tells me I can go home and have the week off, I find my keys on the floor amid my clothes and leave the house naked, bar my bracelet. I fucking well earned this.

It's freezing outside, a typical English morning with a burning pink sunrise and silver frost on the trees. My breath mists the air. My nipples are bruised and hard like bullets—he must have pinched me. I don't remember.

The stony driveway crunches against the soles of my feet, but still, I can't feel a thing.

There's a blanket in the boot of my car, so I get it out to wrap myself up, and then I drive to my apartment.

London is before my very eyes, but I don't see a thing. I'm lost in my mind, trying to focus on anything other than what Maksim has just done to me. It's not as if he hasn't beaten me like that before, but last night felt different. It felt like a different kind of conditioning. Maybe because he's never had penetrative sex with me before.

Pulling into the underground car park, I get out of my car and walk lifelessly into the elevator, and then into my apartment. I drop the bloody blanket on the floor by the front door and patter into my bedroom, heading for the en-suite bathroom.

I'm not in any sort of pain until I get in the shower. The water isn't too hot but the welts on my back are on fire, so sore it's almost too much to bear.

While I wince in agony against the soap, I don't cry. I don't do anything. I simply get clean of semen and blood and Maksim's saliva, and crawl into bed without drying myself. I should clean up the bite mark on my arm with some vodka and bandage it up, but I can't will myself to move.

I sleep for as long as I can, hoping that the next time I see Maksim, he won't be so mad at me.

BLAIRE
(PART ONE)

30

The following week passes in agonizing, numb slow motion.

I wake the next morning, after Maksim beat the shit out of me and sexually violated me for the first time, and I'm in agony. My back is split and crusty with scabs, my hips ache from being banged so hard, and my arm is throbbing, oozing with clear fluid.

I manage to climb out of bed and hobble to the kitchen so I can thoroughly clean the bite mark. I must before it gets infected.

Slumping against the kitchen countertop, I grab a bottle of vodka from the side and twist off the cap, keeping all thoughts at bay—I'm in no right frame of mind to be thinking. I hold out my wounded arm over the sink, shut my eyes, and I pour.

"Aargh!" I scream my heart out, tipping up the bottle to stop the cold, burning liquid from touching my skin. I'm trembling from head to toe, cold sweat clinging to my flesh. My arm feels like it's double the size because it's so swollen and the puncture marks burn like a bitch.

I pour again and scream, again and scream.

By the time the bottle is empty, the wound is throbbing.

Taking deep, steady breaths, fighting not to pass out, I put down the bottle on the countertop and get the medical kit out of the drawer to wrap up the wound, ensuring it's not too tight nor too lose.

I roll the bandage around my arm with caution, wincing at the pressure, the smell of the elastic material reminding me of something clinical.

Done.

I breathe out.

It feels better already, though I'm dizzy from the pain and my mouth is watering like crazy.

I take a moment, holding my dizzy head, trying not to look at the bright ball of fire that is the sun streaming up the sky. I've got such a headache.

Pouring myself a glass of water, I try for a sip but my stomach rolls with queasiness. I don't think I've ever felt such a vast collection of overwhelming sensations in one sitting before.

Needing to rest, I grab my phone from the kitchen side, for if Maksim calls, and I crawl back into bed, my mind still empty of thoughts.

I sleep the day away, occasionally stirring to screams that I recognize as my own; screams that wrack my body with panic and pain. I don't remember any dreams, thankfully—I can't deal with anything more fucking with my head right now. I need to get over what Maksim has done to me.

It's midday when I open my eyes again, the sun burning high in the sky, streaming in. Every limb I have feels heavy and tight and my ass is so sore it's almost unbearable.

There's a text message on my phone from James. He wants to know why I didn't stay with Charlie; wants to know if I'm alright, why I'm not working. I can't even manage a smile about the fact that he cares. I'm too empty.

Pushing the duvet back so I can get up, I grimace, my hips feeling like they've ceased up. When is the pain going to end?

In my grasp, the sheets are wet and heavy. I glance over my bed. The white sheets are covered in streaks of dark red blood. My back must've been bleeding while I slept.

The notion doesn't bother me. Nothing seems to be bothering me. Yeah I'm in pain, and that's overwhelming, but inside, I'm so... numb. It's been a long, long time since Maksim gave me a hiding like that, and I'd usually be sad with guilt for pissing him off so furiously, but not this time. This time I'm just emotionally numb.

My throat is raw. I limp to the kitchen for some water, which doesn't make me feel sick this time. I also try to eat a bowl of cereal, barely registering the fact that there's fresh milk and food in the fridge. Hovering over the bowl, elbows on the countertop, I manage a few mouthfuls of cornflakes but I'm just not hungry. I'm in too much pain to do anything other than sleep.

I use the toilet, heaving at the sight of blood on the tissue, then I slip back into bed and rest for two days without showering.

BLAIRE
(PART ONE)

Day five: the bite mark on my arm is scabbing over. I can feel the scabs rubbing against the bandage every time I move. Lying in bed, I unwind the bandage to let the wound air so it can heal better. I drop the bandage on the floor. Twenty puncture marks I count on my forearm, each one red around the edges and a bit itchy. I try my best not to scratch the wound but it's difficult, like an itch you can't quite reach.

Slugging it out of bed, I use the toilet and manage a full bowl of cereal today, though only because I need to eat—I need to regain my strength if I'm to heal—then I'm back in bed.

Day six: I attempt a shower but the welts and cuts on my body are so sore that even *I* can't bear the pain. I turn off the faucet, then I shrug into a pair of sports shorts and a t-shirt, and I curl up on the couch, watching the sun rise over London with burning orange rays.

Still, I feel nothing. It's so strange. I don't know what's happened to me. It's like, before this moment I'm in right now, nothing exists.

I float in and out of a dark slumber.

Day seven: I endeavor the gym but I can barely make it up the stairs. With one hand, my mobile in my other, I grip the banister so hard that my knuckles turn white, but every step I take is like walking Mount Everest.

Another step and another step. I'm halfway up the staircase now, but I just can't make the rest.

I struggle for another step, fighting with lower body force, and a wound on my back splits.

"Aargh!" I scream through closed teeth, and finally, I break down.

I can't take this numb feeling anymore. I can't stand the pain anymore.

Sliding down the wall, I sit here on the stairs, cradling my mobile, wondering why I don't feel anything. Wondering why I'm so empty. I want to cry but I can't.

Is this a result of Maksim or Charlie?

Charlie...

"Fuck!" I scream so loud that I can feel my voice in the atmosphere. I thrash my fingers into my hair and pull at the strands, inflicting my own pain.

It's the first time I've thought of him since... since...

He shouldn't have sent me home early—a week I could have been with him is a week I've been in pain. He shouldn't have given me this damn bracelet. All of this, the pain and the vacancy in my chest, it's all his fault.

Tears spill down my cheeks, warm tears, and a rush of emotions hit me like a dam has been smashed open.

I don't want to live like this anymore. I don't want Maksim to hurt me anymore. I just want to find some peace.

I felt great peace while living with Charlie, after the first night with him, of course. But even then, he didn't hurt me. It was all mental. I miss waking up to his little notes in the kitchen, saying, *breakfast is in the oven.* I miss knowing he'll be in the gym. I miss that excitement I eventually felt when I knew we'd be having dinner together. I miss... I miss him.

My heart crushing, I scroll through my mobile for his number.

Decena.

The air gets caught in my throat. Tears drip on the screen, making his name look fuzzy. Wiping the tears off with my thumb, I read his number from back to front, storing it in my memory. I delete the name Decena and replace it with Charlie.

Charlie

I can't explain it, but just seeing his name makes me feel better. My chest tightens—no, squeezes, and a strong sense of contentment comes over me. I cannot even feel the pain anymore.

I miss him. I miss him too much.

Before I know it, I'm dialing his number, willing him to pick up because the ringer goes on and on. It takes a moment to register that he's still in England—I can tell by the ringtone—and another moment to wonder why. He said the only reason he was here was for me, and he sent me home, so why hasn't he returned to Mexico?

The ringer dies off but I call him again, and then again. I won't give up until I've spoken to him.

"Pick up," I whisper, blood roaring in my ears. "Please pick up."

"What?" he answers snappily on the sixth call, and my stomach sinks.

"Charlie," I say softly, "it's-it's Blaire."

"Shit, I'm sorry, baby," his voice softens now, the deeper notes melting my bones. "I was expecting a call from someone else."

"Oh... I-well... Shall I call back later or something?"

"No!" he sounds horrified that I'd even ask. "You can call me whenever you want. I've told you that."

BLAIRE
(PART ONE)

I let out a purifying breath of relief, my nose tickling with more tears. It's so good to hear his voice, and it's so good to know I can still contact him whenever I want.

He tells someone to leave the room, then I hear a heavy door shut.

"You took your time, didn't you?" he says. "I texted you a week ago."

Though it hurts stretching out the tight, crusty skin on my back, I lean over with my elbows on my knees and shut my eyes, imagining I'm with him.

"I didn't read your text," I say honestly.

"Why?"

"I..." Pausing, I wonder if I should tell him that I was trying to move on from him, but then I chicken out. "I don't know."

"You don't know?" he snaps, aghast. "I knew I should've called you or just come over to your place." There's a few seconds of silence from him, and I imagine he's thinking hard about something. "So, if you're not calling about my message, then-"

"What did it say, Charlie?" I ask, wishing I read it now. I should have kept it too, and then I could have looked over it when I felt numb and empty like I did only moments ago. It could have been my salvation.

"I wanted to see if you were okay," he says, his voice soft like silk. "And I wanted to tell you that I'm in love with you, Blaire. So in love with you that I can't think of anything else since I sent you home."

I'm wordless, choking up, barely tolerating the hit of his confession.

"You mean everything to me," he says desperately. "I fucking miss you—I want you back."

I whimper in my palm, my emotions imploding. I want to go back but I know I can't, and the thought is like having my heart ripped out.

"Blaire, you still there?"

"Yeah," I squeak out. Covering the speaker with one hand, I stifle back my tears.

"I'm sorry. I don't wanner upset you. I just need you to know that I want you more than anything, Blaire. I want you to come home to me."

Home to him... Fuck, that hurts more than Maksim's torture.

"Where are you?" I ask to divert from my emotions because I cannot stand this chest crushing feeling.

"At the house," he says deadpan. "Have you spoken to Maksim today?"

"No," I shudder at the sound of Maksim's name. "I haven't seen him for a week."

"Why'd you sound like that?" he asks, and I hear a chair creaking, as if he's sitting forward. "Are you crying? Has that motherfucker hurt you!?!"

"No," I lie feebly, wiping my nose with the back of my hand. "I just miss you, is all," I can't believe how easy it is to say that to him.

"Don't be upset over missing me, baby. Everything's gonna be all right."

"It is?" I say, my stomach pooling with hope. I want to go to him. It's such a devastating need. I need him.

"Yeah, course it is. I'm sorting things. I promise."

"Sorting what, Charlie?" I ask, but then my front door clicks open and I freeze.

BLAIRE
(PART ONE)

31

Maksim, James, and a guy I don't recognize, pile up a whole bunch of duffle bags by my dining table.

A weak, shivery feeling washes over me.

One bag is open. There's a ton of money inside.

"Charlie," I curve my hand over the speaker and whisper his name, "Maksim's here. I have to go."

"No, Blaire, wait!"

I hang up on him and switch off my mobile in case he tries to ring back, putting it down on one of the steps. I peer through the banister rails with fearful eyes, scanning the situation.

Ten bags... I count as the pile gets higher, my eyes going back and forth. Twenty bags... Thirty bags...

James and the other guy have to do a few runs downstairs, while Maksim wanders my apartment, his shoes delicately clinking against the marble floors. He's dressed in black slacks and a white shirt that's rolled up at the elbows, revealing a gold watch. He looks like he's ready for business.

As he passes by the staircase, not noticing me, I'm swamped with nerves, trying to figure out why he's here with all that money.

By the time James and the other guy are done running up and down like headless chickens, there are fifty bags piled around my dining table.

I want to go to James. He's the closest thing I have to safety right now.

"My little pet?" Maksim calls out from the kitchen area.

I cringe, trying to be as small as I can.

"You can leave." He turns to James by the front door, his voice deceivingly gentle. "Wait for me in the car."

"I don't mind staying, cэp Maksim," James says, I assume to make sure I'm okay. "I can-"

Maksim only has to give James an iron stare before James head-bows, casts a sneaky glance around my place, and then he's gone.

Shit. I don't want to be alone with Maksim right now. I'm in too much pain and terrified he's going to cause me more.

Maksim saunters through my personal space once more, into the living area and then back out again. He stops at the bottom of the stairs this time, tips his head back and smiles up at me.

"Ah, there you are," he says, a cunning gleam in his golden eyes. "Are you going to come down and see me?"

I nod, then I struggle down the stairs, meeting him on the bottom step. I hug myself, shrinking.

"How are you feeling?" He cocks his head to me, reaches out and runs his fingers down a length of my hair.

"I'm okay." I blink at the floor, unable to endure his wicked gaze.

"Oh, now, my little pet," he tugs on the strand of hair, "don't lie to me."

I cringe again, expecting a blow for lying.

"I'm in a little pain, but I'll be okay," I say softly, focusing on his shiny oxford shoes.

"Of course you will be okay. You're strong." Taking my arm, he helps me hobble over to the dining table, where he insists I sit down next to the duffle bags.

Lowering onto a chair, I wince as my ass feels the pressure of the hard, flat surface, a jolt of pain shooting up my spine.

"Hurting?" Maksim says, amusement in his voice.

Distracted, I nod, peeking over the bags. There has to be millions here in crisp new notes.

"Do you know what this is all about?" Maksim pulls out a chair next to me, scraping it against the floor. "Do you know why I have so much cash?"

I peek up at him, taking a wild guess. "Charlie?"

He said he'd pay Maksim to set me free if he has to, and he's one of the few I know who would have access to this amount of money.

The way Maksim smiles at me... My blood runs cold.

"Clever little pet." He takes one of my hands and holds it in his lap, occasionally squeezing me with long, cruel fingers. "He's paid me to tell you you're free."

My eyes enlarge because there's negotiation in Maksim's voice, but then he gives me this surprised look and I glance away, trying to control the brewing of hope inside me.

"Is this what you want?" he asks, sounding strangely calm. "Do you want me to set you free?"

I shrug. It's all I have. I'm too nervous to say yes. I'm too nervous to tell him that I want to be with Charlie.

Tugging at my hand, making me whine out in pain, Maksim forces me to look up at him.

"Okay." He nods a few times, turning my hand over so he can see the bite mark on my wrist. "You have two options-"

My heartbeat reaches its summit, pounding so hard that I'm sure he can hear it.

"-Option one," he looks up from my wounded arm, right into my eyes, "I'll set you free, but I want you first."

I draw in my eyebrows, studying the expression on his face. Lust?

Does he mean...

Maksim leans closer to me, his soft, shoulder length hair just touching my face. Dropping my eyes to the floor, I sink into my shoulders. I know exactly what he means.

"I want to fuck you," he whispers in my ear, confirming my suspicions.

I quiver as vulgar, disturbing images romp through my mind, the memory of him fucking me with such viciousness.

"I want to show you what you're walking away from, Blaire. I want to kiss every inch of you... make love to you..." He pushes his other hand between my legs and cups my sex over my shorts, making me heave internally. "I want to make you feel good. Know once and for all how much I desire you."

I can't take that deal. I can't even entertain it. Charlie won't want me if I'm tainted by Maksim, and I don't want to be on my own. I'd rather stay with Maksim than be alone.

I wait for Maksim to say, "Option two-" then he pauses for a few seconds, removing his hand from my sex.

I squeeze my thighs together, my toes curling with nerves.

"If you won't let me fuck you," he says, "then you'll stay with me."

Still with my eyes down, I whisper, "Okay."

"Is that what you want, my little pet?" Leaning into me, he kisses the side of my face with suspicious affection, his cold lips chilling me from within. "Do you want to stay with me?"

"Sure I do," I lie, squeezing my eyes shut.

He pulls on my hand again, urging me to face him properly, so I'm practically sitting between his legs. The movement emphasizes how tight and painful the skin on my back is; how new the scabs are.

"Blaire," he says my name, causing me to shrink away, "for us to go back to the way we were before Charlie, you have to get rid of him."

I blink at Maksim then as he sits back, my heart splitting in my chest. I don't want to tell Charlie to go, but if it means Maksim will be nice to me again, I'll do my best to achieve his objective.

"Charlie won't listen to me if I tell him to go, сэр Maksim, but... I'll-I'll try."

A smile, and then Maksim laughs. "No, my little pet. I want you to get *rid!* of him," he elongates 'rid'. "You're the only person I know who can get close enough to slay him. So I urge you-"

"No!" I say too abruptly, too willingly, pushing to my feet. My body floods with pain, but still, I stand my ground. "I won't do that." I point at Maksim, warning, "I won't kill Charlie."

Just the thought of hurting Charlie makes me want to put a bullet in my head. I will if I ever feel the urge to hurt him.

To my utter surprise, Maksim doesn't look annoyed with me. He looks entertained with my daring.

"Then, I guess you'd better take your clothes off, my stunning little redhead, so we can say a proper goodbye."

―――

Maksim gets up from his chair and peels off my t-shirt. I look at the floor the entire time, as he pulls it up over my head, leaving me topless. I couldn't bear a bra when I dressed earlier. I'm in too much pain for anything tight to be touching my back.

I descend into myself, hiding in my waist length hair that curtains my nudity, wishing this moment away.

"You know," Maksim husks out, his vodka clinical breath blowing over my face, "you are a subjectively beautiful girl." He pushes my hair out the way to kiss my neck, making me grimace. "But to me, you are the most stunning little thing." His lips are affectionately inexperienced, rough and hurried as he pecks up my pulsing vein. His kiss makes me think of the way Charlie kissed me, how he took his time when he caressed me, made every touch count, every action executed with tenderness. I never truly understood his attention to detail before today.

I'm not sure I can do this.

"Do you want me to make love to you?" Maksim runs his teeth over my collarbone, sending some horrible vibes through me. "Then you can decide between Charlie and me. For the first time ever, you can choose your own path."

Brutal silence, and I'm mentally trying to block out his closeness, but then, "Or do you want me to fuck you the way I've wanted to fuck you since I first saw you as a little girl?"

I try to speak, *"No. I don't want either offer,"* and while my lips move, words don't come out. I'm silently paralyzed with what's happening.

Maksim grabs a clump full of my hair and tugs my head back. He then licks up the center of my throat until he's sucking my chin, his saliva trailing my flesh.

I shut my eyes, trying to deal with this, but then Maksim thumbs the waist of my sports shorts and I can't take anymore.

"I don't want this, сэр Maksim," I say with a sob. "Can't we just go back to-"

"It's either this," he cuts me off, sharpening his teeth on my jaw line, "or you will end Charlie Decena. You choose."

I press my lips together, suppressing the urge to fight Maksim off my body. I've never felt the urge to fight Maksim before. It's an alien emotion but powerful on another level. Inside, I'm shaking with panic—I just don't feel like I'm *his* anymore.

Maksim slips into the front of my shorts, his dusty arm chafing against my abdomen. He finds my sex with coarse fingers. My stomach rolls with dread. I squeeze my ass cheeks together, enhancing the pain inside for a moment, but then my senses narrow. I feel a single finger being pushed in me, sliding through my folds with violent force.

"No!" I scream, smashing my fists in his chest, forcing him back a step.

The tension skyrockets, our eyes narrowing in on each other's.

"You won't let me have you!?!" Maksim yells after a few seconds, his eyes glowing like golden balls of fire. "Nor will you get rid of Charlie!?!"

"No," I say in defiance. "I won't do either." For the first time in my life, I look right at him with reprisal, balling my hands at my sides. "You don't give a shit about me!" I shout at the top of my lungs, but the effort tires me out. "All you want to do is hurt me," my words come out weaker now, as I stagger back to rest against the wall for support, putting my hands on my knees. "I don't want you to hurt me anymore, Maksim. I just want it all to stop."

"It is Cэp Maksim to you," he says, appalled. "And that's not your decision to make. You're mine to do with as I see fit."

It's a feeble attempt, but I shake my head. "I'm not yours anymore," as I say that, his face changes. "You made sure of it when you handed me over to Charlie, a man who has been kind and caring to me... who made sure I was happy... Why couldn't you ever be kind to me, or even James?" It's like being punched in the chest as I think about my friend and what he's been through in aid to protect me. "We've given you our all and what we haven't, you've taken anyway."

Maksim grinds his jaw, furious, standing there in the middle of my whitewashed apartment.

"Please, cəp Maksim..." Hot tears flood my eyes as I stare at him, the back of my nose tickling to cry. "Tell me why you couldn't be kind to *me* at least. I need to know."

Silence... We look at each other, predator against predator. I'd tear him apart if it really boiled down to it, but he knows my subconscious won't allow me to—or maybe he doesn't. He looks uncertain.

"Tell me," I whisper, my voice cracking. "Tell me. Please?"

"Because..." he's not sure what to say for a second, then, "Because I knew the moment someone tapped into your emotions," he lifts a finger to me, "you'd be lost to me."

"What?" I screw up my face. "But... that doesn't even make sense."

"Oh, it does, my little pet," he husks out, deceivingly calmer now. "I don't think you quite realize what you're capable of. I don't think you realize how important it is to keep you emotionless... to keep you totally loyal to me... I need you, Blaire." His finger circles my frame, emphasizing me. "I trust no one else."

"But... but I'm not emotionless," I say, sure that I'm not. "I've always cared about you."

"Because that's all I've ever allowed you to feel."

I sob then, staring at him through watery eyes. It's now obvious that I could have felt more in my life, been more than what I am, and he stole it all from me.

"Why?" I say, and he hesitates a second time, so I yell, "Why!?!"

"I couldn't risk unleashing your emotions," he says that with no shame, shrugging. "You have to understand, you are so powerful with your Chinese combat skills and your technology skills... If you ever truly understood your merits on the level that we do, and learnt how to be a leader, you'd realize you don't need me—Tatiana wouldn't need me. She'd just want you."

I let my head drop forward and cry quietly, gripping my knees with my nails.

"I did want to be kind to you, Blaire," he says, and he swears it, holding out his hands like he's praying for forgiveness. "But I'm not that sort of man—I hunger for darker things—and I knew that if I ever did have you, if I tried to sexually bond us, I'd unleash your deepest desires as a woman and you would have longed for that sort of affection, affection I can never give you. You'd have left to find something more, as all women do. Women need to feel love once they've had a taste of it, so keeping that sentiment dormant in you was my best option at ensuring you were always mine. And I'm not sorry."

Looking up, I shake my head at him and something in me—my loyalty to him—splinters, because it all makes sense now. The beatings to ensure I was frightened of him. The isolated sexual abuse to connect us on a semblance of an emotional level, as he promised that I was the only one he truly wanted those moments with—

everyone else was just a fuck because he didn't want to rape me. The mental conditioning so I was only able to think of him. His voice in my dreams. The fear that there's nothing else out there without him. The darkness and the coldness that I think was my captivity, which forced me to rely on him for basic things like shelter and warmth.

It was all for his own selfishness.

Charlie understood. That's why he's been slowly breaking me down to gain my trust. Why he's been doing his best to peel away each of my layers with kindness. He knew I'd never felt kindness before. It's the only thing that would have ever worked on me.

"And James?" I say to Maksim, wiping my running nose with the back of my hand as I stand up straight. "Why have you always been so cruel to him?"

Maksim lifts his shoulders, a merciless display. "I just don't love him."

Poor James. My heart breaks for him.

In emotional misery, I hug my breasts to hide my nudity, feeling too exposed. He's ripped out my soul and swallowed it whole, so I'll be damned if I'll just stand here naked and let him look at me.

"I can approach your conditioning from a different direction," he says with a hint of panic, using his hands as a talking point. "We can go back to the way we were—nothing has to change. Not really."

The audacity of him...

"Where did you take me from?" I say with pure hatred. "I know for sure you didn't buy me from a guy in Russia."

He chuckles suddenly, like he can't believe I've just asked that, his face lighting up with impressed amusement. "You're resourceful when I'm not around, aren't you, my little pet?"

I say nothing, just stand here cuddling my nudity, and he tells me, "The IRA was recruiting child geniuses-" He leisurely steps toward me, one hand in his trouser pocket, "-so they created a few cryptic puzzles that were sent out nationally in magazines. Your parents let you have a go at them and posted off your results..." From walking toward me, he changes pattern and wanders from left to right, appearing to be deep in thought. I am in deep thought too. I can't believe I'm Irish. I've always believed I was Russian.

"How does that connect me to you?" I watch him carefully, studying everything he says.

"Well, stories began flying around the underworld about a little redhead girl in Ireland who had executed the cryptic game, and after doing some extensive research, I found out this girl wasn't just talented. She was exceptionally talented—the only person who cracked the code of the puzzles, and that meant she was born for hacking. The IRA wanted you of course—even submitted an offer to your parents for you—that was when Tatiana sent me to get you."

The shock that comes over me is overwhelming. "You stole me from my parents?"

He smiles like a dark angel, as if to say yes.

"Where are they?" I swallow past the growing lump in my throat. "My parents, where are they?"

"Dead," he says without hesitation, unbothered by the fact.

"What?" My heart twists. Any hope I had of finding them shatters right there.

"Did... did you kill them?" I swear, if he did, I'm not sure I won't slaughter him right now.

"No," he says, and I'm swamped with relief. "Your father died two years ago from a natural illness, and your mother..." There's a long, intense pause. "She followed a few months later—maybe of a broken heart." He laughs with sarcasm after saying that, like the idea is weak and pathetic.

Perhaps it is pathetic but I think I understand. If you love someone so much and can't live without them, why not die of a broken heart? It's seems as good a way to go as any.

"Where did you take James from?" I want to find this out for my friend. Maybe he still has someone out there who's looking for him, who loves him.

"Fuck James," Maksim hisses, and I know he won't spill his guts. "Where I took him from is none of your business.

"How long have you known I didn't buy you from a man in Russia, Blaire?"

I keep my mouth shut about how long I've known and how I know.

"He told you..." Maksim spits out, "...Charlie Fucking Decena."

My heart goes a little faster at the mention of Charlie. I should never have left him.

"Don't look at me with those doe eyes because I said his name! He's been using you, you stupid girl. Whatever you feel for him isn't real, and he doesn't care about you either." Maksim taps his own chest, lifting his chin in a pompous manner. "He's been using you to get back at me."

"Lies," I say through gritted teeth, absolutely sure. "Charlie does care about me."

"No, my little pet. I am not lying. He doesn't." Maksim falls silent for a few seconds, watching me in scrutiny, and then asks, "Did he tell you that he's had the map of the bank vault since the day he bought you from me? That he's been ready for the London job for almost three months now?"

I blink at him, screwing up my face, and he nods.

No... I asked Charlie about what was going on with the job and he said it'll happen when it happens. I asked him the first night we had dinner together. He didn't say anything about a map—didn't even tell me he was waiting on one.

"He held off on the job for a reason," Maksim tips his head, "and do you know why?"

Shaking from head to toe in anger, I say, "I don't give a shit why." I can't even think about the reasons why. I don't want to consider that Maksim is telling the truth. Charlie *does!* care about me. He does!

"You and me," I point at the ground between us, cuddling my breasts in one arm, "we're done."

"What?" Maksim's eyes enlarge with horror.

Running on adrenaline, I stagger past him and up a few steps to grab my mobile. I switch it on with fumbling fingers, trembling impatiently as it loads up.

"What are you doing?" Maksim says from the bottom of the staircase. "Blaire!"

BLAIRE
(PART ONE)

When my mobile screen blinks white at me, signaling it's ready, I call Charlie. I choose him. I should have chosen him all along.

His phone rings a few times, while Maksim is shouting, "What are you doing!?! Who are you calling?"

"Shut up!" I yell with all the force my body will allow, moaning against the pain in my back. "Just shut up."

"Blaire?" Charlie says on answering.

"Yes," I whimper his name in relief, desperate to go to him. "Come get me, please? I don't want to be here."

"What's going on?" I can hear he's in the car, the engine roaring with speed. "Is he still at your place?"

"Ask him," Maksim whispers, nodding a couple of times. "Go on, my little pet. Ask him."

"Yes," I say to Charlie, holding Maksim's golden gaze the entire time. "He is here. He's-" I go quiet, and I'm not sure if my master is fucking with my mind, but I suddenly can't focus on anything other than the need to know if Charlie really has had the map of the bank vault for all this time, so I ask. "Don't lie. Just tell me."

I hear the car pull over to a sharp, screeching stop.

"Blaire," Charlie says my name with caution, "listen to me, I dunno what he's told you, but-"

My heart splits in two. Maksim is telling the truth. I know it. I can sense it in Charlie's voice.

"Told you," Maksim says, fueling my fire.

"Just give it to me straight!" I scream in frustration down the phone, but then I whimper in pain, my back feeling stretched out. "I'm sick of lies, Charlie."

"Don't trust his word," Maksim says, coaxing me. "He will lie his way out of this. He knows you care about him. He will use that to his advantage."

I'm scowling at Maksim, furious and heartbroken that he might be right again.

"Tell me, Charlie!" I scream, my voice breaking.

"All right, all right," he says warily. "Just calm down and I'll tell you." There's a moment of unsure silence, his breathing heavy down the speaker, then he confesses, "Yeah, I've had the map for months."

"No..." I gasp, having to grab my stomach because it feels like there's a sharp knife in me. I'm physically in tatters because of what Maksim did to me but inside... The emotional pain hurts a lot more. "Why didn't you-"

"I used you to get back at that bastard, okay? And I held off on the job just in case I needed a reason to send you home early. Fuck...!" he says the one thing I never thought he would and my stomach twists in more pain. "I served four fucking years in a Russian jail because of him."

Agonizing silence. No one says a word for a moment, but then I want to know why Charlie ended up in jail. I search Maksim's face as I ask, expecting him to tell me. He doesn't. He's as impassive as ever, standing there with his arms hanging by his sides.

"We did a bank job," Charlie says, "it went wrong and I was the only person with the kahunas to hold off the police chase. Maksim told me not to worry, that if I got caught, he'd get me out of jail, but he lied about how much control he had over his government, and I was forced to serve my sentence."

"He-he left you in jail?"

"Yeah, he did," Charlie says, "so I bided my time—used the time you and I had together to break you down, to make you fall for me so I... so I could teach Maksim a lesson." He hesitates once more, I imagine gutted that he has to tell me all this. "I wanted you to hate him. I've wanted you to hate him for so long..."

It's anguish to know he really was using me. Of course I've suspected all along but hearing it...

"When you said you wanted me from the moment you saw me..." I have to squeeze out every word because my throat is restricted with burning tears. Does he really care about me? Has he ever?

"Course I fancied you—you're a pretty girl—but I won't lie. I had an agenda, and that was to turn you against Maksim because I'd heard from every person in his inner circle that you were his most valued possession—his Achilles' heel." Every word he says is like taking a slug to the gut. "Then I was going to send you back to torment him, whether it be physically or mentally, and I was going to leave feeling satisfied that the four years I spent in jail were redeemed. Losing you is worth far more than four years, trust me, I know..."

I'm not moved by his sweet nothing. I'm too hurt.

"Why didn't you just kill him, Charlie?" I say, striving to control this possessing urge to cry. It's the most obvious question. If Charlie is so powerful in this world and feared by so many, why not just kill Maksim and be done with it?

"He's too calculating for that," Maksim butts in, and I look down on him. "He fancies darker things than I do, Blaire—four years of revenge has satisfied him nicely, I will bet."

"Death is too easy," Charlie says eventually, sighing with aggravation. "And that motherfucker knows it—expected it."

I'm sure Maksim did. It must have come as a surprise when Charlie asked to hire me, instead of putting a gun to his head.

"None of that matters to me now, Blaire—you have to believe me. I don't give two fucks about Maksim or what he did to me anymore. I just want you. I'm so in love with you it's insane."

"You could have told me all this, Charlie." My voice is breaking with tears. I feel like I can't breathe properly. "All those times we talked in the kitchen... And you sent me home? Did you send me home to torment him, as you planned?"

"No! I told you I didn't want you to go!" he yells that with such passion, desperate to convince me. "Don't you get that? I wanner take care of you—give you anything and everything you desire..." I hear him punch something, probably the steering wheel. "Please, don't let him do this. I fucking care about you, Blaire! How many times do I have to tell you?"

I can feel the urgency in him—I believe him. He does care about me... And that's all I need to hear, that he loves me. If his plan was to make me hate Maksim and leave me here to torment him, he wouldn't be asking me to come back.

"I do get that," I croak out. It's crazy how I trust him so explicitly, but he's... he's Charlie.

Keeping a suspicious eye on Maksim, who's now practically blowing steam because he can see that I'm weak to his adversary's spell, I again tell Charlie that I want him to come and get me, that I can't live like this anymore. "I don't want to be with Maksim. I want to be with you."

Charlie exhales down the speaker. "You don't know how long I've waited to hear you say that."

James... He pops into my mind.

"Can James come with us? Please, I can't leave him here."

"If that's what you want, baby," he says, and I hear that he's smiling. "I'll be with you in less than an hour— I'm already half way to London. Put that fuck down if you have to and leave your apartment. Don't pack anything. Just meet me by the river."

"What about James? I don't know where he is..."

"Don't worry. I'll have my men get a hold of him. Just get away from Maksim."

A great sense of hope makes me smile, even through my tears. I should never have doubted him. I know he truthfully cares about me.

"Okay," I whisper, nodding to myself, "I'm going to leave and wait for you by the river."

"No you're not!" Maksim dashes up the staircase then. I kick him back down, knocking myself over in the process. I drop my mobile to grip the banister rails, gasping out in pain as I bump down a few steps.

Glancing back on instinct, I see Maksim unfolds his tall body from the floor and slowly gets to his feet, the look of the devil in his eyes. His hair is ruffled and his bottom lip is bleeding. Thick claret slithers down his smooth chin, dripping on the collar of his white shirt.

"You've gone too far, my little pet," he says, his lips thin as they curl against his teeth. "I feared this day would come—the day you feel something other than the need to protect me—but this is beyond the latter."

"And whose fault is that?" I say through gritted teeth.

I reach for my mobile because I can hear Charlie yelling something, but then I see Maksim pointing a shiny silver gun at me.

I go cold in place, lifting my hands in defense, my mobile in one.

"Put the phone down, Blaire, and I mean it." He clicks back the hammer, gripping the weapon in both hands.

"You wouldn't dare," I say, holding his golden iron stare.

"No?" He laughs at me, the skin around his eyes crinkling.

"No." I gain strength on my feet, and while my back is killing me, I lift my chin with nerve. "You won't do it," I say, almost sure. "You need me more than I need you."

"Oh, Blaire, if you are lost to me, then what use are you to me?" there's something like sadness in his voice. "I'd rather you were dead than leave me for that Latin fuck!"

"Drop the gun, Maksim," someone says from the open front door. "You shoot her and I'll blow a fucking hole in you."

I whip my head in that direction, as does Maksim. It's James! He's stalking in across the kitchen space holding a long gun in both his hands.

"No..." Maksim growls like a dog, his golden eyes blazing. "How dare you even think about pulling a gun on me!?!"

BLAIRE
(PART ONE)

James isn't fazed by Maksim's disappointment and anger toward him, but I'm suddenly so terrified for my friend that I don't know what to do. When it boils down to it, James won't shoot. He can't. We're not wired that way.

"Ten years I've spent on you both and look at yourselves." Maksim screws up his nose, shaking his head. "Blaire is a lovesick puppy for my enemy and you're pointing a gun at me? You should be ashamed!"

James walks up behind Maksim and points the gun at the back of his head. "You steal us from our childhood beds and we should be ashamed?"

"You too?" I say, my stomach flipping. "You know what happened to us?"

"Oh yeah," James nods at me, "I know everything, especially the fact that you're my little sister." He jabs Maksim with the gun, knocking him forward a step.

My face drops, and I stare in mute shock.

James is my brother...

I grab my mouth, barely believing what I'm hearing.

I had a whole family!

"How do you know?" I say.

"You were gone for months, Blaire, I had to find you, so I broke into his office and found the files he has on us. Have you told her why she can't remember anything before you?" James prods Maksim with the gun again. "He used a Chinese experimental drug on us called Wángjí. It literally means 'forget' in traditional Chinese."

I'm not surprised by that. I have often wondered why I can't remember a thing past Maksim.

Our master isn't saying a thing, just standing there at gunpoint, shaking from head to toe with pure wrath.

"Ten years you've stolen from us," James says, tormenting him by poking him with the gun. "Ten years we could have been with our parents and now they're dead!"

The way Maksim glares up at me... I really, really fear for James now. I've no idea why—he's the one with all the power at the moment. But Maksim's face... If looks could kill...

"You have to leave," I say to James. "I-I don't want anything happening to you too."

James slowly shakes his head at me. "I won't let him hurt you anymore. I've done my best to prevent him from sexually abusing you but not enough to stop him from hurting you. I won't let him hurt you anymore," he repeats, as if it's all he cares about in the world. "I won't!"

BANG

A flash of spitting yellow, and then a sharp pain jolts through me, making my entire body quake.

"No...!" James yells.

BANG

BANG

A moment of total quietness follows.

I feel like I'm floating.

In the distance I can hear someone screaming. I think it's James. I think he's in pain. I can also hear Maksim screaming, saying this is our fault. "If neither of you broke protocol, none of this would be happening!"

Pressing one hand to my own stomach, I touch a small wound, soaking my fingers in warm, thick liquid—blood.

He did it. He shot me.

BLAIRE
(PART ONE)

My body plummets to the ground.

BLAIRE
(PART ONE)

32

It's like watching something in slow motion, life actually flashing before my eyes, just like they say it does. I remember the first time someone whipped me to the point where my flesh ripped open.

I am on all fours against a damp, concrete floor. My body is buzzing with a doped-up-confused sensation. I can't remember my own name or how old I am, but I'm young. A man is telling me that if I call for Maksim, he'll stop the beating.

Wa-tch!

He strikes, forcing me to arch to evade the next blow.

This is the first time I truly need my master.

"Maksim!" I beg for him and he comes; pushes open the heavy door to my cell and lets in a tunnel of light.

After this day, I start to recognize his presence as protection. When he begins beating me himself, I recognize it as punishment, nothing more, so I try to be good.

"Your name is 'Blaire' when you are in trouble and 'my little pet' when you are not." Maksim is crouched

down in front of me, looking into my eyes as he brainwashes me. *"Anything before now doesn't exist."*

The memory of being strapped down on a chair pulls me in. My eyes are taped open. my arms are hooked up to wires and machines that read my pulse. There's a television hanging on the wall in front of me but it's blank white. I cast a troubled glance around. My cell is dark and cold, causing my breath to mist the air. It smells like piss and something stale.

Image after image flickers across the television screen, attaining my attention. It's a story about a girl who will do anything to defend her master. She's holding a sword in one hand and a gun in her other, symbolism that she's a warrior. She's me: long red hair, wearing a black combat outfit. Her master stands there at her side with pride, one hand on her shoulder. He's smiling just like Maksim does, as if he has a hidden agenda.

The images turn into a video. She slices open throats with one clean swipe of her sword, punishment for those who have done her master wrong. She cuts out hearts to prove that she does not have one.

"She's no longer responsive to fear," Maksim says. He un-cuffs me from the chair, peels the tape off my eyes and stares at my deadpan face. *"Perfect."*

Charlie... I suddenly think of him. I visualize I'm smiling at him, reaching out to touch him but he's just too far away. He is the muse of my affections. I don't think I've ever cared so much about someone in all my life.

"Please stop," I beg for Maksim's voice playing on repeat to stop, curled up in the corner of my cell. My hair

is just past my shoulders and I'm nothing but flesh and bones.

How did I get here?

A small window up on the back wall brings in a channel of daylight. Dust is trickling through the air, small particles of dirt that are visible in the light. I gaze around, my tear varnished eyes recognizing everything. This cell was my captivity until I was fourteen.

There are numbers written in white chalk all over the dark brick walls, some smeared because the ceiling is leaking, water dripping down in places.

The dripping drives me insane.

I wrote those numbers. Maksim said they were secret agent codes and that it was my job to remember them all. To prove I could, I covered my cell, the order of sequence just like it was written down in the file. My hands rubbed against the chalk for so long that I had sores on my palms. The sores bled but I kept going.

"You're becoming a good fighter, girl," Demetrius says, dragging me to another memory. He's my trainer, a famous Asian Wing Chun artist known throughout the underworld.

"I'm learning from the best," I tell him, flexing my hands because my knuckles hurt.

"Yes, you are," he says, panting for breath as we stand opposite each other. The space under Maksim's house where we train, just down the hall from my cell, is huge but you can't see how high because the ceiling is pitch black. *"Maybe one day, you'll beat me,"* he adds with sarcasm.

I attack him then, going for his face but I change my attack at the last minute.

The images in my mind zoom in and out of focus.

"This is James," Maksim says, introducing him to both Demetrius and me. *"He will be training with you."*

We look at each other as the seconds tick by, while Maksim is ordering Demetrius to teach James one style of fighting—to kill. James is wearing a leash that's attached to a black leather collar wrapped around his neck and a pair of black trousers, nothing else. He's slender, and I imagine hungry. His skeleton ribcage is a disgusting sight, the bones all but screaming their way out of his tightened flesh. He eventually lifts his lips in a smile like he knows me, and I blink at him with confusion, glaring in character. He doesn't know me. I don't even know myself.

The only thing I know is Maksim.

Numb to emotions, I stand there day after day, night after night, and watch Demetrius beat James half to death. He will keep beating him half to death until James fights back.

James begins to fight back and I feel admiration for him. It's the first thing I remember feeling except for fear.

When we're alone after training, he starts talking to me, asks if I know who I am.

"Blaire, when I'm bad," I say, because my master has told me I can talk to him, *"my little pet, when I'm good."*

"It's the same for me," he says, *"though I'm just called, my pet."*

"We should leave," James says from within my cell this time, as we flicker to another time. He's pointing at the open cell door, my cell door, shaking from head to toe. *"Now's our chance."*

BLAIRE
(PART ONE)

My instincts come over me for the first time, like a red mist erupting.

I will never leave Maksim.

I shove James up against the damp, watery wall with my forearm pressed across his now strapping chest, growling in his face, *"Disloyalty means punishment! Disloyalty means punishment!"*

"He won't know," James begs for me to just leave with him. *"We won't get another chance!"*

"There's nothing out there for us without Maksim," my voice comes out detached, but this is me now. *"If we're good, we're rewarded with his good mood. If we're bad... you know what happens."*

"You've passed," Maksim says from behind, *"take the boy and tag him."*

After this, I see more. So much more. The years go by in my mind faster than I thought they would.

Maksim leaves me out in the cold unmanned. It's dark and I can hear rustling in the nearby bushes. He's testing me again. Though I remain on alert for if trouble breaks out, I don't move. I stand there under the trees in my master's garden until he returns and pets me...

...In Russia, it's so cold. My teeth chatter and I can feel the chill in my bones.

Maksim leaves me outside Tatiana's house to stand guard. That's when I hear them, the Turks, speaking badly about my master and his master. I pull a knife from my belt and give the first Turk a smiley, slicing through his mouth, unresponsive to the blood pouring over my hands. I cut out the next Turks tongue so he cannot speak poorly of my people again and shove it down his throat. James watches me, doing nothing.

My reward doesn't come but neither does a punishment, so I'm okay.

I flash to a corner in my cell, cowering under Maksim who is looming over me, disappointment ruling his expression. His eyebrows are drawn together, making him look evil. He pulls up the zipper of his trousers.

"I'm sorry," I sob, sliding down the cold, damp wall. I stuff my head in my naked knees as I pull them up to my chest. *"I'm sorry for saying no."*

"Please don't hurt her," James stands there in the doorway, pleading with glossy blue eyes to our master. *"I'll do whatever you want, just please, don't hurt her."*

It's just about to happen—the first time I ever see Maksim fuck James—and then...

...I go to a place where I want to be this time. I dream I'm lying in bed with Charlie, embraced in his arms. He's playing with my hair, his fingers running through the strands. Maksim is nowhere to be seen and I like the idea. It's just us.

"Don't leave me," Charlie whispers in his familiar, raspy voice. Cupping my face in one large hand, he turns me into him, putting us eye to eye. His are glowing with fear, bluer than I've ever seen them.

Why the fear?

"You hear me?" he says, raising his eyebrows. *"Don't. Leave. Me, Blaire. Stay with me."*

Why would I leave him? I'm not missing a moment of this.

I sigh with content and snuggle in his masculine chest, but then somewhere in the back of my mind, I'm sad. I can't feel how warm he is and I can't smell him.

BLAIRE
(PART ONE)

It didn't happen like this. I can always feel and smell him.

"Wake up, my little pet..." Maksim's voice resounds as if under water. "Wake up..."

I feel like I'm under water, hovering in and out of certainty.

Am I dead?

I pull at my hands but I'm paralyzed, my limbs heavy and restrained by numbness. I must be dead—Maksim shot me—but there's a dull ache in my stomach and a tight hotness across my lower back. The pain forces me to register that I'm still alive.

James... I heard two other shots go off. Maksim must have shot him because he is here and James isn't!

I pull again. Nothing. It's exhausting. My breath is woozy as I breathe in steadily, whistling from the deep of my throat.

Another breath. I can smell burnt flesh and warm metal.

What's going on?

I try to open my eyes. They flutter and spasm but won't open fully. I'm so... tired.

So tired.

Charlie...

"I'm going to leave and wait for you by the river."

He's waiting for me. He needs to know where James is.

"Get the doctor," Maksim's words wave through the air in vibrations. "She needs stitches."

Strong hands close around my wrists and ankles, elevating my body. Taut heat races across my lower back like fire. *Fuck,* it hurts. It hurts so much that I have to forcefully center myself on the weightless sensation of being carried through the air, but then I'm dropped onto a hard, flat surface, whacking my forehead against the pane.

"Awh..." I gasp out, my skull throbbing.

The surface is cold, making me aware that my skin is clammy and sweaty, my face soaked in damp lengths of hair. I try to bend my knees so I can get up but the pain in my stomach... it's excruciating.

I heave against the agony, trying to add pressure to the wound but I can't move. Why the fuck can't I move?

"Wipe up the blood," Maksim says.

I'm still bleeding. That's not good.

Charlie... He has to know that I care about him. Before I die, he has to know. And I have to find James! I have to know he's still alive!

Pushing into the hard surface, I strain against my own heaviness, willing myself to get up and fight free of Maksim so I can see Charlie just one last time and find James, but I fall back down with a heavy thud.

Fuck. I really am so, so tired.

I suck in another whistling breath to gather my strength, my head hazy, stuffed with cotton wall.

I need to get up. I need to get up.

Come on, Blaire, get up!

I struggle against the surface once more, but then—

Wa-tch!

I jolt in reaction to the hot lick of a belt across my back, enhancing the ache in my stomach with the sudden movement. It's not a dull ache anymore. It throbs with fire.

"Welcome back to the land of the living, my little pet," Maksim says from a distance.

I blink open my eyes though all I can see is blackness.

"Сэр Maksim?" I croak out, turning my face to the left where his voice came from.

"Yes, my little pet." His gargling voice comes from the right this time. "Now you're fully awake, I'll make you completely mine."

Am I awake?

"Let us first list your wrongdoings-"

Wa-tch!

I hiss in pain, squeezing my face to handle the torture.

"-A whip for talking back to me-"

Wa-tch!

"-A whip for refusing to end that Latin piece of shit-"

Wa-tch!

"-A whip for refusing me-"

Wa-tch!

"-Do you know what you've caused?" he says with strange calmness. "I'm in hiding, for your lover wants my head on a spike."

Wa-tch!

The beating goes on and on, sending me into a fucked up zone, and when it becomes too much to bear, I plunge into a hell-like slumber where the beating goes on without me...

...Wa-tch!

"Ouch!" I grab the edges of the surface, my entire body shuddering awake.

"Ah, you're back," Maksim says from beside me, his chest heavy with pants. "I was starting to worry."

Click, click, and then I hear the faint hissing of a flame. My mind is too messed up to really register what's going on, but then after a few seconds, I smell metal being warmed up, the metallic scent almost strong enough to taste.

I remember that smell. I remember it well because it reminds me of when Maksim burnt an M into my back.

Now I'm awake.

"It's time for the last few letters," Maksim says with lust in his voice. Something hits the floor at my side with a shallow clang: the belt. "Stay still, Blaire," he warns, and then he burns my lower back with a scorching branding iron.

"Aargh!" I scream through my teeth, clawing the surface I'm lying on. I can't move because my limbs still feel tied down. I manage to shake from left to right, thrusting my hips trying to get free, but my efforts are useless.

"How does that feel, my little pet?" Maksim says, laughing at me. "Like home?"

He peels the branding iron off my skin and I slump in relief, panting like a dog, cool sweat veiling my flesh.

The silence of pain. I want to scream some more but I can't.

"Cэp Maksim," I gasp his name, turning my head to the other side, wheezing for breath. "Why?"

"Why... it's the age old question, isn't it, my little pet?"

Quietness. I can hear sizzling and feel pure heat beside my face.

"Once my name is burnt into your flesh," Maksim strokes wet lengths of hair back out of my face, "you'll know who you belong to."

"Your name?" I gasp in horror. "You're burning the rest of your name into-Aargh!" I scream out desperately as he puts the hot iron to my skin again. It crackles, melting through layers of flesh. I beg him to stop. I beg him to forgive my disobedience. I have no idea where my vocal strength has come from but it's fucking useless. I'm drowning in my own pleas.

"I'll stop when I know you're loyal to me again, my little pet." He holds the iron to my skin for longer this time, causing me to blackout from the pain...

...Cold droplets of water rain down on my skin and I sigh, relaxing, basking in the tenderness.

"Cэp Maksim?" I croak out his name, wondering if it's him treating me. *Please don't let it be him. Please, please don't let it be him.*

"Yes, it's me," he husks and I whimper, all hope of being free of him fading. He kisses between my shoulder blades, making me wince, then a cool waterfall washes over me. "It feels good, doesn't it, my little pet?"

I moan, wishing for more cold water.

He lays a heavy, cold piece of material over my back and my mind propels to where the darkness is.

BLAIRE
(PART ONE)

33

The next time I wake up, the room is spinning.

I pant so hard to catch a breath, feeling my heart is pulsing on the outside of my ribcage.

I'm trembling uncontrollably.

What's wrong with me?

Closing my eyes, I try to center my world and focus on my breathing but I can't. If anything, I'm panting faster now, drying out my throat.

There's this hot sensation in me too. I am burning from the inside out, warm sweat trickling down the sides of my face, gathering near my eyes.

High temperature... abnormal breathing... abnormal heart rate... I'm in trouble. If I can't control my own body, I know I'm in trouble.

The first thing I do is push against the bed I'm lying on to rise on all fours. I'm no longer tied down. I pull up my knees to rest on them but my stomach throbs and my back is so raw and taut that I sob out in pain.

BLAIRE
(PART ONE)

Hunched over on my palms, gasping through my nose, the torture comes back to me in flashes of white light.

The gun shot.

The beatings.

The branding.

Fuck. What has Maksim done to me?

Peering through hazy eyes, I glance about. I'm alone in a strange bedroom with gleaming white walls that won't still, and again I realize I'm not tied up.

I need to get out of here while I can. I need to get away from Maksim. He's never been so violent in such quick succession and I've never felt so disorientated.

Rolling onto my side, I fall off the bed and hit the floor.

"Aargh!" I screech, my knees and palms buried in glass. The wound on my stomach pulses and I vaguely feel blood slithering down my navel.

I try to ignore the pain and the blood because I need to focus. I need to get out of here before Maksim returns.

Trembling with fatigue, I fight to my feet, groaning through closed teeth as I stand on the broken pieces of glass, each shard piercing the soles of my feet.

Why is the floor covered in broken glass?

My head swirls when I'm upright. I press a hand to the wall but slide against the smooth surface, my hand seeping with blood.

I don't understand what's wrong with me. I've not been drugged. I know that feeling all too well. No. This isn't the sensation of being drugged. This is an illness.

Blinking about, I search for some clothes because I'm naked—even my bracelet is gone.

BLAIRE
(PART ONE)

My bracelet.

Charlie...

My heart twists, but I urge myself to pay attention. I can find Charlie when I'm out of here. Hopefully, he knows where James is. Hopefully, James is still alive.

Stretching across the far back wall are a collection of white doors. Wardrobe doors? They're too far away. One step, and I'm walking on glass. At the foot of the bed, there's a white shirt. I fall onto the bed with a bounce, enhancing the throbbing in my stomach. I shuffle for the shirt and slip my hands down the arm holes, struggling to shift it up over my shoulders. Every motion is agony, drawing my focus to the splits across my back. As I button myself up, I'm very aware that the cold material clings to my back, like it's soaking through with water or something.

Blood. It has to be blood.

Before I get up again, I try once more to calm my heart rate and my breathing, but neither will slow.

I touch my chest; feel my heart hammering against my palm.

Maybe Maksim has drugged me? That's all I can make sense of.

If he has, that means my mind will be clear in a few hours. I just need to find a few hours of freedom then I can battle for more.

Thinking on a subconscious level, I knock the pillows off the bed, onto the floor, and use them as a bridge over the glass. My legs are fragile, rickety under me, and I go off balance as my feet sink into the pillows, soaking them through with blood.

BLAIRE
(PART ONE)

At the door, I pull down the handle and stagger out of the bedroom, clutching my stomach.

Music. I can hear music booming from downstairs. A party.

That means Maksim will be excited on drugs and booze.

I swallow past the dry-tightness in my throat, willing myself to be as quiet as a mouse.

Gripping the banister rail, I stumble down the stairs and across a small oval entrance hall, my vision a mazy vapor. Everything is enhanced with colors, giving me double vision.

Front doors. I blink a few times. Definitely front doors. Pulling down the handles, I yank them open and fall through, landing on my bloody palms. I don't scream out, even though I want to. That hurts. With a heavy, pounding head, I negotiate to my feet and stagger across a paved driveway, between tons of flash cars, leaving a trail of blood in my wake.

The air is so cold it's hard to handle, making my eyes feel like balls of ice in their sockets.

A country lane. I gasp in relief, though I have no idea where I am. I'm not near London, that much I'm sure of.

It's dark. The trees are tall and thick, clawing over me. As I stumble onward, the moon flickers through the leaves in silver streams of light.

I'm not sure how long I wander around for until I see blinding white headlights. I shield my eyes with my forearm, squinting to see who that might be. I haven't passed another house. Maybe *that* is one of Maksim's friends?

My heart drops through me.

The car stops with a jagged screech and I hear a door clicking open. I stop there, frozen to my core, struggling to focus my eyes.

Please, don't be Maksim or one of his friends.

"Oh my god!" a woman says with shock. "Are you okay? What-what's happened?"

I blink up to see who she is but my vision is so blurry.

"Where am I?" I say, wobbly pattering onward. Unable to bear the weight of my own body, I fall into her like deadweight. She catches me around the waist and I scream out in agony, her fingers digging into the shot wound.

"Ohhh, I'm sorry! I'm sorry!" she cries, helping me sit down on the curb side. "Here. Just sit here."

I grab my face, noticing the heat in my cheeks. My skin is really hot.

"What's happened?" that woman asks. "You're bleeding and you... you don't look-"

"A phone," I pant, wiping my hair back. "Do you have a phone?"

"Yes!"

Fumbling through her pockets, she pulls out a mobile and passes it to me. I grab it in both hands and try to dial Charlie's number—he's the only person I can think of who'll come get me. I'm not sure James is okay or even alive.

My fingers won't still against the digits. My hands are trembling like mad. With the screen glowing, offering me some light, I pause, studying the color of my skin. My hands are really red and blotchy with thin red streaks. Has Maksim poisoned me?

"Miss," that woman says, touching my knee, "we should call an ambulance."

"No!" I yell at her, then I slowly and shakily dial Charlie's mobile.

The ringer hums on and on and then it dies off.

"No," I whimper, redialing him, panic setting in. "Come on, Charlie," I beg.

It dies off again, and now I feel sick with panic—literally. I swallow back a heave. *I won't be sick. I won't be sick.*

"Look, I don't know what's happened, but I really think we should get you to a hospital. I can take you." That woman leans in to scan my face. "You look very poorly."

"No, please, just wait," I plead to her.

I try Charlie's phone one last time and he picks up, asking warily, "Who is this?"

"Charlie, it's Blaire." I hug the phone to my ear with both hands.

He gasps my name with what sounds like relief. "I've been looking for you for over a week." He turns his attention to another, saying, "It's Blaire."

"Charlie, listen to me," I gulp down a lung full of air, hunching over to put my head between my knees, "I don't know what Maksim's done to me, but I'm sick."

Silence... It's the longest few seconds of my life, then Charlie goes into toil-mode. "Track this number," he says to someone. "Get the chopper up. Get the men in their cars—get every fucking person we have on our side in cars with guns! Blaire, baby, do you know where you are?"

I peer up at that woman with watery eyes. "Where are we?"

"Kent," she says. "Sevenoaks."

"Did you hear?" I say to Charlie.

"Who's that?" he asks, his tone taking a chilling edge.

"Some woman who just pulled over to help me."

"Take her car and go to a police station," he says in a bizarrely calm voice, then he yells at someone else, "Get a fucking move on!"

I flinch against his voice. It rings in my ears.

"Blaire, you hear me, baby?" Charlie says. "Take that woman's car, get to a police station, and call me from there. I'm coming."

"No!" that woman screams, staring over me with wide, horrified eyes.

I don't know what happens, but I feel a heavy whack to the back of my head and I think I faint.

"Charlie warned you not to hurt her," is the next thing I hear. "He warned us all with death threats, so what the hell are you playing at, Maksim-Markov?"

Maksim's here.

That's enough to knock me out cold again.

For hours I float in and out of perception, sweating my ass off, my heart hammering nineteen to the dozen.

When I can open my eyes again, I find I'm in the same state. I'm loosely aware that I'm in Rumo's snooker room, slumped in a chair. It's the smell of mucky cigar smoke that gives my location away. No other place on this earth smells like this snooker room.

There's something cold on my head—a flannel?

"Where are you going to take her?" Rumo says. I only assume it's Rumo because I'm in his house.

"It's best that you don't know, my friend."

Maksim...

Maksim is here.

My heart is already racing through my ribcage, so it cannot possibly go any faster without forcing me into cardiac arrest.

There's someone else in the room too, saying something in Spanish. Carl?

"Speak English," Maksim snaps. "I can't fucking understand Spanish!"

"Why are her hands and feet covered in cuts?"

Maksim laughs like he's proud. "I had nothing to tie her down with, so I scattered glass across the floor to prevent her from escaping. Though, it seems shattered glass is no match for my little pet."

They talk about me for a while. Carl wants to know why I'm in such a state. "What did she do to reap your wrath like this?"

I study the voices, trying to regain my strength so I can get out of here. I can't go back to Maksim. He'll make me suffer gradually and painfully, until I die. I know he wants me to die. I want to die too after all the pain but not like this, and not before I see Charlie once more. I have to see him. And I have to know James is okay!

When the voices leave the room, I stumble off the chair, landing on gory hands. The room is whirling and the back of my head is throbbing like a bitch. I cup my face in one hand, straining to my feet. I sway, the soles of my feet tender and shredded to pieces.

Using the snooker table for support, I make my way out of the room, blinking rapidly to steady my vision.

In the welcome hall, I hear voices by the front doors; Maksim and Rumo.

"I'll pull up your car," Rumo says, "but that's it, Maksim-Markov. I'm not getting in any deeper. I'm not going to be a part of Blaire's death."

I can quite honestly say that in all my life, I've never felt so hurt by someone's words—Maksim really does want me dead.

"I understand, my friend," Maksim drawls. "I just want to thank you for bringing her back to me. I owe you."

"I don't suppose I can talk you into giving or selling her to me?" I think Carl says.

Maksim laughs his head off, his voice echoing. "I want her death. Not money. I have enough of that now I have Decena's cash. Pull up my car, Rumo. I need to go."

Panic races through me. I've not got long. If Rumo is pulling up the car that means Maksim intends to leave now.

Pushing open a set of doors, I struggle into a room I've never seen before.

A living room.

It's dark and the air reeks of old musk.

I lean against a wall and fold over on my knees, gasping for breath.

"Where's my little pet gone?" Maksim says from the entrance hall.

I whip up my head too fast and rock off balance.

Shit.

I'm either going to have to fight my way to freedom or beg him to just kill me.

I'll beg him to take mercy on me. He has to see reason. In that dark soul of his, there has to be some kindness in there somewhere—even I have kindness in me.

"She must be in there. The door was closed," Rumo says, and all thoughts of begging go out the window.

Fuck knows how I manage it, but I dart across the living room, stubbing my toe on something.

"Ouch," I gasp under my breath.

Another door. I shove it open and stumble through, finding myself in the hall that leads to the ballroom where James and I fought. The floors are so cold that they burn my wounded feet.

Running my hand along the wall for stability, I make my way to the ballroom, knowing French doors lead off there, into the garden. I can get out of the house through the ballroom.

"Blaire," a voice whispers from behind me and a red mist descends. All my pain fades into the background and the only thing I can think about is escaping Maksim.

I spin around. It knocks off my equilibrium, but I'm well aware who I come face to face with. Carl.

"I won't go back to Maksim," I say under my breath, and acting on instinct, I swipe for his throat with wicked pursuit. "You hear me?"

He gasps as I pinch his windpipe, digging in my nails so hard that I draw blood.

"I won't go back to Maksim," I hiss in his face, squeezing my teeth shut for strength.

"Let me go," he chokes, clutching my wrist with both hands. "I-I'm trying to help you."

I'm numb to his plea. He's slowly fading, and I'm slowly ripping into his throat. I don't want to do this but I can't go back.

"I'm sorry," I whimper, watching Carl drift away.

"Blaire!" someone yells from down the hall.

I freeze then, staring at Carl's bloodshot eyes, my own blood roaring in my ears.

Heavy footsteps come toward me, followed by a fuss of voices.

Tears stream down my face, bitter tears. Maksim. He's going to take me.

A hand closes around mine and pries me off Carl, who crashes to the floor in a pile of skin and bones. That black switch goes off in my mind. I can't stop it. I don't want to stop it. It's the only thing keeping me alive.

Screaming at the top of my lungs, I pound at god knows who—I'm not even sure if it's Maksim. I don't give a shit if it is. I won't go back to him.

"Calm down!" Maksim fights to restrain me but I'm going wild, clawing at anything and everything. "Calm down, Blaire! It's me, Charlie!"

Not Maksim. Charlie.

I stop dead.

BLAIRE
(PART ONE)

34

"Charlie..." I sob out his name, craning my head back to look up at him. I squeeze my eyes shut a few times because I so desperately want to see him but I can't make out a face.

"Yeah, baby, it's me," he says, and I know it's true. I recognize his voice now. "Where did Maksim shoot you?"

Bursting into tears, I fall into him, letting my vulnerability take over.

"He's back there." I swallow down my nerves, hiding in Charlie's body. "Please, don't send me back to him."

"I'll never send you back to him again." Charlie wraps his arms around my shoulders, burying my face in his chest, embraces me with safety. "S'all right. Don't cry. Everything's gonna be all right."

He smells like home, clean and soapy and musky. I hold him like I'll never let go. It's so bizarre that in just a few short months, he's come to mean more to me than anyone in this world.

"Baby, you need to sit down so I can check you over." He tries to urge me backward. "I know Maksim shot you. I need to make sure the wound-"

"No!" I protest, clinging to him. I don't want to sit down. I don't want to be anywhere than where I am right now.

"All right," he says. "All right. Just stay calm."

I distantly listen to a commotion behind, which I assume is Carl coming around, and then Charlie starts barking orders to god knows who. "Guard this entrance. Guard the front entrance. Have the Scour Detail ensure our exit is safe and get back to me. We need to leave as soon as possible." A long, questionable pause, then, "Whoever brings me Maksim gets a bonus."

"I'm on it, boss," someone says.

"Where did he shoot you, Blaire?" Charlie asks again, kissing my damp forehead. "I need to make sure the wound is clean and bandaged up."

"In-in the stomach. And my back... he burnt my back."

Charlie urges me back an inch so he can look down on me but I step into him, gripping his shirt with desperate fingers, not wanting him to let me go.

"Baby, s'all right. I'm not going anywhere. I just wanner check you over and wrap up your wounds."

I sob then, shaking from head to toe. "Please, just stay with me."

"I am. I'm not going anywhere, I swear." Holding me to him in one arm, he lifts my chin with his other hand, forcing our eyes to align. His enlarge and glaze over with guilt. "Your face..."

He's seeing the bruises where Maksim slapped and punched me. He touches them, my black and blue cheek; my eye.

"James didn't mention this..."

"James?" I heave his name. "James was at my apartment. He... he..."

"S'all right. He's okay. I found him with a few shot wounds to his shoulder-"

"Shot wounds?" Anger comes over me, bubbling in my stomach with such rage I swear if Maksim was here I'd fucking shoot him!

"James is fine," Charlie says, reassuring me. "He's had an operation and he's fine."

Relief sweeps through me but it only serves to make me feel ill. I squint through the lights in the hall, a warm rush of nausea coming over me. "I don't feel well, Charlie."

"Sit down then, please. It won't be long before we can leave." He manages this time to sit me on something hard. The concrete cools the backs of my naked thighs.

I blow out a long, exhausting breath, and shut my eyes, holding the edges of whatever I'm sitting on. The sound of material being ripped apart, and then I feel pressure on my left knee. It makes me moan in pain.

"I'm sorry but I need to stop this bleeding." Once Charlie is done bandaging up my right knee, I hear that ripping sound again and then he's wrapping something around my palms, first my left, and then my right. It doesn't hurt so much having him fondle my hands.

Next, he lifts up the shirt I'm wearing and bundles it around my chest. Cool air blows over my skin. It's so refreshing. I'm too warm.

BLAIRE
(PART ONE)

There's a long moment of silence between Charlie and me, until something much thicker is being ripped apart.

"Aargh!" I scream through clenched teeth, as he wraps something around my waist, over the burn on the low of my back and the bullet wound in my stomach. I grip his shoulders instinctively, panting through my nose.

"That's it. Just take easy breaths." He lifts my left arm from his shoulder and turns it from side to side like he's assessing me, the bite mark, then he yells in a panic, "Andres!"

He lays something heavy over my naked legs—his leather jacket. The material is cold but welcomed.

Charlie crouches down in front of me and I can feel that he's staring at my face. I sit forward, elbows on my legs, trying to control my breathing. Years and years of meditation and I can't control my breathing? I know something isn't right.

"Is that her?" a man says in a Latin seasoned voice.

I glance up with blazing eyes, ready to attack.

"Relax." Charlie grabs both my arms on my legs and holds me there. "That's Andres."

"Your brother?" I say in a shallow tone, peering back at Charlie.

He nods at me, his face tight with anxiety, then he looks up at his brother. "We need to go, Andres."

"Dios mío!" his brother says. "She's the Irish girl from the missing person's report I got this morning. Her and her brother were kidnapped from their home in Ireland ten years ago. She-she looks exactly the same as the girl on the newspaper article."

"Yeah," Charlie says, "the boy we've got at the house... he's her brother."

Charlie knows James is my brother?

A blazing pain shoots through my lower back. I screw up my face, reaching around to touch the burn.

Gaining height on his feet, Charlie leans over me and a hand lifts the shirt at my back. The anger that comes off his body in waves is stark.

"I'm gonna murder that motherfucker," he says. "We haven't got time to wait for the Scour Detail. I think she's got blood poisoning."

"No, no! Stop, Charlie!" Andres says in a fluster. "If we run into trouble, she might not make it. Just wait. Keep her calm."

I feel Charlie's presence move away from me, and then I hear the low murmur of his voice, "He's branded his name in her back, bit her arm, shot her, and I'm pretty sure she's got blood poisoning. If we don't leave now she won't make it anyway. She's dying."

Another hand touches my back where the burn is under the bandage, causing me to whine in pain. "Please, don't touch my back."

"Jesucristo," Andres gasps. "James must've been telling the truth when he said Maksim shot her."

Charlie's anger rises, and he says sarcastically in Spanish, "You think?"

A tall guy whose features I can't really make out squats before me. "Blaire, I'm Andres," he says in a deep voice. "I'm not going to hurt you. I'm just going to look at your arms."

"We don't have time!" Charlie yells.

"Brother, let me check her over," Andres says, and I imagine he's giving Charlie a serious look because nothing else is said.

I blink up at Charlie standing at my side, and he nods, so I let his brother examine me.

He gently grips my hands and turns them over. I let my head hang then, coming down from my rush of adrenaline-panic, but as I do, the tension in my back and the wound in my stomach become unbearably painful, and the fuzziness is back, the throbbing in my head making my skull pound.

"You're right," Andres says. "She does need medical attention but she's got time." He touches my inner elbow, which stings a little. "That pig has been giving her fluids, I think, so she's hydrated. If you stay calm, Blaire, you'll be okay," he says in my face, warm puffs of air blowing over my cheeks.

"Did you know he was doing this to her?" Charlie asks someone. "Because if you did-"

"No," Carl chokes out. "I swear. None of us knew." He tells Charlie between coughing Maksim was warned a few years ago by Tatiana that he's not allowed to whip me anymore. "She's the reason Blaire has money, a car, and an apartment."

What?

"How'd you know this?" Charlie sounds dark with intrigue.

"Maksim's other pet—James," Carl clears his throat, "he told me. A few years back Blaire apparently overheard the Turks bad mouthing Tatiana behind her back and slaughtered the lot of them for it off her own

BLAIRE
(PART ONE)

free will—no orders needed. Tatiana found out and commanded Blaire's freedom."

I knew it. For years I've wondered about her involvement in my freedom from Maksim's house, but now I know for sure.

"I don't know any fine details," Carl says, "but James said Tatiana was swooned with Blaire's natural loyalty to her and Maksim, and she rewarded her for it, granted her with freedom and protection."

"So, why's he still whipping her then?"

"I don't know," Carl says. "Rumo is just as confused—and before you think he's betrayed you, he was trying to delay Maksim from taking Blaire tonight. That's why he brought her here and didn't take her back to the whorehouse."

Someone butts in and tells Charlie the coast is clear. "We need to leave now if we're to avoid a showdown."

"Call the Lone MD's," Charlie says to Andres, his words coming out strained and fast. "Tell them to get to the central hospital now. Tell them what's wrong with Blaire so they're equipped."

"I'm already on it," Andres says, pushing back from me. "Give her this, just for if anything happens, and put pressure on that wound. It's bleeding too much."

Charlie grabs one of my hands and puts something heavy in my grasp. A gun. He then grabs my other and forces me to hold the wound on my stomach. I whimper because it's agony to touch.

"I'm sorry. I know it hurts, baby," he says softly, stroking my hair back out of my face, "but you have to press on the wound to stop the bleeding. I'm gonna pick you up now." He swathes one arm around my shoulders, the other behind my knees, and lifts me into his chest.

"Aargh!" I scream, feeling like my back is being stretched out.

"I'm sorry but I've gotta get you outa here," he says. "Let's go."

My mind coils as I feel the steady gait of his movements—he's running. An array of heavy footsteps follow.

With the pain and the tender feeling of being ill, I just want to go to sleep. I want to wake up and feel better. I'll feel better if I get some rest.

"Don't let her sleep," Andres puffs out. "She'll slip into a coma."

"You hear that, Blaire? Don't go to sleep," Charlie warns, though it's almost too late. I'm so tired.

"Look at me," Charlie snaps, his strides long and powerful, knocking me back and forth in his embrace.

With all the might I have, I open my eyes and lift them to his but I can't really see him.

"Keep your eyes open," he says in clatters of breath. "Don't. Go. To. Sleep."

I think I nod at him, but I do shut my eyes. I'm just so, so tired.

Outside, the cold air hits me. My stomach rolls. I'm going to be sick. But then we come to a sharp stop that makes me wince, pulling me back from the sickness and the tiredness.

"Maksim..." Charlie's tone deepens as he says his name. "I fucking warned you not to hurt her. Did you think I was joking?"

He's here. Maksim is here.

Still holding the gun in one hand, I cover my face with both arms, cowering, panic coursing through me.

"Put-put her down," Maksim says, his voice dripping in fear as he stutters, "Put-put her down and let's talk, Charlie. Let's not start a war ov-over one girl."

"She's not just one girl, you fucking fool—she's *the* girl," Charlie's voice vibrates in his chest with raw, inhumane anger. "Andres," he says, and then I feel someone else's arms around me. Charlie is passing me to his brother, who huddles me in a hard torso, careful not to hold my back.

Bile rises through me then, burning the back of my throat like acid. I lean over quick enough to spew on the ground and not on Andres, gagging and coughing up. I'm not sure what's coming out of me but it's not food. I haven't eaten in a while.

"Oh, shit," Andres curses, carefully putting me down on my knees where I let go of the gun. "Blaire, just let it all out. Don't try to stop it."

"Maksim," I retch, trying to stop the nausea, "he's-"

"Don't you worry about him." Andres is on his knees with me. "If you need to be sick, just be sick," he says.

Holding myself up on all fours, I toss up my guts—I can't seem to stop. Someone gathers my hair at the back of my neck—Andres, I'm guessing. I heave harder and faster, projectile vomiting through my nose and my mouth, my stomach panging in pain.

I think I'm spewing up blood.

I can't hear anything but my own choking, then, "You're dead, as are your lackey's," Charlie says in a voice that's strangely unfamiliar to me. A loud commotion trails, which I'm sure are guns going off-

BLAIRE
(PART ONE)

BANG
BANG
BANG
-making my ears ring.

I cup my ears and hunch over, curling up in a small ball.

BRATATATAT

Fuck, my head hurts and I can't see. My vision is so woozy.

I suddenly think of Maksim and that he might be a danger to Charlie somehow—if he lives, he could be a danger to James!

My new instincts kick in and I don't know how, but I swipe the gun from the ground and battle to my feet in a state of vertigo. There are soldiers everywhere firing guns, lighting up the night with flashes of burning yellow. More soldiers than I think there really are.

Double vision.

Maksim... I squint but can't see or hear him.

There's a large man standing next to me—one of Charlie's men. He's firing a powerful machine gun at what's left of Maksim's security detail, blowing them away. The shots are so close that I can feel my ears pop with each blast.

"Aargh!" I screech as steely arms close around me from behind. I buckle at the knees, the pain excruciating. The gun goes off in my hand with a powerful jolt that sends a shooting pain up my arm but it's nothing compared to having someone flush against my back.

"Blaire, stop fighting, we're here to save you..." Andres says in my ear, using his full strength to hold me down.

"Let me go, please!" I beg, burning up with a fever. I claw to get free but I can't. I think I call out again but I cannot hear my own voice anymore.

In the distance by a stretch of SUV's, I see Charlie kneeling over someone, pounding him in the face with a clenched fist. He's strangling the man with his other hand, ensuring he cannot escape.

Maksim.

He has to pay for what he's done. He has to pay for shooting James.

"Let. Me. Go!" I scream so loud, a burst of energy coming over me. I fling out my arms, forcing Andres to release me, and stagger to my feet once more. Through the firework of gunshots shaking the atmosphere, I stumble over to Charlie and Maksim, barely registering any pain now.

It seems adrenaline has overcome me.

"Blaire..." Maksim's golden eyes, swollen and full of blood, widen at the sight of me. He's gripping Charlie's wrist in an attempt to get free.

Charlie stops his attack and turns his head to look at me, his face covered in specks of blood. The devil is in his eyes, blazing with fury.

"You shot him." I lift the gun to Maksim and click back the hammer, trembling from head to toe. "You've done some terrible things to James but shooting him? Me?"

"I'm sorry," Maksim splutters, "I went too far—I realize that now."

"Sorry isn't enough," I say, cold of emotion. Finally, I feel nothing but hatred for him.

Releasing Maksim, Charlie pushes away from him and stands at my side, his breathing ragged. He puts one arm around my shoulders to hold me, steadying my stance. I notice the gunshots have stopped. It's so quiet. There's an eerie feel to the night.

Staring right at Maksim as he stares at me, I consider two options for him. Suffering or death.

"He has to die," I croak out, my lips wobbling with uncontrollable tears.

"I'll do it, Blaire," Charlie says, but I tell him no.

I try to crouch down to my master, to put us eye to eye, but I buckle at the knees. Charlie doesn't let me fall. He controls my equilibrium, gripping my shoulders tightly in his hands and carefully helps me to my knees.

Maksim is coughing up blood, straining to stop himself.

"Blaire," he chokes, reaching out for my hand with cold fingers, "you can stop this. You can save me." Holding my hand, he pleads physically, squeezing me. "Don't let him kill me," he says under his breath in Russian so only I can hear him.

"Why not?" I search his eyes, blinking a few times to clear the white film in my vision. "There is nothing for you anymore."

"I won't go to hell yet!" he yells with all the power his body will allow, hunching over on his side in pain to cough up some more. He pulls me with him and I moan at the pain of my back being stretched out, but then Charlie snatches my hand out of Maksim's.

"I cannot go to hell yet," Maksim's voice softens as he says that, and I think he's crying. "I am not ready, my little pet."

BLAIRE
(PART ONE)

I blink tears of sadness and rage, knowing I've failed to do the only thing I've ever known—keep him safe from anything and everything in the world.

I lean over to say in his ear, wincing in agony, "Hell is ready for you." And putting the gun to his temple, I squeeze the trigger and blow him away with a thunderous *BANG*.

My body doesn't react to the sound, and I don't move away from him.

I'm not sure if I shut my eyes, but the world goes black and I feel a strange sense of weight being lifted off my shoulders, like his soul is leaving me.

We're safe now. James and me. Nothing can hurt us anymore.

"I'll see you again someday," I say under my breath, so only Maksim can hear me, "I'm sure."

BLAIRE
(PART ONE)

35

I can't recall a time I felt like this, so... neither empty nor fulfilled. Somewhere in the middle.

Must be the drugs that doctor just gave me, keeping me in a hazy state of limbo, but still, I can't deny there is this strange emotion lingering within me, something I've not experienced before. I've just slaughtered my master and all I want to do is get up from the hospital bed I'm lying on and walk out that door right there in front of me, escape the captivity of this tiny room and this horrid clinical scent of the hospital. I'm not sure where I want to go. Perhaps I want to stand under the rain and smile while the moon glows on my face, because it is raining outside, I imagine washing away Maksim's blood from Rumo's driveway.

I can't leave though because I'm sick with infection, lying on my side with cushions propped against my back, keeping me in this position. My right upper arm is wrapped up in a tight blood pressure reader and there's a plastic clip attached to my index finger, reading my pulse. A long, droning beeping near my ear.

BLAIRE
(PART ONE)

Beep...Beep...Beep...

"I want a full medical report while she's unconscious," Charlie says from outside the door open to ajar, dragging my attention, "internal and external examination, swabs and blood tests, the lot. Don't leave an inch of that girl unchecked."

"Do you suspect she's been attacked sexually, Mr. Decena?"

"Oh, I don't suspect," Charlie's voice is harsh with rage, carrying over the noise of the waiting room, "I know-"

Of course he knows. Maksim must have confessed what he did to me when Charlie was punching his lights out.

"-And while you're removing that burn from her back, be fucking delicate or we're gonna have a problem. I've seen the way some of you surgeons handle your patient's."

"We will be extra delicate, Mr. Decena. I've called in the best surgeons to assist your girlfriend so once we get her blood pressure under control, we'll take her down for surgery. You have my word she will be handled with the best care."

I sigh, glad it'll all be over soon, my every sense buzzing with this strange relaxed sensation. The doctor has given me far too much pain relief because I can't really feel anything. There is no pain. I'm not disappointed by my actions and I'm not relieved either. I'm just... hazy.

The door creaks open fully and Charlie wanders in to stand at my side, the force of his presence dominating the small room. The balding doctor follows in, scribbling

477

something down on a pad in his hands. He is dressed in a long white coat, a stethoscope hanging around his neck. Dr. Shyam he said his name was. It's fitting. He's Indian with light chocolate brown skin and matching brown kind eyes.

Weakly lifting my head off the pillow, I look up at Charlie. His arms are crossed over his chest and even though he looks lethally evil in his pose, he smiles at me with a mixture of guilt and pure affection. "You all right, baby?"

The muse of my affections, he is. His tan is darker against the pale green room we're in, and his unruly hair looks death black under the lights. He's still painted in Maksim's blood, specks marrying his skin under those striking blue eyes. It was the first thing the receptionist noticed when he carried me into the hospital not an hour ago, the blood. But then she saw me in his arms, covered in my own blood and on the verge of death by infection and pain.

"I think so," I say to answer Charlie's question, "though I do feel a bit... unclear."

"That's the pain relief but s'all right." Charlie tips his head, gazing down at me like there's nothing else in the world. "I don't want you in pain."

I smile back at him, feeling safe in his company. I know he won't let anyone hurt me.

"Blaire," the doctor says my name softly, reaching for my left hand, "I'm going to fit you with a cannula so we don't have to keep poking you with needles."

Tearing my attention from Charlie, I tug against the doctor's subtle grasp, glaring to warn him off. I don't know him. He's not allowed to touch me.

Or, is he?

"Give it here," Charlie says, taking the cannula, "I'll do it."

He'll do it, just like he undressed me from that bloody shirt I was wearing and helped me into the hospital gown I am now wearing. It's an off white color with pallid blue dots, falls to just below my knees. It doesn't cling to my wounds so I feel comfortable in it.

As I look up at Charlie again, he tips his head to the other side and watches me with curious blue eyes. "Baby, hold out your arm and give me your hand."

I do, staring at his gorgeous face the entire time. He takes a tray of things from the doctor and puts it on the bed by my stomach, pulls up a chair and sits there in front of me. He gently grips my hand and wipes my skin clean of possible germs with an antiseptic wipe. Focused in his pursuit, he wraps a yellow elastic band around my wrist and tightens it so the pale blue veins pop out of my hand. I can feel my blood flow slowing, pressure gathering there.

"This is gonna feel like a sharp scratch." Charlie glances up from my hand at my eyes, then back down to where he inserts the needle, piercing through my skin.

It doesn't hurt at all. There is a slight scratch that pierces my skin, as he just said there would be, but it's nothing I can't handle. The doctor passes a length of surgical tape and Charlie sticks it across the needle now buried under my skin, and then he hunches down to kiss me there.

"All right?"

I nod against the pillow, satisfied to have him attending to me.

BLAIRE
(PART ONE)

"When are we leaving for Mexico?" I say. It's all he was talking about on the ride over here from Rumo's house, just after I murdered Maksim. I think Charlie was trying to break through my numb barrier, and it worked. While I was curled up on his lap, his brother driving the car, he told me again what Mexico will be like, as he used to tell me when we spent our days talking to each other; how he misses the sun and how much his house will feel like a home once I'm there.

Charlie flashes me his most handsome smile, stroking over my knuckles with the pad of his thumb. "As soon as you've had the operation to fix up the shot wound and clear up the burn on your back, we'll go to Mexico."

"Today?"

"Maybe tomorrow morning, baby," he says softly, reaching out with his other hand to give my chin a gentle, loving squeeze. "You'll still be asleep but by the time you wake up, we'll be home."

Home... It's so weird to hear him say that.

He winks at me, and a familiar warmth spreads through my chest.

"I'd like that," I whisper, lifting my lips in another dazed smile. "And James will come with us?"

Charlie told me in the car that James is waiting at his house for us. He blames himself for what's happened to me and can't find the will to see me at the moment, not while I'm in this state. I understand. Though I don't blame him for anything that's ever happened to me, I understand his guilt.

Charlie nods a couple of times. "If he wants to. I've already told him he's welcome to come live with us as I assumed that's what you'd want."

"Yes. He's my brother," I remind myself, unexplainably glad that I still have some family left in the world. "I want him to know that while Maksim is gone, he still has me."

I feel nothing for Maksim at the moment but I reckon that might have something to do with my medicated state. Neither do I care that Charlie and I are talking freely in front of this doctor who is trying to act invisible, writing god knows what on that pad.

"Us," Charlie corrects, raising his thick eyebrows at me, and I have no idea what he's talking about. "Anything James wants or needs, we'll sort it together."

"Oh..." I nod, my emotions for him all but bursting out of me. "Yes. Us."

I'm oddly vulnerable right now, saying things I wouldn't usually say, but I want it to be like this with Charlie. I want us to be a team. If I need him, I have to know that he's there and vice versa.

"Mr. Decena-" the doctor interrupts our conversation, and Charlie lets go of my hand; turns around in his chair.

"-She's ready for the next shot of antibiotics." He lays out two syringes on the tray, gesturing that one is a strong antibiotic and the other is the anesthetic. "Anesthetic last, once her blood pressure reads one-hundred and thirty over ninety on this screen." He leans over Charlie and turns the monitor toward us, so Charlie can see it properly. "I'll give you both some time alone. When you're ready for me, I'll be waiting outside, as will my medical team." He gives me a courteous yet pitiful smile, pivots away and leaves through the only door in the room.

As soon as Charlie and I are alone, my vein rushing with cold because Charlie injects the antibiotics, I can't help thinking about when we lived at his house. How at home and safe I felt there. I'll never forget the first time I fought Charlie in aid of the rights to my body. The first time I felt bad for hurting him when I put him down. The times we shared together eating in the kitchen, talking and holding each other.

"Blaire... you with me?"

I blink up at Charlie, coming back from my thoughts.

"You know," I say, my tone low and soft, "maybe we can put Mexico on hold for a while. Maybe we could go back to your house here and it'll be just like before when it was just us, though obviously James will be there now." My foggy head likes to imagine life as it was. It was perfect. There was no Maksim, just Charlie and me. Just how I want it to be.

Just as it is now.

"If that's what you want, baby," Charlie says, dropping the syringe on the tray. He wipes a few loose strands of hair back out of my face and cups my cheek.

"Really?"

He nods at me, his eyes crinkling because he's smiling. There's something about his mood tonight. He's not completely content but neither is he angry. I can't tell what's wrong with him.

"Yes..." I smile to myself regardless of his weird mood, recalling the first morning Charlie and I woke up together in my bed—when I really let myself go and allowed my feelings for him to come out. I felt so whole, like I was right where I was supposed to be.

"I miss waking up next to you." I take Charlie's hand from my face and hold it; fiddle with his long, callous fingers. "I miss my room at your house. We can stay in my room again, right?"

"Course we can," he says. "If you wanner go back to the house for a while so you can recover, then that's what'll happen. You want us to stay in your room, then that's where we'll be."

I smile again, somewhat staying in my thoughts—my memories. "Maybe we'll go have dinner like you wanted to?"

"We will," he says, his eyes glancing up and down between my eyes and my mouth. "We'll do whatever you wanner do, baby."

Feeling tired, I rest my eyes with a sigh. Something brushes over the bandage on my wrist where Maksim's bite mark will forever be—where my bracelet should be.

My bracelet... I hate that it's gone. It hurts that it's gone.

"You could get me another bracelet like the one you gave me before." I open my heavy eyes to look at Charlie. "I'm sorry I lost it."

"Now why would I buy you another one when I have this?" Pressing his foot into the floor, he lifts his hips up off the chair so he can dig through his pockets, and shows me my bracelet.

I can't even put it in words how I feel... Despite it all—the suffering and the pain, broken by the thought that James might be dead, thinking I'll never see Charlie again and killing my master—I think I'm happy, finally.

Charlie unclips the pulse reader from my finger and slips the bracelet over my right hand this time. He puts the pulse reader back on, clicks the clasp shut on my bracelet, and lifts my hand to his mouth; kisses my inner wrist, sending some intense vibes through my body.

"Maybe I'll get you the gold one to match," he kisses my wrist again, his eyes dazzling with something raw, "and you can wear them together."

"You will?" I say, hungry for that moment again—the moment he first gave the bracelet to me. I was beyond anxious but I just didn't understand what was going on between us. Now I do, I want all those moments again and more.

"Sure I will. Anything you want, you can have it, Blaire."

He keeps saying things like that—*whatever I want*. I swear if I asked for the sun he'd go right up there and get it for me.

He glances at the monitor and I notice the beeping has slowed.

"I'm gonna inject the anesthetic now," as soon as he says that, I'm utterly frightened. Some people don't wake up from anesthetic, and given my physical state, I'm frightened I won't make it through the operation. I'm frightened I'll be joining Maksim sooner than I have to.

"Charlie," I blink at him with obvious fear, "if I don't wake up, you'll take care of James, won't you?"

"Hey," he leans into me so we're eye to eye, his widening in what almost looks like anger, "don't say things like that, Blaire. You're gonna wake up. You're gonna be fine. I'll be there while you have your operation and I'll be there when you wake up, okay? Nothing bad is gonna happen."

I swallow down my nerves, shakily nodding.

BLAIRE
(PART ONE)

"Don't be scared, baby. You know I won't let anything happen to you." His eyes search mine in a desperate attempt to connect to me. "The sooner the operation is done, the sooner we can leave and go home and everything will be fine. It'll be just like before except there'll be no one between us, all right?"

The idea that it will be just us is comforting.

"And then we can be together properly, right, Charlie?" It's all I want now, for us to really be an *us*.

I don't even need to elaborate on what I mean. He knows.

"Once you're better, yeah. Just try and stop me." He winks at me, making my stomach roll with need for him. For us to be together.

I stare at Charlie for a while, urgently storing the image of his face in my memory for my dreams, so I can dream of nothing else but him.

"Thank you," I whisper, just if it's too late.

"Thank you?" His eyebrows draw together, and he entwines his fingers through mine to hold my hand, causing my hand to pinch against the cannula needle. "Thank you for what?"

"You came for me."

His eyes enlarge again. He looks insulted. "I came for you because I love you, Blaire, and I'd do it again, and again, and again."

He loves me... I'll never tire of hearing him say that.

"You don't have to thank me for anything," his voice comes out dark and hurt. "If anything, you should be telling me that you fucking hate me—it's my fault you're in this state."

He kept apologizing in the car earlier too, blaming himself as James blames himself. What is it with the men in my life? One minute they're so twisted and cold, and the next they can't do enough for me.

"You shouldn't have had to do *that* tonight," Charlie says, reminding me that I shot my master, "and I'm sorry for that too. I'm sorry for everything but I promise, I'll make it all up to you."

"Tonight couldn't have gone any other way," my lips wobble as I say that, emotional pain seeping through the cracks of my medicated numbness. "If you or anyone else ended him, I'm not sure how I would have reacted, and I don't want to hurt you, Charlie... I'd rather die."

Sighing, Charlie cups the back of my head and draws me closer to him, so we're mere inches from each other. He's holding the wound where someone whacked me but it doesn't matter. I want him near. His clean-musky scent... the warmth of his body... it calms my nerves.

He kisses my lips with the softest of intentions, like if he kisses any harder I might break. My heart squeezes. It's like all those times before when my chest squeezed but I now realize it was my heart all along.

"I love you, Blaire," he says softly against my mouth before sitting back, putting too much distance between us. Reaching out for the anesthetic on the tray, he inserts the needle into the cannula attached to my hand and presses down on the syringe. My vein floods with cold, filling my bloodstream with a warm, dopy sensation that will take me in a deep slumber.

"Now close your eyes, baby, and think of something nice."

BLAIRE
(PART ONE)

THE END

Thanks for reading guys. I hope you've enjoyed Blaire and Charlie's story. It doesn't end there. Part Two will be out in 2017.

If you leave a review on Amazon and Goodreads, and e-mail the link to itsanita@hotmail.co.uk, or post it on my facebook page/Twitter, I will send you a scene from Blaire in Charlie's POV. Please state your desired format (mobi or Epub).

If you want to be notified when any of my new novels are coming out, sign up for my newsletter.

I love chatting to readers (and not just those of you who have read my book) so find me on facebook, twitter or Goodreads; Anita Gray Author. Tell me what you think about Blaire. Tell me what books utterly consume your mind. I've devoured my reading list so I'm in need of some advice on what to read next. My reading suggestion, Twist Me by Anna Zaires. It's a trilogy but has been finished so there's no waiting around for the next book. Be warned, it's not for the faint hearted but if you love Dark Erotic Romance with a bit of Action, it's for you. In my opinion, Julian Esguerra is what Christian Grey wishes he could be. (Once you've read Twist Me, you'll get my drift).

I'd like to thank everyone who helped with Blaire;
Emma,
Lisa,
Nero, who is also Blaire's cover designer,
Desert Wolf aka Bill,
Melissa, GR,
Regine, GR,
Lisa, GR
Melissa, GR,
Sahara, GR,
Nicole Wescott, GR,
You all know who you are, and you've each played a significant role in helping Blaire grow. Your thoughts, comments, sleepless nights and support is priceless. I'll never forget what you have all done for me.

I'd also like to thank a dear friend of mine, as Shane would call her, Pickle. You have been a huge part in the spring of Blaire, when it was a stem with no petals. Together we spent days and nights helping Blaire bloom, and now we have this, a rose in the making. I hope you enjoy. xoxo

I dedicate everything to the love of my life, Shane, and my boy, Bradder's. You're both incredibly patient with

BLAIRE
(PART ONE)

me, given I lock myself away for hours on end to write.
It only makes me love you more (if that's even possible).
xoxoxo

Printed in Great Britain
by Amazon